The Expendable Spy

(A tale of World War II)

by

Maximilian Lerner

ALSO BY MAXIMILIAN LERNER

Fiction

The Improbable Spy

Non-Fiction

Flight and Return: A Memoir of World War II

ABOUT THE BOOK

From the deserts of Libya and Egypt to the icy lakes of Scotland, from London under the Blitz to German occupied France, from Alpine glaciers to the stately homes of Britain, this book ranges over the landscapes of World War II.

Its protagonist escapes from Austria with a burning desire for revenge after the murder of his parents by an SS officer. He becomes a British agent, is involved in numerous missions against the German enemy and at the same time hunts for the killer of his parents. At the climax of the book, just as he finds the murderer, he is ordered by his chief to sacrifice his life and the life of the woman he loves to ensure the success of the invasion of Normandy. Will he comply-and is it necessary?

FOR LENORE

CONTENTS

CHAPTER 1

It was inevitable that his colleagues at Christchurch College in Oxford would call Adam Bede the Venerable Bede. It was not only his name and his studious habits that made this nickname appropriate. While there are no photographs or paintings of the eighth century churchman whose name Adam shared, Adam looked exactly as one would have imagined the original Venerable Bede to look. He was short, round and prematurely bald, with a fringe around his skull. This looked exactly like the kind of tonsure his namesake was likely to have sported.

Adam was the greatest expert on ships the world had ever known, or at least, so he told his students or any one else who would listen, as frequently as possible. If you wanted to know exactly what types of ships were involved in the battle of Actium, ask Adam Bede. If you needed to know precisely how many sailors manned each of the vessels which made up the mighty Armada, the Venerable Bede would tell you. And if you were at all curious about how many kegs of rum were aboard the British or the French fleets at Trafalgar, Adam would enlighten you in more detail than you really needed.

Unfortunately for some one so obsessed with ships, Adam tended to get seasick even when he watched a movie depicting a sea voyage. So, he spent his life as a good Oxford Don should, studying musty records and drawing up detailed charts. In the process, however, he had developed a methodology which aroused the interest of his country's intelligence services.

By ascertaining the types of supplies and quantities of such supplies being sent to the home port of a naval vessel, Adam could deduce with uncanny accuracy not only the duration of its mission but often also its nature. Simply put, as Adam liked to explain, if you knew the complement of a ship, and the quantity of toilet paper loaded on it, you could judge the maximum duration of the voyage on which it would embark. In fact, Adam's method was far more complex, but it was efficacious.

Adam had perfected his method during the first world war, which he spent in a cubby in Whitehall, from which emerged a steady stream of advisories to the Navy. Some of them were even listened to, and Adam acquired a reputation for prescience.

He spent the interval between wars back in his beloved Oxford, where he again immersed himself in the lore of sailing ships instead of modern and unromantic naval vessels. Once the war started, he was immediately recalled to his old post, this time in a more senior position, with assistants to whom he could teach his methods.

On this lovely June day in 1940, Adam arrived in his office, punctually as ever, turned on his radio, shed his coat, and began to brew his morning cup of tea.

The news was uniformly bad. After the "phony war" which had begun in September of 1939 and lasted throughout the winter with not much action on any front, German troops had burst out, occupied Denmark and Norway, slashed through the Netherlands and Belgium, almost destroyed the British Expeditionary Corps, occupied Paris and forced the French government to sue for an armistice.

Adam Bede shook his head as he was drinking his tea. How will Britain cope, he thought. This is the worst situation for his country he, a historian of note, could imagine.

The door to his cubby burst open. A young man in ensign's uniform rushed in.

"Mr. Bede? Admiral Morse wants to see you. Now. Please hurry."

The ensign hustled Bede back into his jacket and practically pulled him out the door. Adam had trouble keeping up with the taller and younger man. He was huffing and puffing by the time they had reached the street. The ensign rushed him across traffic clogged streets without regard for the imminent danger of getting crushed by an army lorry or a bus, through passages Adam did not recognize, into a stately building in the heart of Whitehall, and up the stairs to a suite of offices.

This, apparently, was the lair of the legendary Admiral Morse, chief of military intelligence, and nominally, Adam's boss.

The anteroom was crowded with high ranking officers of all services, all clamoring for a moment of Admiral Morse's time, and all being denied with exquisite politeness and yet absolute firmness, by an attractive Wren, a member of the newest branch of the Royal Navy, the Women's division, guarding the door. Nevertheless, when Adam arrived, the Wren beckoned him forward and opened the door to the inner sanctum. " Mr. Bede," she announced as if she had known Adam from childhood.

Adam almost stumbled into a large well furnished office. He saw a large desk, in one corner, two leather armchairs with a small table between them, book cases filled with leather covered volumes along the walls, and a large French window behind the desk. An indistinct figure rose from the armchair behind the desk and came forward. So this is the Admiral, Adam thought.

Morse was medium size, compact, wearing a full beard, cut square in the fashion of the old sailor he once had been, and glasses which obscured his very penetrating eyes. His hair had once been black, but now was shot through with gray and white. Adam guessed his age somewhere in the fifties.

The Admiral motioned Adam to one of the two armchairs in the corner.

"Come in, Mr. Bede. Please sit down.", the Admiral said. "May I offer you a glass of sherry? "

Barely able to catch his breath, Adam complied and gratefully accepted the drink.

"Thank you," he said. "But what can I do for you, Admiral?"

"All in good time. Please tell me about your relationship with Admiral Theberge."

"Bobo? We're very good friends."

"Bobo? Is that what you call him? I hope my friends have more mature names for me." Admiral Morse grinned.

"Well, his name is Paul, but when he was a baby his mother called him Bobo, and the name stuck, at least among his intimates."

"I'm glad you're one of them. How did you meet him?"

"I spent some time in Paris in 1919 as an adviser to the government in fashioning the naval aspects of the peace treaties. During that time, I lectured to some military classes at St.Cyr about my methods. Bobo - Admiral Theberge - was a senior instructor there at that time. We got to be friends, very good friends in fact."

"I take it you speak French?"

"Yes, with an accent that Bobo says, you can cut with a knife. And I have always teased him about his horrible mispronunciations of English."

"How did this friendship develop?"

"What you are saying, Admiral, is that a friendship between a high-ranking French officer and an Oxford Don is unlikely. Perhaps. We share a passion for ancient naval design and we could argue for hours about the specific advantages of Roman triremes against Viking ships."

"Did you see him frequently?"

"Every time I could get to France, when he was not at sea. And he and his family often came to England."

"His family?"

"He has a lovely wife, Clemente, and two beautiful daughters. Now may I ask, why all these questions about my friend?"

"Admiral Theberge is in command of a French squadron presently in harbor in Oran. With the surrender of France, there is considerable danger that this squadron as well as other elements of the French fleet will be turned over to the Germans for use against us. I don't have to tell you, of all people, what the addition of the French fleet to the German Navy would mean for us."

Adam paled. "It would be a disaster. Is that conceivable?"

"Not only conceivable, but very likely. The Prime Minister has decided that rather than risk this possibility we must attack and destroy the elements of the fleet in port in Oran. That is, unless…"

"Unless what, Admiral?"

"Unless you can persuade your friend, eh, Bobo, to surrender his squadron to us. Then we would have it as an addition to our forces."

"I? Why would he listen to me? And how could I contact him?"

"Because you are his friend he would see you. And you will contact him in person. Leave that to me."

"But, Admiral, I'm not a field officer, I'm a bookworm. And besides...."

"Besides what?"

"I get terribly seasick," the Venerable Bede admitted with considerable embarrassment, "just crossing the channel to get to France is a major problem for me."

"Well, we all have to make sacrifices for the cause," the Admiral said unconcernedly. "Now, listen. You will have twenty four hours in Oran to either persuade your friend to surrender his squadron to us, or at least to open the seacocks and sink the ships to prevent them from falling into German hands. In the latter event, at least we will not be forced to attack a former ally, and to suffer the negative publicity that will create."

"But Admiral, isn't there any one else...." Adam stuttered, horrified at the prospect.

"You are the man for the job. I'm sure you'll give it your best."

* * *

Adam Bede was hustled into a waiting car, driven to an airfield somewhere, dressed in an aviator's sheepskin and squeezed behind a laconic pilot in a tiny aircraft. *There is not enough room here, I can't breathe*, he wanted to say. But the plane was already taxiing down the runway, and he held on for dear life. Hours later he saw below him an aircraft carrier which looked like a toy in a large pond. The noise from the engines was deafening. Adam was sure that his hearing had suffered permanent damage. The pilot turned, gave him a friendly grin and pointed down.

What are you doing, Adam wanted to say. *He can't possibly expect to land on the deck of this tiny ship.* But that is precisely what the pilot proceeded to do. *We're going to die*, Adam knew, and tried to think of asking for forgiveness of his sins, but before he could start enumerating them, they had landed.

The pilot gave Adam a cheery wave and disappeared. Adam slowly relinquished his grip on the plane. "Hurry up, sir, please," a friendly voice addressed him. A large Petty Officer pulled him out of the plane, and propelled him to the side of the carrier, toward a contraption attached to one of the masts.

"Just get in here, please, sir." The Petty Officer strapped him into a bucket, and the bucket began to move.

Oh, God, what now? Adam saw that there was a wire strung from the aircraft carrier's mast down to another much smaller vessel floating besides it, and that his bucket was inexorably descending to that vessel. It reached the deck, strong hands grabbed it and lifted him out.

"Welcome aboard, Mr. Bede. I'm Lieutenant Commander Tolliver, Captain of His Majesty's Destroyer Drake. We'll try to get you to Oran as quickly as possible. In the meantime we'll try to make you comfortable aboard our ship."

Adam could not breathe. The ship had started to move and was cutting through the waves with great speed. The aircraft carrier was already far behind. The deck was lurching up and down, side to side, and the masts - the masts were dipping and rising, rising and dipping. Adam stumbled to the railing and heaved, and heaved.

"Oh, I'm sorry you do not feel well," Tolliver said. His face showed total equanimity, but Adam was sure that a contemptuous grin was lurking somewhere. He knew the attitude of those fortunate mortals who were immune to seasickness toward those so afflicted. They thought it funny.

Adam pulled himself up to his less than considerable height and said with as much dignity as he could muster: "Please show me to my quarters."

"Certainly." The captain signaled to one of the junior officers near him. "Ensign Roberts will accompany you."

"This way, sir." Adam followed the Ensign toward a stairwell leading down into the interior of the vessel. The Ensign began to climb down and Adam attempted to follow. At that point, the ship appeared to encounter a larger than normal wave. There was a sharp sideways movement, and

Adam lost his footing and plunged down, down to the bottom of the stairwell.

* * *

Pain. Pain. Adam's head hurt, and his left leg was in agony. He tried to open his eyes, but the swaying of the ceiling above him made him dizzy. He closed his eyes again, and mercifully lost consciousness.

He had no idea how much time had passed when he woke again. He opened his eyes and tried to look around. The ceiling was still swaying rhythmically. He closed his eyes briefly. *Ah yes, I'm on a ship.* He looked around. He was lying on a bunk bed. Another bed on the other side of the room - cabin, he realized, contained a figure completely swaddled in blankets. At the other side of the cabin were shelves and a table filled with medical equipment. There was the unmistakable smell of disinfectant associated with doctors' offices.

He remembered where he was. *This must be the sickbay aboard the destroyer. What happened to me?* He took inventory of his body. There was a bandage on his head, but he felt little pain there. What seemed more serious was his left leg. He felt with his hand. The leg was completely encased in a cast reaching almost up to his groin.

What a disaster! This is my fault for not holding on to the railing properly. He remembered his mission. *How am I going to get to Bobo in Oran, when I'm incapacitated?*

He closed his eyes again. The swaying was making him ill. But above all, he felt sick about himself. *The first time, my country asks me to do something important, and I fail before I even get started.*

When he opened his eyes again, Captain Tolliver was sitting on a chair pulled up to his bunk.

"How do you feel, Mr. Bede? " he asked gently.

"Rotten. Please tell me exactly how I am."

Captain Tolliver waved to a figure behind him. "I'll let our ship's surgeon do that."

The doctor bent over Adam. "You have a bad wound on your forehead. It took twelve stitches but I think we have that under control. I can't tell yet whether you have a concussion, but I doubt it. Your eyes are clear and your evident dizziness can be attributed to seasickness. We'll have to watch that. The principal problem is a fracture of your left femur. I have set it to the best of my ability and immobilized it with a temporary cast, but it should really be X-rayed as soon as possible. Unfortunately, we don't have X-ray equipment aboard."

Adam closed his eyes for a moment in despair. Then he looked at the Captain.

"I must find a way to accomplish my mission in Oran. It's vital."

"Well, Mr. Bede, my orders are to get you to Oran as quickly as possible, to get you ashore in the most circumspect manner in some cove out of sight of the French Navy, and to pick you up again, if possible, after you have accomplished your mission. And come what may, I must rendezvous with my squadron by July 2 at certain coordinates. Normally, I could have given you twenty four to thirty six hours in Oran. I don't know or want to know what your mission is, but I don't see how you can get around without help."

"That is obvious. Would any of your ship's complement volunteer to help me? I can assure you that my mission is crucial."

"No," Captain Tolliver said, regretfully. " I can't allow any member of my crew to go ashore in potentially enemy territory. You are a civilian, Mr. Bede, but if one of my men is caught in civilian clothes, he would be treated as a spy. And given the secrecy of your mission, I can hardly imagine that you could accomplish it accompanied by someone in a Royal Navy uniform."

A voice croaked from the bed on the other side of the cabin: "I'll do it. I can help you."

* * *

"Who is that?" Adam asked with astonishment.

"This is someone we picked up from a sinking boat just a few hours ago. I don't know any more than that," the Captain said.

The figure in the other bed sat up, and hesitatingly made his way to Adam's bed. It revealed itself to be a young man, dressed in torn pants and a badly torn shirt. His face showed total exhaustion, his lips were crusted and swollen and his voice barely audible. Unshaven and filthy as he was, Adam could see that if he were properly cleaned up, he would be a handsome young man. At a shade over 6 feet, he towered even over Captain Tolliver, who was well above average height.

"My name is Kurt Auster." He spoke in slightly accented English. Then he turned to the Captain. "Thank you for rescuing me, I don't think I could have held out much longer. May I have something to drink, please."

"Certainly." The Captain signaled and a glass of water appeared immediately and was placed in Kurt's hand. Kurt drank it gratefully and asked for another. Then he continued.

"I'm a Jewish refugee from Austria. I tried to get away from the Germans occupying France and had the brilliant idea of rowing from France to Spain. As you can see I'm no sailor. If it hadn't been for you, I wouldn't be alive. All I want to do is fight the Germans. If your mission," he turned to Adam, " is against them, I'll do anything to help."

"Wait a moment." Captain Tolliver interjected. "I'm sure we appreciate your offer, but I don't know whether we can trust you."

"Did your people bring my backpack aboard when they rescued me?" Kurt croaked.

"I believe so."

"You will find my Austrian passport and my French Carte d'Identite. And if you need to be convinced that I'm Jewish and thus a bitter enemy of the Nazis, I'll gladly demonstrate." Kurt smiled as he started to remove his pants.

"Hold it." Adam said. "How long before we reach Oran?"

"Three days." The Captain replied.

"Then allow me the time to get acquainted with this young man. This may be my only chance to accomplish my goal. I'll be the one taking the risk. So, I believe, the decision should be mine."

"As you wish." Captain Tolliver nodded.

* * *

A remarkable rapport developed between the middle aged scholar and the young refugee. The Venerable Bede was pleased to learn that Kurt was fluent in French as well as his native German. He felt that this might be helpful on the mission. He listened very carefully to Kurt's account of his life. He was aware that the young man did not tell him everything, but came to the conclusion that Kurt was trustworthy and resourceful.

Kurt took over the nursing duties and admired the iron will that Adam Bede demonstrated in attempting to get up in spite of his injuries. The ship's machinist had constructed a pair of serviceable crutches. Kurt helped Adam practice with them whenever the sea was reasonably calm. Kurt did not ask the nature of the mission in Oran. He knew that he would not be told, but it was enough for him to feel that he was making a contribution in the war against Germany.

And then the idyll in the sick bay was shattered. Captain Tolliver appeared.

"Can you explain why you are carrying a German Luger in your knapsack?"
"You looked in Kurt's luggage?" Adam exclaimed. " That is not cricket. Isn't there any sense of privacy any more?"

"No, Mr. Bede. There isn't. Not in wartime and when the safety of my ship and your mission is at stake. Now, young man," the Captain continued grimly. " I am waiting for an explanation."

"I took the gun away from a German dispatch rider I encountered South of Bordeaux. And I delivered his dispatches to Captain Corcoran of HMS Dauntless."

"What do you mean, you took it away? No German soldier would give up his weapon and his dispatches without a fight."

Kurt hesitated. Well, he had to speak the truth.

"I killed him. I attacked him from behind with a rock. I'm not proud of it. It wasn't a fair fight."

Adam exclaimed: " A fair fight! An untrained youngster against an armed, trained soldier. And you think it wasn't fair?"

Captain Tolliver frowned. "I think I'd better see if we can contact the Dauntless and verify this story."

Another day passed. Adam was getting a little stronger. The ship's surgeon was no longer worried about a concussion, and Adam felt a little more confident about being able to maneuver on his makeshift crutches. That is, once he reached terra firma. He couldn't wait for the moment when his world would stop rocketing about, his stomach would no longer attempt to empty itself when it was empty, and his head would stop hurting.

Captain Tolliver visited the sick bay. " Fleet headquarters confirms that they received some information supposedly coming from German dispatches. However, the bad news is that the Dauntless has gone down with all hands, after an attack by a German U-Boot."

With an inarticulate cry, Kurt Auster dashed out of the cabin. After a few moments, Captain Tolliver followed. He found the young man at the railing staring out at the unforgiving sea. .

"Please forgive me," Kurt said quietly. "A traveling companion was allowed to board the Dauntless."

"Someone you were fond of?" Tolliver asked with sympathy. Kurt did not answer.

When Kurt and the Captain returned to the sickbay, Adam Bede noted that the young man's eyes were red, but that his expression was harsh and bitter. Adam thought that he would not like this look to be directed against him

"I don't even know how to handle a gun." Kurt turned to Captain Tolliver.
" Would you, please, explain the workings of the Luger to me. Mr. Bede, I would like to take it with me when we disembark."

Adam Bede understood the young man perfectly. "I see no objection to taking it along. Who knows, it may come in handy. But, Kurt, you must promise me that you will use it only when I give you permission. Now, Captain, can you teach Kurt how to use it?"

"Well, " Captain Tolliver replied, " I can't teach you how to hit what you aim at, that takes practice. Just point it in the right direction and try to be as close to your target as possible. Now the workings: The Luger is a gas powered pistol. Here in the grip is the magazine. This version contains eight bullets. Here is the safety. To fire, you first turn off the safety, then make sure there is a bullet in the chamber like so " and he demonstrated, - and pull the trigger. Be prepared for a strong recoil when you fire, and hold the pistol very tightly.

I have no ammunition aboard that would fit this pistol, so you have only the eight bullets in the magazine. It's too late to give you a chance to fire one of the other guns we have aboard, so that you could at least familiarize yourself with the general idea. I hope that you'll not be called upon to use this gun."

The next evening the Drake approached the African coast not far from Oran. Kurt and Adam Bede disembarked into a small rubber raft and Kurt rowed to shore. He had been given a Very Pistol, so that he could signal their return to the same spot the next night by firing off a flare. It was made clear that the Drake would be waiting off shore only during that night, and would leave at dawn for its rendezvous with the squadron. If Kurt and Adam did not make it back by then, they were on their own in French Algeria.

Kurt beached the rubber raft, jumped out and pulled it in shore as far as possible. He then carried Adam inland up the sandy beach toward a road. Even though Adam was short, he was quite corpulent, and it took every ounce of Kurt's strength to achieve that goal. Kurt then returned to the raft, pulled it up toward a dune and tried to conceal it as much as possible behind a cluster of rocks. He picked up the crutches and his backpack and rejoined Adam.

This was Kurt's first venture to a new continent - Africa. He felt that it was different. There was a warm wind coming from the land blowing toward the sea, a wind laden with mysterious smells, cinnamon and other spices, or was this only his imagination? He pictured exotic sights, strange animals, veiled women and wondered how the reality would meet those romantic expectations.

"We have to stop a car and get him to drive us into Oran." Adam said. "I will tell you now where we are going. I need to see Admiral Theberge. He's the commander of the French Squadron in port here, and he's also Port Captain. He may occupy the Port Captain's residence above the Naval port. If he is not there, but on his flagship, our task will be much more difficult. It is important that my visit to the Admiral is as circumspect as possible. That would be much easier on shore."

It was a warm night, the sky filled with stars, the sea glimmering along the beach, and the sandy expanses of the beginnings of the Sahara stretching out on the other side of the road. There were few cars coming along, and Adam was reluctant to stop a private car.

"We need someone who will take our money without asking any questions, a small truck, a local farmer or worker." he said.

After a while the right kind of vehicle made its way toward them. It was a small panel truck of indeterminate age, stuttering along, with occasional puffs of dark smoke from its exhaust. Kurt ran into the road in front of the truck and waved his arms wildly. "Arretez, s'il vous plait, arretez."

The driver was a dark faced Arab, with a big handlebar mustache, dressed in a brownish robe, with a kaffiyeh on his head. He looked incredibly exotic to Kurt.

Kurt held a handful of francs in front of the driver's eyes. "Vous nous emenez en ville, au port maritime?"

"Bien sur, Patron." The driver opened the door to his cab and snatched the money out of Kurt's hand. Kurt helped Adam into the front seat, stowed the crutches next to him, and swung into the back of the truck. He saw some ladders, rakes, spades and other garden tools.

As the truck went on its way more habitations appeared on the side of the road. The highway left the shore and entered the town. It began to climb and curve. There was no longer a view of the sea. Expertly, the driver wound through narrow streets, left turns and right turns. Kurt was totally lost. After a while the road opened again. It turned into a corniche with cliffs on one side, below which Kurt could hear the sea battering the shore. The road descended and widened. On one side there were a number of military looking buildings, on the other side the port. A number of warships of different types and sizes rode at anchor or were tied up alongside a series of jetties jutting out into the harbor.

The driver pointed to a large house in the center of the port area. "Voila, la residence du capitaine du port. Ou voulez vous descendre?"

Adam Bede motioned to the driver to continue on. He had noted a sentry pacing at the front entrance. "Drive around the corner," he told the driver, " and we'll get out there."

Kurt handed the Arab another bill. "Pour votre silence." "Merci, merci, Patron." The driver sped off.

"There must be a back door. I don't mind knocking and waking the help, as long as we don't get the Navy involved." Adam said.

Painfully he moved along the wall surrounding the building. It was his first attempt to use the crutches on land for more than a few steps, and it was more difficult than he had thought.

There was a back entrance. No sentry. The gate was easily unlatched. "The same kind of security that allowed the Germans to enter France by the back door. Won't they ever learn?" Adam muttered.

They made their way through a garden to what appeared to be a door toward the kitchen. There was a light shining through a window. Kurt stepped over some plants and looked through. A heavyset woman was busy at the oven. Kurt rapped on the window. She looked up in shock. He put a finger to his lips and motioned her closer.

"I have a secret message for Admiral Theberge. A matter of national security. Is he here?"

"Yes, he's asleep. I am baking his croissants. He must have his fresh croissants for his breakfast. You'll have to come back later. How did you get in here, anyway?"

" I assure you the Admiral will be grateful to you if you wake him. You don't even have to let us into the house. We'll wait right here. Just tell him, that Adam Bede wants to talk to him. I know you're a patriotic Frenchwoman. I promise you that this is important for France."

With a doubtful glance at Kurt and an even more questioning look at the smaller man holding on to his crutches for dear life, the woman withdrew, took off her apron and left the kitchen.

"Do you think she'll wake the Admiral, or will she alert the guards?" Adam wondered.

"Well, we'll have to wait and see."

After what seemed a long while, the cook returned. She opened the door and beckoned, "Par ici. " She led them through a corridor toward the front of the house into a large room. At one end of the room there was a heavy desk with a comfortable armchair behind it, at the other end a couch with several armchairs. Paintings of naval vessels decorated the walls. A large book case and a liquor cabinet stood along one wall. A small French flag was furled on a stand behind the desk. Two more straight backed chairs facing the desk completed the furnishings.

"Asseyez-vous," the cook pointed to the two chairs in front of the desk and left the room.

Adam sat down gratefully on one of the chairs, placing the crutches on the floor next to him.

"Something's wrong," he whispered. "The Bobo I know would have run down to meet me in his pajamas, particularly since I'm dropping in so unexpectedly."

The door opened. In strode an Admiral of the French Navy in full uniform, and behind him another naval officer, clearly of lesser rank. Kurt was not familiar with the insignia of rank in the French Navy, but there was a lot less gold braid and fewer stripes on the other man's uniform.

The Admiral sat down behind the desk, the other officer stood behind him.

"You wanted to see me?" the admiral addressed Adam coldly.

Adam Bede fought his way out of his chair, onto his crutches and stumbled around the desk. "I have a message for you." he whispered. Involuntarily, both the admiral and the other officer leaned forward so that they could hear better. At that point, Adam seemed to lose control of his crutches, pitched forward and in the process of trying to regain his equilibrium, managed to hit the younger officer in the stomach with the metal tip of the crutch.

"Scheisse," the officer exclaimed, doubling over.

Kurt jumped up, grabbed a heavy paperweight from the desk and hit the officer in the face with all his might. Blood and brain tissue flew about. The body collapsed.

The Admiral jumped up. "How in hell did you know, Venerable, and what happened to you?" Joyfully he embraced Adam Bede. Kurt looked at the tall Admiral and the roly-poly Englishman and wondered at the vagaries of friendship. He noted coldly, that he had just killed another man and that his conscience was perfectly clear. He wiped his hands on the dead man's clothes, sat down and waited for the two older men to stop babbling and to begin to discuss matters of substance.

Admiral Theberge bent over the body and came up with a small revolver in his hand. "This is why I couldn't greet you the way I wanted," he said to Adam Bede, "there are two more Germans guarding Clemente and my daughters. This bastard gave the other guards instructions to kill my family if we are not back there by," the Admiral looked at his watch, " in another thirty minutes. He told me smilingly to, as he said, encourage me to get rid of you quickly. We have to do something about them. I will call for help."

"Hold it." Adam placed his hand on the Admiral's arm to prevent him from using the telephone. "Please explain first."

"This man wearing a fake French naval uniform and two men in civilian clothes presented themselves to me. All three are German. I believe that this one," he touched the body contemptuously with his toe, "was the only one who spoke French. They informed me that a British attack on my squadron is imminent and ordered me to take my squadron out to sea and to fight. To ensure my compliance, they kept my wife and daughters prisoner in their bedroom. I was arguing with them when the cook knocked at the door with news of your arrival. My captor was afraid that you would start a commotion if I did not see you. My instructions were to get rid of you quickly."

"Wait a minute," the Admiral continued. "Is it true? Is the British fleet going to attack? I don't understand. We're Allies?"

"Never mind that now." Adam Bede replied. "Let's get rid of the other two men, then we'll have time to talk about everything. But I urge you not to call for outside help. I think privacy is essential until we have had our talk. I wish that I could help," he looked ruefully at his cast, " but do you think that you and Kurt here could handle those two Nazis?"

Kurt spoke up. "What is their position? Where are they and how are they armed?"

"They have Walther revolvers like this one." The Admiral hefted the gun he had taken from the body of the fake officer. "One is seated in the corridor in front of our bedroom door and the other on the balcony outside the bedroom. Both of my daughters are in the bedroom with my wife."

"Is there any way to get to the balcony from the outside?" Kurt asked.

"Over the roof, perhaps. But what about the guard in the corridor?"

"Here is what I propose." Kurt said.

* * *

Gunther Hesse was extremely nervous. Here he was, in civilian clothes, in enemy country where he did not understand one word of the language. His commanding officer, the only one who knew what they were doing, had disappeared with the French Admiral. It is true that he had sworn obedience to the Fuehrer's orders when he joined the SS, but he had expected to fulfill those orders in his beloved black uniform in the company of his SS brothers. Then he and his companion were picked out of their unit, given civilian clothes and placed under the orders of a Naval Officer. What does the Navy have to do with the SS?

The Sturmbannfuehrer in command of his unit had spoken to them: " I have chosen you because of your reputation for absolute obedience to orders. You may be called upon to do things that you may find difficult or even distasteful. Just remember that the Fuehrer knows best, and that his Will is transmitted to you through the officers set above you. Whatever you are ordered to do you will do. It is all for the good of the Fatherland. I rely on you. Heil Hitler."

Within twenty-four hours, the two SS men and their leader had been flown to this exotic place in Africa, and were now guarding a Frenchwoman and her daughters. Their orders were very specific. If the Admiral and their own commander did not return within the next thirty minutes, go into the bedroom, shoot the three women, and escape, if possible, to the German consulate. The difficulty was that they had not been informed of the location of the German consulate, and not speaking French, would have a lot of trouble finding it.

So Gunther was very nervous. He kept looking at his watch, and wondered how his partner was doing out on the balcony.

Someone is coming. Gunther jumped up and pulled his revolver out of its holster. A young man, carrying a tray with two cups and saucers. "Halt." Gunther barked, raising his gun to cover the young man.

"Alles ist in Ordnung. Ich bringe Ihnen nur Kaffee. Die Probleme sind alle geloest."

Oh, a German. Gunther relaxed. *And he's bringing coffee. I guess the Navy settled things.* Gunther lowered his gun, as the young man approached.

Kurt slammed his knee with all his might into the German's groin where he was most vulnerable. With a barely audible "Oof, " the German doubled over, instinctively grabbing at his testicles to protect them. Kurt hit the German's head with the Luger he had concealed under the tray, careful not to drop the tray so as to keep the noise down as much as possible. It was essential to disarm the German without alerting the man on the balcony, so Kurt could not use his Luger to shoot. Admiral Theberge ran up from the corridor, and started to wrestle with the German. Now Kurt was able to aim his blows better. The Nazi collapsed under the hail of blows.

"Quick, let's get him out of here," the Admiral panted. They pulled the German's body down the corridor, where Adam Bede was waiting. "Here," Kurt gave Adam the German's gun. " Make sure he stays quiet."

"Trust me. This I can do." Adam said grimly.

"Now the other man. How do I get up to the roof?" Kurt asked.

"Through this window. Can you swing up? I'll help you." The Admiral pushed and Kurt pulled himself up into the roof. Fortunately the building was constructed in the Mediterranean fashion, where a flat roof was often used for sleeping quarters during the hottest part of the year. Kurt thought that it would be much more difficult to climb over the high gabled chalets of his native country. He crawled over to the edge of the roof overlooking the balcony and peeked over the side.

The German was leaning on the balustrade with his back toward Kurt. He was smoking and his gun was not visible. *It must be in his pocket,* Kurt thought. This is my chance.

Kurt jumped from the roof directly onto the Nazi. The German's body broke his fall, but for a moment Kurt was stunned by the unexpected shock. The German recovered quickly and grabbed Kurt by the throat. Kurt was able to break his grip, but both men were wrestling on the floor of the balcony, with neither gaining a clear advantage.

The German was strong, and certainly better trained than Kurt, who had no experience in physical combat. Kurt felt himself weakening, and the Nazi again was able to get both hands around Kurt's throat. Kurt scratched and clawed at his opponent's face but the man held on and tightened his grip. Kurt was beginning to lose consciousness. Desperately he kept clawing at his enemy's face. Then his hand found an eye, and he squeezed with all his might. He felt something give. The eye.

The German screamed. He let go of Kurt's throat, and clutched his eye. Kurt tried to catch his breath and at the same time attempted to hit out at the Nazi. At that point, the Admiral finally burst through the bedroom door onto the balcony. The German saw the Admiral waving a gun. He realized that the other side had the upper hand, jumped over the balcony and disappeared into the night.

The Admiral leaned over the balcony looking for something to shoot at.

"Stop." Kurt said. "You can look for him later. First we must talk."

"Very well. I'll join you in my study in a minute. Let me reassure my family first."

This time Kurt did not have to climb over the roof. The Admiral escorted him through the bedroom to the door into the corridor. Kurt couldn't help seeing the Admiral's wife and daughters huddling in their nightclothes on the large bed, but the Admiral did not stop to make any introductions.

"What are we going to do with this one?" Adam Bede said, pointing to the German. The man was slowly regaining consciousness, but did not move when he saw Adam's gun pointing at him.

The Admiral entered. "We'll tie him up and lock him in this closet, until we have had the talk you so desperately want. Then I'll call in the security detail. He should be able to tell us a few things." Admiral Theberge disappeared and returned with some rope and expertly tied the German hand and foot. "Old sailors never lose their skill with knots," the Admiral muttered. The body of the Nazi in the French uniform was still lying next to the Admiral's desk.

"Come on, let's sit down here." The Admiral pointed to the couch and the two armchairs, " it's very early but I believe we are entitled to a drink." He brought a bottle of Armagnac from the sideboard and filled three glasses. "Welcome, Venerable, and thank you, young man. Now talk, old friend."

"I have been sent here by my government precisely because of our old friendship." Adam Bede began. "You know about me and the sea - we do not get along. I got injured on the way here. Fortunately, my young friend Kurt here volunteered to come with me."

"Yes indeed, fortunately for all of us," the Admiral agreed with a friendly nod to Kurt.

"But what does your government want from me?"

"Your squadron." Adam Bede replied bluntly.

The Admiral jumped up. "Do not go beyond the bounds of friendship, Adam. I am an Admiral of France, and I do not betray my colors."

"Please listen to me, Bobo. Let me assure you that I do not believe that anything I ask of you is either dishonorable or would be damaging to France. I know you better than that.

You know that at this time, Britain is fighting for her life against the overwhelming might of Germany and Italy. If the Germans get hold of the French fleet, our island will be in truly desperate straits. We know that under the armistice agreement Germany has undertaken to allow your fleet to remain neutral, but, particularly after your experience with those" and he pointed at the dead German,
"Can you believe that such German promises will be kept?"

"I am a soldier, not a politician, Adam. My duty is to obey my government. And my government has signed an armistice agreement, and has ordered me to keep my squadron in port. And that is what I must do."

"But you saw that the Germans wanted you to go out and fight against us?"

"I can assure you that I had no intention of doing so, regardless of personal cost, without express orders from my government. And this brings me to the other question. Is there a British fleet on the way to Oran to attack me?"

Adam did not answer. "Bobo," he said entreatingly, " we are allies in a war against the forces of darkness. Who is that government you speak of? The Petain group has no legitimacy, they are the ones who surrendered..."

"My dear Adam, all the French territories along the Mediterranean, Morocco, Tunisia, Algeria, Syria and Lebanon, have accepted the legitimacy of Marshall Petain. Half a million men under arms in those territories obey his government. Who do you want me to obey?"

Adam Bede paled. "I did not know that. I had hoped that they would go with General de Gaulle and his French government in exile in London."

Admiral Theberge laughed. "That upstart? Who appointed him? For heaven's sake, Adam, I outrank him and there are half a dozen Generals and Admirals in the territories who outrank him. He's a megalomaniac traitor and a tool of your government."

"Bobo, without you and your help, it is entirely possible that Germany will win this war. Do you want this on your conscience? Do you want that gangster Hitler to rule Europe?"

"Oh, Adam, all governments are corrupt. What does it matter? I have good friends in Germany, just as I consider you my dear friend. The sooner the war is over, the fewer people will get killed, and the better for everybody."

"Bobo, I can't believe what you're saying. How can you even consider the possibility that Hitler and his unspeakable henchmen emerge victorious? Do you know how they are treating the populations of the countries they have conquered? And what they are doing to the Jews?"

"Have another drink, Adam, and don't get so excited." The Admiral smiled. "What they are doing to the conquered populations is done during wartime. Once the war is over things will ease up. I don't think they're acting any differently than we did in territories we conquered. And as for the Jews..."

"Yes, what about the Jews?" Adam asked.

"Well, they may be going a little overboard, but I can't disagree with their premise. There are just too many Jews in positions of influence. This is true for France as well. Why, you can't read a book, see a play or read a newspaper, without getting the Jewish point of view. And as for politics, it wouldn't be so bad for France if we had a masterful figure like Herr Hitler. We need some discipline and order."

During this entire conversation, Kurt sat in complete silence. Adam Bede was totally dumbfounded and could not even reply. Kurt got up and walked over to the window. Dawn was breaking.

"Please forgive the interruption," Kurt addressed the two older men. "I can see that Mr. Bede is totally exhausted. As his, " he chuckled, " nurse, may I suggest that we can give him some time to rest, and resume the conversation later? And, may I ask, Admiral, what will you do about the two Germans, dead and alive?"

"You are absolutely right, young man. I am a bad host, Adam." The Admiral rose. " Let me help you to a guestroom. Both of you could use a few hours sleep. We will have dinner tonight en famille, and we can talk further then. There is no urgency, is there, Adam? There is no British fleet on its way here, Adam?"

Adam Bede was very subdued. "I know nothing of British fleet dispositions. What about the two Germans?"

"Leave that to me. After all, I am in command here. I fought off an intruder, and the surviving German will be kept incommunicado in our jail until we can interrogate him further. Perhaps, your friend here can assist us with that tomorrow, since he speaks the language. But first, you must get your rest. Come with me, let me get you settled, and I will see you at dinner tonight."

* * *

.

"I don't understand, I don't understand. A friend of twenty years, and I never knew how he felt. This is dreadful." Adam Bede was almost in tears. "What do we do now? We've got to get back to the Drake and tell them I've failed."

"I think what we do now is rest. We'll leave here tonight. We can't rendezvous with the Drake until night. Perhaps by then we can think of something. Come, let me help you to bed." Kurt said.

A few hours of sleep, and a bathroom in which Kurt could clean himself and assist Adam, and in spite of Adam's great disappointment, the world looked brighter. The evening sun was sinking lower as Adam hobbled on his crutches to the dining room, accompanied by his "nurse."

The dining room was filled with flowers. White damask tablecloths, silver cutlery, crystal wine glasses, and the Admiral in full uniform, gave the room a festive appearance. *If this is the way an Admiral lives*, Kurt thought, *maybe I should consider that profession.* And he smiled to himself. *Of course, an Austrian Admiral. Or, since I am no longer Austrian, a Jewish Admiral. Of a Jewish Navy no less. What a dream.*

"I have asked Clemente and the children to dine by themselves, since I am certain that you want to continue our discussion. Clemente sends her best, and hopes to see you later, and young man, she also told me to thank you for your help with those intruders."

The Admiral seemed to have accepted his own story about intruders without reference to the political implications. He continued: "I am doing this for the sake of our old friendship, Venerable, but I beg you to be very circumspect in what you are asking of me.

In fact it would be so much better if we could ignore the present situation and consider only the problems we have enjoyed so much in the past. For instance, what kind of ships, do you think, Hannibal used to transport his war elephants across the Mediterranean.?"

A magnificent meal, served by the same middle aged woman who had first called the Admiral, wonderful wines which Kurt did not know enough to appreciate and from which he abstained as much as possible, and conversation about the arcana of ancient ships, made the time pass quickly. Every time Adam Bede tried to resume the discussion about the present political situation, the Admiral politely but firmly changed the subject to their mutual hobby. Kurt spent the time mostly in silent contemplation.

It was midnight. "We must leave," Kurt interjected into a discussion evaluating the merits of Hawkin's flagship versus the flagship of the Duke of Medina Sidona, leader of the great Armada. "We need transportation. Will you help us, Admiral?"

Admiral Theberge hesitated. "Venerable, I want your assurance that there will be no British attack on me."

"How can I give you such an assurance? I am not privy to the decisions of my government. And if I don't answer that, what are you going to do, Bobo, keep me prisoner? Don't be silly."

"You are right, old friend. I will get my car and driver to take you wherever you want to go."

"Excuse me." Kurt spoke up. " I don't think it would be wise to publicize our presence here any more than necessary. It isn't terribly far. Would you drive us, please, Admiral?"

Theberge looked at Adam." Do you really think that's wiser?"

"Indeed, I do."

"Very well." The Admiral picked up his phone. "Bring my car to the front door. I am going out. I will drive myself."

"One more question, Admiral. " Kurt said politely. "You have made the decision to obey the Vichy government in all things. Do you think all your men agree with that decision? Wouldn't you want to ask them? Perhaps you might call an assembly and have them vote for Petain or De Gaulle?"

The Admiral laughed. "You are very naïve, young man. This is a military organization and there is only one commander. I make the decisions and no one else."

Kurt gently took the German Luger out of his backpack and placed it on the table in front of him.

"Well, Admiral, I think it would be wise to get all your men off the ships and assemble them on the parade ground we drove past on the way here. And I ask that you make sure that all your men are there no later than 6 A.M."

The Admiral jumped up. "So there will be an attack. Well, thank you. We will know how to defend ourselves."

Kurt picked up the pistol, clicked off the safety and faced the Admiral.

"Sit down, Admiral. Quickly, before this gun goes off. I am no expert on guns and it could happen easily."

Slowly the Admiral lowered himself into his chair. "Do you approve of this?" He turned to Adam. "You are no better than the Germans. And you have lied to me."

Adam Bede was speechless. He looked at Kurt in despair.

"Now, Admiral." Kurt said quietly. "All I want is to help you save the lives of your men. Get them up on the parade ground and they will be safe. Leave them aboard your ships and many of them will die."

"You're not going to shoot. I'm going to warn my ships and we will fight any attacker, British or German. That is our duty."

The Admiral began to get up from his chair. Kurt leaned over the table, grabbed the Admiral by the neck with his left hand, and slapped the officer with all his might, left and right. Theberge collapsed in his chair. Kurt picked up the pistol again, pointed it at the Admiral and said quietly.

"Please, Admiral, make no mistake. I will do what I have to do to save the lives not only of your French sailors, but also those of the sailors in the British fleet against whom you want to fight."

Adam Bede finally found his voice: "Bobo, please do what the young man asks. There is nothing dishonorable in saving the lives of your men. You cannot defeat the British squadron and in any case, I do not believe that you really want to fight against us."

Kurt had never seen anyone looking at him with such naked hatred. "No one has ever treated me like that," the Admiral muttered. "Go ahead, and shoot."

Kurt moved around the table and stood over the officer. "You still do not believe that I will kill you. You saw that I killed a German without hesitation. You have made killing you easy. I heard what you said about Jews." Kurt took the Admiral's face in his hand and forced him to look up. "I am a Jew. Now save your life and the life of your men. Give the order to assemble them all on the parade ground. One word out of line and you are dead. And after that, if you have any doubt about complying, know that I will shoot your wife and daughters as well."

"Kurt, no, you can't do that." Adam Bede exclaimed.

"I can and I will. The world will be better off with fewer anti-Semites. Now will you make the call, Admiral?"

Admiral Theberge gave Kurt a long look. Then he picked up the telephone. "Give me Adjutant Michaud, please. Michaud? Sorry to call you so late. I want you to assemble all the men on the parade ground at 6 A.M. All of them. Do not let any one stay on the ships. What? Oh, we're in port, no need for a skeleton crew on each ship. I have an important announcement to make and I want every man on the parade ground. Is that understood? Good. See you there. Au revoir."

"Thank you, Admiral. Now, please take us to your car." Kurt continued to point the pistol at the officer.

"Just one minute." Adam Bede said. "Do you realize what will happen to you after the attack, Bobo? It will be evident from the order that you just gave that you were aware of the attack and assisted in it. You will be court-martialed."

"Oh God, you are right, Venerable." Admiral Theberge sank into his chair. "What have I done? I should have let you kill me."

"Let me make a suggestion, Bobo." Adam Bede got out of his chair, stood up with the help of his crutches and moved toward the Admiral. "Come with us. Bring Clemente and the girls and join De Gaulle in London. With your rank you will be received as a hero. You will certainly receive a ministerial position in the French government in exile. And I promise you that what happened here to persuade you to join our side will remain our secret." Adam Bede turned to Kurt. "Will you make the same commitment to the Admiral?"

Kurt smiled grimly. "Yes, I will. We need all the help we can get to fight against Germany, even someone like you." He could not hide his contempt for the Frenchman.

"We must leave." Adam Bede said. "You will drive us alone and we will leave you on the shore out of reach of a telephone, or we will take your family with us and all of us will board a British vessel. What is it to be, Bobo, a triumphant arrival in London or disgrace here?"

* * *

On July 3, 1940 a British squadron commanded by Vice-Admiral Somerville attacked the French fleet in port in Oran. The French battleship Dunkerque was badly damaged and aground; the Provence and the Bretagne were destroyed, the seaplane tender Commandant Teste and two destroyers were sunk. Casualties were extremely light.

Kurt had watched the attack from the deck of the Drake. He saw planes dropping bombs, long range guns delivering their deadly cargo, and explosion after explosion in the area of the port. But he saw no resistance, heard no answering salvos.

Getting back to the Drake had been a close call. Once Admiral Theberge was persuaded to come with Adam Bede and Kurt, he had to gather his wife and daughters. To wake three Frenchwomen out of a sound sleep, tell them to pack within fifteen minutes and leave their home forever, seemed to Kurt a far more difficult task than to convince the Admiral. He could not consider the use of his pistol a viable option, even though he had threatened the Admiral that he would shoot the ladies. He was shocked that Theberge had believed him, and attributed that fact to the Frenchman's anti-Semitism. After all, Jews must be capable of the most heinous acts, because they are Jews.

Captain Tolliver had been as good as his word. Once Kurt fired the Very Pistol from the beach near the spot where they had landed, the Drake approached the shore, sent a boat, and the transfer to the ship was accomplished.

The moment that Adam Bede found himself alone with Kurt, he pulled him aside and whispered: "How did you have the nerve to do what you did? If your bluff hadn't worked, we'd both be in a French jail."

"Never mind that now." Kurt answered. "We have to report immediately that the Germans knew about the plan to attack Oran. How did they know that? And they must have known it days in advance, so they could send their bullyboys to Admiral Theberge."

"You're right. I forgot about that." Adam Bede sighed. "I'm just not thinking like an intelligence operative but you seem to have a natural talent for it. This is very serious. We must find the leak. We must inform the Captain."

"The question is," Kurt asked, "whether the Germans got the information from intercepting ship's radio communications, or whether there is a spy in your organization in London."

"That is true. I think we'll keep that to ourselves until we reach London. In the meantime, I will strongly suggest to Admiral Somerville that his radio communications may be compromised."

When Vice-Admiral Somerville learned of the presence aboard the Drake of Admiral Theberge and his family, he detached that vessel from his squadron and ordered it back to England at full speed. Obviously he felt

34

that Admiral Theberge's presence in London would be useful. This caused Captain Tolliver no end of problems. A Royal Navy destroyer is not equipped for passengers, particularly very demanding female passengers. The Captain gave up his quarters to the Admiral and Madame Theberge, arranged for the wardroom to be transformed into quarters for the Admiral's daughters, and doubled up with his executive officer. Adam Bede returned to his old bunk in sickbay. Kurt joined him there.

The passage was swift. Adam was as seasick as ever and spent most of his time in his bunk. It was very hard for him to get around the destroyer on his crutches. He was afraid of falling again and aggravating his injury. Kurt assisted him as much as possible, but found plenty of time to spend on deck, observing with admiration the disciplined workings of a Royal Navy crew.

During one of the few moments the Venerable Bede was not retching and complaining, Kurt asked: " What will happen to me when we reach England?"

"I don't know." Adam replied. "But I can tell you this. I'll have to report to my superiors for a debriefing. I am sure they will want to hear from you as well. After that...tell me what you want to do."

"There isn't any choice for me. I want to fight against the Nazis and I can't make any other plans until they are defeated."

"That's what I thought. I will certainly recommend that you are given the opportunity. I think you could be very useful to my masters. But I fear that my recommendation may not carry much weight. After all, I failed in my mission." Adam said despondently.

"That," Kurt said, " may be a matter of interpretation."

A destroyer does not have the promenade deck of a luxury liner. Frequently, when Kurt was on deck, leaning against the railing and enjoying the fresh air and sunshine, particularly after spending time with Adam Bede in the fetid atmosphere of the sickbay, he encountered the Theberge family. Admiral and Madame Theberge, followed by their daughters, attempted to walk up and down the narrow deck as if indeed it were a promenade.

Admiral Theberge studiously ignored Kurt, even when he brushed by him on the narrow confines of the deck. Madame Theberge gave him a cordial smile the first time this happened, but after that, probably on instructions from her husband, followed the Admiral's example. This gave Kurt the opportunity to observe the Theberge ladies with impunity.

Clemente Theberge was at least fifteen years younger than her husband. She was tall, slim and elegant, with black hair streaked with premature white, that made her face look more youthful than her age of barely forty.

Of the two daughters, the younger one was probably thirteen or fourteen. She had all the awkwardness of a yet unformed woman, but her black hair and regular features promised good looks when she matured.

The older daughter was a beauty. On the threshold of maturity, slim and well formed, her black hair cut short like a helmet, framing a pert face, unexpectedly blue eyes sparkling with humor, she was a pleasure to behold.

Because of his rank, on occasion, the Admiral was invited to the bridge where he could discuss the ship's progress with Captain Tolliver. One evening, while Theberge was so engaged and Kurt stood at his usual place at the railing staring out to sea, a soft French voice interrupted his thoughts.

"Why is my father angry at you?"

Kurt turned. The beautiful young woman looked at him questioningly.

"I'm sorry, Mademoiselle...?"

"Solange. My name is Solange. What is your name?"

"Kurt, Kurt Auster. I'm sorry, I can't tell you why your father feels about me the way he does. You'll have to ask him. And I fear you may get into trouble if you are seen speaking to me. I'm a pariah as far as the Theberge family is concerned."

"Don't worry. What can my father do to me? I'll talk to whomever I please." Solange said tossing her head. "But I don't understand. I know that you helped save us from the three Nazi soldiers and that you assisted in our escape from the Vichy regime. I know, my mother, my sister and I are very grateful to you. So why is my father so angry? You've given him a chance to fight for France."

"Really," Kurt said regretfully, " I can think of few things I dislike as much as disappointing a beautiful woman, but I can't answer your question. And I think I'd better say good night." And Kurt left his accustomed place along the railing and returned to the sickbay.

* * *

"You were absolutely right not to say anything to Solange." Adam Bede said. "We have committed ourselves to support Admiral Theberge's contention that he left Oran voluntarily in order to join de Gaulle and fight for a free France."

"Can he be trusted to do that, Mr. Bede?" Kurt asked.

"First of all, my dear young man, we have been through so much together, that it is time you called me Adam. In fact, if you choose, you may even use the nickname only my dearest friends are privileged to use, Venerable."

"I heard the Admiral call you that, Adam, but I didn't understand where that nickname came from."

"Well, there was an eighth century church historian in Britain named Bede, and he was called the Venerable Bede. We know little about his life except that he was monastic, but we do have his histories of the church in Britain and they are very valuable. You can see why my friends would apply that name to me. Now, as to your question regarding Admiral Theberge's trustworthiness. I don't know the answer. He served with distinction against the Germans in the first World War, but time and promotion may just have made him too comfortable in his present position. Well, you shattered tha! Can he be trusted? Perhaps. He is, as I have found out, an opportunist, and now he has no choice but to be an ardent supporter of the Free French."

"I know," Kurt mused, " that we promised to be silent about his attitudes and that we had to force him to cooperate with us. But my feeling is that we must reveal the whole story to your superiors in the Intelligence Service, so that they can be aware if there is another shift in his loyalties."

"Oh, I fully agree with you." Adam Bede nodded. "It was always my intention to report everything at our debriefing and I promise that you will get full credit for what you have done. I must say, Bobo and I had been friends for so many years, and I never knew or understood him. This is a great disappointment to me. I thought I was a better judge of character."

"War changes people drastically, Venerable." Kurt said, trying the "Venerable" for the first time. " I did not know what I would become, and what I am capable of. I'm not happy about it but I have to be realistic about the world we live in, and to learn to deal with people and situations in ways I would never have dreamt about two years ago."

"You are wise above your years, Kurt. "Adam Bede said. "Do you know what bothers me? And how silly it is? That Bobo does not even take the trouble to visit me. I guess our friendship is at an end. But if he came here, and we talked, perhaps it could have been saved. Perhaps, I could have convinced him that he did the right thing in ordering his men off the ships and in joining our fight against Nazi Germany."

"I doubt that he could ever forgive me for slapping him and for forcing him to leave his command. And you were a witness to his humiliation. Too bad. I would have enjoyed getting to know Solange."

* * *

The next evening, Kurt stood at his usual spot along the railing looking at the phosphorescent wake the ship left in the swift trip toward England Night fell late, there was an ocean of stars - so many more visible than from the cities in which Kurt had spent most of his life. *I have no control over my environment until we reach London. And then, what will happen to me? Technically, I'm an enemy alien. Will the British accept me and allow me to join their army? I never expected to be a soldier, but now that seems the best thing I could do. Winning the war against Germany must be the highest priority, and I've got to do what I can.*

"You look very sad. What are you thinking about?" A soft hand touched Kurt's elbow.

"Mademoiselle Solange. Forgive me, I did not hear you." Kurt said with some embarrassment.

"Tell me. Why are you so sad?"

"You know you're going to be in trouble with your father if you talk to me." Kurt smiled at the lovely girl.

"Look, you don't want to tell me why my father hates you, and I asked him, and he doesn't want to talk about it either. He just told me that you're not the kind of man a well educated jeune fille should associate with. Well, I'm old enough to make up my own mind. So, if I promise not to bother you about what happened in Oran, can we talk about other things?"

How could any young man refuse to talk to a beautiful young woman, whose astonishing blue eyes look at him pleadingly, whose hand gently caresses his elbow, and whose black hair glitters in the starlight. Kurt was probably more susceptible than most to feminine charms. And so he surrendered.

"Very well, let's talk."

* * *

During the next three days, or rather evenings, Kurt spent many hours with Solange. He did not know whether the Admiral was aware of these conversations, but noted that Solange appeared alone only late, when presumably her parents and sister had retired for the night. During the daily promenades, when Admiral and Madame Theberge strolled past him on the narrow deck, followed closely by their daughters, Solange never spoke to Kurt, but she favored him with a complicitous smile whenever her father's back was turned.

Kurt learned that the Admiral had been away from home at sea for much of Solange's youth. The command at Oran was the first time that he was stationed on shore long enough to have his family join him. Life in Oran for a French Admiral and his family was far more luxurious than in metropolitan France. The quarters were much more commodious, there were many more servants, and the social life among the elite of the colonial power was active and glittering. Solange reported that her mother was not at all happy about the Admiral's sudden decision to give up the glamorous life they had led among the high society of French Algeria for the life of an exile in a foreign country at war.

Madame Theberge complained that she should certainly have been consulted before such a decision was made. Solange felt that a rift had developed between her parents. Solange, on the other hand, was an ardent patriot. She admired her father enormously for his action in giving up everything so that he could fight for a free France.

Kurt was tempted to disabuse the lovely girl by telling her the circumstances of the Admiral's patriotic decision, but remembered his promise and so kept silent. Had there not been a war, Solange would have returned to Paris in the Fall to enter the Sorbonne. She had no idea where her university career would have led her, but the Sorbonne was the next logical step for a jeune fille bien elev.

Now she was concerned about what she would do in London. She did not speak English at all. She wanted to volunteer to help with the war effort, and wondered whether there would be any place for her among the Free French. And she kept asking Kurt how quickly he had learned his languages and whether he would be around to help her learn English.

Of course, Kurt had no idea about his future. He had told Solange little about his past, just that he had escaped from the Nazi dominated continent of Europe, and had come along to Oran to assist the injured Adam Bede.

When Solange asked why the Nazis were after him, he told her that he was Jewish and waited for a reaction. Surely, the daughter of Paul Theberge had to be as anti-Semitic as her father. But, to Kurt's pleasant surprise, that did not seem to be the case.

Solange made Kurt promise to try to find her in London so that they could expand on their friendship. It was easy for Kurt to make such a promise to the lovely girl, subject of course to his ability to move freely around that city. He shared his own concerns about his future with her, fully aware that he was not likely to be able to spend much time in London.

And then the British coast appeared on the horizon.

Captain Tolliver sighed with relief. They had encountered no submarines, no German planes, no German warships. He thought they had been very lucky. His passengers had no idea of the dangers they had been running during the voyage, They must have thought this was a pleasure cruise. He couldn't wait until he was rid of them, and his ship could resume her duties as a man-of-war.

When the Drake docked at the jetty in Portsmouth, Captain Tolliver stood near the gangplank to say good bye to his guests. Two cars were waiting on the pier: One limousine with a French flag and a French naval officer was waiting for Admiral Theberge and his family. A smaller car waited for Adam and Kurt. As Kurt was helping Adam navigate the gangplank on his crutches, he caught a glimpse of Solange entering the limousine. She glanced at him and waved. Admiral Theberge gave Kurt and Adam a look of pure hatred.

"I guess he really does not like me any more. Too bad." Adam muttered. "I'll miss our talks."

* * *

London had changed drastically during Adam's short absence. What Winston Churchill had called " the Battle of Britain" had begun in earnest. Every night masses of German bombers dropped their murderous cargo on the city. The Royal Air Force, handicapped by a shortage of men and planes, did a miraculous job. The Germans paid a heavy price, but the bombings went on and on.

The first sight Kurt and Adam encountered as they approached the city were the barrage balloons floating high in the sky, attached to the earth by heavy wires. They were supposed to prevent bombers from approaching their targets too closely. Large numbers of sandbags were piled along the streets and buildings. Every Londoner carried his gas mask over his or her shoulder. Wherever it was possible, glass storefronts were covered with plywood. And here and there empty lots filled with rubble, where houses had once stood, demonstrated the efficacy of the enemy.

Even Admiral Morse's office in Whitehall had changed. Heavy curtains covered the windows and were not opened even during daylight. Admiral Morse's desk, which had been near the largest of the windows from which he was accustomed to enjoy the view of the park, had been moved to the center of the room, as far away from potentially exploding glass as possible.

"So you think you failed?" Admiral Morse chuckled after Adam had made his report. "Well, let's analyze that.

Imprimis, you found out that there is a leak here in Whitehall. It is definitely not the naval transmissions that gave the Germans warning of our intention to attack Oran, the timing would be wrong. No, we have a bad apple here, and I can guarantee that I will find him.

Secundis, you ensured that our attack succeeded with almost no casualties, not even casualties on the part of the French, who, in spite of everything, are still putative allies.

Tertius, you brought back a French Admiral, the commander of the squadron in Oran to join de Gaulle's Free French. Certainly to say the least, a propaganda victory.

And finally, you killed one German agent and injured or captured two other enemies.

I wouldn't really call this a failure."

"Admiral, you are very kind, but I did not accomplish the mission you gave me. And besides, "Adam said earnestly, " all the accomplishments you listed so generously were not mine. Credit must go to my companion, Kurt Auster."

"Ah, the young man who is waiting in the anteroom. Tell me more about him."

"All I can tell you is that without him, this mission would not even have gotten off the ground. And now I believe that it would be best if you spoke to him directly, Admiral, but I am convinced that he could be of great service to our cause, if you give him a chance."

"Well, we'll see. I'll certainly consider what you have said. And now off with you. You must get proper medical care. Call me from the hospital and tell me how you are doing and when you can get back to work. Thank you for your efforts."

"May I see Kurt to say good bye to him?"

The Admiral hesitated. "No, I don't think so. I want to know what this young man is made of. I'll let you know what I've decided about him, and you'll probably get to see him later. You'd better leave by this door. John " the Admiral turned to the aide who had brought Adam in, " see to it that my good friend gets the best care at St. Elizabeth's and then report back to me."

* * *

Kurt had been sitting in the Admiral's anteroom for a long time. Finally he was called in to the presence. Admiral Morse did not get up from behind his desk, nor did he invite Kurt to sit. He addressed Kurt in fluent German.

"I'm Admiral Morse. I've heard interesting things about you. What do you want?"

"Defeat Germany." *If he's going to be blunt, so will I be.*

"Hmm, a consummation devoutly to be hoped. What do you want to do about it?"

"Join your army and fight." Kurt said quietly.

The Admiral shifted to French.

"Adam Bede speaks very highly of you. You have demonstrated to him that you can think quickly and act decisively "

Kurt got tired of standing in front of Admiral Morse's desk like a schoolboy in the principal's office. He sat down. The Admiral took no apparent notice of this action, but something like a smile may have appeared behind his beard.

Now the Admiral shifted to English. "I may be able to use you. Do you want to work for me?"

"Doing what?" Kurt asked.

"Whatever I tell you to do."

"Thank you, Admiral, but I won't make an unconditional commitment like that. Obeying without question is what got Germany into her present mess."

Admiral Morse clearly hid a smile. But he said sternly.

"Are you telling me you'd refuse to obey a superior's lawful order? What kind of a soldier do you think you'll make?"

"One who won't abandon his right to think for himself."

The Admiral leaned back. " I'm glad to hear you say that. Now, again, do you want to work for me?"

"Sir, I don't want to sit in an office and shuffle papers. I want to fight."

"Well," the Admiral smiled, " I have no intention on wasting your talents shuffling papers. You'll risk your life more than you know, and you'll fight. But I must warn you, before I make a final decision to take you on, I'll have you vetted. By the time my people are through with you, I'll know every breath you ever took. If there is anything you don't want me to know, you may walk out of here now."

"And then what happens to me?"

"You're an enemy alien. You'll be interned for the duration. It will not be terribly comfortable, but it will be safe."

Kurt smiled. "That is not what I want, Admiral. I have no objections to telling your people all about me as long as they understand that there are things I had to do to survive of which my mother might have disapproved. But I have one request."

"Go on."

"I want British citizenship. I do not want to be stateless and after the war have no place to go. I'll fight for Britain, but I want British papers."

The Admiral snorted. "Don't you bargain with me, young fellow. One word from me, and you'll spend the war years in a camp."

Kurt got up. "Thank you for your time, Admiral." He turned and walked toward the door.

"Come on back," Admiral Morse said with a smile. "Can't scare you easily, eh? What would you have done, if I had sent you to an enemy alien camp?"

Kurt smiled without answering.

"Oh, you think you'd escape and go your way? Don't forget, Britain is an island, it's not so easy to leave here. Anyway, never mind. I can only promise to try to make you a British subject as soon as possible. I'm going to be dealing with bureaucrats and their damned rules and regulations, but I'll give it my best shot. And now get out, my people will take you in hand. God help you if you're not who you say you are."

Kurt stood up. "Please forgive me, Admiral, but where is Adam Bede? I'm responsible for him. He can't get around without help."

Morse smiled. "He's in good hands. When we're through with you, you'll be able to see him. Now go on."

* * *

A silent young man led Kurt to a waiting car and an equally silent driver sped off. To Kurt's question: "Where are we going? " there was no reaction. *Very well, I'm in their hands.* Kurt thought. In due course, the car left the city and eventually drove through ever narrowing roads into a very pretty section of countryside. Hedges ran along side country roads, there were flowered borders, trees and occasional small streams. With all the twisting and turning, Kurt had no idea whether he was North, South, East or West of the capital. Then they turned into a long driveway.

This must be one of the famous stately homes of England, he thought at his first sight of the building. It was a rambling structure with large windows facing a garden full of flowers, with many chimneys, dormer windows on the top floors and large French doors leading outside. The garden and building were surrounded by a low brick wall. Had Kurt known anything about architecture, he might have identified the house as basically late Georgian, with numerous subsequent additions.

He got out. The driver did not give Kurt a glance, but drove off immediately. For a moment, Kurt stood in front of the large entrance door, feeling somewhat lost.

A big, heavyset man in uniform came down the steps.

"Here you are then." The man did not smile. " I'm Sergeant Hawks. I'll try to make you comfortable. And you'd better get started. Come along."

He led Kurt inside, took him into a small room and seated him at a desk. "Here's paper and pencil. You've got three hours until dinner. Write the story of your life. As detailed as possible, please. Full names and addresses, phone numbers if you've got them. If you don't finish before dinner, you can continue afterwards."

"And then what happens?" Kurt asked.

"Tomorrow the interrogators will start in on you. So you'd better be accurate - and truthful." Sergeant Hawks still did not smile. " Bathroom is down the hall on your left, and I'll bring in some tea and cookies to keep you from starving." The sergeant left.

Kurt sat down and looked at the blank sheet of paper. *Where do I begin? And what do I leave out?*

He walked over to the window and looked out at the beautiful formal gardens. For a moment, he rested his head against the windowpane. He did not see the English roses. He saw the snow covered sidewalks of Vienna two and a half years earlier.

The bitterness of his loss welled up in him. He turned resolutely, sat down and began to write.

* * *

CHAPTER II

For a long time, Kurt Auster remembered his eighteenth birthday as the last time he had been truly happy.

When his alarm rang on that day, he snuggled for a moment longer under the down quilt in his warm bed, then, gritting his teeth, jumped up into the cold room. The fire had gone out as usual. A huge tile oven was built into the wall to heat his room and his parents' adjoining bedroom. But the heat only came out when the fire was lit. And the fire did not stay lit through the night.

Kurt looked out through the double window. Ice crystals had formed on the outer glass. He saw that a fresh blanket of snow had covered the streets during the night. It was still dark. Daylight would not come for another two hours. It was a typical February day in Vienna, but it was his birthday.

Quickly Kurt jumped into his clothes. He rushed to the bathroom to brush his teeth and wash his face with cold water. Briefly, he looked longingly at the complicated gas powered contraption that would heat the water for his weekly bath in the large tub. He had two more days to wait for this sybaritic pleasure.

He looked at himself in the mirror. *Eighteen*, he thought. *Well, that makes me a man.*

Kurt was just a shade over six foot, with black hair combed straight back, brown eyes and a strong nose. His expression was normally quite cheerful and there was something innocent about his face, as if he had never encountered a problem bigger than the grade he would get on a Latin examination. He had lived a pleasant, sheltered existence, occupied primarily by his studies and his family and his friends.

When he entered the kitchen, his mother was there already. As always, she had lit the gas oven to take some of the chill out of the winter air. His coffee and croissant were waiting at his seat at the kitchen table.

By long standing family tradition, his birthday was not mentioned. That would come tonight, at a festive table with his parents and his best friends. But there was a little extra warmth in his mother's morning kiss.

Kurt's father had already gone downstairs to dispatch the trucks that would fan out into the countryside to pick up fresh butter, cheese and eggs from the farmers who supplied Auster Provisions, the family firm.

As usual, Kurt rushed out the door to get to his school, and as usual he was called back by his mother who had prepared "a little snack for my growing boy."

That evening, indeed, Kurt's birthday was celebrated with pomp and circumstance. His mother had made his favorite dishes, particularly the apricot dumplings he loved. His father opened a bottle of wine, and Kurt's birthday present was the new pair of skis he had hoped for.

He would never have occasion to use those skis. Three weeks later, German troops crossed into Austria.

* * *

"You have been ordered to come here, so that I can explain your new status to you."

Professor Schmidt paused and looked at his audience. The assembly hall of the Akademische Gymnasium, one of the most prestigious schools in Vienna, was packed with all of the school's Jewish students. Schmidt stood in the well of the large room with ascending rows of seats made shiny by a hundred years of use.

"You may no longer consider yourselves citizens of this country."

There was a movement among the students - an in-drawing of breath, shock visible on some faces. Schmidt looked sternly at his audience and waited for quiet before continuing.

"For too long your vicious race has dominated and ruled honest Aryans through your insidious machinations. Finally, as a result of the heroic leadership of our Fuehrer, Adolf Hitler, Austria has come home into the Reich. Now he will defend us against your foreign influences which have so damaged our German soul and spirit."

The students were seated by classes; the youngest, the ten and eleven year olds in the front, and the oldest, at seventeen or eighteen ready for graduation after eight years of rigorous studies in the last rows.

"Do not believe," Professor Schmidt continued, while looking at the students directly in front of him, " that you can escape the evil heritage of your race by aspiring to a Germanness to which you can never belong. You have tainted blood."

Even in a school and in a country where Professors were respected above all, and where they had almost god-like powers to quiet an unruly classroom with a glance, these statements aroused some of the students to attempt to move in protest. Schmidt waited for a moment before continuing.

"The history of your race is such, that all methods are justified to defend our pure and innocent Aryan character against you. Your degenerate influences have come to an end. The sooner you understand that we will no longer tolerate you among us, the better for you.

"You are no longer students at this school. The Akademische Gymnasium prides itself on its long history. It is the school that taught Franz Schubert, Hugo von Hofmanstal, and many other good and famous German men. In the last generation, it has become infested by you Jews. No more. This school, like all other educational institutions, will be purged of all foreign influences and will return to its mission of educating German men.

"You will return to your homes. Perhaps at some time, the Fuehrer in his wisdom will arrange for you to continue your education in circumstances more appropriate to your present status. But first, a graphic demonstration of where you are today. Each of you will be issued a toothbrush and lye and a bucket of water. You will scrub the sidewalks around the school which you have polluted for all these years. You will scrub and scrub and scrub until all traces of Jewish contamination are gone!"

Some of the younger students in the front rows started to weep. Older students in the back began to protest. Schmidt ignored them and continued.

"You are dismissed. Take up your new duties."

Kurt Auster, watching one of his favorite professors from the back of the auditorium, felt the bile of bitter and impotent rage mounting in his throat. *I can't believe that Schmidt was a Nazi all along*, he thought. *He had always been so pleasant.*

As he and his fellow students left the auditorium, they found themselves surrounded by groups of uniformed Hitler Jugend, the Nazi youth movement. Kurt recognized some of his non - Jewish classmates among them.

The young Jews were organized into groups of six, received their equipment and were marched out into the pale March sunshine. Behind them rose the huge baroque building that had been the center of Kurt's existence for almost eight years; across the street, the small Beethoven Park, with the composer's statue in the center; across the Ringstrasse, the main boulevard circling Vienna's inner city, the skating rink where Kurt had spent many pleasant hours. Kurt looked around as if he had never seen this area before.

Kurt's group was marched around the corner. "Get on your knees and start scrubbing," the leader of their Hitler Jugend guards ordered. Kurt obeyed. He looked up. People from the neighborhood crowded around to watch. A policeman was there to keep order. When Kurt caught his eye, the policeman grinned and said to some of the people watching, "High time that those Jews found out what honest work feels like."

Kurt and his companions got on their knees, moistened the toothbrushes in the bucket of water mixed with lye, and started to scrub. He did not look up, but he heard some of the comments and the general laughter from the onlookers.

March could be very cold in Vienna. Kurt's hands soon were frozen, burned by the lye, and scratched by the pavement. He was glad that he wore long pants. He thought of the younger kids, still in short pants, without any protection against the cold and wet pavement.

Kurt glanced up at the policeman. All his life, his parents had taught him respect for law and order, and for the police who enforced it. He remembered his parents' instruction when he was first allowed out on his own, that the police were there to assist him if he ever got lost. And now, the police were there helping the Nazis persecute the Jews.

He began to feel panic. What had happened to his city and his country? He had always considered himself a patriotic Austrian. He had studied the thousand year old history of Austria with the same fervor as the four thousand year old history of the Jewish people. He had never felt that there was a conflict between his being a good Jew and being a good Austrian. Now, his country rejected him.

Suddenly, there was movement in the audience. Several adults were pushed down next to the group of students to participate in the sidewalk cleaning . Kurt recognized Director Marcus, the principal of the Akademische Gymnasium, and Professor Lackenbacher, who taught Latin and Greek. Lackenbacher had been Kurt's homeroom teacher for almost the entire eight years.

The student next to Kurt whispered something unintelligible.

" No talking, Jew, just work," came a voice from above, and a powerful kick landed on the student's posterior. He fell flat on his face and the bucket spilled.

"You," the voice of authority ordered Kurt, " take the bucket and get some more water."

Kurt obeyed. He grabbed the bucket and withdrew from the group standing around the scrubbers. As he turned the corner, he saw that he was not observed by any of the uniformed guards. Dropping the bucket, he ran away from the open Beethovenplatz into the narrow, winding streets of the Old City, the Innere Stadt. He did not look behind him, but there was no pursuit. Blindly Kurt rushed through the twisting alleys of the oldest section of Vienna. His heart was beating, partly in fear and partly in anger. Finally, he stopped, leaned against a wall and started to breathe. In front of him, just across Michaelerplatz, stood the church of St. Michael, one of the most beautiful baroque churches in Vienna.

Kurt entered the church. It was dark and silent. There was a faint scent of incense. In the gloom, Kurt saw an occasional worshipper seated on the benches. Kurt collapsed in a pew as far away from the entrance and as far way from the pulpit as he could. He shivered, not from the cold, but in recollection of his feeling of panic.

What have I done? he thought. By running he feared he had exposed himself to further punishment. He took some deep breaths. *I've got to think this through,* he said to himself, *I can't take any chances that Papa and Mama get into trouble because of me. I should have stayed and done the work.*

Kurt realized that with the Anschluss - the absorption of Austria into the German Reich -his life had changed drastically, and that any plans he had made for graduation and University were now unrealistic fantasies. He began to believe Professor Schmidt's warning that there was no longer any place for Jews in Vienna.

Kurt decided to wait in the church for a while. The crypt had been the repository of the sarcophagi of Hapsburg emperors and their families for many centuries, and there were frequent guided tours, but at that time, barely a week after the occupation of Austria by German troops - to a jubilant reception by most Austrians - these tours had not yet resumed, and the church remained quiet. Kurt had been there many times. He had always felt that the Hapsburgs were his emperors, and their glory, his glory as an Austrian. Now he began to feel like an alien intruder. Schmidt's words had had their effect.

Two hours later, Kurt emerged from the church. He had tried to clean himself up as best he could, and looked no different from any other teenager - except for one glaring difference. There was not one "Aryan" Austrian who did not sport a swastika in his lapel. Foreign citizens were quick to place emblems showing the flags of their countries there. Austrian Jews had no insignia, and thus were easily recognized.

Kurt walked home as quickly as he could, continuously glancing over his shoulder to see whether he was being observed or followed. He suddenly felt totally unsafe in his own hometown.

When he returned to his street, he paused for a long moment near his parents' door. He looked around. He was afraid that there would be police or Hitler Jugend members waiting for him. *You're not that important*, he finally scolded himself, as he entered.

Both his parents were waiting for him. This was the first day of school after the Anschluss, and they were eager to know how the day had progressed. What Kurt told them, confirmed their worst fears.

Kurt's mother wrung her hands. "What are we going to do? And just before Kurt's graduation. " She looked at Kurt's father pleadingly, as if he could come up with an answer.

The older Auster tried to be calm, even though it was clear that he was very upset at the treatment Kurt had received.

"Let us hope that this anti-Semitic eruption will pass as soon as Austria is completely absorbed into the Reich. After all, we have lived here for centuries, and we have withstood anti-Semitism before."

"But this," Kurt's mother would not be pacified, "making Kurt scrub the sidewalk? That's just terrible."

"I know how you feel about our son," Kurt's father chuckled. "You're a lioness when your child is mistreated. But let's be calm. No harm came to him, except to his dignity. Let's just wait and see."

Kurt's father sat down in his favorite armchair, waited for his wife and son to sit as well, and continued.

"There were only 600.000 Jews in all of Germany, when Hitler came to power in 1933. That's out of over 60 million Germans. Some of them had it bad, and others left, but by and large, if they kept their nose clean, they got along. There are 200,000 Jews in Vienna, 10% of the population. They can't get along without us. And what do you think the world will say about uncivilized behavior like what we saw today? Do you think, Hitler wants the world to think of him as a bully? No. He wants to be considered a statesman. Hitler got what he wanted, the Anschluss, and now he'll want to improve the economy and be respectable in the eyes of the world. At least, that's what I think. I'm sure, things will improve."

* * *

In 1934, barely one year after Adolf Hitler took power in Germany, a group of Austrian Nazis invaded the Chancellery in the Hofburg, shot and mortally wounded the Austrian Chancellor Engelbert Dollfuss, and proclaimed a Nazi government. Hitler massed troops as the Austrian border, ready to march in as requested by the Nazi Putschists.

At that time, however, Mussolini, the Fascist dictator of Italy, had no desire to have Germany directly on his frontiers. He sent a few divisions to the borders himself, and thus forced Hitler to abandon his plans.

Dollfuss bled to death without being allowed to have either a doctor or a priest. In a well orchestrated military assault by the Austrian army, most of the Nazi attackers were killed or arrested. This was probably the last victorious engagement in which Austrian troops participated.

Education Minister Kurt von Schuschnigg became Chancellor after Dollfuss's death. The Nazi party was banned, as the Communist party had been after an earlier brief civil war. Austria was ruled as a benevolent dictatorship by Schuschnigg and his very conservative Christian-Socialist party.

The Nazis continued to recruit and to intrigue, and many Austrians were "illegal" party members.

By 1938 German diplomacy had succeeded in forging the German-Italian Axis of Fascist powers in Central Europe and Hitler was ready to try again. Mussolini would no longer object to Hitler's plans.

Hitler called Schuschnigg to his aerie in Berchtesgaden and threatened war if Schuschnigg did not agree to the immediate absorption of Austria into the Reich. Hitler insisted that all German speakers must be under one flag and under one leader.

Schuschnigg returned to Vienna and set the date for a plebiscite - a vote on whether the population of Austria really wanted to join Nazi Germany. The plebiscite was scheduled for Sunday, March 15, 1938.

However, Hitler did not want to take any chances. Two days before the plebiscite, on Friday, March 13, German troops crossed the Austrian border and the Anschluss was a "fait accompli". Schuschnigg was arrested and spent the next seven and a half years in a German prison.

Shortly after the Anschluss, there was indeed an election in Austria. Of course, Jews were not allowed to vote. According to official German figures, more than 99% of the voters chose annexation to Germany. Judging from the jubilant masses which received Hitler on his triumphant entry into Vienna, it is unlikely that this 99% figure had to be corrected by the impartial Nazi vote counters.

* * *

Vienna was beautiful. Two months after the Anschluss, the excitement had not subsided. Flowers were blooming everywhere in one of the sunniest Mays in history. The city was festooned with Swastika banners and Nazi party slogans - "Ein Volk, ein Reich, ein Fuehrer (One people, one Empire, one Leader)," "Juda verrecke (Jews Croak)," "Wir danken unserem Fuehrer (We thank our Leader)," or "Die Juden sind unser Unglueck (The Jews are our misfortune)." There was an atmosphere of joy and patriotic fervor. Colorful uniforms were to be seen everywhere - SS in black, Army in field gray, and even Navy in blue. Austrians who had not had a seaport since 1918 could again aspire to serve in a Navy, albeit a German Navy.

Here and there, a few outsiders who did not share in the general pleasure skulked along the streets, trying to be as inconspicuous as possible. Some of Vienna's two hundred thousand Jews had no choice but to risk the danger of the streets. They had to run some errands to stay alive.

Kurt Auster was one of them. Since his expulsion from the Akademische Gymnasium, he had stayed home and attempted to help his parents keep their business going. But even that did not work. Many of the farmers who had supplied his father for many years suddenly decided that it was unwise to deal with a Jew. Many of the customers who had been served by the firm immediately abandoned it in favor of Aryan suppliers. There was little to do, and yet his father did not dare to fire any of his Aryan workers, who showed up only on payday to collect their unearned wages. The situation was becoming untenable, but Kurt's parents were not yet ready to abandon the home and city their families had known for generations.

Whenever Kurt felt stifled in the apartment, he wandered the streets of Vienna. He knew how dangerous it was, but he also knew he needed to get out. He knew that it was no longer his city, that Austria was no longer his country, and he wanted to absorb as much as he could of the new Nazi Vienna, because, subconsciously, he felt that this would make it easier to leave when his parents decided that the time to do so had come.

That day, as he was on his way home, the sky darkened and suddenly it began to rain. Kurt had not anticipated this change in the weather and had no raingear. He ran as fast as he could toward his street, but the rain turned into a deluge just as he approached his home. He took shelter under the overhang of the building across the street from his apartment. *This storm can't last much longer*, he thought.

Across the street something was going on in front of his building. A military truck stopped in front of the entrance. Two men in uniform jumped out and went in. A moment later, they emerged carrying a long, wrapped object and unceremoniously threw it into the back of the truck. They returned to the building and came back with another similarly wrapped object which they threw into the truck as well. Then they drove off.

A cold premonition of disaster gripped Kurt's heart. Mindless of the rain, he rushed across the street and upstairs into his apartment.

He opened the door. Sprawled in his father's best chair, smoking a fat cigar and drinking his father's best Slivovitz - the plum brandy only used for the Kiddush on Friday night - was his father's foreman, Maresch.

"Ah, young Kurt - poor young Kurt. I did not mean this to happen, young Kurt. After all, a fellow has the right to try to better himself, doesn't he? You got to take your oppo - oppr- opportunities when you can. Right, young Kurt?"

"You are drunk, Herr Maresch. What are you doing here? And where are my parents?"

"Ah, poor young Kurt. I live here now, young Kurt. And if I want to get drunk, who's to tell me not to? Not a young Jew. You're lucky you weren't here, young Kurt. But I did not, I did not, I did not mean this to happen. Believe me, I did not. Not my fault, young Kurt, not my fault. It was the SS -they're the ones, not me."

"What happened? Where are my parents?" Kurt grabbed Maresch by the throat, "Where are they, where are they?"

"They're gone, young Kurt. Gone, gone, don't you understand? They're gone."

"What do you mean, they're gone? Where are they?"

"They're dead, young Kurt. They're dead. But I didn't mean it, I didn't have anything to do with it, it's not my fault, not my fault."

"Dead, both of them? I don't believe you. This is a sick joke. Come on, tell me the truth."

"It's the truth, young Kurt. He shot them both. He shot them both, and when he catches you, he'll shoot you too, young Kurt. But it's not my fault, it's not my fault. You'd better get out of here. Get out of here, because he'll shoot you too, as sure as can be."

Kurt looked around. The Torah which his father had inherited from his own grandfather, a renowned Rabbi, and which had rested on its own stand for as long as he could remember, was lying amidst the ashes of the fireplace. Its silver crown and breastplate were missing. As he looked further, he noticed dark spots on the carpet.

Kurt sank to his knees. Blood? Could this be his parents' blood? Could this horror be true? He looked at the pathetic drunk in front of him. *It's true, it's true, they're gone - Papa - Mama - they're gone. What am I to do? What am I to do?*

For a moment, the drunk appeared sober. He pulled Kurt up from his knees.

"You'd better go, young Kurt, better go." He pulled and pushed Kurt toward the door.

"He told me to keep you here, if you showed up before him. But I can't, I can't do it. He'll be back, he'll be back, and he'll kill you too. Better go, go."

Kurt stumbled out the door, his eyes full of tears - then he stopped and turned around.

"What is the murderer's name, what's his name? Tell me his name."

"Ratzersdorfer."

* * *

Kurt Auster sat on a rock high up in the mountains overlooking the Valley of the Inn. In the distance the lights of Innsbruck glimmered. On his left he could see the Isar Mountain, from which the Tyrolean national hero, Andreas Hofer, had conducted his guerrilla forays against the soldiers of Napoleon Bonaparte until he was betrayed and executed. All around Kurt was the wondrous beauty of the Tyrolean Alps, where he had skied and hiked so often. But Kurt saw nothing. He sat there contemplating his great loss and his shattered life.

He thought of his father. He remembered him intoning the Sabbath prayer at the dinner table on Friday nights. He remembered as a little boy going to the synagogue with him and being enfolded in his father's Tallis, the prayer shawl inherited from his grandfather, and which Kurt fully expected to inherit in due time.

He remembered he had never in his life felt so safe.

He thought of his mother, who always, always protected him. He remembered her going to school with him and fighting for him like a lioness for her young, when he had been falsely accused of some prank. She had kept on until she elicited an apology from the teacher. He thought of her helping him study his Latin vocabulary, of intoning " Vacca - Cow, Iter - Road " even though her own education tended toward Hebrew and not the languages he was studying.

Once, when he was eight or ten, he had an ear infection and the great Professor Neuman stood at his bedside to perform a small surgical procedure. He was transferred into his parent's large bed, and he remembered his parents hovering about him anxiously until Professor Neuman's assistant shooed them out the door. And he remembered waking up from the anesthesia to see them both at his bedside, their faces full of love and worry. Never again would he hear his mother's voice singing old melodies while she was preparing dinner. Never again would he listen to his father's stories of his youth, or tales of his business ventures. Never, never again.

Kurt had rushed out of the apartment and had blindly wandered the streets of Vienna for hours, mindless of the rain drenching him. He had found himself near the Westbahnhof, the railroad station from which he had so often taken a train on his trips to the Tyrolean countryside. He boarded a train without thinking. His eyes full of tears, his mind full of the horror he had learned, he had entered a lavatory, locked the door, and stayed there weeping helplessly.

It was night by then, and the train was almost empty. Eventually it left the station and began to make its way west. Many hours later, Kurt realized that the train had stopped. He opened the door and saw the sign "Innsbruck". He left the train. He wandered through familiar streets and started to climb on familiar paths higher and higher into the dawn.

And now he was sitting on a rock overlooking the valley and attempting to accept the unacceptable.

He started to shiver. It was cold, much colder than it should be in late May, even at this altitude. He looked down into the valley. It was gone - the lights of Innsbruck were gone. He was surrounded by fog. It looked as if he was in a box of cotton. He could hardly see more than a few feet in front of him.

And then it began to snow. Large, wet, heavy flakes coming down so rapidly that drifts accumulated as he watched. He realized that he was not in a fog, but in a low lying cloud, and that this was a late spring storm, not unusual in the Tyrol. Kurt was dressed for a spring day in Vienna, with city shoes, thin jacket, and spring coat, and a hat, which he had become accustomed to pulling low over his forehead. He was not immune to the Nazi propaganda that any good Aryan would immediately recognize a Jew by his Semitic features.

It was obvious that he needed shelter until the storm passed. Should he try to make his way back into the valley? With the low visibility, this would be risky. A small misstep, and he could be tumbling down some of the sheer cliffsides he had passed on the way up.

He did not know exactly where he was. On his way up he had been too absorbed in his thoughts, but he knew that there were some Alpine meadows ahead. Meadows meant huts. In the summer, the local peasantry would bring their cattle up to spend the good weather feasting off the fresh, green grass, and the cowherders would spend these months in comfortable Alpine cabins. The other consideration for Kurt was of course, that he could not feel safe back in the valley, surrounded by Nazis, where he was in constant danger.

Kurt was amazed at himself for thinking so clearly about his immediate predicament. His pain about his parents' death did not diminish, but he knew that he wanted to survive. He was not ready to give up, nor was he ready to make any plans for the future. But he was not willing to allow a little snow to stop him from at least thinking about what he could do with his life.

So he started to walk uphill. He attempted to stay in the center of any path he could discern, and tried to feel his way onto ground that was as level as possible.

The storm continued with full force. Drifts grew larger and deeper, and it got more and more difficult to advance. The cold got more intense. It became an enormous strain to move. In the thinner air of the upper reaches of the mountain, Kurt began to find it difficult to breathe. His clothes were soaked, partly from the inside by the perspiration caused by his efforts to advance, and partly from the outside by the wet and heavy snow.

Kurt looked around in the desperate hope of finding a hut or even a cave where he could shelter. The snow was coming down so heavily now that he could see nothing. He realized that shelter could be ten feet away, and he could pass it by.

But I have to keep going. I must, he exhorted himself. *If I stop, I will die. The snow will cover me, and they will find my body in the summer. Would that be so terrible? I would join Papa and Mama. We would be together. And I won't have to think about them, mourn them, weep for them, any more. I could just sleep and wake up in their arms.*

But I must not do that, they would not want me to. Papa and Mama wanted me to have a life. They did everything for me to give me every chance. And every time we went to synagogue, we listened to Moses' words: " I have set before you good and evil, death and life, therefore choose life..."

Choose life... but it was getting more and more difficult to do that. He was getting so tired, so tired. He had hardly slept in more than twenty four hours, nor could he remember the last time he had eaten. The drifts were getting higher, the snow heavier. A sharp wind tore at his face. He tried to call out in the desperate hope that there was someone, somewhere who could help, but the whistling of the wind was louder than his voice. He trudged on, and on, and on.

And then he fell. He got up with difficulty, but a few feet further on, he fell again. *I'll just rest a little, I'll catch my breath, I'll get up right away* ---and the snow came down on him, soft and silent and protective.

* * *

Maria Brettauer was the oldest of the four children of the Brettauer clan. Her father's farm was one of the biggest and best run in the Inn Valley. Maria had been helping with the chores, milking, taking care of the farm animals and working in the kitchen and the fields since she was a small girl. Now at twenty, she was a robust young woman, strong and capable. She was not beautiful like the movie stars she worshipped, but she had the charm of youth, and her fiancé, Alois, thought the world of her. Or at least, so he said. He had been urging her for some time to allow the banns to be posted at their church, so that their wedding could be planned right after the harvest in the Fall.

But Maria hesitated. Alois was a good man, and by marrying him, she would eventually become the mistress of Alois' father's farm, which was close to the Brettauer farm. Her life, then, was preordained. Within a year or so, she would have her first child, and she would continue to work and live in her beloved Inn Valley, surrounded by some of the most beautiful mountain scenery on earth. Why was she not certain that this was what her life should be?

Maria was a reader. She devoured romances, and loved reading about strange and foreign places, strange and foreign people. She had hardly ever been out of the valley, except for climbing and skiing her mountains. She had never even been in Vienna, the distant capital. And before she settled down, she thought she might want to know something more of the world.

But Alois did not want to wait. He wanted the marriage to take place as soon as possible. He had even hinted that there were other eligible young women in the valley, if she proved recalcitrant much longer.

She knew that she had to make a decision. And when her father said that it was time to prepare their alpine hut for the summer, and to take their cattle up to the meadows, she volunteered to do so. A little bit of solitude in her mountains was just what she needed to do some thinking.

She loaded her rucksack with supplies, and started out before dawn. She knew every shortcut and thus reached her goal, the hut in their meadow, within four hours of hard climbing. It was a trip she had taken every year in early Spring for many years. When the herd of cattle was driven up to the meadow, it would take much, much longer. They would have to zigzag to be able to avoid the steepest climbs, and of course, their cows were not as fast as a healthy young woman with a lot on her mind.

She opened the cabin and threw wide all the windows to the fresh mountain air She brought the bedding out to air in the sunshine, brought in wood from the pile cut last summer, and filled the water containers from the well. Then she sat down, looked out at her view and considered her future.

She smelled the air - *there will be a storm, for sure. I should have waited another few days before coming up here. Winter is still not over. We'll get another blast. The question is, should I try to make it home, or stay here and wait it out? They won't worry about me if I stay overnight. They'll know I got here before the storm broke. Come on, I wanted some time to myself. Take it now.*

Soon the snow began to fall. She brought the bedding back in, and closed the hut against the storm. It was a much stronger storm than she had expected and in a short time the hut was almost buried in snow drifts. The wind howled around the small chalet, but inside Maria was comfortable and warm. She had made a fire in the stove, brewed herself a pot of coffee, and relished the unaccustomed inactivity and solitude.

What is this banging? The wind must be stronger than I thought. Is there damage to the hut? She slipped on her loden jacket and forced the door open against the wind.

Someone is there, she thought- *there's a body lying on the snow.* She went out and grabbed the body by the shoulders. Using all her strength, she pulled and pulled and finally succeeded in manhandling the body into the cabin and slamming the door against the wind and snow.

It's a man, a young man, and he'll freeze to death if I don't do something fast, she said to herself. Maria knew what to do. She was an experienced mountain dweller, after all. Quickly she stripped the stranger of all his wet and frozen clothes. Then she rubbed his feet and arms with particular attention to the fingers and toes to restore circulation. When she saw that some feeling appeared to be restored to the man's extremities, she pulled and pushed him into the trundle bed, and piled blankets high on him. She put more logs on the fire, and then caught her breath.

He's still unconscious, poor lamb, she thought. *I wonder what he was doing up here in this weather, dressed in city clothes? What a handsome young man. So different from Alois and all the others around here. Tall and slender and much more refined looking than my Alois. And his hands are soft. I bet he never did a day's work in his life. He looks a little like the busts of those Roman emperors in the museum in Innsbruck.*

But there is something odd about him. I noticed it while I was rubbing him, but I can't think of it now. What is it? And who is he?

Well, he'll tell me about it when he wakes up, I'm sure. What a break that he found the cabin and that I heard him. He'd certainly have frozen to death.

Maria picked up the stranger's clothes, shook them out and hung them to dry near the stove. She found his shoes and stuffed them with newspapers so that they too would dry properly. Then she slipped off her dress, found another blanket to wrap herself in, made herself as comfortable as she could on two chairs she put together, and fell asleep.

Kurt was dreaming that he was in his own bed, and that his mother was sitting next to him and holding him in her arms. Then he opened his eyes. His mother was dead. His father was dead. The knowledge hit him like a sword in his guts. He winced at the pain.

But where am I? What happened? He remembered the struggle in the snowstorm, his last fall, and finally, finally being able to get up once more and stumble onward. And he remembered almost hitting the cabin wall, banging against it with his last strength and then collapsing.

He realized that he was nude under the covers. He looked around and saw the inside of a typical Alpine hut. His clothes were hung up to dry near the stove. The fire had gone out, and it was cold in the room, but there was sunshine coming into the windows. Clearly the storm was over.

"So, you're awake." A young woman looked down at him. "You'll have to explain to me what possessed you to come up into the mountains in those clothes," she continued." But first, breakfast."

She set about lighting the stove. "Wait a minute," she said, "your clothes are not dry yet. I'll find you something."

She rummaged in a closet and emerged with a long, green loden coat. "This should do for the moment. Here, put it on."

Kurt suddenly became aware of his nudity. He started to maneuver the coat trying to protect himself from the young woman's level gaze. "Come on, who do you think got you undressed, rubbed you all over, and put you to bed?" His hostess smiled. "You haven't got anything I haven't seen. Come on, get up."

Kurt crawled out of bed and into the coat. He realized that he was blushing. The thought that this attractive young woman had not only seen him, but handled him when he was unconscious, was actually quite exciting. For a moment, the agony of his parents' death receded a little into a dull ache. After all, Kurt was a normal, healthy young man, and the circumstances in which he found himself created all kinds of interesting sensations.

Maria busied herself making coffee. She then put out bread, cheese, sausages and jam, all of which she had brought up to the cabin in her rucksack. "Breakfast is served. First we eat, then we talk," she said.

Kurt had not realized how desperately hungry he was until he saw food before him. He started to wolf it down. "Stop, stop," the young woman cried out. "Eat slowly or you'll make yourself sick."

It was exactly what his mother would say when they broke their fast at the end of Yom Kippur, the Day of

Atonement. Tears came to Kurt's eyes and he turned away. " Now, now," Maria said, "Can't be that bad, can it?"

Oh yes it can, Kurt thought, chewing more slowly. *What does she know? But she saved my life, I can't take it out on her because she doesn't understand.*

"All right, I'll begin," the young woman said. "My name is Maria Brettauer. My father owns the Brettauer farm in the valley. I came up here to prepare the cabin for our summer stay, when we bring our cattle up to the meadow. I got caught in the storm, and fortunately found you lying at my door. And here you are. It's as simple as that. And now your turn. What are you doing here in city clothes?"

"It's not quite that easy to explain." Kurt said slowly. "First of all, you did save my life. For that I will always be in your debt. As for the rest, I really cannot say."

"Come on now." Maria smiled. "You owe me something." She took another sip of coffee. "It's not just idle curiosity. If you're in trouble, maybe I can help you."

"Very well. I will tell you one thing and then we will see. I am a Jew."

Maria recoiled involuntarily. In her entire life she had never met a Jew. Oh, it was possible, even probable that some of the tourists who infested her mountains during the summer and in the skiing season were Jewish, and that she had spoken to them to give them directions or to sell them some of the products of the farm. But she had never sat across the table from a Jew, alone, in a hut with no one nearby to help her.

All her life she had heard bad things about Jews; the priest in her church would often describe the Christkillers or talk about the bloodsucking qualities of the people who denied her Lord, and in the last few months the new German government had done even more to explain how dangerous and villainous Jews were.

Suddenly, she realized what was so odd about the young man's body. His penis looked quite different from Alois'. She recalled stories of how Jews ritually mutilated their male children. Her thoughts about that part of men's bodies, and the uses it could be put to, made her face turn crimson.

Kurt smiled bitterly. "You see. We really have nothing to talk about. You must be sorry now, that you rescued me. But what's done is done. I apologize for inflicting my presence on you."

He got up and walked over to the window. The world outside was covered in deep snow. The sun was warm, and there were sounds of water dripping from the eaves of the hut.

"It does not appear that I can leave right away. I will have to wait until at least some of the snow is gone, and that may be a day or two. But, I will try to stay as far away from you as possible, so I do not contaminate you with my presence."

Kurt pulled a chair over to the window, turned it around and sat down with his back to the living area of the cabin and to Maria.

Maria looked at him, sitting there quietly with his back toward her. *He does not seem to be dangerous, and he's so good looking*, she thought. *How could a nice, young man, so soft spoken, so educated, be a Jew? Jews are supposed to be slimy, nasty creatures with big hook noses. They want nothing more than to take advantage of young Aryan maidens so that they can adulterate our German race. At least, that's what the papers say, and the radio, and all the men when they talk about the politics of the new unified country* we *live in. Isn't that true?*

You want to know something about the world outside your valley, girl. Well, here's your chance. Ask him. Go on. Ask him.

She went over to Kurt, knelt down next to his chair, took his hand and said, "Tell me."

"Tell you what?"

"Tell me about being a Jew. Tell me about your life. Tell me who you are. Tell me why people hate you. I really want to know. I have never met a Jew before."

Kurt looked at the young woman. She looked back at him, her eyes wide and questioning. He began to talk.

He talked about his home, his school, his youth. Mostly, he talked about his parents. He described their love, their devotion. He talked about celebrating holidays, like the Passover Seder, and explained what was being celebrated. He talked about the teachings of the Torah. His father had tried to live by them and had tried to instill their lessons in Kurt. He described his mother and the time and effort she had spent in her work as a hospital volunteer. He talked about his father making sure that he contributed to charity out of his allowance, so that the habit of giving to others was firmly engraved in his character.

He returned time and again to the warmth of his home, and the love of his parents. And the tears welled up in his eyes as he talked, and he could not stop them.

"But what happened? Where are your parents? Why are you here now?" Maria asked.

"They were murdered by an SS man who came to take my father's business away from him. And, if I get caught by the SS, they'll murder me too. Because we're Jews, and Jews are not allowed to live in your new Third Reich."

"Oh, my God. How dreadful. You poor thing. I'm so sorry, so sorry." Maria could not help but put her arms around the young man. *He's just a boy*, she thought, *and now he's all alone. Even Jews do not deserve this, and it doesn't seem to me that all Jews are so terrible. He and his family certainly sound like good people.*

For Kurt, talking like he did was a catharsis. For the first time since he found out about his parents' death, he began to believe that he could really go on and survive and make a life. His agony about them became a dull, permanent ache, but he looked around with new eyes. And in front of him, cradling him in her arms, was the young woman who had saved him.

So he kissed her.

And she kissed him back.

The snow would not allow these two young people to leave the cabin, but they found wondrous ways to entertain themselves in the hours that followed.

Two days later, the snow had diminished sufficiently so that they could leave. Maria wanted Kurt to come down into the valley with her, but she recognized that he would not be safe. It was essential that he leave German territory as soon as possible. She found a pair of old ski boots in the closet, and with those and the loden coat, Kurt was much better equipped to hike the mountain trails west toward the border.

Maria drew maps of the trails for him as far as she knew the route, but her knowledge of the area was limited to her valley and the surrounding mountains. "Just keep going west, and sooner or later, you'll get to the borders with Liechtenstein or Switzerland. And you promise, you'll write to me when you're safe?"

" I owe you my life and more." Kurt said tenderly. " But don't you think a letter from a Jewish fugitive would endanger you? I'm afraid we can't take a chance."

"I'll never hear from you again? " Maria was upset.

"You have to go on with your life. But I'll remember you always." Kurt said sadly.

"Go on, then. Here are some sandwiches I made for you. I don't know how you'll eat when they're gone. What will you do? You've got to stay away from people."

"I don't know what I'll do. But don't worry. It will work out. And thank you again."

A last hug and he was gone. Maria stood outside the cabin door as long as he was in view. Then with a sigh, she assembled her things and started on her own way home.

Alois will want my decision when I get home. What will I tell him?

* * *

This time, Kurt had no problems with the weather. The sun was warm, and he made good time skirting the valleys of the Tyrol, and staying on or near the crest of the lower hills, mainly out of sight of people. When he encountered a passer by, his loden coat and ski boots made him appear sufficiently like a local, so that he aroused no suspicion. A muttered "Gruess Gott" and he went on his way.

At night he found shelter in other huts, easily located when there was no snow to obscure his vision. Once or twice, he moved down into the valley, and slept in barns as far removed from the main farmhouse as possible.

Food was a problem. He stole eggs when he came near a farm. At times he found some canned food left in the cabins. He did not starve, but he was always hungry.

He did not know how many days he spent on the road. The days and nights blended into one another. He kept going.

One day, he saw a small town in a valley. As he got closer, there was something different from all the other towns and villages he had seen from a distance. At first, he did not know what it was. Then he understood. The ubiquitous Nazi flags were missing. Other towns and villages he had seen were covered with black and red swastika flags. Could it be that he was no longer in German territory?

He was not sure whether he had crossed the border into Liechtenstein already or whether the border was ahead of him. It seemed unlikely that there would not be border posts everywhere, but perhaps, here in the mountains where there were only footpaths, he might be lucky.

He stayed away from the paths, and kept to the higher altitudes and advanced very cautiously. He approached the town. Could this be Vaduz, the capital of Liechtenstein? Above him was a medieval looking castle, perhaps the residence of the Prince of Liechtenstein, ruler of that tiny, independent country. But what if it wasn't? What if it was just one of the many castles which dotted the Austrian mountains?

He had to make sure. He waited until dusk and dared to approach a main road. There was a sign: " Vaduz center 2 kilometers." He was out of German territory.

But was he safe? He did not think so. Liechtenstein was too small to oppose Germany. It could survive only if it accommodated itself to the wishes of its giant neighbor. If he reported to the authorities and asked for asylum, would it be granted or would he be returned? He could not take the chance. He had to go on.

He climbed above the castle in order to be able to circle the town. From his height he could look into the castle's courtyard. He watched a small open truck being loaded with suitcases and trunks. A large black Mercedes stood nearby.

I wonder where that one is going, Kurt mused. *It must be the Prince, or some members of his family. With all those suitcases, they're not going next door to visit their neighbors. The question is, are they going to Germany, or to another country. If I only knew for sure that they're not visiting Germany. I could sneak aboard the truck. My immediate problem might be solved.*

Kurt climbed down from the heights very carefully, hiding as much as possible behind bushes and trees so as to avoid being seen from the castle. Finally, he found himself in the darkness of the broad gate in the castle wall. A few moments later, the truck drove slowly past him. Taking a chance, Kurt grabbed the tailgate and vaulted into the back of the truck. Immediately, he threw himself down on the floor. Near him, there was a trunk with a tag attached to it: "For cabin use SS Queen Mary."

They must be going to America! Oh how I wish I could go along, Kurt thought longingly. *But where will they catch the Queen Mary? I don't think she docks in any German port, so it has to be Le Havre, France or Southampton, England. Either way, I'd be in good shape. I'll risk it.*

After a while, the truck stopped. Kurt overheard the driver talking to what sounded like customs officials. "This belongs to the young prince. He's going to America to go to college. All covered by diplomatic passport. Here are the papers."

The truck moved on, and Kurt saw behind him a customs barrier being lowered. And the flag, a white cross on a red background. Switzerland!

Thank God, Kurt thought. I should be safe here. *Might as well stay aboard as long as I can, and get as far away from the German frontier as possible.*

Hours later, the truck stopped again. Kurt peeked out and saw a sign: "Kloten Airport." The next time the truck halted, Kurt scrambled over the tailgate and ran to the side of the road. He waved gratefully to the driver, who must have acquired a high, and perhaps unwarranted, opinion of Swiss friendliness.

There was a sign: "Zurich - Centrum", and Kurt started to walk in the indicated direction. *In Zurich there are Jews. All I have to do is find some, and I won't be alone.* He had no money, he was filthy and hungry, and there was the constant pain when he thought of his parents. But he whistled as he walked.

* * *

CHAPTER III

Kurt walked for a long time. He followed the signs toward the center of the city. He was getting more and more tired and hungry. In fact he realized that it had been more than twenty-four hours since he had eaten.

Eventually, he approached the more elegant section of town and in the distance saw the shimmering waters of a large lake. He kept walking. He was worried that a Swiss policeman would consider his disheveled and dirty figure worthy of attention. He needed a place to rest.

How wonderful, he thought. *This is just what I need.* He saw a large square building with a sign: Beth Israel Synagogue. A number of people were entering its wide doors. *A service must be about to begin,* he said to himself.

He entered, found a bathroom and tried to make himself more presentable. But nothing would hide the old, torn loden coat that had stood him such good stead in the mountains. The service had begun. He picked up a Tallis - a prayer shawl - and pulling his hat firmly on his head, entered and found a seat in the rear of the sanctuary.

In spite of his tiredness, he found it comforting to be able to participate in the worship. He intoned the familiar prayers and when, toward the end of the service, the congregation rose to pronounce the Kaddish, the prayer for the dead, he participated with a full and grieving heart. He realized that this was the first time that he could share in this ritual on behalf of his parents. He broke down weeping, and while he was trying hard to stifle his sobs, they were not unnoticed.

Kurt noticed a figure sitting next to him. A small, middle aged man, cleanshaven, with an intelligent face, looked at him. "My name is Edward Langler. I think you need help. May I offer it?"

Kurt looked up at the kind face of a fellow Jew. "My name is Kurt Auster. I'm from Vienna. The Nazis murdered my parents, but I was able to escape. I've just arrived in Zurich. I'm penniless. I don't know what to do."

"And you crossed the border into Switzerland illegally?" Langler asked.

Anywhere else Kurt might have hesitated to answer. But in a synagogue and to a fellow Jew, he felt safe. "Yes," he said.

"Come with me," Herr Langler told Kurt. "You need food and rest. My wife will be glad to provide that. Then we'll talk."

The reference to the man's wife reassured Kurt. He followed the little man to an apartment building a few streets away. Mrs. Langler met them at the door. Whereas Herr Langler was small and thin, she was comfortably upholstered, and slightly taller than her husband. "This young man just escaped from the Nazis. He needs help" Herr Langler told her.

Mrs. Langler looked at Kurt. "First he needs a bath and clean clothes. Come with me, young man. I'll take care of you."

Kurt burst out crying. "That's what Mama would have said," he sobbed.

"I'm sure your mama was a good Jewish mother. We're all sisters when it comes to our children," Mrs. Langler said, as she led him away.

* * *

Kurt felt completely renewed. Bathed, shaved, dressed in clean clothes that had been borrowed from a neighbor, and fed with the kind of food his mother would have given him, he was a new man. He was ready to tell his story to the Langlers, but decided to do a little judicious pruning about the incident with Maria Brettauer.

When he was finished, Mrs. Langler put her arms around him. "You poor dear. So young and orphaned."

"I don't know how to thank you for your help." Kurt said.

"Oh," Herr Langler smiled. "I'm sure we'll figure out a way to help you and to help us as well. Now, I have some contacts in Vienna. You'll stay with us a few days and I'll see what I can find out. I would advise that you don't go out until I can arrange for a temporary residence permit for you.

The Swiss are notoriously inhospitable and if they catch you, they will return you across the German frontier."

"Can you really help me?" Kurt asked.

"Trust my husband," Mrs. Langler chuckled. "He handles things very well."

* * *

"I have heard from Vienna. The word was given out, that your parents and you moved to Poland, where they came from originally...."

"Poland", Kurt interrupted, "my parents and grandparents were all born in Vienna..."

"Let me continue," Herr Langler said. "As I said, the story was given out that the three of you moved back to Poland, and that your father sold his business at a fair price to Becker and Grotze. Do you think that there is a possibility that your parents are still alive? "

"I'm afraid not. I am convinced that it was their bodies I saw being thrown into the truck."

"I agree with you. There is no point in harboring false hopes. Unfortunately there is no way to find out what happened to your parents' bodies. I'm sorry to mention such a painful subject, and we can only hope that they were treated with a measure of dignity."

"I doubt that very much," Kurt frowned, " those bastards, those damn bastards..."

"Yes, I know, and I agree with your sentiments. At this point, until there is a change of government in Germany, I do not think that you can do anything. When, as it must, a new and more civilized government takes over, you can pursue claims for your parents' estate, and perhaps even get justice from your parents' murderer. But for the moment, Hitler seems very much in power.

Now," Herr Langler continued. "I have obtained a temporary visitor's permit for you. It will protect you if you are stopped in the street, but it does not bear very close examination. So I advise you to be circumspect when you wander around Zurich."

"You mean this is a fake document?" Kurt was somewhat aghast that this nice man would actually do something illegal.

"Do you have any problems with that?" Herr Langler grinned. "Would you rather report to the authorities and be returned to German control?"

"No, of course not." Kurt said hesitatingly. But he winced as he said it. He had been brought up to be rigorously honest, and now he found himself in the position of not only breaking the unjust laws of Nazi Germany, but also the laws of his host country.

"Well now, you take a look at Zurich, and let me think about how else I can help you." Herr Langler said pleasantly.

"How can I thank you? " Kurt asked.

"Never mind, " Herr Langler smiled. "I'll find a way."

"May I ask, " Kurt stammered a little, - I hate to ask my benefactor, but, Herr Langler, what is it you do?"

Langler laughed out loud. "I was wondering when you'd get around to this. I'm an intermediary. I help people. I find people who need each other and bring them together. And I help solve their problems. Perhaps you'll be able to assist me in one problem that comes to mind."

And that is all he would say at that time.

* * *

Kurt wandered around Zurich. He admired the elegant stores, the beautiful park along the Lake, the old city center along the Limmat River. Langler had advanced him some money so that he could stop and buy a cup of coffee in one of the many outdoor cafes. And he thought.

I must make some plans. I can't wait around until the Swiss come and intern me, or return me to German control. I've got to find a way to start my life again.

Herr Langler clearly is involved in all kinds of illegal or extralegal activities. Do I want to get involved with that? What are my choices now?

And I want to fight those murderers. I'm not going to let them get away with it. I don't know how, but sooner or later there'll be a chance to fight them.

Listen to me talking like that. What nonsense. Who
do you think you are, Kurt? Right now, what you need to do
is find a place where you can stay in safety, and never mind
such grandiose ideas.
  No, I will fight. I will do something.
  And I won't forget Ratzersdorfer.

* * *

In Vienna, after the Anschluss, passers by,
particularly those without the swastika in their lapels, were
often stopped by the police and asked for their identity papers.
Kurt and his parents had been in the habit of carrying their
Austrian passports with them, and that document was still in
Kurt's possession. Of course, any country which recognized
the absorption of Austria into the German Reich would no
longer recognize an old Austrian passport as a valid travel
document. Kurt, in fact, had become one of the large and
growing group of refugees considered in the nice
bureaucratic term "Stateless".

The League of Nations had begun to issue travel
documents to such stateless persons. They were called
Nansen Passports, named after the great Norwegian explorer
and activist, Fritjof Nansen. The League of Nations
headquarters was in Geneva, but a branch office in Zurich
accepted Kurt's application for such a passport. However, the
official handling the request did not hold out much hope.

"We are swamped with applications. In any case,
most member states will no longer recognize such a
document, even though they are required to do so by the fact
of their membership. All countries are just afraid to be
flooded by refugees. Even though the need is great, no
country wants to be the first to admit a lot of penniless
people."

"What you really mean is that no country wants to
take in any more Jews than they already have."

"I did not say that, but realistically...." The official
did not continue.

In fact, in July 1938, shortly before Kurt had made it
to Zurich, the Western powers, including the United States of
America, had met at a conference in Evian, France on the

shores of beautiful Lake Geneva, to discuss the growing problem of Jews escaping from Germany. The conference was a total failure. No country was willing to take in more than their usual small number of immigrants. It became very clear, not only to the desperate Jews, but also to the Germans, that emigration from Germany was not the solution. If Germany wanted to be rid of the Jews in its territories, another way would have to be found. And of course, eventually, it was.

It was obvious to Kurt that Switzerland would make every effort to preserve her neutrality. If that meant expelling or interning Jewish refugees, that would be a small price to pay.

If there would be a war, he might have a chance to participate in it and fight Germany. There might be an army he could join, although it was problematic whether anyone would take a stateless Jew. In any case, he had to get out of Switzerland into either France or Britain, the two countries most likely to stand up to Hitler eventually, even though they would do it most reluctantly.

One evening, after Frau Langler had served one of her mountainous dinners - Kurt could never understand how Herr Langler preserved his slight figure, accustomed as he was to such food, - his host said:

"I have a proposition for you that can help you and me."

Discreetly, Frau Langler retreated to her kitchen, from which the sounds of washing up could be heard.
"Do you ski?" Herr Langler asked.

"What?" Kurt was nonplussed by what appeared to be a non sequitur.

"Trust me. There is a purpose to my question. Are you a good skier?"

"Fair enough. I have spent a lot of winter vacations in the Alps. But why?"

"Are you good enough to cross the Alps into France, if you have help, equipment and a guide?"

"That depends on the terrain, but I should think I could. I never thought of crossing the border in the mountains. Wouldn't that be very difficult? I already had one experience in the mountains that almost killed me."

"Listen to me," Herr Langler leaned forward and fixed Kurt with his eyes. " I trust you. I have learned about your background and observed you. I have to deal with a lot of people and I have to make up my mind quickly. I do not think you are a thief."

"Thank you, but I don't understand.."

"I must transfer a package of goods into France. It is a small package, but quite valuable. It can easily be carried in a rucksack, but it cannot cross the border where it may be opened by the customs authorities."

"You are talking about smuggling."

"Indeed, I am. You have smuggled yourself across frontiers illegally. Do you have any problem with smuggling goods?"

Kurt thought for a moment. It was easy to be honest in the safety of his home in Vienna. Now he was floating in mid-air, penniless, stateless and homeless. He had to act, and here was an opportunity.

"What is in the package?" he was not sure Herr Langler would answer, but the little man did, with a smile.

"Currency."

"Currency?"

"Yes, Dollars, Francs, Lire, Pound Sterling, Swiss Francs, even Reichsmarks, whatever. There are lots of occasions when funds have to be transferred from one country to another without going through the banking system. The free market exchange rates are often much higher, and it is at times vital not to have governments aware of these transfers. Don't forget, Zurich is one of the great financial capitals of Europe. Do you feel better now? Or do you still have scruples?"

"No, that's fine. But why do you need me?" *Certainly, partly because I'd be the one to go to jail if I'm caught, and not you.*

"Because I trust you. The temptation of disappearing with a large sum of money is great. I can arrange for you to be fully equipped with skiing gear. I will get you a guide through the mountains whose business it is to help people cross the frontier. But of course, he won't know what you are carrying.

All this costs a lot of money and takes time. I am willing to make that investment in you. You will deliver my package to an address in Paris, and receive a small sum for your trouble, enough to allow you to survive there for a few months, while you make other arrangements. We will both be served. If you agree, we must begin preparations soon."

France. Certainly I would have a better chance to fight the Germans from there. Perhaps the Foreign Legion? Kurt remembered reading romantic adventure stories about that famed corps. *But they fight Arabs. I want to fight Germans.*

Herr Langler continued. "Do you speak French?"

"No. I studied Latin and English in school."

"Well, you can't leave until there is enough snow in the mountains. Besides it is much safer to travel during Christmas/New Years, when there are a lot of tourists about. That gives us at least four months, maybe a little more. I will need that time to make my arrangements. I will get you a French tutor, so that you can get yourself to Paris after you've crossed the border, and we'll consider that a bonus. And you can continue stay with us until your departure. Are we agreed?"

"Agreed."

* * *

In September of 1938 Hitler struck again.

In 1919, at the end of World War I, the victorious Allied powers had dismantled the Austro-Hungarian and German empires. Among the new countries created from the former Hapsburg possessions was Czechoslovakia, composed of Czech speaking Bohemia and Moravia, and Slovak speaking Slovakia.

In their desire to inflict as much damage as possible on the defeated Central powers, the victorious Allies included in the new country a large segment of ethnic Germans, at the German - Czech border, in an area called Sudetenland.

Hitler insisted that this section of Czechoslovakia be transferred to Germany, on his principle that all German speakers had to be part of his Reich. Czechoslovakia refused to be dismantled. The country was tied by mutual defense treaties to France and Britain.

Hitler threatened war.

At the instigation of the Italian dictator, Mussolini, by now a firm ally of Germany, a conference was convened in Munich, Germany, close to Hitler's mountain retreat of Berchtesgaden. The French Prime Minister, Edouard Daladier, the British Prime Minister, Neville Chamberlain, Benito Mussolini and Adolf Hitler decided on the fate of Czechoslovakia. The victim country was not even invited to the conference.

The Western powers agreed to Hitler's demands. The Sudetenland, which included some of Czechoslovakia's armament factories and its best defense installations against possible German invasion, was surrendered to Germany. The Czech Army, which had been prepared to fight, had to abandon its territory without firing a shot.

When Neville Chamberlain returned to London from the conference, he waved the treaty in his hand and announced that he had insured "peace in our time". He also proudly announced that "Herr Hitler has promised that he had no further territorial ambitions in Europe."

Hitler kept his promise for six months. Munich has become a name for appeasement.

* * *

In his wanderings around Zurich, Kurt often passed the German consulate. It was located in an elegant building, with a large Swastika prominently displayed. Sometimes, Kurt fantasized about going in there with a submachine gun, like the Chicago gangsters in the American movies and just killing all the Nazis he saw. Then he reminded himself that he could no longer think like a child, but had to reason like an adult.

Unfortunately, another young man in France did not have Kurt's maturity.

On November 8, 1938, a seventeen year old Polish Jew, Herschel Grynszpan, whose parents had been terribly mistreated by the Nazis, walked into the German embassy in Paris looking for the Ambassador. He found only a minor legation secretary named Ernst vom Rath, and shot and killed him. Ironically, vom Rath was not a Nazi and had spoken out against the Reich's racial policies.

Hitler took full advantage of the opportunity this tragedy presented to him. On November 9, 1938, well orchestrated "spontaneous" demonstrations erupted through the length and breadth of Germany. Jewish owned stores were destroyed, synagogues were burned, homes were attacked. In the morning, Heinrich Himmler, the head of the SS, the paramilitary organization of the Nazi party, reported to the Fuehrer that 815 shops had been destroyed, 171 homes had been attacked and 119 synagogues were in flames. Over 20,000 Jews had been arrested. This was a low estimate, as the riots continued.

That night went into history under the name "Kristallnacht", the night of shattered glass. The Nazis imposed a fine of one billion Marks on the Jewish communities in Germany, which, in effect, meant confiscation of all Jewish property.

Any illusions that Jews in Germany may have had were now as shattered as the store window glass that gave that night its name. Frantically, Jews tried to leave, but there was no place for them to go.

The only spot on the globe to which one could get without an entry visa, was the treaty port of Shanghai in China, and a good number of Jews braved the rigors of the Trans-Siberian railway to get there. They were well received by the local Jewish community. Others tried legal and illegal methods, and many other destinations. Most did not escape.

* * *

And then the day of Kurt's departure came.

Kurt dressed in his recently acquired skiing togs, and inspected the skis, poles, and boots. " I have made quite an investment in you," Herr Langler grinned as he inspected Kurt. " Don't disappoint me."

"I won't." Kurt said warmly. "You and your wife have been very kind to me, and I won't forget it."

"Here is your rucksack, and here the packages you will carry for me," Herr Langler said, and showed him two oilcloth covered packages the size and heft of bricks.

"Now, Kurt, here is some Swiss currency and some French Francs, to enable you to get to Paris. You will take the train from Zurich to Martigny, and from there a bus into the foothills of Mont Blanc to Orfieres. In that village there is only one inn. Ask for Hans Huber - and so you can identify him, he is a tall, blond young man, with a very large mustache. He is expecting you and will guide you across the slopes, skirting Mont Blanc, to the French border. He has been paid, and all he knows is that you are a refugee from Germany without any papers who wants to get into France. I have used him before, and he is very reliable.

With any luck, you will get across the border in two days of hiking and skiing, and ski down into Chamonix in France. The entire area, on both sides of the border is a skier's paradise. You should be able to disappear among all the tourists. From Chamonix you just take a train to Paris. As a Swiss citizen, I have no problems travelling to France, and I will personally meet you in the Hotel Paris-Rome, 4 Rue de Provence, in Paris. The hotel is just off the Faubourg Montmartre near the Boulevard des Italiens, you'll find it easily.

As a fall-back, if I am not waiting for you at the hotel, look for me at a kosher restaurant, the "Galil" in the Rue Richer, not far from there. The owner, Rene Mayer, is my cousin, and you can trust him.

One more thing: In France every traveler staying in even the smallest hotel or pension, must fill out a fiche with all his vital information, and must show his identity papers. The police check all these fiches very frequently. So you cannot under any circumstances sleep in a hotel until after you have arrived in Paris and delivered the packages to me. After that you will be able to make some arrangements to regularize your papers."

And if I can't regularize them, Kurt realized, *at least I won't put Herr Langler's money at risk.*

* * *

The inn at Orfieres was surrounded by dark fir trees. It was at one end of the sole street of that small village. This early in the season, there was just enough snow to cover the roadway so that one could ski right up to the door of the inn. The low building was alive with skiers who had just come down from the slopes and, full of the joy of a day of strenuous exercise, clamored for relaxation and beer. Outside, the ski racks were filled to capacity. The sinking sun illuminated the slopes on which the hardiest of the skiers made their last run of the day.

Kurt had been sitting in a corner of the inn at one of the many wooden tables, nursing a beer. He did not like beer, he did not like the noise, the smoke, the boisterousness of his surroundings. *Don't these silly revelers know what's going on in the world? Don't they understand that there is a monster abroad, a monster that will soon devour them, and their world? All they seem to be interested in is the speed of their last descent and how many moguls they encountered without falling.*

He kept looking for a tall, blond man with a very large mustache, but no one resembling that description showed up. *The bartender keeps looking at me. Either I'll buy another beer, or I have to leave. Well, might as well take a chance.*

Kurt went up to the bar. "Another Pilsener, please. And incidentally, do you know Hans Huber? Do you expect him to show up soon?"

"Huber? The poor fellow. You won't see him here so soon. Just yesterday, the ski patrol brought him down from the mountain, badly injured. He's in the hospital in the valley, and they'll try to patch him up. It's strange, he's such a good and careful skier. I can't imagine what happened to him."

Kurt brought his beer back to his corner. *This is terrible. My first contact and it's gone wrong. The poor guy. But what do I do now? Should I go back into the valley and telephone Herr Langler? Or should I go to the hospital first, and see whether Hans Huber can give me some advice? Or is there a way to go on and get across without a guide? That would be foolhardy, but the longer I sit around with what I'm carrying in my rucksack, the more dangerous it becomes. I've got to think about this and make a plan of action.*

Suddenly, Kurt became aware that he was being looked at with more than casual interest. The stranger came over and sat down across the table from him, carrying a mug of beer.

"Hi there. Did I hear you ask for Hans Huber?"

Kurt saw a middle aged, middle sized man, dressed in the usual skier's outfit, dark hair, no special facial features, the kind of man who could disappear in any crowd because of his very average looks.

"Do you know Huber?" Kurt asked.

"He's my cousin. I'm Walter Huber. The poor guy broke a clavicle and both legs. We're all very worried that he may never ski again. I can't believe this happened to him."

"How did it happen?"

"I guess a moment of carelessness and a slip on ice. But Hans was usually so careful. He's a very experienced skier. But now to you. What did you want with him? You don't seem to know him."

"Oh, somebody had mentioned his name to me as a potential guide into the higher reaches of the mountains." Kurt said with some hesitation.

"Well, he would have been the second best guide around here. By why not talk to the best guide?"

"And who would that be?"

"You're talking to him," the man said with a smile.

"Oh."

"Come on, don't you have a sense of humor? Hans and I have been rivals all our lives as far as knowledge of our mountains and our skiing ability is concerned, but apart from that we're the best of friends. Now, listen to me." The man turned serious and leaned over to talk to Kurt more quietly. "Hans told me that he expected a client who needed a special guide. That usually means, someone who needs to get across the border into France. Would that be you, by any chance?"

Do I dare? This may be my opportunity. But what if he goes to the authorities? Take a gamble.

"How would you go from here to Chamonix?"

A broad smile appeared on Walter Huber's face. "I thought so. You're the client Hans expected. Well, come on."

"Where are we going?"

"Up to my cabin. We'll catch a few hours of sleep," Huber looked at his watch, "very few hours. We'll start at daybreak, and I'll have you across the border by late afternoon. You'll have to camp out overnight, but I'll point you in the right direction, and you'll be in France tomorrow night. Now, let's go."

"How can I thank you?"

"Oh, I don't want to ruin my cousin's reputation. Don't worry about it."

Huber moved up the mountain path with long strides and so quickly, that Kurt had trouble keeping up with him, encumbered as he was by his skis and backpack.

"Here, let me help you. Give me your rucksack. You're not accustomed to the altitude."

"Thank you, but that's all right."

By the time they reached Huber's cabin, they had covered at least two miles horizontally and several hundred feet vertically. Kurt was exhausted.

The cabin was a small, neat, wooden hut. It was set on a ledge overlooking the village and the valley below. Behind, Mont Blanc reared up into the clouds. A ski rack outside with several pairs of skis, one large room with the usual woodstove, two beds, a wooden table and a few chairs, gave the cabin a spartan and functional look.

"Leave your skis outside, just take off your boots. We'll sleep in our clothes, so we can start very early. I'll just make a fire and then get some rest, too." Huber said.

Kurt followed his instructions. But what to do with the rucksack? He slid the bed away from the wall just far enough so that he could wedge the rucksack between the bed and the wall, slid his arm through the straps, and allowed himself to stretch out and relax.

Huber watched these preparations in silence. Then he turned and busied himself with the stove.

* * *

He couldn't breathe. An enormous rat in a black SS uniform sat on his chest. He couldn't make out its face, something stopped him from seeing, something stopped him from breathing. He struggled to free himself from the enormous weight. He flailed his arms and legs, but it didn't help. Blood suffused his face, his eyes, his lungs were bursting.

Suddenly he could breathe again and see again. Huber lay on the floor holding the pillow with which he had tried to asphyxiate Kurt. In his struggles, Kurt had managed to free his arm and had slung his backpack so it had hit Huber. The weight of the bricks of currency did the rest.

Kurt jumped up from the bed. Huber, only slightly stunned, jumped up too. The two faced each other.

I've never been in a fight. What do I do? He's certainly stronger and more experienced than I. He tried to murder me!

"Now listen," Huber said. "Just give me the rucksack, and I'll let you go, and for all I care you can get yourself to France."

Kurt retreated, the rucksack in his hand, the table between him and the guide. He still had not completely caught his breath, but he could see more clearly by the light of the woodstove, and he started to think.

"Come on," Huber said, "if I have to go after you and take the rucksack, you'll regret it, or " and he laughed, " you may not have time to regret it at all." The guide reached behind him, and a very large knife appeared in his hand.

Kurt kept circling the table to stay away from Huber. The guide followed, constantly trying to reach over to attack Kurt. In the small space, Kurt had very little maneuvering room.

Something's got to give. He'll grab me and then it's all over. I've got to find a way out.

As he circled, Kurt tried to get closer to the wood piled up near the stove. Then he risked everything.

With both hands, he threw his rucksack at Huber's face. In the same motion, he grabbed a log from the pile, and with all his might hit Huber's head. The guide had grabbed at the rucksack and ducked to protect his head. Kurt just managed to hit it a glancing blow. But the blow was sufficient to stun Huber momentarily. Huber slid to his knees. Kurt followed up the first blow with a second, then a third. Huber collapsed on the floor and lay motionless.

Oh, God, I killed him. I'm a murderer. How could I do this? I had to, I had to.

Sobbing from the strain, Kurt bent over Huber's body. *Thank God, he's not dead.* Huber was breathing, but breathing very heavily, and blood welled out of the wounds Kurt had inflicted to his head.

I've got to get out of here, before he wakes up. Quick, my boots, my backpack, and let's go.

Kurt ran out of the cabin, put on his skis, grabbed his poles and his precious rucksack, and started to ski off. Then he turned and for a moment looked at the other skis in the rack. He undid his own skis again, grabbed the other skis, ran to the ledge, and flung them as far as he could into the valley. *Now, let him go after me.*

One more glance into the cabin. Huber was still lying motionless and breathing loudly. *He needs medical attention, he might die without it. But he tried to kill me. I can't help him.*

Kurt had little experience in cross country skiing, he was better on the slopes. It was still a long time to daylight, but there was a moon, and the stars were very bright on the snow. Visibility was good, fortunately. This would have been impossible on a dark and moonless night.

Which direction? Away from the village, of course. But where am I going? I've got to think this through.

Kurt remembered studying the maps of the area with Herr Langler. *If I keep the peak of Mont Blanc on my left, ultimately I will skirt it and get to the French side. A guide would have known all kinds of short cuts, and doing it my way will take much, much longer. And then, there is the problem of the border patrols, both Swiss and French. A local guide would know how to avoid them.*

I have no choice. I must go on. This time, if the weather turns bad, I had better find shelter fast, no more foolhardiness like in the mountains near Innsbruck.

I have to be prepared to travel several days. Anytime, I can find a hut to shelter in, I'd better do it. Now as to food, all I have is what good Mrs. Langler gave me; just as well I did not eat it on the train but indulged myself with the cake and hot coffee they brought around. Oh, what I wouldn't give for a cup of hot coffee now.

It was still early in the season, and there was just enough snow to allow Kurt to make good time. The air was cold, the snow glittered in the starlight. For some reason, in spite of his desperate situation, Kurt felt good.

As he advanced, always trying to keep the peaks of Mont Blanc on his left, he also moved upwards on the slopes whenever there was a choice. *I may be wrong, but it seems to me that the border patrols are more apt to stay on the lower slopes.*

After some hours of progress, there was a flash of red in the sky, then another and another. Soon the sun had come up and illuminated a beautiful vista of steep mountains and wide fields covered with snow. On his left, the sharp rocks and high cliffs of the main peaks threatened the valleys on his right. Kurt permitted himself a short rest and half a sandwich and slugged on.

This man Huber who tried to kill me, must have been waiting for me. Obviously, he knew the contents of my rucksack. I wonder whether Hans Huber's accident was really an accident. It is unlikely that Huber was really Hans Huber's cousin. If he knew what I am carrying, someone betrayed Herr Langler. I'd better keep that in mind before I show up at the rendezvous in Paris, that is if I make it to Paris.

Kurt felt himself getting very tired. He had slept very little in the past twenty-four hours. The physical exertion at an altitude to which he was not accustomed, together with the excitement of having to defend his life against a brutal attacker, began to take its toll. He started to look around for a shelter, a hut or a cave.

Something is different in that rock face, there. The sun reflects more from one spot than another. Let's check it out.

Kurt removed his skis, shouldered them, and climbed painfully up to the cliff. There, another flash. As he approached, he realized what he had found.

An opening was cut into the rock, closed with a metal door, which had reflected the sunlight. A large protruding lever enabled Kurt to open the door. On a ledge, next to the entrance on the inside, Kurt found an oil lamp and some matches.

Kurt made sure that he could open the door from the inside, and then closed it. He lit the lamp and looked around.

Switzerland had maintained her neutrality for several hundred years by being prepared. Every Swiss male had to serve in the Army and had to be in the reserves with annual training up to the age of fifty. Every male had his Army rifle at home, ready for use in case of emergency.

By making it very clear, that it would be very costly to invade Switzerland, and that the Swiss would fight for every hill, every mountain and every lake in their beautiful country, the Swiss had managed to deter would-be invaders for centuries. As part of these preparations, the Swiss had hidden depots throughout their mountains. Kurt had the good fortune to stumble on one of them.

He found himself in a large room filled with crates, barrels and boxes. First of all there was food, tin cans, preserves, even some smoked meats that could be maintained in the cool atmosphere up here. There were sleeping bags, blankets, boots and boxes that seemed to contain bandages and medicines. And there were guns, from rifles to small howitzers, and boxes of ammunition.

Kurt wondered why there was no lock on the door, and then understood that any traveler lost and needy would be welcome here, in the spirit of hospitality personified by the famous St. Bernard dogs.

Clearly, the careful Swiss would inspect and replenish this depot periodically. Kurt hoped that this would not be too soon. He made himself a bed out of some of the blankets, put out the light and almost instantly fell asleep.

Of course, it was dark when he woke up. It is always dark in here, he realized. He lit the lamp again, and first went over to the door. *It's snowing hard, this is a good place to stay.* He ate the last of Mrs. Langler's sandwiches, and went back to sleep.

This time, when he woke up, he was ravenously hungry. *I wonder how long I've slept?* His watch had stopped. He opened the door to brilliant sunshine. The fields and slopes were covered with fresh snow. *Time to go.*

He fixed himself a meal out of the provisions he had found, loaded his backpack with more tin cans, and slung a sleeping bag over his shoulders.

Oh, Papa, oh, Mama, look what's become of me. I almost killed a man, now I'm a thief stealing from the country that gave me temporary asylum, and I'm a smuggler as well. But, I don't feel like a criminal. I do what I must.

Heavily laden as he was, and in the deep snow, he progressed only slowly, but he was no longer tired and felt that he could keep going for a long time.

When night fell, he found a cleft in a rock, stretched out in his sleeping bag, and in spite of his misgivings about the morality of his actions, slept the sleep of the just. Or at least, the sleep of the exhausted.

Fortunately, for the next two days the weather held, and he kept going following the same routine. Once he reached a sheer cliff face, and had to backtrack a considerable distance. By constantly keeping the peak on his left, he thought that he was making progress.

Since he never encountered another skier he felt that he must be in the border region away from the normal tourist areas. Then, on a wide slope, he saw two skiers in the distance behind him. They were coming on fast, and he saw rifles on their shoulders.

Border patrol. I must get away. Lighten my load. He dropped the sleeping bag, which hampered his progress, and moved as fast as he could.

They're catching up. They're much better skiers than I am. What do I do now?

He schussed down the slope at maximum speed, afraid that he would fall and injure himself or that he would come to a cliff. The pursuers came on relentlessly.

There were trees, firs and pines. *I must be getting closer to a valley, away from the tree line.* The slope got steeper but there were substantial clumps of trees on one side now.

I can't outrun them. Where can I hide?

There was a cliff. Kurt stopped, took off his skis, and pushed them hard. They went over the cliff, and their tracks were clearly visible in the snow. He took off his backpack, pulled it behind him to obliterate his traces and got to the trees. *Now, down behind the trees.* He hugged the ground.

The two pursuers came by fast. They stopped at the edge of the cliff and peered over it. They took off their skis, one of them held a rope and the other rappelled down the cliff.

They're looking for my body. How long, before they realize I'm not there?

Kurt walked as fast as the deep snow permitted and as silently as he could away from the cliff. Once he was out of sight and hearing, he scrambled downhill over rocks and boulders through stands of pine and fir. Downhill, downhill. He fell several times and rolled at others. Finally, he stopped and looked around.

In the distance there was a structure. A ski lift. *I am back in civilization. But where am I?*

He made his way laterally toward the ski lift, scrambling over rough terrain, and always downhill. And then he saw the flag at the top of the structure, - blue, white and red - France.

Kurt stood still. He wanted to laugh. *I have not laughed since that horrible day in Vienna. What am I feeling?* He understood. He was happy. The pain of his parents' death was still with him, and always would be, but he suddenly felt good. *This was fun, the excitement, the danger, coping, the adrenaline filling me, and I handled it. I handled it.*

He turned into the mountain and yelled with all his might: "Papa, Mama, I'll make it. I'll make it. Whatever happens, I'll make it."

And then he turned once more and yelled:
"Ratzersdorfer, I won't forget."

* * *

After his escape from Vienna, Kurt realized he had returned to the cocoon of a warm and loving family because of the kindnesses he had received from the Langlers. In fact, he now understood that he had only been half alive in Zurich - he had not really assimilated what had happened to his parents and to him, and he certainly had not taken control of his life.

But now, he knew that he could act. He felt a confidence that he had never felt before. No more long range plans, he decided. First, he would fulfill his obligation to Herr Langler, and then he would arrange to stay in France and support himself and await an opportunity to fight Nazis. And somehow, somewhere, he was sure, he would meet Ratzersdorfer and deal with him. There would be a war, he was sure, and that meant that such an opportunity would come.

The village, where he emerged from the mountains, was far to the northeast of Chamonix, but that did not matter. Kurt had found that he had a reasonable talent for languages. The time with the tutor Herr Langler had provided in Zurich, together with his background in Latin and English, enabled him to communicate in French quite adequately. He also noted how rapidly his facility increased as he found himself immersed among French speakers. He had no difficulty in finding transportation to the nearest railroad station and getting a train to Paris. In fact, he even found a public bath where he could clean up after his stay in the mountains.

The Hotel Paris-Rome was a small hotel in a narrow street on the right bank near the Rue Lafayette. Kurt sat in a café with a view of the hotel's entrance, drinking coffee. He had been there for hours, partly camouflaged with the Figaro. He had glanced through that newspaper many times without losing sight of the hotel entrance. Fortunately, café owners in Paris were accustomed to having people sit in their establishments for hours over one or two coffees.

If Herr Langler was in Paris, he should be going in or out of the hotel, and I will catch him on the street somewhere. I think going into the hotel may be risky, after my experience with the fake Huber.

By now it was quite late. *If Langler is in, he must be asleep by now. And I'm getting very tired myself. But I can't go to a hotel, remember Langler's warning.*

Kurt left the café and wandered the streets. He came to the Boulevard des Italiens, and walked on. What a beautiful church, it looks like a Greek temple. He saw that the square was called Place de la Madeleine, and presumed that that was the name of the church.

As he stood there, admiring the building, he felt a hand on his arm.

A lovely young woman stood before him.

"Tu viens avec moi, mon petit? On va bien s'amuser."

Kurt understood that it was not his manly grace or his charm which had attracted the young woman, but that she was merely proposing a business transaction.

But this might be a solution of his immediate problem.

"Combien pour la nuit?" he asked.

"The whole night? That's expensive, I have a living to make."

"I only want to sleep - no sex. I need a bed for the night." Kurt was not sure that his newly acquired skill in French was good enough to communicate his need, but he did not have to worry.

"Oh, I understand. Police is after you?"

"No, but I have no papers."

The young lady mentioned a price. "I'll find you a bed, no questions asked, and then I'll go back to work."

She led him to a small hotel. "Give the concierge twenty Francs. I have to go up with you or he'll be suspicious."

She took the key and a small towel handed her by the concierge, who barely looked up from his newspaper while completing this transaction. Kurt followed her up a narrow stairway. Looking at the lovely legs ahead of him, he began to regret not having taken her up on her first offer. After all, he was young and healthy and the interlude with Maria was far away and long ago.

They entered a small room. A shabby bed, a wash basin and a rickety chair filled almost all the space. Madeleine - or so Kurt thought of her, since he had never asked her name, looked at him with a smile.

"Such a handsome young man. Are you sure, you don't want me to stay?"

"Perhaps another time," Kurt replied - and it cost him a great deal to say so, "but I am too tired now. Thank you for your help."

"Well, you know where to find me. I'm always around the Madeleine." She disappeared down the steps.

Kurt wedged the door shut with the chair, and stretched out on the bed. *What a fool I am. And she did not look like a prostitute. But she is - and these girls have all kinds of diseases. The last thing you need is to catch something. Yes, maybe, but she was so attractive, and so willing.*

And finally, Kurt fell into a fitful sleep.

* * *

The next morning he took up his vigil again. He counted the money Herr Langler had given him, and saw that he might have enough for one or two days, if he again spent the night in the same manner as before. Of course, he had Herr Langler's currency, but he felt himself honor bound not to touch it.

Another day went by, and there was no sign of Herr Langler. Finally, Kurt made a decision. He telephoned the hotel.

"Monsieur Langler, s'il vous plait."

"Un moment, s'il vous plait."

The phone was picked up. "Hello."

"Monsieur Langler?"

"Oui."

"It's Kurt, Kurt Auster."

"Oh yes. Where are you?"

What a cold reception. I thought something would be wrong, and it is.

"I expect to be in Paris tomorrow morning."

"Good, come to room 214."

"I will. Oh, one more thing, I promised to send a postcard to the French tutor you had provided for me. I've got his address but I can't read his writing. What's his last name?"

Well, it's clear that poor Herr Langler is not alone, and in fact, probably in the hands of the same people who had sent Huber after me. He gave me a wrong name for my tutor in Zurich. That is enough of a signal. Now, I have a choice.

Whatever goes on between Langler and his enemies is not really my affair. I don't even know who the rightful owner of the currency is. I should just take the money and disappear, get on the next train to some seaport, like Marseilles or Le Havre, and with that kind of money, bribe my way out of France to Palestine, or England, or even America. I could live a long time on what I'm carrying.

But Langler was good to me, and he trusted me. And Huber tried to kill me. I can't abandon Langler, and I won't let Huber get away with it. But what do I do now? Of course, the police is out of the question. Langler had given me the name of his cousin, Rene Mayer, as a fall back. But I don't know whether I can trust him.

Now that they know that I'm around, they'll be looking for me. Kurt did not stay in the café any longer. It got dark very early at this time of year. He wandered around to the back of the Hotel Paris-Rome, trying to find a way in without passing the lobby.

There was an alleyway, with several garbage cans. Kurt hid behind the cans. A door opened, and a man in an apron lugged out another trash can. Kurt waited a while, then gently opened the door. He found himself in a hallway. On the right, he saw two big swinging doors opening into the kitchen. He could hear a great clatter of dishes and a lot of shouting back and forth. On the left, another door.

Someone is coming. Kurt opened the door on his left. A small room was filled with shelves containing bedding, tablecloths and napkins. Kurt wedged himself into the far corner, and tried to push linen in front of him so that he was not readily visible from the door. Then he waited.

Twice the door opened. Twice a waiter came in, grabbed some tablecloths and disappeared. Both times, Kurt's heart beat so loudly, that he was sure that the waiter would hear him, but both times, he remained unobserved.

Eventually the noises from outside his hiding place quieted down. *It is getting late. Dinner is long over. They will have locked the doors, and most people will be asleep by now.*

Kurt had a plan. It was not much of a plan, but the best he could do.

He waited a while longer. Two A.M. Now may be the time. He left his hiding place, trying to be as quiet as possible. *Good, no one around.* He entered the swinging doors of the kitchen. There was a night light so that he could get around easily. A rolling pin. *Good. It can be used as a weapon, just like the log that saved my life from Huber's attack. And a long, sharp knife. I can't imagine using a knife on a human being, but I'll take it.* He stuck the knife into his belt.

Ah, this is what I need. A large, iron pot. Some kitchen rags from the stove. A newspaper. Matches I've got.

He left the kitchen and found the stairs. Up one floor - no room 214. One more floor.

Not a soul in sight. Wonderful. Ah, here's 214, right in the middle of the corridor.

He placed the pot filled with the greasy rags and paper toward the end of the corridor, and lit the paper. The rags caught fire, and emitted just what he had hoped for, a considerable amount of smoke. The corridor was filled. He put the lid on the pot, putting out the fire. *I don't want to burn down the hotel. Now, let's go.*

"Feu, feu," he screamed, "Fire, fire," and ran up and down the corridor banging at all the doors. "Sortez, sortez vite," he yelled, "get out, get out, quickly."

Doors started to open. Disheveled, half undressed people started to mill about. They smelled the smoke, and someone started to scream in panic. A crush developed near the stairs. Hotel guests were pushing and shoving to get out.

The door to room 214 opened. A man stepped out. His head was heavily bandaged. Huber. Kurt swung his rolling pin with all his might, and Huber collapsed. In the panic, none of the guests who were cluttered near the stairwell noticed.

Kurt rushed into room 214. No one. *Where is Langler? Ah, a connecting door.* Kurt dashed in - Langler was stretched out on the bed, hands tied to the bedpost, a gag in his mouth, trying desperately to free himself.

Kurt pulled his knife from his belt and sawed through the ropes attaching Langler to the bed. *Quickly, before Huber wakes up.* He hoisted the little man on his shoulder. By now, the hotel guests had managed to get down the stairs. In the distance, he heard the distinctive sound of fire engines. He carried Langler down the stairs. At the bottom, he freed Langler from the gag, and the rest of his bonds. "Quickly, let's get out of here." He pulled and pushed the man toward the rear of the hotel. Out the door in the back, away from the alley, several blocks down the Faubourg Montmartre to the Boulevard des Italiens.

Here there are people, pedestrians, cars, even at this hour of the night. He found a bench, and collapsed on it, pulling Langler down next to him.

"Hello, Herr Langler. How are you? Please forgive my rudeness. I should have greeted you sooner."

Langler looked at Kurt with astonishment and admiration. "Kurt, you saved me. I thought all was lost. How did you, what did you…how can I ever thank you?" and then, looking around, "and where is your rucksack and the money?"

"The money is safe, I hope. Tell me, what happened to you and who this man is who kept you prisoner."

"Not here, not now." Langler shivered. Kurt realized, that the poor man was dressed only in a shirt and pants, and that he was barefoot. Not the outfit to wear in Paris on a night in late December. "Where should we go?" Kurt asked.

"Have you been in touch with my cousin Rene Mayer?"

"No. I did not know whether he could be trusted."

Langler looked at Kurt appreciatively. "An old head on a young body," he mused. "He can be trusted. Can we get a taxi? And have you got enough money to pay for one?"

"Yes and yes," Kurt answered.

* * *

Rene Mayer's apartment reminded Kurt of his parents' home. Heavy, dark furniture, oriental carpets, a feeling of warmth, and redolent of good food and drink. Rene Mayer was as short as his cousin, but there the resemblance ended. He was round and jovial. *He must taste all he sells in his restaurant,* Kurt thought, *it's a good thing I didn't have to lug him downstairs at the Hotel Paris-Rome, I'd never have made it.*

In spite of the lateness of the hour, Mrs. Mayer had provided hot tea and cookies, and they all sat around the large, heavy dining room table, the Mayers in robes and

Langler still in the only clothes he had. A lamp with a fringed shade gave a warm light. Kurt began to feel safe and comfortable.

"The man you call Huber is really Werner Bender. He is, or I should say, was, the trusted assistant of my principal in Zurich, and thus was fully aware of our plans. I suppose, he thought he could get the money away from you, because you are young and inexperienced. If he had succeeded in killing you, he would have made you disappear in the mountains. We would all have thought that my faith in you was misplaced and that you had absconded with the funds. Bender would have been perfectly safe in that case. He could have remained with us with no one the wiser. Eventually, he could have retired with all our good wishes and lived on the money in some more pleasant climate.

Once you foiled his plan, he knew he could not stay around any more. The only way he could attempt to escape the long reach of his superior would be with the money."

"He tried to murder me, and he probably is responsible for the injuries suffered by Hans Huber."

"Yes. After you gave him such a beautiful headache, he got himself to Paris, overpowered me, and waited for your arrival. If you had just walked in.... I can't even think what would have happened. How intelligent of you to give me a chance to tell you that something was wrong."

"What happens now?" Kurt preened a little. Everyone enjoys a compliment.

"Are you sure the money is safe?" Herr Langler asked anxiously.

"It's in a locker at the railroad station."

"Well, we'll have to hope for the best, then. You did remarkably well. In the morning, I will call the recipient of the funds...."

"Don't you think, you could tell me who he is?" Kurt was getting a little annoyed by Herr Langler's circumlocutions.

"You are right, you have certainly earned my confidence. Anyway, in the morning I will call Monsieur Silvio Goldoni to whom the funds belong. I will tell him about Bender's betrayal, and I suspect, Bender will have a headache even greater than the two you have inflicted upon him. I will also ask Goldoni to send some of his assistants here to go to the station with us to pick up your rucksack, just in case Bender tries again."

"Who is this Monsieur Goldoni?"

"Oh, an investor."

"What kind of an investor?" Kurt pressed.

"The kind who does not want his business publicized. Am I making myself clear? But, I will introduce you to him. He owes you a lot, not as much as I do. He would have made me responsible for the loss of the money if Bender had succeeded, and if Bender hadn't killed me, I would have had to face his displeasure, and I would not have enjoyed that."

* * * .

Monsieur Goldoni lived in a beautiful old house on the Place des Vosges. The square is one of the most attractive and historic in Paris, the houses were all seventeenth century, with a lovely park and fountain in the center of the square. *I could easily imagine d'Artagnan or Cyrano de Bergerac dueling in this square,* Kurt thought.

Goldoni's office covered half a floor. It was thoroughly modern, a large functional desk, leather armchairs, a coffee table with several armchairs on one end of the room, book shelves, paintings, and several telephones, a teleprinter and in one corner a huge safe. Monsieur Goldoni was a tall, swarthy man in his early fifties, with a small mustache and piercing eyes. He looked at Kurt for a long time.

"You have done well, young man. You have done me a service. What are your plans now?"

"I need a residence permit here in France. I have no papers."

"And what makes you think I can help you with that?"

"I'm certain you can," Kurt smiled. "The question is, will you?"

"The young man has courage as well as brains," Goldoni said to Herr Langler. " Perhaps I could use him."

"Up to a point. " Langler said. "He has a sense of honor. He has demonstrated that by what he has done. I wonder what kind of disadvantage that could be in the world in which we live."

"Very well," Goldoni said to Kurt. " I will help you. But you must understand, that my help comes at a price. I will call on you to return the favor."

"If we're talking an exchange of favors," Kurt said boldly, " I believe that you are in my debt."

Monsieur Goldoni burst out laughing. " Very well, I'll accept that. Now, here's what you do. You will need a passport photograph. Go to the studio of my friend Odette, here's the address, " and he winked at Langler, "Odette will enjoy meeting this handsome young man."

"Then," he continued, " see Monsieur Andre Demines at City Hall. Mention my name and don't pay him more than 100 Francs."

"How will I find him?"

"Aren't you supposed to be a debrouillard, young man? Eh bien, debrouillez vous."

Kurt was not familiar with the term, but understood that this would be another test of his resourcefulness. Very well, he would handle it.

"I'll need some money," Kurt said to Herr Langler. " I've just about run out of the funds you gave me in Zurich."

There was an interchange in rapid French between Herr Langler and Monsieur Goldoni, too rapid for Kurt's comprehension.

"Oh, very well, " Goldoni added. " Here. It is a loan which you will repay with interest in due course. Now, I own the two buildings to the left and to the right of this one. You can stay in one of them until further notice. Go see Marthe, the housekeeper, and she'll fix you up. Now get going. I need to talk to Langler alone."

* * *

Odette's photo studio was only a few blocks away. Kurt climbed two narrow flights of stairs - *isn't anything on the ground floor?* - and entered a reception room furnished with a couch, a few chairs and a table covered with magazines. From the back, a voice called out: "Just relax, I'll be with you in a little while."

Kurt sat down and picked up one of the magazines. Oh, how interesting. The lead article - if that is what one could call it - was "Tarzan dans la banlieue" (Tarzan in the suburbs). There was very little written text, the article consisted mainly of full size photographs, but the story line was very clear. The first picture represented a well built young woman, totally nude, sunning herself on a lawn. In the next series of pictures, an athletic young man in a loin cloth appeared, had some conversation with the young woman, whose body was very clearly visible in every detail in every picture. The conclusion of the photo essay was a photograph of the young man holding the naked young lady close to his chest, while her hand fumbled with the drawstring on his loincloth.

Kurt was fascinated. He had never before seen anything approaching pornography. He fantasized himself in the place of the suburban Tarzan, and almost felt the young woman's lovely breasts against his own.

A whiff of perfume, and someone bent over him. "Oh, I see you appreciate my work." And a hand touched him where his interest had become totally expressed. "How reassuring that my pictures have such an effect. And what a nice effect."

With a friendly squeeze, the hand was withdrawn. Kurt blushed a deep red, and finally had a chance to look at the woman before him.

Odette was one of those ageless French women anywhere between 30 and 60, whose looks were of no importance, because they exude so much charm, and above all sexual energy. In this, she was a direct descendant of Diane de Poitiers, Madame de Pompadour or Madame de Stael, who bewitched royalty and intellect not because of their looks, but because of their character and charm.

"How can I help you?" Odette asked.

"Monsieur Goldoni sent me. I need photographs for my residence permit."

"Come along, then. " She seated him on a chair in her studio, fixed bright lights on him, and quickly and professionally snapped two pictures. She then removed the plates from the camera and vanished into her darkroom. This was done with such efficiency and dispatch, that Kurt could hardly imagine that this was the same woman who had touched him in so intimate a manner just a minute ago. Had he dreamed the moment?

Odette returned and stood in front of him, leaning on the arms of the chair and bringing her lustrous eyes to bear with full force on Kurt's.

"We have a little time, while the pictures are developing. Is there anything you would like to do?"

Kurt was silent. Oh yes, there was, but how could he say it?

"Come on, my pretty one. Isn't there anything more I can do for you? Say it." She continued to look into his eyes, and her hand snaked into his lap.

* * *

A very satisfying two hours later, Kurt left with his photographs in his hands. "Could I see you again?" he asked.

"Of course not, you're half my age. But it was fun, and I envy all the young women of Paris who will have a chance at you now. Good luck, and tell Goldoni thanks for sending you to me."

What a city, Kurt thought. *What a fabulous and wise woman. And there are so many more, and so much more to do. How exciting life can be.*

And now to find Monsieur Andre Demines at City Hall.

The residence permit section was filled with people standing in lines. Some of them appeared to be refugees from Germany or Austria, others looked like Arabs from France's Middle Eastern possessions, and there were a good number of blacks, clearly from the African colonies. Here and there, Kurt could see Asiatics with their entire families, and he could not tell whether they were Chinese, Japanese or from French Indochina. In Vienna he had not had any experience with such a polyglot assembly, and he found the atmosphere and the Babel of languages very exotic.

Well, let's find out the procedure. He did not trust his French sufficiently, so he approached a German speaking couple.

"I've just arrived. Could you please explain to me what I have to do?" He asked politely.

"You have to wait in line. That's what you have to do. That's what this system is designed to do. And they treat you like criminals. After all, we came here legally."

The speaker was a well-dressed man of middle age, clearly unaccustomed at the treatment meted out to him.

"I understand, but could you tell me the system, please?"

"First, you wait in this line to get an application. Then you fill it out, and attach your two photographs and your passport showing your entrance visa. Then you wait in this line to buy tax stamps. The amount you have to pay depends on your age and on your country of origin. Then you attach the stamps to your application. Then you wait in that long line over there to have your application checked. If you haven't made any mistake, and if you get to the head of the line when the official is not having a coffee break or a conversation with someone else, and when he's in the mood for work, he'll accept your application and give you a receipt. Then your application goes on that pile. Eventually, someone picks it up, issues the residence permit and your carte d'identite non-travailleur and puts it on another pile. You stand in that line over there, and if your permit has been issued, you'll get it, and if not, you'll come back and try again."

"That's a very inefficient system."

"Keep in mind, your time has no value here. Only the bureaucrats behind the desks are important. They earn less than a cleaning woman, but they represent La France, and their importance increases every time they can make one of us jump through hoops." The man said with total disgust.

"Well, thank you very much for all this information." *Which one of those officials is Andre Demines?*

* * *

"I must say it again, you have done very well," Monsieur Goldoni said. "How did you find Andre Demines?"

"Oh it was no problem. I decided that the man who issued the residence permits was most likely the one who could be bribed. So I looked him over carefully, waited until the office closed, and then followed him. I had intended to follow him to his home, where I could have verified his name without difficulty, but he made my life easier. He stopped for a drink at a café where he was evidently well known. I confirmed his identity with the bartender and then joined him. I will pick up my Carte d'Identite tomorrow."

Goldoni looked at Langler, and then back at Kurt. "Do you want to work for me?"

"Within limits." Kurt said. " There are things I will not do. But if you don't mind my making my own decisions in each situation, I'd be glad to work for you."

"Oh, I think, we'll get along."

* * *

CHAPTER IV

In March of 1939 Hitler broke his solemn promise that he had no other territorial ambitions in Europe. Germany annexed Bohemia and Moravia, the Czech remnants of Czechoslovakia. Slovakia became a German satellite, nominally independent, but in practice totally subordinate to the Fuehrer's whims. The Anti-Jewish laws were now extended to the entire former country of Czechoslovakia, and another large number of Jews were cast adrift. The flood of refugees grew, but still there were no countries to take them in.

By now even the most optimistic and most deluded appeasers, such as British Prime Minister Chamberlain and the French Premier Daladier realized that war was coming, and France and Britain finally began to rearm. But it was very late in the game.

On August 23, 1939 the world was stunned by the news that Hitler and Stalin, who had been bitter enemies, had signed a non-aggression pact. Only later did it become clear that this pact included another division of Poland.

On September 1, 1939 Germany attacked Poland with all her forces, destroyed Warsaw with vicious bombing attacks and advanced on all fronts. Britain and France, tied to Poland by mutual defense treaties, had no choice but to declare war. The monster of world war had risen again.

Within three weeks Poland did not exist any more. Soviet troops entered Poland from the East. Three quarters of Poland were in German hands, one quarter in Russian.

Poland had been the center of gravity for European Jewry. More than 10% of the population of Poland, over three million people, were Jewish. In Warsaw, one third of the city's population of one and a half million was Jewish. There was a rich intellectual life, with schools, academies, newspapers and books, theaters, and many, many synagogues, hospitals, orphanages and old age homes.

All of them were now at the mercy of the Nazis.
And there was no place for them to go.

*   *   *

Now that France was at war with Germany, Kurt considered joining the French Army so that he could participate in the fight. But France had no use for a stateless person with fake papers. If he asked for induction the likelihood was that he would be interned as an illegal immigrant, perhaps even as an enemy alien.

The only unit that would accept him, no questions asked, was the Foreign Legion. In his childhood Kurt had devoured books about this famed corps and its heroic adventures in the desert. However, he saw no advantage to giving up his life in Paris for the privilege of fighting Arabs in North Africa. They were not his enemies and he did not believe that the Foreign Legion would be employed against the Germans. After all, the French Army was one of the strongest in the world, wasn't it?

After the defeat of Poland nothing happened.

Britain and France had declared war. But nothing happened.

After World War 1, when they had almost been defeated by German attacks and German troops had reached the outskirts of Paris, the French had built an impregnable defense line of underground bunkers, forts, and artillery emplacements. This line was named after the minister of defense who had first proposed it, the Maginot line. It stretched from the Swiss to the Belgian border, protecting France against its ancient and hereditary enemy, Germany. The French felt totally secure behind it. So they sat.

The British sent an expeditionary force to France to back up the French, and they sat.

And nothing happened. The winter of 1939/1940 passed very peacefully. On occasion, there was a small artillery duel or an encounter between German and Allied planes, but essentially nothing happened.

After a while this period got the name: "Drole de Guerre" (funny war). In English it was called, perhaps more realistically, "Phony war".

In April 1940 Germany occupied Denmark in one day, without resistance, and in a few days, occupied Norway. While the West conceded that this gave Germany substantial strategic advantages, still nothing happened. The British sent a small expeditionary force to Narvik, in Northern Norway, but it was withdrawn when it became evident to the British that they could not inflict much damage to the German occupiers there.

Kurt was now twenty. He was much older in spirit and experience than the average twenty year old.

He was one of the hangers on at the court of Monsieur Goldoni. Goldoni never paid his people. He gave them connections and allowed them to use them for their own benefit. But they had to be available to him when he called.

Kurt had used his contact with Andre Demines to help other refugees to obtain residence permits and cartes d'identite. If in the process of transmitting funds from the briber to the bribee, he took a commission, who was there to object?

Goldoni frequently sent him on trips from one end of France to another, mostly either to deliver cash or to pick up cash from one of Goldoni's well paying investments. After all, Kurt had demonstrated his trustworthiness. In the process Kurt made contacts with a number of people who could provide hard to get goods. These contacts became even more valuable as the war began and rationing was instituted. In the sudden need for rearming the French military, shortages of various kinds of materiel developed. Kurt was soon one of those facilitators who could obtain scarce goods at a price.

Langler always made it a point to dine with Kurt on his frequent visits from Zurich, mostly at Rene Mayer's restaurant. Once Kurt asked him:

"Whatever happened with Huber? Or at least, that's the name I remember him by. Did they ever find him?"

"Don't worry about it. He won't bother you again." Langler answered reluctantly.

"But what happened to him?"

"You are better off not knowing. And I suggest, you'd better always keep on the good side of Monsieur Goldoni." Herr Langler was very serious.

It was then that Kurt decided that it was better to begin to distance himself from Goldoni as gently and as quickly as he could.

With Goldoni's permission, he moved out of the house on the Place des Vosges into a small apartment in the Marais, the old section across the Seine from Notre Dame. His income from his various ventures was enough now so that he could live reasonably well.

Kurt had discovered many things about himself. He had found a talent for languages, a talent for business and a talent for intrigue. He had matured into a competent, capable man, resourceful enough to merit the title debrouillard.

He missed his parents dreadfully. He wanted to be able to bring them word about his successes, to have them console him about his failures. Whenever he could, he attended Sabbath services in one of the synagogues of Paris and recited the Kaddish, the ancient prayer for the dead, and that gave him some comfort.

Kurt had developed the idea that it was essential for him to know English as well as French. In the back of his mind, he remembered his thoughts of going to the Holy Land, which was occupied and ruled by the British. He studied English, and when his finances improved hired a tutor, whom he found through the British consulate. And he studied French and French culture and literature as well. In fact, he worked harder at these two pursuits than he had ever worked in school under the well meaning spur of his parents.

He was very lonely. He had no friends, only a lot of acquaintances. There was an unbridgeable gap between the young man of Viennese Jewish background and the French members of the milieu - the twilight world between crime and legality - that he inhabited now.

Kurt loved to walk the length and breadth of Paris, from the Place du Tertre high up on Montmartre, down the Rue du Bac to the elegant Grands Boulevards and the Champs Elysees; from the Place de la Concorde along the beautiful Seine to the ancient Ile de la Cite; along the Boulevard St. Michel on the left bank, where the students from the Sorbonne congregated, to the Museums of the Louvre, of Rodin, of the Ecole Militaire at Invalides, and even to that great tourist attraction, the Eiffel Tower.

He loved the wheeling and dealing with which he made his living. He particularly loved helping some paperless refugees to the reassuring security of a Carte d'Identite, and when his funds permitted he would do so without charge.

He never forgot Ratzersdorfer. At first, he tried to get some information about the man from the German consulate. He even went so far as to walk into that lion's den and to ask whether he could obtain the address in Germany of a long lost friend. The official began to fill out a form and asked: " First name?" Of course, Kurt had no answer, he mumbled something and fled. Once the war started the consulate was closed, and that potential source of information dried up.

By May 1940 the phony war came to an abrupt end. In complete violation of neutrality treaties Germany invaded the Netherlands and Belgium. The armies of both small countries were no match for the overwhelming German forces. Then German troops rushed onto French soil along the entire undefended Belgian border with France.

How unfair of the Germans not to attack in front of the Maginot line where they were expected. How beastly of them to come in through neutral Belgium.

The British Expeditionary Force was surrounded and escaped through the port of Dunkirk because of heroic deeds by British sailors, civilian and naval. But while the men of the force returned to Britain, to fight again some other day, all their equipment was lost.

The French army attempted to stand against the German juggernaut but failed dismally in its endeavor.

By early June there was nothing between German troops and Paris. On June 10, to complete the debacle, Italy declared war against France and Britain, and totally aligned herself with Germany.

Monsieur Goldoni summoned Kurt to his office. Kurt had never seen the man so depressed. This was a man, who never showed his emotions, who always seemed to be in perfect control. Now he was almost in tears.

"All is lost, we have lost the war. Oh, France, my poor France."

Kurt was astonished. He had never considered Goldoni a fervent patriot. This was a new aspect of the man's character.

"Are you certain?" Kurt asked, "In 1914 there was the miracle of the Marne..."

"Yes, yes, I know. The taxis of Paris bringing reinforcements to the front to stop the German army. But not today. We have no army left, we have no generals. No, no. The war is lost, and we'll have to live with it."

"What are you going to do?"

"Never mind me. I'm staying in Paris. I will manage even under German occupation. A man like me can be useful to the occupiers, and I will have to adapt to the situation. But I'm concerned about you. You are Jewish, and there is no safety for Jews anywhere in Europe. You've got to get out."

Kurt was touched. In all the time he had known Goldoni, there was never a hint of feeling. Kurt always thought that he was an instrument that Goldoni could use when it was to his advantage and could discard the moment it was no longer useful. Now he realized that somewhere in his black heart Goldoni had developed affection for him.

"I really appreciate your thinking about me. What do you advise?"

"First, get out of Paris as quickly as you can. I am sure German troops will be here in the next forty eight hours. Do you know that our government has already fled? No, you wouldn't know. It's not public knowledge and it won't be announced because it would create panic. But I know that the ministers all have left Paris. They have begun negotiations for an armistice, which means a complete surrender."

"Where should I go?"

"Go south. See if you can get to Marseilles or Toulon. You know my contacts in both ports. You have been there before. Get on any boat that will take you out of France. I am sure that Britain will have to surrender too, or the Germans will invade and destroy the British. They are just too strong. So do not stay anywhere in Europe or in any of the French or British possessions in Africa. They'll all be German before long. Go to the United States if you can and save yourself."

Kurt saw that Goldoni was panicking. He could not believe that the situation was as black as Goldoni saw it, but he agreed that it was certainly better to get out of Paris and probably France, if he could manage it.

"Thank you for your advice. I will follow it. And thank you for all your kindness to me."

Goldoni jumped up, gave Kurt a bearhug, kissed him on both cheeks, and exclaimed: "Good luck, son, and may we meet safely in better times."

Kurt concealed his astonishment at the emotional outburst. He went home, packed his trusty rucksack, removed all his money from its various hiding places, put some into a money belt and distributed the rest into various pockets. Then he rushed to the Gare de Lyon.

The railroad station was packed. Evidently, the flight of the government from Paris and the imminent approach of German troops had not remained a secret very long.

Thousands of people thronged the station. Lines in front of ticket counters snaked around the block. There were the usual incomprehensible announcements of train departures and arrivals over the loud speaker. There was total noise and confusion.

There is no point in waiting in line for a ticket. I'll just get on the next train out and then see what happens.

At the entrances of the tracks frustrated railroad officials attempted to stem the flood of would be passengers and to allow entry only to those clutching tickets in their hands. But the crush was too great and the overwhelmed officials finally gave way. The crowd surged onto the platform and began to fill every available place on the train. Kurt followed leisurely. There would always be room for one more, he felt.

"Young man," a commanding voice with a heavy Spanish accent called out to him. "Young man, come here."

He saw a huge pile of very expensive luggage, suitcases, hat boxes, carrying cases and even a small trunk. Seated on the trunk was a middle-aged, rather corpulent woman wearing a simple traveling outfit and no makeup. But she exuded an air of authority that was almost imperial.

"Come here, young man, and help stow this luggage on the train. I need you."

It was clear that the woman expected unquestioned obedience. Kurt looked closer.

"Madame Esperanza Gonzalez? Is it you?"

"Yes, yes, now get the luggage on the train."

Madame Gonzalez was the principal singer of the Paris Opera. Kurt had acquired a taste for Opera from his mother who had often taken him to the Staatsoper in Vienna. As soon as he could afford it, he began attending the Paris Opera. At first, he went standing room, high up and far away from the stage, so that he could hardly make out the performers. Because of the wonderful acoustics of the Palais Garnier, he could still enjoy the music. As his financial fortunes improved, he obtained seats lower down, and closer to the stage.

How many times had he thrilled to Madame Gonzalez' voice. She was a superb Butterfly, an impressive Tosca, a magnificent Turandot. No wonder that a diva like her, admired and adored by the opera-loving public, was accustomed to command.

The window in the compartment next to the pile of luggage opened and two hands beckoned. Kurt swung the suitcases and hatboxes up and they were received by those hands, and disappeared into the compartment. He finally wrestled the small trunk up through the window and looked around. Madame Gonzalez had disappeared.

What, not even a thank you? Well, I might as well get on the train here rather than anywhere else. Kurt swung up into the car, as the train began to move with a great clatter.

Of course he realized this was a first class car, but since he had no ticket of any kind, he would be just as well off there as in the overcrowded second and third class sections of the train. He found it remarkable, that even in its panic to board the train, the public maintained its discipline and only got into the cars appropriate to its class. He walked down the corridor to the compartment he had helped fill with luggage, entered and sat down comfortably.

"This compartment is taken", Madame Gonzalez announced.

Kurt ignored the diva. He looked at the other person in the compartment. He was instantly in love.

He had admired beautiful women in Paris - even though, mostly from afar. But this one was something special.

She was tall and slender, with blond hair piled on the top of her head, blue eyes and very fine features. But what really appealed to Kurt was a sense of elegance, an almost aristocratic manner of movement, that came across even while she was quietly seated at the side of Madame Gonzalez.

"I have seen and heard you so often at the Opera, Madame," Kurt addressed the Diva, without being able to take his eyes off her companion. "I want to thank you for the great pleasure you have given me so many times."

"Well, thank you," La Gonzalez preened. "Clearly, you are a young man of taste and discernment."

The train began to move. "Close the window shades," the Diva ordered. "I can survive train travel only if I sleep through it."

She covered her eyes with a sleep mask taken out of her capacious hand bag, stretched out as far as she could, and instantly fell asleep. Her lovely companion looked at Kurt with a smile, and leaned back. Neither of them dared to disturb the silence in the compartment.

Almost two hours later, the train came to a screeching halt. Kurt looked out the window. Fields of sunflowers in full bloom appeared on both sides of the train but no station was in sight anywhere.

"Young man, make yourself useful," Madame Gonzalez commanded. "Find out what's going on."

Slightly amused that he had been preempted as the diva's man-of-all-work, Kurt moved down the corridor to the stairs. A conductor ran past. Kurt grabbed him by the arm.

"What's happening?"

"The tracks ahead of us have been bombed. This train will go back to Paris. If you want to go on, you'll have to walk to the next station, and maybe there'll be a train there to take you onward."

"Maybe? Don't you know?"

"Who knows anything? There's a war on, haven't you heard?"

The conductor tore himself out of Kurt's grasp and stormed on.

"Just a moment, how far to the next station?"

The conductor replied, but his voice was carried away by the wind.

Kurt returned to the compartment and explained the situation.

Madame Gonzalez turned to her companion and began speaking to her in English.

"Excuse me," Kurt interjected in the same language, "If you are speaking English for the sake of privacy, I have to tell you that that won't do."

"Oh no," Madame Gonzalez said, " but Sarah doesn't speak much French."

Sarah! What a wonderful name for this goddess. Kurt turned to her and explained the situation in English.

"I guess the only choice we have is to continue on foot until we have passed the damaged section of track and to get to the next station."

"That is true for you young people," Madame Gonzalez said, " but as for me, I'm going back to Paris."

"But you can't. The Germans will be there," those were the first words Sarah had spoken. *Oh what a beautiful voice, and her upper class English accent!* Kurt felt himself totally entranced. He crossed his legs to avoid giving any evidence of his infatuation.

"So the Germans will be there. So I'll sing Wagner. The little man with the mustache is supposed to love Wagner. I'll be all right. Don't forget, I'm a Spanish citizen. The Germans aren't going to do anything to me. But you, my dear, you're English. You can't fall into German hands. And if they discover who your father is, they could make life very difficult for him and for you."

Kurt spoke up, "I'll be glad to assist Mademoiselle Sarah as much as I can." *What an opportunity to be together with that wonderful girl.*

"There, you see. This young man will interpret for you. He looks trustworthy. You just go with him. What's your name, young man?"

"Kurt, Kurt Auster."

"And this is Sarah, eh…Brown."

"Happy to meet you." Kurt said. *So her name is not Brown. I wonder who she really is, and who her father is.*

"Very well," Sarah said. "I hate to leave you like this, but you're right. Let me just get my suitcases." She began to move a medium sized suitcase and a hatbox down from the shelf above the seat.

"May I make a suggestion?" Kurt asked. "There will be a lot of walking, I assume, and it may be wiser to take only what you absolutely need."

Sarah looked down her perfect nose at him. "Thank you, but I'll take all my things."

Madame Gonzalez jumped up and hugged and kissed Sarah. There was an exchange of words between the two women, too low for Kurt to hear. Then Sarah somewhat tearfully walked out of the compartment onto the tracks.

Who appointed me porter? Much as I admire the girl, I have to put a stop to this immediately.

Kurt took his rucksack, bowed to Madame Gonzalez, and left the compartment.

"What about my suitcases?" Sarah demanded.

"If you want them, you'll have to carry them. But I would again advise repacking the smallest one with just what you absolutely need."

"You're not going to carry them for me? You're not a gentleman."

"I guess I'm not. Now look, most of the passengers have started to walk. If you want to follow my advice and repack a small case, please hurry."

"No, thank you. I don't need you. I'll carry my own."

"As you please."

Sarah stumbled along, laden down by the suitcase and the hat box. Kurt walked slowly next to her, occasionally stealing a look at her profile.

"You'll get wrinkles if you keep looking so angry," he said. "It's still time for us to go back and take just a small bag."

Sarah did not answer but kept on walking.

Most of the passengers from the train were way ahead of them by now. Suddenly, Kurt grabbed Sarah and shoved her into the ditch next to the tracks. He covered her with his body.

"What are you doing!" Sarah screamed. "Help, help, rape."

There was the sound of motors. It became louder and louder. Two German planes appeared and flew low over the tracks. Suddenly there was the crackle of machine gun fire. The passengers ahead of Sarah and Kurt scattered, but Kurt saw some bodies lying on the tracks. People were screaming and running in all directions. The planes made two more passes, machine gunning the passengers. Then they disappeared below the horizon.

Ahead, the passengers slowly gathered near the tracks. A number were on the ground, some moaning and some ominously silent.

Kurt realized that he was still on top of Sarah and that the nearness of her bewitching body made him feel wonderful in spite of the mortal danger they had just escaped. Reluctantly he got up and held out his hand to help the girl rise.

"You've saved my life, " she said. "How did you know the planes were coming?"

" I must have heard them, the rest was instinct. Look, they may be back. We've got to get away from the tracks."

Kurt looked around. Several hundred yards into the field, there was a small stand of trees.

"Run over to those trees and wait for me, please. I'll get your things and join you." He jumped back on the tracks, grabbed the hat box and looked for the suitcase. But the suitcase was torn to shreds, some of the machine gun bullets had ripped through it.

Kurt held the suitcase together with both hands as well as he could, and with the hat box and his own backpack burdening him, clumsily made his way across the field to the stand of trees. Sarah looked at her torn and shredded suitcase.

"This could have been me!" Sarah said, and her look of gratitude made Kurt want to take her into his arms immediately. But he restrained himself.

"Look," he said, "sort out what you can use, and we'll put as much of it as possible into your hat box. The rest, I'm afraid, has to be abandoned. What you need most of all, is

116

stouter shoes or boots, if you have any, a warm jacket and raingear. Do you have anything like that?"

Kurt looked up into the sky. The sound of another plane's engine drifted toward them. High up, there was a single plane, but a much larger aircraft than the two which had attacked earlier. "A bomber," Kurt said. "We should be all right under the trees, but if he attacks I feel sorry for the other passengers."

Suddenly, the plane went into a steep dive. As its nose almost seemed to hit the ground, a cluster of sticks appeared. The plane came out of its dive and swooped up into the sky. Time seemed to stand still as they watched the bombs fall. The explosions shook the ground they were standing on, but the bombs had hit near the cluster of passengers, far away from them.

Sarah shook her fist against the sky. "Where are our planes? Where is the Royal Air Force? Oh, one day, one day, we'll get you, we'll get you."

"I certainly hope you're right, but now we'd better get out of here. Let's get your things together and go."

Fortunately, Sarah found a pair of boots, a beret and a raincoat among her possessions. Regretfully she abandoned some lovely hats and dresses. She crammed what she could into the hat box, and off they went.

"Where are we going?" Sarah asked.

"First as far away from the tracks as we can, and then South. Perhaps eventually we can find a train again, but here that seems a little risky."

Walking across the field was slow and tiring, but after a good while they reached a narrow country road.

"I've got to rest for a while," Sarah said. " My feet hurt, I'm tired and so thirsty."

"Well, let's relax for a few moments." Kurt agreed. They stretched out at the side of the road.

Sarah looked totally exhausted. Her face was smudged with dirt, she perspired, her clothes were disheveled. She looked altogether adorable.

Kurt noticed Sarah glancing back toward the area they had just left. The railroad tracks were no longer visible, they had come too far.

"You are worried about your mother." Kurt said, "I understand that. We can only hope that the train she was on reversed course and returned to Paris without being attacked."

Sarah looked at Kurt with total astonishment.

"How did you know she's my mother?"

"Elementary, my dear Watson," Kurt smiled. "There was a lot of affection between you. Clearly you were not a hired companion, your ignorance of French precludes that, and you are too young to be merely a good friend. Do you want to tell me about it?"

"My parents divorced when I was a baby. It was quite an acrimonious divorce. At the time my mother's career was just taking off and she would have had trouble caring for me, so my father evidently persuaded her to give me up. My father is British, and after he remarried I was brought up by his wife, whom I really consider my mother. I never knew I wasn't her daughter or that my brother is only my half brother. I found out about my real mother accidentally just a few weeks ago, and immediately wanted to get to know her. My parents objected, but I came to Paris anyway to meet her, and I'm very glad I did. She's a wonderful person."

"And your father, who is he?"

"Oh, he's a civil servant. But what about you? Who are you?"

"Time for us to go," Kurt said. "We can talk as we're walking."

He got up and stretched out his hand. Sarah took it and allowed him to assist her up. "You're right, Sherlock," she smiled.

As they walked, Kurt told Sarah a bit about his past. He excised judiciously the story of his illegal activities in the past two years. After all, he was very anxious to have Sarah hold only the highest opinion of him. Sarah cooperated by not asking too many specific questions about how he had supported himself. Perhaps her background was such, Kurt thought, that the need to obtain money simply would not occur to her.

In June in France the days are very long. It was still full daylight even though the time was well past 8 p.m. Kurt felt a substantial gnawing in his stomach, and was sure that

Sarah, too, would be feeling hunger pangs. As they walked South, he looked around for signs of life.

"There's a farm house ahead. Let's stop and see whether we can buy some food. It might be better if you hide out here," Kurt suggested. " Who knows whom I might encounter."

Sarah stayed in a little copse of trees, while Kurt walked over to the farmhouse. In a little while, he returned in triumph.

"Come along, we're all set. I've got bread and cheese, and a small bottle of vin ordinaire, and permission for us to sleep in the barn. What's more, I know how we can go on from here."

Kurt had acquired considerable expertise in sleeping in barns on his trek out of Austria. They climbed to the loft and Kurt pushed piles of straw together to make comfortable beds. Then they feasted on the provisions he had obtained.

"We have to get up at dawn. There's a freight train that stops just around the bend every morning to take on water. It goes to Bordeaux, and if we can get on it, we should be all right. That is, if we can avoid any German bombers, but we have to take a chance." Kurt enjoyed very much how attentively Sarah listened to his words.

Sarah took off her boots and massaged her feet. "I'm so tired, I can't even think straight. I've never slept in a barn before." She stretched out. "Thank you for all you've done for me, Kurt. Good night."

"Good night," Kurt said. *What's the matter with me? I'm with this beautiful girl, I'm crazy about her, and I don't even try? She'll think I don't want her, or worse, that I'm not interested. But she trusts me, I can't just grab her. She's so different from any of the other girls I've met.*
Kurt set his interior alarm clock for dawn - some times it even worked - and fell into a fitful sleep.

* * *

The small railroad station even provided a primitive bathroom where Kurt and Sarah could make their morning toilet in a very limited way. And, as the farmer had promised, a freight train rolled up. The locomotive stopped under the water tower, and the engineer started the procedure of taking on water.

"Quickly, let's go." The two young people dashed to the last of the five freight cars. Kurt opened the doors, they jumped in and he closed them. They looked around. Apart from some cases in one corner, the car was empty.

"Interesting that there is so little freight being shipped," Kurt mused, " but just as well for us."

In due course the train started again. As they looked out through the slats of the door, they saw the countryside whizzing by. The tracks evidently led through a very rural area of central France. "This must be a special freight spur," Kurt said. " We don't seem to be passing many cities."

It was hot. After a while, the rhythmic sound of the wheels lulled the young people to sleep. They had not slept very well in the barn and could use the rest.

Kurt woke with a start. Sarah was sleeping in his arms. Her head was on his shoulder, her lovely hair tickled his nose, and his right arm was completely asleep.

In spite of the dangerous situation he found himself in, he was unreasonably happy.

After a while, the train came to a stop. Sarah woke up, realized where she was, and gave Kurt an embarrassed grin.

"Where do you think we are?"

Kurt looked through the slats. The train was in a huge freight yard, tracks on both sides, many occupied by other trains.

"If this isn't Bordeaux, it's another major city," Kurt said, "I think it's time we got out."

They left the railroad car, and climbed over many tracks until they came to the end of the freight yard.

"Do you know what I really want now?" Sarah asked.

"A bathroom?"

"Yes, yes, but above all, a cup of tea."

"Well, we should be able to arrange that. There must be a café close by."

They walked on, past the freight yard, into city streets. In the distance, they saw a big building. The sign above the doors said: "Bordeaux, Gare Principale."

"Well, we've made it. There should be a way for you to get back to England from here." Kurt said. "And here's a café."

They settled down with a sigh of relief. Sarah disappeared into the bathroom, and Kurt ordered tea with milk for her, and a double coffee for himself, with croissants and jam.

Sarah emerged with her face scrubbed and glowing, her hair combed and even her clothing straightened out and brushed. She looked absolutely lovely, Kurt thought.

She took a big swallow of her tea, a bite of her croissant, and said "I'm beginning to feel human again."

Suddenly, their peace was disturbed by the roar of many engines. A German motorized column drove past them.

Sarah jumped up in panic. Kurt pulled her down. "Let's not call attention to ourselves," he said.

"They got here before us. We're going to be caught. It's all my fault. I should have left earlier. My poor daddy - if they catch me, he'll have to resign…"

"They haven't got us yet. Drink your tea, and then we'll see what we can do. But why should your father have to resign? A simple civil servant?"

"Oh, you don't understand. If I'm a German prisoner, they'll think they can use this as pressure against him, and they won't trust him any more. He's in trouble anyway, because he was against this war for so long."

"Who is they?"

"His superiors in the government. Never mind, it's too complicated to explain. Let's just get out of here."

"That, I think, is the right move." Kurt agreed.

Sarah and Kurt walked back in the direction of the freight yard. Tracks left the yard in three directions, North, East, and South. To the West was the Atlantic, and it seemed logical that German troops would occupy the coast as quickly as possible.

"We'll follow the tracks South as far as we can." Kurt said. "Then we'll try to find country roads. Not all roads will be occupied so quickly. Let's aim for the Spanish border."

After two or three miles there was a grade crossing. The railroad track turned East, but the highway followed a southern direction. It was wide and straight. Yet, there was no traffic.

"This is too important a road, "Kurt said, " but it's going South. It seems to be deserted because of the Germans, but perhaps we can find a French car or truck where we can hitch a ride."

The crowds of refugees fleeing from the German invasion must be well ahead of them. This alone was an indication that they were behind the German advance line.

Napoleon Bonaparte had ordered that shade trees had to be planted along all French roads so that his troops could march in comfort without suffering from the summer heat. In the 150 years since that edict most of the trees had grown to substantial sizes, and walking along a road in France at the height of summer was almost like walking through a leafy tunnel. The pleasures of the road were of course far from the mind of the two travelers. They kept looking behind them, constantly expecting to hear the sound of German motors.

They kept on for several miles. The road was rising and after a while the Atlantic Ocean was in view below them.

"At least we know we're going in the right direction as long as the ocean is on our right." Kurt said.

There was a look out point at the height of an incline, and then the road seemed to begin to go downhill.

"I must rest a bit. " Sarah threw herself on the ground and took off her boots and socks. "Oh, my poor feet," she said, massaging her toes.

The long June day was coming to an end. Kurt began wondering whether they would find a place to spend the night, or whether it would be wiser to continue their advance in the dark. He tried to remember whether there had been a full moon or at least close to one the night before, which could help them navigate at night.

What they had been afraid of, happened. They heard the sound of an engine.

"Quick, into the bushes." Kurt pulled Sarah with him. "Let's see who's coming."

A German soldier atop a motorcycle, rifle slung diagonally across his shoulder, drove up. He stopped, got off the motorcycle, looked at the lovely view of the ocean below him, and comfortably began to urinate over the ledge.

This was the first time Kurt had been close to a German soldier since he had left Vienna. *These are the Nazis who killed my parents, who are murdering and torturing my people.* An enormous feeling of rage rose in him. He looked around. *Aha, a large rock.* He grabbed the rock with both hands, lifted it high over his head, and with an inarticulate cry jumped out of the bushes at the soldier.

The German turned and for a split second, Kurt saw an astonished face. Then the rock descended on the trooper's head. The German fell backwards. Kurt jumped on top of him, and seated on the man's chest, kept pummeling and pummeling his head.

"Stop it, stop it. The man's dead." Sarah cried, holding on to Kurt's arms with both her hands.

Slowly, the rage subsided. Kurt looked at what he had done. The soldier's head was crushed. He saw blood, brains and bones. Kurt's hands were bloody. He had never seen a dead body before. *I've killed him! I've killed him!* Kurt got up and was violently sick. He heaved, and heaved until there was nothing left.

Sarah approached him. "Here, let me clean you." There was a water fountain nearby, and she used a small lace handkerchief to dry Kurt's face. "Give me your hands, " and she tenderly washed the blood off his hands.

Kurt allowed her to deal with him. He was totally numb. *What have I done? I'm a murderer. He was no older than I am. Maybe he wasn't a Nazi, just a soldier. How could I do this? How could I? I'm no better than Ratzersdorfer.*

Slowly he collected himself. Sarah looked at him with compassion. He couldn't meet her eyes. "I'm sorry, so sorry. I lost my temper. They killed my parents, you know."

"Yes, I know. You told me. Look, they're the enemy. It's war."

"That's no excuse for me. Anyway, we can't talk about it now. We've got to get out of here. If I only knew how to ride a motorbike. I don't even know how to drive a car."

"I do." Sarah said.

With great reluctance, Kurt approached the body of the German soldier. Flies had already settled on the bloody mess that had been his head. *He must have been a dispatch rider. I'll take his pouch, there may be valuable information.* A pistol was on the man's belt. Kurt had never held one in his hand before. He hesitated, then drew it out of its holster, and put it in his backpack. There was some ammunition - he did not know whether it was for the rifle or for the pistol, but he took it any way. *If they catch me with that I'm dead, but hey, I'm a Jew, I'm dead anyway if I fall into their hands.*

"I think I can handle the motorbike," Sarah said. "Do we dare ride it? What if we get caught?"

It was getting dark. It will be even darker under the trees. "Let's risk it. If we see the lights of other vehicles, just be ready to turn out your lights, and we'll get off the road as quickly as possible."

Sarah got on the motorcycle, with Kurt behind her holding on to her slender waist. With some difficulty she got it started and off they went. Normally, Kurt would have enjoyed Sarah's proximity, the feel of her body against him, her hair tickling his face, but he was still so full of what he had done, what he had found himself capable of doing, that he could not think of anything else.

They rode through the darkness, the wind in their faces, the light from the motorbike's single bulb illuminating the road. The moon rose - indeed it was almost full. "Turn off your light," Kurt advised, "we'll be less visible."

They rode and they rode. Hour after hour the road flashed before them. Then the motorcycle's engine began to sputter, catch, sputter and finally stop.

"I think we're out of petrol." Sarah said.

Here again, the road went along a cliff. Below they could see the ocean, phosphorescent waves crashing against a rocky shore.

They pushed the motorcycle to the edge of the cliff, and with a mighty shove pushed it over. They could hear it tumbling and crashing down the rocks until there was silence.

"We've come a long way. Let's go on as long as we can. Can you hold out a bit longer? " Kurt asked.

"I'll try. We've got to get away from here anyway."

Hours later, they watched the dawn come up from the vantage point of a haystack along the road. They napped for a while in the fragrant hay, then went on.

There was a crossroad, the first they had seen in a long while. Their road widened.

"This is a primary road now." Kurt said.

As the morning progressed, there was traffic. At first, Kurt and Sarah hid in the bushes every time a vehicle came by. Most of them were farmer's trucks, occasionally a small private car.

"Where are the Germans? Did we get past them?"

Suddenly Kurt ran out into the road waving his arms. A bus was coming along, filled with people. The bust stopped. The driver stuck his head out.

"Where are you going?" Kurt asked.

"St. Jean de Luz. But I don't think there's an inch more room inside."

"We'll find room. Please take us along."

Sarah and Kurt ran to the back door of the bus, and started to crowd in. Before they had finished climbing in, the vehicle started with a jerk, and Sarah found herself thrown into the lap of a motherly woman. Kurt remained in the stairwell, holding on for dear life.

"Pardon, pardon," Sarah used one of her few French words, as she got up. Kurt also apologized, and then started a conversation with the people around him. After all, they had been on the road for several days. What had happened to the war?

They were told that the French government, led by Premier Paul Reynaud, who had taken over from the appeaser Edouard Daladier only last March, had fled Paris. It resigned en masse in the face of the overwhelming defeat of the French forces.

On June 14, Pierre Laval, an anti-Semitic and pro-German minister, had brought the eighty four year old hero of the battle of Verdun in the first great war, Marshall Philippe Petain out of retirement. Petain, who may already have been approaching senility at that time, was named Chief of State, in complete violation of the French constitution.

On June 17, Petain asked the Germans for an armistice. It was, in fact, a total surrender.

Most German troops halted their advance while the armistice was being negotiated.

It was during this small window of opportunity that Sarah and Kurt had made their escape from Bordeaux. Their bus, filled with people trying to get away from the Germans, was destined for St. Jean de Luz, on the Atlantic Coast, near Bayonne and Biarritz and close to the Spanish border.

It was late evening by the time the bus arrived at its destination. Both of the young people were totally drained. Standing in a crowded bus for many hours after their experiences on the road had brought them close to collapse.

In front of the bus station there was a sign: "Hotel de la Gare."

"We've got to rest." Sarah said. "I can't think straight. Tomorrow we'll find a way out, tomorrow, tomorrow…"

A middle-aged woman sat behind the counter of the small hotel.

"Excuse me, Madame," Kurt approached her, "would there be any rooms available?"

The woman looked at the two tired and disheveled travelers.

"Have you got any money?"

"Yes, yes, " Kurt said, pulling out his wallet.

"I have one room available."

Kurt looked at Sarah. One room only. She took his arm and squeezed it. He did not know whether she had understood that there was only one room, but he registered and got the key.

"Up one flight and down the hall. Room 11, " the Patronne said. "The bathroom is three doors down."

"One more question, Madame. Can we get anything to eat? It's been a long day."

"There's a café across the street, but it's closed by now. Sorry."

Kurt did not say anything, but he looked at the Patronne pleadingly.

"Wait a moment," the woman said as she disappeared behind a curtain in back of her counter.

"This is the best I can do," and she handed Kurt two apples.

"Thank you very much."

Their room was very small. It was dominated by a large double bed, which took up most of the space. There was a small dresser, one chair and one window, and a sink in one corner. It was very hot. Kurt opened the window and leaned out. A slight breeze brought a briny tang to his nostrils. He turned.

"The ocean must be very close."

But Sarah did not answer. She had slipped out of her dress and shoes and crawled into bed. By now, she was sound asleep.

Kurt looked at her tenderly. Then he followed her example and slipped into bed in his underwear. He positioned himself as far away from Sarah as he could, partly out of fear of waking her, and partly because he was afraid that his desire for this beautiful creature would overwhelm his sense of judgment. Then he, too, fell asleep.

* * *

There was blood on his hands, so much blood. He was straddling a body and like a metronome, he was beating the head. The face below him looked at him reproachfully. It was the German soldier. No, it was his father, then his mother's beloved face. And he couldn't stop. He was moving, moving and hitting, hitting.

"No, no, no. No more." He cried out, jumping up and banging his head against the headboard.

"Sh, sh, you're dreaming. Everything is all right. Just relax, relax, " a dear voice spoke, and soft arms enfolded him, and held him tight. Kurt shivered uncontrollably, and finally woke up from his nightmare.

"Sh, sh," Sarah continued, and she drew his head to her breast, " just sleep, just sleep. Don't worry. You did the right thing, you did right."

Slowly the shivering stopped. Kurt relaxed and finally fell asleep again, this time feeling protected by Sarah's arms.

Bright sun filled the small room. Kurt opened his eyes. His head nestled in Sarah's bosom, her arms were around him. In front of his eyes an adorable nipple peeked out from under the brassiere which had slipped during the night. Kurt felt himself harden. He could not resist kissing the tender spot.

He raised his eyes. Sarah looked at him with an unreadable expression. Then she jumped out of bed. "I'm starving, let's get some food and see what we can do."

"Of course." Kurt said, considerably embarrassed. Then he added, "I'm sorry that I woke you during the night."

"Never mind that. Let's just go. My turn first in the bathroom." Sarah drew the blanket around her, and marched out the door. When she returned half an hour later, she was clean, her hair brushed and even with a touch of lipstick adorning her face. Kurt had managed to shave in the small sink. Then he withdrew into the bathroom for a short time.

As they walked out into the bright sunshine, the Patronne appeared. "If you want to keep the room for tonight, you'd better pay me now. Rooms are hard to get at this time."

Kurt complied. If they did not find a way out, at least they'd have a bed. After all, this was the first night they had slept between sheets since their departure from Paris, many days ago.

The café was packed with travelers. While they were looking for a table, Kurt heard not only French, but many other languages. There were mostly family groups, people who had fled the approaching Nazis and now did not know what to do.

After they had finally been seated and ordered their breakfast, Kurt looked around more carefully. There were some men in uniforms, some French, and some he assumed to be Polish from their distinctive five pointed caps. The buzz of conversations made it almost impossible to conduct a private talk.

"I'm sure of it," a man at the next table expounded. "The Germans will occupy all of France. The armistice is a complete surrender. They'll be here tomorrow."

From another table, Kurt overheard: "The British Fleet will save us. Didn't you see the ships in the harbor? They're going to evacuate all those who have reason to fear the Germans."

"No way," came the reply. "They can't evacuate the entire population of France. They're here just for their soldiers and the remnant of the Polish troops who got here."

Another conversation: "The Spanish will open their borders. There's a Spanish consul in Bayonne, who's issuing visas. We've got to get there."

"The Spanish? Franco is Hitler's ally. He's not going to do anything the Germans don't like."

Around the square in front of the railroad station there were many more people, laden with suitcases, some on carts which they had pulled with their possessions who knew how far and how painfully. Children of all ages, as children will, played around their parents, or cried and complained. French gendarmes tried to maintain order, but as authority figures they were constantly stopped and asked questions they could not answer.

With full stomachs and a night's sleep behind them, Sarah and Kurt felt on top of the world in spite of the danger they faced.

"Let's go down to the harbor." Kurt suggested. "I overheard someone talking about the British fleet evacuating Polish troops."

The port of St. Jean de Luz was very small. It was designed for pleasure craft and a number of small boats were at anchor. There was one pier jutting out toward the jetty. It was filled with people sitting on their suitcases. "The British are coming, the British are coming." People told each other, hopefully.

But there was no sign of any ships anywhere on the horizon.

Along the corniche circling the bay, there were a number of luxury hotels. "This is where we should have gone last night," Sarah said.

"Let's not complain, at least we had a bed."

Sarah blushed. Seeing that gave Kurt a wonderful, warm feeling.

Next to the entrance to the port there was a large bulletin board with a map of the area.

Kurt studied it.

"The Spanish border is probably twenty/twenty five kilometers south of here. Bayonne is just down the road along the coast highway. That's where the Spanish consul is supposed to be issuing visas. But that's probably just another rumor." Sarah said.

"What do you think would happen if you entered Spain illegally, since Spain is allied to Germany?" Kurt asked, without even considering his own situation.

Sarah shrugged. "Spain is still neutral. I'd certainly be better off than in German hands. There's a British Embassy, and they'd help me."

"Then here's my plan." Kurt said. "We'll make our way to Bayonne and see if indeed there's a Spanish consul there who would issue us visas to enter Spain legally. Frankly I doubt it. So, my fall back plan is to wait until night, try and steal a boat, and see if we can get into Spain that way."

"Do you know how to handle a boat?"

"No, but I've got a strong back, and I'll row if you'll navigate. Look at the map, all we have to do is get past the frontier."

"But what about you, Kurt? I'm British, I'll be protected. You're Austrian and there is no Austria. The Spanish won't let you in."

"Don't worry about it. We'll find a way." But Kurt knew perfectly well that Sarah was right. He was not going to get into Spain, and even if he was successful in entering that country he would at best be interned for the duration of the war, if not returned to German control. That is not what he saw as an acceptable alternative for himself. But remaining in France with German troops arriving momentarily - for he agreed with that prospect - was not a solution either.

In any case, first I've promised to care for Sarah. Once she's safe, I'll think about myself. If necessary, I'll hide in the mountains and come down at night and kill Germans.

Stop being a romantic. You're not going to fight the entire German Army single-handedly.

But I killed one of the bastards. I can get more of them, and I will.

Spoken like a true murderer. Is that what I want to be? Is that what my parents wanted me to be?

Again, Sarah and Kurt began to walk along a French road. This time, there was plenty of traffic, mostly toward the Spanish border. Most cars and trucks were so overcrowded, that it seemed pointless to ask for a ride. Finally, a wagon appeared. On its seat, there was an old man, wearing a large straw hat, indolently flicking a whip at the back of a spavined horse. The wagon's speed did not exceed their own by very much.

"Could we ride along with you for a while?" Kurt asked, as the wagon began to pass them.

The man looked at them, spat, and nodded. They hopped into the rear of the wagon. There were a couple of empty barrels, and a bit of straw.

"We're not getting very far very fast, " Kurt said, " but it's less strenuous than walking."

They stretched out, and relaxed to the clip clop of the horse's hooves.

A while later, the wagon stopped. The driver turned around.

"I'm going down to the port. If you're going to Bayonne, you'll have to get out here."

"What port? " Kurt did not remember a port between St. Jean de Luz and Bayonne on the map he had studied.

"Oh, the naval base. They just built it in time for the war."

"We'll go down there with you, if you don't mind."

As the horse and cart moved slowly down a twisting road, Kurt whispered to Sarah:

"We may have hit on something. There's a naval base that was not on the map. I think it's worth investigating."

The road took another turn. Below them, there was a small port, several trucks disgorging men, and two large motor boats tied to a jetty. In the harbor, at a distance, a naval vessel rode at anchor, the cross of St. George on its mast.

"British, a British ship," Sarah exclaimed jubilantly. "We're safe, we're safe. Let's go, let's go."

Kurt did not share her enthusiasm for himself, but Sarah's safety was important to him. He was astonished at how important it was.

"Thank you," he said to the driver, " we'll go on from here."

They ran down the hill as fast as they could. At the entrance of the jetty, a soldier in a strange uniform stopped them.

"Nyet, nyet" or some words to that effect. Polish? It was not one of the languages Kurt was familiar with, but the troops descending from the trucks and lining up to get on the motor boats were clearly Polish.

"Let me through, let me through," Sarah screamed. "I'm British, I'm British."

No comprehension. The guard stood his post.

Kurt started to scream at him, too. The soldier unslung his rifle, and approached Kurt in a menacing manner.

An officer approached from the motor boat. He clearly was British.

"Here now, what's all this commotion? Sarah, is that you? I can't believe it. What are you doing in this god-forsaken place?"

"Pudgie, oh how good it is to see you, " Sarah exclaimed, throwing her arms around the officer's neck. "I need a ride home, Pudgie."

Kurt stepped back. Well, it was too good to last. She's back among her own.

"Pudgie, this is Kurt Auster. He saved me and got me here. You've got to give him a ride too. Kurt, this is Ensign Ivor Crane, better known as Pudgie to all who love him. He's one of my brother's closest friends, and mine too."

Kurt nodded to the officer. Sarah kept babbling on, telling him about their adventures. He noted that she avoided talking about the German he'd killed or about their last night.

While they were talking, the Polish soldiers filled the first boat to capacity, and it took off toward the ship. The rest of the men filed toward the second boat.

"Hold it." the Ensign said, "I'll have to signal for permission to take civilians on board. Are you British too? " he addressed Kurt.

"No, I'm not."

"Well, we're under radio silence, but I'll signal my captain." The Ensign called over one of his sailors and gave him quiet instructions. The sailor got a signal lamp out of the boat and started to send his message by a series of flashes.

"Why did you tell him you're not British?" Sarah whispered to Kurt.

"Wouldn't they have found out from my accent? And from my lack of a British passport? I have no papers. There is no point in lying."

Ensign Crane came back. "I have permission to take you on board Sarah, but, I'm sorry, " he turned to Kurt, " I can take no non-British civilians."

"Then I'm not going. " Sarah cried." Tell your Captain that Kurt saved my life and I wouldn't be here without him. Tell him, my father will…."

"If it weren't for your father, I don't think the Captain would take even you, Sarah." Ensign Crane interrupted sternly. Then he continued in a slightly softer tone. " There's no room for a woman on a warship. We're overcrowded enough with all these Polish troops. And don't forget, we'll face the German Navy on our way home. But the Captain decided leaving you here would endanger you more than taking you along."

"Well, that's his worry." Sarah said. "Come on, Kurt, we'll get home another way."

"No, Sarah. You're coming with us. Those are my orders." Ensign Crane stepped in front of her.

"Pudgie, what are you doing? Are you out of your mind? Wait until my brother hears of this. Don't you touch me." Sarah was very upset.

Kurt intervened. "You must go with him, Sarah. It's the only way. You'll be safe and you'll get back to England. Remember what you told me about your father."

Sarah gave Kurt a long look. "Don't you want me with you?"

Kurt took both of Sarah's hands in his. "Oh God, how much I want you. But I want your safety more. I'll come to you in England. I promise."

Kurt turned to the Ensign. "Here is a German dispatch case I took from one of their soldiers. It may have information your people might find useful."

"Kurt, just wait here," Sarah put her arms around Kurt's neck. "I'll make the Captain pick you up. He'll listen to me. What's his name, Pudgie? Have I ever met him?"

"I don't know. He's Lieutenant Commander James Corcoran."

"Captain Corcoran? You must be joking."

"I'm not," the Ensign said, "and you'd better not even smile when you meet him. That name has been the bane of his existence ever since he was appointed Captain."

Kurt did not understand the reference at all. What was the problem? It seemed to him a perfectly good British name. He looked at Sarah, so animated, so happy to be back among her own. *What was I thinking? A relationship with this golden girl, clearly a member of the British aristocracy? Who am I? A penniless, stateless wanderer. How stupid of me.*

"Now promise me, you'll wait here. I'll make the Captain send a boat back for you. Don't you worry."

"Of course you will." Kurt said with a sad smile. *And I think the dear girl really means it.*

Kurt gave Sarah a quick hug, and turned away. The Polish troops had completed boarding the second tender and Ensign Crane led Sarah to the boat. She kept turning around to look for Kurt. There were tears in Kurt's eyes, but he resolutely kept walking away toward the end of the pier.

Suddenly, he turned and ran back. The boat had just left. He screamed: " Sarah, Sarah, what's your name, what's your real name?"

Sarah yelled back. But he could not hear what she was saying. The engine noise and the wind made it impossible for him to understand her words. But he could make out on the stern of the tender the words "HMS Dauntless."

Slowly, Kurt walked away. There was a great pain in his heart. *Will I ever see her again? I doubt it. Even if I get*

*to England, which is very questionable, and even if I can find
her without knowing her name, will she even remember me
now that she's back among her own? We spent a few days
together on the road. If she talked to me as she did while we
were walking, if she revealed herself to me, spoke about her
life, her dreams, her feelings, it was to pass the time. And it's
always so much easier to talk to a stranger whom you never
expect to meet again.*

Ah, but I know you Sarah. And I will never forget you.

* * *

There were a number of rowboats at one end of the
pier, and one or two small, gray naval looking vessels on the
other side of the port. A few men in French naval uniforms
busied themselves around them.

Kurt found a crate and sat down. Sarah's tender had
reached the "Dauntless." He watched as its passengers
climbed aboard the vessel, watched as the anchor was hoisted,
and watched as the ship began to move away from shore
toward the distant horizon.

*Goodbye, my love. Have a good life. And think of me
some times.*

* * *

For two years, ever since he had lost his parents on
that horrible day in Vienna, Kurt had been alone. He had
experienced the kindness of strangers, notably the Langlers,
but he always knew that he was on his own. For a few days,
on this voyage, he had had a partner who had shared his fears
and worries. And now it was time to accept that he was
alone again.

Kurt shook his head, wiped some tears from his eyes,
and decided that he must go on. *Remember, the preservation
of life is the highest commandment, let's see how I can
preserve mine.*

*Perhaps, my original plan is still valid. I'll wait until
dark, steal one of those rowboats, and try to get into Spain by
sea. How difficult can it be to just row along the shore, until
I'm past the frontier? Maybe I should get some food and*

water? Maybe, but if not, how long could it take for a few miles?

He walked around the port. Near the naval vessels, there was a small building that looked like it may have been a canteen, but it was closed and locked. Kurt took note of its location. Then he found a quiet nook behind some crates and stretched out in the hope of getting some sleep.

But sleep escaped him. He thought of Sarah. *I should have told her how I feel about her. I shouldn't have been such a gentleman, at least we could have made love last night. How stupid of me. Now she's probably in bed with Pudgie or one of her other aristocratic friends laughing about the poor Jew with his accented English who admired her.* He woke up full of anger at Sarah. *She deserted me.*

Slowly, reason took over and he stopped blaming the girl. *If I don't forget about her, I'll ruin my chances of survival. I've got to concentrate on that.*

Night had finally fallen, very late at this time of year. The port was deserted. Kurt walked as quietly as he could to the building he had identified as a canteen. It was not difficult to smash the lock with a rock he had picked up, but it was noisy. Kurt withdrew into the shadows. *Good. No one is coming.*

Indeed it was what he had hoped, but there was very little food as far as he could see. He found four cans of peaches, two tins of sardines, and a bottle of beer. *Well, it will have to do.*

Back on his side of the port he climbed into one of the rowboats, made sure that there were two oars in the boat, and sawed through the rope attaching the boat to the dock with his knife. Then, before starting to row he remembered the pirate stories of his childhood.

They always rowed with muffled oars when they did not want to be heard. How do you muffle an oar?

Well, what would produce sound? Slicing through the water. That can't be helped. And the metal of the oarlock. Aha.

He removed two socks from his backpack, and tied one around each of the oars at the oarlock. That did it. The metal on metal sound was indeed muffled.

He started to row out of the port toward the open water. He was totally inexperienced and so very clumsy. Sometimes he rowed stronger with one hand, and sometimes with the other. The boat was zigzagging. He understood that he had to try to make the strokes more even. *Oh, if I only had a navigator. Don't even think about her.*

He kept turning around to make sure that he was going toward the open sea, and every time he did that, he lost the proper rhythm of his strokes.

This is not as easy as I had thought.

And then he left the enclosed port area. Suddenly, he was in the open sea. This was the Bay of Biscay, notorious for high tides and wild waves. He tried to control the boat, but the waves were too powerful. *This may have been a mistake. Perhaps I should go back.* He tried to row, but there was a strong undertow, and his efforts failed. The boat was caught by the waves. Saltwater hit his face, spray and waves engulfed him.

He pulled the oars into the boat and held on for dear life. He could see nothing. The boat rode the wild waves, up one, down the next, and he could only hope that it was seaworthy enough not to be swamped or overturned. The wind rose and the waves got higher. He began to despair. He crouched in the bottom of the boat, held on, and prayed.

He was soaked to the skin. On the shore it had been a soft Summer night, out here on the open sea the wind was cold and biting. He began to shiver, he was freezing. *It wasn't that cold in the Alps.* He ducked as far down as he could to escape the wind and the spray, closed his eyes and held on. *Just hold on. Hold on.*

He did not know how many hours had passed, but the wind died down a little and there was a glimmer of light at the horizon. The sun rose. The waves subsided a little.

Then as the sun rose higher the sea became calmer. He looked around. There was no sign of land.

As the sun rose higher and higher he felt warmer. He felt a little more comfortable, but he was incredibly thirsty. He opened one of the cans of peaches, ate the fruit and drained all the sweet liquid. Then he used the can to bail out the boat as much as he could. It was remarkable how much water had accumulated in the bottom of the boat during the night.

Where am I? The sun rises in the East, and it rose over there, so land should be in that direction. He began to row toward what he considered to be the East.

He had no idea whether he was making any progress at all. There was nothing to measure it. The sea was much calmer than during the night, but there were still fairly high waves, and they seemed to move in the direction in which he was rowing. But was that an illusion? Kurt was no sailor.

Rowing was hard work particularly for an inexperienced young man. His back was beginning to hurt, his hands blistered, and worst of all, he had no sense of accomplishment. Was there any point to this effort?

He looked around. *Maybe there'll be a ship. I need help. But what if it's a German ship? I'll worry about that then. Let there be a ship, any ship.*

He pulled the oars back into the boat, and collapsed, totally worn out. The sun was at its zenith, broiling him. *First I froze, and now I'll burn,* he almost smiled, *what a stupid idea to take this boat.*

At least Sarah did not come with me. At least, she's safe.

Exhausted, he stretched out, tried to cover his face with his jacket against the relentless sun, and began to doze.

Evening, and no ship. He had no idea where he was. The waves began to rise again, and the spray began hitting him again. He endured another night bouncing from wave to wave. He crouched low down, wet through and through, and shivered from the cold. He had finished all his food.

Another morning, and again a calmer sea as the sun rose higher and higher. There was no point in rowing, since he did not know where he was.

He spent the day again crouched in the well of the boat. He attempted to cover himself as much as possible against the sun. The constant battering of the waves was getting harder to endure. He was almost out of his mind with thirst. *I deserve this, I'm a murderer. I did it to myself.*

The sun took its daily bath in the Atlantic and he began to shiver again. *I must have a fever,* he thought. *It's not even that cold.* He let go of his jacket, he let go of everything. *I must be delirious. I'm not even uncomfortable. Is this what dying is like?*

* * *

CHAPTER V

Kurt flexed his fingers. Writing the story of his past two years had been difficult. Too many painful memories had made him stop frequently, and it always took a major effort for him to continue.

"I was unconscious when I was lucky enough to be picked up by the Drake," Kurt completed his report." I woke up in the Drake's sick bay."

He thought that this was the end of the vetting process, but it was only the beginning. For the next four days teams of interrogators asked questions, eliciting answers Kurt did not know he had. Eventually, the ordeal was over.

Kurt Auster was brought back to Whitehall and into the presence.

This time, Admiral Morse received him warmly.

"Sit down, sit down, my boy. Now, here's my offer to you. You will spend the next six months as a private soldier in an elite unit of the 46th Royal Scots. You will be trained in the use of weapons, in unarmed combat, tactics, discipline and close order drill, in short in anything that a soldier must know. If you survive this training - and I warn you, that will not be easy, - I will bring you back here and I will use you for whatever missions may require your particular talents. I will tell you now, that I will consider you expendable. If you are not prepared for this, I will allow you to enlist in any other branch of the British Army, and take your chances like all other soldiers. What do you say?"

"I'll be happy to work for you, sir, and I'll do my best to pass the training. What about my becoming a British subject?"

Morse smiled. "Persistent cuss, aren't you? If you survive the training and start working for me, you'll get it. Now, one more thing. You are not to mention to anybody - anybody, you hear me,- that you know me and that you expect to work for me. Is that clear?"

"Yes, sir. Is there any way I can see Adam Bede before I leave London?"

"He's still in hospital. They had to operate on his leg, but I believe he'll be all right. Yes, you can visit him. Then you'll be taken to the recruiting office and sworn in. I hope you'll make it and that I'll see you in six months. This is going to be a long war. If we want to win it, we have to learn how to fight. I wish we had had the brains to begin training for this war a long time ago, but our masters were totally unrealistic for too long. Now we're in it up to our necks. Good luck."

* * *

After a short visit with Adam Bede, who made Kurt promise that he would see him whenever he came to London, Kurt was delivered to an army recruiting office. His minders left him there. Kurt was received by a sergeant who obviously had been notified of his destination, if not his identity. He was sworn in and given traveling orders to the training camp of the 46th Royal Scots.

As he raised his right hand and swore to obey the King and the officers he appointed and to protect the British Empire, Kurt reflected for a moment on his strange destiny. In his heart of hearts, he still saw himself as his parents' son, a student in Vienna, following the usual career path to University. Now he was a British soldier fighting against the culture that had been responsible for so much in his life, and his parents, his poor parents, were gone. *It's what I wanted - to fight against Germany - and I'll be trained for it. And if I am serving in Intelligence, perhaps I'll be able to find Ratzersdorfer one day. I won't forget him.*

The sergeant wondered what made this young man look so grim as he took the oath.

Apparently, in spite of the name, the camp was in Northern Ireland. Kurt traveled North by train, took a ferry across the Irish Sea to Dublin and another train to Derry. There he reported to the station master, as instructed. A phone call, and an army vehicle picked him up and brought him to the camp. As he found out later, the camp was on the vast estate of Lord Londonderry. On occasion during the training, he could see the impressive manor house in the distance, but that area and the gardens surrounding it, was of course off limits to the troops.

Kurt reported to the Sergeant Major. At that point, he found out how limited his knowledge of English was. What he spoke, was the King's English, what he heard was a heavy Scottish burr laced with the standard military scatological interjections. As a result, he frequently did not hop as quickly as he was told to hop. There were often unpleasant consequences in terms of extra details.

But at least, he was finally in British uniform. Apparently, his unit consisted only of volunteers ready to be in the forefront of battle. The training cycle of his unit would not begin for a week or ten days, he was told, until all the men arrived from their various previous assignments. So in order to introduce him to military life, Kurt was assigned to K.P. - kitchen police - until further notice.

Since all other volunteers had already undergone their basic military training, and Kurt was the only recruit coming directly from civilian life, the sergeant major assigned a permanent cadre corporal to introduce Kurt to the necessities of military life - how to salute, whom to salute - essentially everybody who moved - close order drill, how to keep his gear in his footlocker, how to make his bed the proper way, and principally, to hop when told to hop. The corporal was not happy with this assignment which cut into his free time, since Kurt was only available to him after his K.P. duties were over, and he made Kurt feel his displeasure.

After a week of this regime, Kurt wondered whether he would not have been better off in an enemy alien camp, where he might at least have been allowed to sleep. Then the other men of his unit arrived and the real training began.

Now Kurt found out about the tremendous varieties of spoken English which existed on that little island. He had become accustomed to the Scottish burr after a fashion, now he tried to understand the broad Lancashire drawl, the musical Welsh, and most difficult of all, the Londoner's Cockney. And he waited with some anxiety for the moment when he would be allowed to leave the camp for a few hours to try to communicate with the Irish inhabitants of Derry.

After a few days of training, Kurt began to regret the relatively easy time he had had on K.P. His day began before dawn with a four-mile obstacle course with full field pack and carrying a rifle. This involved climbing fences, crossing creeks by swinging over them on ropes - shades of Tarzan - crawling through fields over which machine guns fired bursts of supposedly live ammunition, to make sure, as the sergeant said, that you keep your butt down.

After that, there were lessons in the use and care of all kinds of weapons, from the bayonet and a short gurkha knife, through pistols and carbines, to rifles, machine guns and B.A.R.'s - Browning Automatic Rifles. There was unarmed combat, and training in explosives. There was training in communications equipment and Morse code. There were lectures on German and Italian uniforms, insignia and ranks. There were classes in Order of Battle, describing both the British military organization, and German and Italian military systems. Kurt and his companions had to learn how to recognize German warplanes and distinguish them from British planes; they studied German and Italian vehicles and even German and Italian Navy vessels.

When German paramilitary units were studied, Kurt paid particular attention to the description of the SS - the Schutzstaffel - the elite unit formed by Heinrich Himmler, one of whose members was Ratzersdorfer, the murderer of Kurt's parents.

At one point, Kurt's lieutenant found out that Kurt did not know how to drive a car. "You must know how to drive before I let you go. We'll find some spare time and I'll teach you." The lieutenant was as good as his word. On the one day a week, when Kurt's companions in misery rested exhaustedly in their bunks, or with the energy of youth shared a beer in the enlisted men's mess hall, Kurt was taught the rudiments of driving.

Three months after the training began, Kurt was considered proficient enough by his lieutenant to be allowed to forego any further driving instruction, and for the first time was given a day pass. With one of his comrades, a Londoner named Harry Broll, he hitched a ride into Derry, or as the British called it, Londonderry.

After they had been wandering the streets of the town for a while, looking at houses and stores as if they had never seen any before, Kurt saw a relatively luxurious looking hotel. "Here, let's have a nice lunch in a decent dining room," he suggested.

"That's not for me, I'm no toff, I won't feel comfortable in there." Harry said.

"Come on, we'll eat at a table with a table cloth and be served by a waiter. It'll make such a difference from camp." Kurt urged.

And indeed it did. The dining room was large, with high ceilings. The table was covered in snow white linen. The maitre d' looked at the soldiers askance, but Kurt spoke to him with the authority and upper class manner he had observed among his officers, and they were seated courteously.

Kurt felt as if he were back in civilization after a long sojourn in the jungle. Harry kept looking around at the dignified, well dressed customers in the restaurant, and pointed out to Kurt that the only other uniforms in the room belonged to officers, in fact, mostly higher grade officers.

"Our money is as good as any one else's," Kurt reassured him. "I haven't spent a penny in the last three months, so lunch is on me." And he ordered a carafe of wine.

Britain and of course Northern Ireland were subject to very stringent food rationing regulations. Individuals had ration cards, soldiers were fed by the military authorities. In restaurants, there were strict limitations as to how much you were allowed to spend on food. Naturally, these limitations varied with the class of restaurants, and Kurt and Harry were in the most expensive class. Nevertheless, there was just so much they were allowed to spend, and Kurt found that he still had plenty of money left over after paying the bill and tipping the waiter.

As they left the restaurant, Harry nudged Kurt. "The Colonel" and they both snapped to attention.

Lieutenant Colonel Wheat, Commandant of the training battalion, stood in front of them.

"Did you enjoy your meal here, privates?" he asked.

"Yes, sir," they chorused.

"It might be better if you picked another restaurant the next time you are in town. One more suitable to your station. Is that clear?"

Kurt was furious.

As the Lieutenant Colonel turned his back to walk away, Kurt yelled out:

"Sir"

Colonel Wheat turned back. Kurt continued in his strongest, most military voice:

"Sir! Private Auster apologizes for polluting the colonel's air. Sir!"

Lieutenant Colonel Wheat stepped closer to Kurt and looked at him. Kurt kept his face totally expressionless.

"Are you making fun of me, Private?" The Colonel asked.

"No, Sir!" Kurt yelled out. Then he continued in the same voice:

"Sir! Private Auster apologizes for giving the Colonel the impression that he is making fun of him. Sir!"

Colonel Wheat looked Kurt up and down. Kurt stood at attention, keeping his face totally blank. After a long moment, the Colonel turned his back and walked away.

"You have some nerve" Harry Broll was almost stuttering with fright. " Do you think the colonel will let you get away with this?"

Kurt did not answer. But he felt very satisfied with himself.

* * *

Why do I want to be a British subject? I admire the British for being the only country willing to stand up to Hitler. I particularly admire the people of London who are holding out against the nightly raids that are destroying their city. But I can't stand the class system. There is an automatic assumption of authority and subservience based solely on your accent. Because I'm a foreigner, I'm exempt to some extent, but even here there is an automatic distrust of all things foreign that is evident among all classes. In the long run, I do not believe that this is the country I want to live in.

Right now, of course, we'd better win this war, and I'll accept anything if it brings the defeat of Germany nearer.

* * *

In September of 1940 Germany, Italy and Japan signed an economic and military treaty of cooperation - the Rome/Berlin/Tokyo Axis was born. And Britain under the indomitable leadership of Winston Churchill was the sole country standing against German might.

During the presidential campaign for his third term, President Franklin D. Roosevelt of the United States promised his electorate that he would not send their sons to fight in foreign wars. And yet, realizing that Britain could not count on help from the United States, Britain held on.

The bombing of London and other metropolitan centers continued without respite. But the Germans paid a heavy price. Their Heinkel and Dornier bombers were unprotected by fighter escorts, because the Messerschmitt fighter the Germans used did not have the range to reach Britain. And swarms of Spitfires and Hurricanes tried to defend British cities. The bombing went on, but the German bomber squadrons suffered heavy casualties.

By February 1941, Kurt's training was complete. Only one more test remained - a parachute jump. Kurt's companions were very nervous about this last event and Kurt shared their worry. The sergeants, as sergeants have done since Roman Army days, had no sympathy for the concerns of their charges, but instead joked about the number of broken limbs and broken necks that each unit produced.

Kurt's squad of twelve were driven to a nearby airfield, shown how to fold their own parachutes and how to put them on. Then they were herded into an aircraft which took off immediately. "Now, listen here," the jumpmaster announced, "it's no worse than a jump from a three story building. Just tuck your legs under and roll with the momentum. And don't let the parachute drag you. Now above all, keep the parachute neat and clean, don't get any blood on it. That's hard to clean."

And then the door opened, and one by one the men were ordered out. Kurt stood in the open door his face buffeted by the slipstream, holding on for dear life. "Go on, stop dawdling," he heard and a mighty boot in his back propelled him forward. Down, down, cold and windy. *Where's the grip? Ah, here. I'm supposed to count to ten, is it time? I can't see the plane It must be too late. Pull the ripcord. Pull. It won't release. It did.* A jolt that rattled his bones, and he was floating, softly floating. *The ground, it's coming up so quickly. Hold tight, roll over, here it is.* Boom, every bone felt broken. But no, he was all right, bruised perhaps, but all right.

Kurt got up, collected his parachute and limped to the edge of the field. By the time he reached the next group waiting to participate in their ordeal, he had straightened out and walked briskly, in spite of the pain of his bruises.

"How was it?" he was asked.

"Piece of cake," he replied nonchalantly.

And then the training was over.

The men in his unit left for destinations unknown. Kurt had largely kept to himself, and become friendly only with Harry Broll. A warm handshake, and "I hope we'll run into each other again," and that relationship seemed over.

Kurt was alone again, and since his orders had not yet come through, back he went to the bane of the unassigned soldier's existence, K.P.

And then, finally, he was instructed to report to the Sergeant Major, handed his travel documents and ordered to report to a certain destination in London.

A train from Derry to Belfast, another crossing of the Irish Sea by ferry, this one in the middle of winter was as unpleasant as possible - how Adam Bede would suffer - and a train to London.

The young man who got off the train at Paddington Station was far removed from the callow youngster who had fled Vienna in a panic after the murder of his parents. He had filled out, was enormously fit after the training he had undergone, felt comfortable in his body because of what he had learned, and was secure in his ability to cope with whatever would come along.

Now it's time for me to rejoin the war. And perhaps, one day, I'll meet you, Ratzersdorfer.

Kurt walked to Whitehall from the station. So much more of London had been destroyed since his previous visit, that entire streets were gone. The Admiralty Arch was covered in protective sheeting and surrounded with sandbags. Admiral Morse's office had been moved into the basement. This time, there was only a small desk behind a temporary partition, but it was the same imperious Admiral Morse.

"Private Auster reporting as ordered, sir." Kurt stood at attention and saluted.

"At ease. It's good to see you, my boy. Sit down. I hear you've done well and that your instructors were pleased with you. I did have a negative report from the commanding officer. He claims that you have a tendency to be insubordinate. That is no great surprise to me. Do you have anything to say about that?"

"No, sir. " Kurt said nothing to defend himself.

"Well, I won't let you get away with anything, is that clear?"

"Yes, sir." Kurt replied.

"Are you ready to go to work?" Admiral Morse continued.

"Yes sir, very eager in fact."

"I have one problem with you. Your French is excellent, but you have a slight accent. I will arrange to have you see someone who will help you get rid of it. I will need you in France and I don't want you to arouse suspicions because of your accent. You'll stay in London for a while for that purpose."

Morse pulled out a small cigar, lit it with some ceremony without offering one to his subordinate, and went on.

"Now, de Gaulle's Free French have been more trouble than they are worth. No French possession except for a small colony in Equatorial Africa has gone with them. In the meantime, they're being supported by us and are a drain on our resources. There is a lot of backbiting and maneuvering among their officers. I need to know whether de Gaulle is going to be able to maintain his dominance over the others, or whether we should throw our support to someone else, like Admiral Darlan or Admiral Theberge. I'm going to assign you as liaison officer. I want you to keep your ears open while you work on your accent. Oh, and you'll be commissioned lieutenant, can't have enlisted personnel involved with those highfalutin frogs.

Adam Bede has suggested that you might board with him, while you're in London. Here's his address. You'll report first to Army Headquarters on Regent Street for your commission, then go see him. And now get out of here, and let me get back to work."

"Yes, Sir. Thank you, Sir." And Lieutenant Kurt Auster of the British Army left the Admiral's cubby.

* * *

Adam Bede lived on the second floor of an old Victorian mansion in an unfashionable part of Chelsea. Most of the bombed area of London covered the East End, primarily the section around the docks, but German bombs were notoriously inaccurate, and even the West End was scarred with lots filled with rubble. Miraculously, Adam Bede's street had escaped any damage so far.

Lieutenant Auster wearing his newly issued officer's uniform, proudly sporting the "pips" indicating his rank, rang the bell under the card showing Adam Bede's name. An upstairs window opened, and Adam's head appeared. "Kurt, welcome home, how good to see you. Come on up, quickly."

Kurt entered a rather dim hallway and walked up one flight of stairs. Adam Bede stood at the entrance of his rooms, with both hands out gripping Kurt's.

"It's good to see you too, Venerable, " Kurt smiled broadly. "How's your leg?"

"Oh, those butchers cut me up twice and say they repaired it as well as possible. I'm getting along all right, but I'll be limping the rest of my life. But I get to use a cane, and everybody says that that makes me look distinguished. The doctors say I should have rested the leg, instead of doing what we had to do. They don't understand there's a war on." Adam grumbled as he led Kurt into the apartment.

There was a small entrance hall, with a coat rack on which there were several overcoats, an umbrella stand and a rack for galoshes. Adam led Kurt into the parlor, filled with several armchairs, a small table, and above all, bookcases along every wall overflowing with books. A gas operated fireplace gave the room a warm feeling.

"Don't blame me for the furniture," Adam continued. "Only the books are mine, I couldn't live without them. One day, you'll see my digs in Oxford. That's the way a man should live. But this will do. Look here," Adam led Kurt into the back. "This is my bedroom, and here's a small room that you can use whenever you're in London. I have a feeling that you'll be away a good deal. And here's the kitchen and the bathroom, you don't mind sharing, do you? Now come and sit down, have a cup of tea, or would you prefer a sherry, and tell me all about your last six months."

Kurt looked at his voluble host fondly. "I have to tell you again how glad I am to see you. You're really making me feel at home, and I'm very grateful to you." He sat down, stretched out his legs, accepted a cup of tea, and they began to talk.

* * *

Marcel Levesque had been an actor in his youth. He would tell you that he performed in the great heroic parts on the French stage, Le Cid, Cyrano, d'Artagnan. But if you looked at him, you might have doubts. He was very short, quite stout, and almost bald. He would explain to doubters that he had come to live in London for the love of his wife, a native Londoner who refused to live in France, and that his stoutness was attributable to her excellent cooking and his hair loss to advancing age. This did not explain how he could have portrayed the great heroes of the stage while looking up from his level at heroines who normally would tower over him. But who would be discourteous enough to ask that question?

He had been supporting himself and his wife as a French teacher for many years. Their income was augmented very substantially by his wife's job as cook for a titled family whenever that family was in residence in London. And now he had been hired, not to teach French, but to improve a young officer's accent in that beautiful language. His instructions were to devote as much time as necessary, but that the officer had to sound like a native Frenchman in the shortest possible time.

And so Kurt found himself in Marcel Levesque's flat in Soho from early morning until late in the afternoon, repeating and practicing sounds he did not know he could produce. His teacher had no problems with Kurt's knowledge of the language, nor with Kurt's very comprehensive understanding of French grammar. Kurt attributed his facility with both French and English grammar to the sound foundation of Latin that Professor Lackenbacher had forced into him during his years at the Akademische Gymnasium in Vienna.

But there are sounds that are different in every language. The sound for R for instance was different in German, in French and in English. And Kurt found himself spending hours with Marcel Levesque, with a tissue in front of his lips to see the movement of air, pronouncing R R R R until Levesque declared himself satisfied.

In the evening, Kurt often dined with Adam Bede. And then, came the nightly bombing raid. By that time, most children under fourteen had been evacuated from London to anyone willing to take them in the presumably safer countryside. Most adults spent the nights in the shelters of the Tube, the vast subway system. The trains stopped running at midnight, and by that time, every inch of space on the platforms was occupied by families of Londoners bringing their bedding down and sleeping as well as they could next to strangers. In the morning they emerged into a city they sometimes did not recognize because of the destruction wrought during the night, to see whether their homes had escaped that night's devastation.

In the early days of the Blitz, the underground stations were places of companionship, where it was not uncommon for groups to sing cheerful songs, and to have impromptu parties where food and drink were freely shared. But now, after eight months of nightly attacks, the mood had soured. Lack of sleep, lack of comfort, and constant danger, had eroded the Londoner's spirit. But not enough, never enough to consider surrender. On the contrary, the determination to get back at Jerry grew with every raid and with every day.

Adam Bede refused to sleep in the Tube. He was not willing to give up his comfortable bed for the safety of the underground. "One has to be fatalistic about this," he would intone. "Survival may be too high a price to pay for the abandonment of civilization."

Of course, this meant that Kurt slept in his own bed as well, in the small room assigned to him. He would never abandon Adam Bede or show that he did not have the same courage or in fact foolhardiness as the older man. But privately he hoped that his assignment away from London would come soon.

Then he got word that his appointment as liaison officer to the Free French had come through, and that he would begin his duties by attending a function at the French embassy. There he could be introduced to General de Gaulle, and meet his French counterpart.

* * *

Major Bill Thompson cursed the day his parents had moved to France. Because his father was in the wine business, because his father's firm had sent him to France to buy and ship French wines, because his father had insisted on spending his three year stint with his family, Bill had had to learn French. He was twelve when the family moved to France and fifteen when they came back to England. He had hated every moment in a country not his own, where no one was interested in cricket, where he could not get his favorite fish and chips and where the boys his age were far more interested in girls than in sports. And he was forced to learn French. He could never master the accent, but after three years, he spoke and understood the language.

He blamed himself for the worst mistake of his life : When he entered Sandhurst to begin the career in the Army he had aspired to practically from the day he was born, he had listed among his accomplishments his knowledge of French.

And then some officious clerk in Whitehall found that information in his file. So, here he was. Instead of fighting the war as Adjutant of his battalion, instead of being with his troops and doing the soldier's job he loved, he was a glorified errand boy and maid-of-all work for the Free French officers billeted in London. What they were doing there, and why Britain had to pay any attention to people who had turned tail and lost their war, was beyond Bill Thompson's understanding.

Major Thompson was a tall, rangy man with a short graying military mustache, always immaculately uniformed, and accustomed to going by the book. He was convinced that the Army knew best, and that the British Army Manual and British Army directives were the word of God.

Bill Thompson sat in his office bemoaning his fate. He was the first field grade officer found by the bureaucrats, whose knowledge of French was adequate. So he had been pulled from his unit and assigned the job of head of the liaison office in London. And what did this job entail? Constant complaints from French officers about their quarters - as if it were so easy to find accommodations in a London devastated by the bombings - complaints about insults to the dignity of France, if General de Gaulle or the Admirals and Generals surrounding him were not accorded equal status with British General Officers in the planning and execution of military and naval strategies. And this, when the French officers lived off a stipend generously allocated to them by His Majesty's Government, a stipend for which they not only were not grateful, but about which there were streams of complaints because of its "inadequacy." And these officers were, after all, considered traitors by their own people in France and in the French colonies. If those officers had troops of their own to command, Bill Thompson would have a little more sympathy for them, but at this point, there were very few French troops in Britain, just the handful who had escaped alongside the British from the debacle at Dunkerque.

Kurt reported to Major Thompson with the military snap he had so recently acquired.

"Ah, another victim of too much knowledge." The Major greeted him. "I'm told that your assignment here is only temporary, so there's no point in giving you a desk and a specific task. Just do me one favor: keep the French and their demands and complaints as far away from me as you can, and you'll have my thanks. And to begin with, do you think you can handle tonight's reception without me? Just introduce yourself around. You'll meet Captain Reynaud, who liaises with us, and he'll show you what's what. He's one of the less objectionable frogs."

In June 1940 when France fell to the German onslaught and was forced to sign its humiliating surrender, and Charles de Gaulle arrived in London to establish the French government in exile, the French Ambassador to the Court of St. James was placed in a dilemma. Should he obey the new government of Marshall Petain which had signed the surrender and return to German occupied Paris, or should he throw in his lot with that upstart de Gaulle and remain in his luxurious quarters in the French Embassy. The French are nothing if not practical, and so it was not surprising that the Ambassador and his entire staff became part of the Free French movement.

Charles de Gaulle and his wife occupied quarters in the French Embassy, all other members of his government in exile, officers and supporters were quartered all over London with the reluctant help of Major Thompson. And of course, none of the living arrangements were commensurate with the rank and dignity of the personages assigned to them.

The British government had second thoughts about its hasty recognition of General de Gaulle's government in exile. Contrary to what had been hoped, almost no French possessions had joined his cause. Most still obeyed the Vichy government of Petain and Laval. And in metropolitan France, de Gaulle's call for resistance against the Boche largely fell on deaf ears. The great industrialists in occupied and unoccupied France were doing very well for themselves producing for the German war machine. The people in general, with admirable realism and logic, were waiting to see who would come out the victor in the conflict before committing themselves. And in early 1941, the momentum for ultimate victory very clearly was on the side of Germany.

The reception at the French Embassy was designed to impress the opinion makers in Britain: politicians, the press, the highest ranks of the Army, Navy and Air Force, and as many cabinet ministers as could be prevailed upon to show up. It had to demonstrate that there was a Free French Government in exile, that, in spite of all adverse information, it had the support of the French people, and that it was in Britain's interest to continue to support it.

London was totally blacked out. It got dark very early in the winter. Any time some poor civilian dared to show a light, the local Air Raid Warden would appear and sternly order him to close the blackout curtains and sometimes would even impose a fine. The few cars that were on the road, at a time of severe gasoline rationing mostly government vehicles of one sort or another, had their lights totally covered with black paint except for a small circle which gave so little light, that the fact that there were so few accidents had to be attributed to the scarcity of automobiles.

Kurt decided to walk to the Embassy. He carried a flashlight, standard equipment together with his gas mask. As he walked down Regent Street to the West End location of the Embassy, he was stopped a few times by ladies of the evening offering their services. During wartime, the competition from volunteers who wanted to snatch a few moments of joy from a generally depressing time was so keen, that earning their keep was very difficult for the professionals.

It was their practice to approach a soldier, glide their hand along his arm and shoulder to establish his rank - not visible in the blackout - and then name their price accordingly.

Kurt was accustomed to this and found himself saying " No, thank you, no, thank you", as he walked.

The French Embassy was a large imposing building, surrounded by a high fence. Kurt identified himself to the French soldier at the gate, who used his flashlight to make sure that Kurt's name was on the guest list. "Ah, yes, Lieutenant Auster. Please go on in."

Kurt walked up the steps and entered a large reception area. He was directed to the left and entered a ball room. Heavy blackout curtains covered every window, but Kurt was overwhelmed by the impression of glitter and light. He stood at the entrance for a moment to orient himself.

The large room was filled with men - and some women - in uniform, but Kurt's attention was drawn to the many women of varying ages dressed in the height of fashion. During the Blitz, London was generally drab, but there was no drabness in the scene he observed.

Bare, white shoulders adorned with jewelry, perfume, exquisite coiffures - beautiful ladies laughing at the compliments paid to them by the men in uniform or the handful of civilians in dinner jackets, waiters circulating offering flutes of champagne, an orchestra playing cheerful dance music - Kurt felt a little overwhelmed.

"You wouldn't think there's a war on," a voice spoke to him in French.

Kurt looked at a man in his late thirties, black hair, with a small mustache on an intelligent face, well built but a head shorter than Kurt, wearing the uniform of a Captain in the French Army.

"You are right, mon Capitaine. " Kurt answered. " I admit I haven't seen anything like this in a long, long time."

"You are Lieutenant Auster, are you not?" The Captain asked.

"Yes, how did you know?"

"You are the only officer of your rank invited to this august gathering. And even I, who outrank you a little, am here only because of you. I am Louis Reynaud, your liaison."

"Enchant, mon Capitaine," Kurt offered his hand which Captain Reynaud shook warmly. "But why am I responsible for your presence here? "

"Because le grand Charles wants to meet every officer assigned to us, and because it is my task to introduce you to him when he finally makes his appearance. In the meantime, let us have a drink, get acquainted, and admire the beauties spread out before us." Captain Reynaud took Kurt by the arm, and walked him into the ballroom, snagging two flutes of champagne from a passing waiter.

"A votre sant, mon Capitaine," Kurt accepted the drink and clicked glasses. "Tell me, how long have you been here?"

"Not long. I was transferred here from Africa because I speak English, and I must tell you that except for the small discomfort of the German bombs, this is a much more amusing post. From your admiration of the white shoulders and bare arms, I have a feeling that we share similar interests."

Kurt smiled in embarrassment. It was true that he had a hard time keeping his eyes away from some of the beautiful ladies surrounding them. "It's been a very long time since I've been in the company of beautiful women," he confessed.

At that point, he saw Admiral Theberge, followed by his wife, making his way toward them. The Admiral looked at Kurt without recognition, then came back and looked again, taking particular note of Kurt's uniform. With a stern glance, he then deliberately turned his back to Kurt and walked on. Captain Reynaud had watched this scene with some amusement.

"An old friend, Lieutenant Auster?" he smiled.

"Hardly a friend, mon Capitaine. Unfortunately, I had occasion to displease the Admiral and he is unforgiving. I guess I'll have to live with his disapproval."

"That may actually be to your benefit," Capitaine Reynaud said. "Admiral Theberge is neither liked nor trusted by de Gaulle. He has never explained to de Gaulle's satisfaction why he did not bring his entire squadron to our side, but left Oran only when the British fleet began its attack on our ships. You wouldn't know anything about that, my friend?"

Kurt smiled without answering. "Tell me where were you stationed at the time of the Armistice - or should I say, surrender?"

"Ah, you are very good at changing the subject. After all, we all like to talk about ourselves, n'est ce pas? I was in charge of the Gendarmerie in one of our North African possessions. I must admit I haven't seen any action, and I would be very happy if the only action I see in the future is with some of the charming ladies here. And I see, one of them is very anxious to talk with you. Go ahead, I'll find you when it's time to present you to the General."

Kurt saw Clemente Theberge standing alone near the wall, trying to catch his eye. When he looked at her, she motioned to him to approach. Kurt followed instructions.

"Bon soir, Madame Theberge. You look very beautiful tonight."

"Thank you," Madame Theberge said abstractedly. "You are the young man who saved us from the Germans in Oran and escorted us here, are you not?"

"Yes, I am." Kurt admitted.

"I must see you, but not here. Please come to visit me tomorrow. Here is my card with my address. Come at four in the afternoon, please. Promise me, you'll come."

"I'll be glad to," Kurt said with some astonishment. "But you know, that your husband dislikes me and will be very displeased with my visit."

"Paul is leaving tomorrow morning on an inspection tour of a shipyard where one of our destroyers is being refitted. He won't be back for two days. I need to talk to you. A demain, alors. I'm counting on you." Clemente Theberge turned her back, and began an animated conversation with a passing group of people.

Well, I was instructed to find out what's going on with these people, so I will certainly pay Madame Theberge a visit. I wonder whether Solange is here, too. It would be nice to see her. But that lovely girl was not in attendance as far as Kurt could see.

Suddenly, there was a change in the atmosphere. General de Gaulle had arrived. True to his nickname, Le Grand Charles towered over everyone in the room. Like iron filings to a magnet, the guests were drawn toward him, and Kurt found his part of the ballroom emptying.

"We'll go over there in a little while, let him dispose of the pushiest hangers on first," Captain Reynaud was at Kurt's elbow. "In the meantime, tell me about your conquest. Clemente Theberge is ripe, but very appetizing. I wouldn't mind tasting a bit of that. It should be particularly pleasant, considering how her husband feels about you."

Kurt smiled at Reynaud's amoral attitude. " I am sorry to disabuse you, but it's nothing like that."

"I don't believe you. Frustrated wives are a fertile field for conquest. Trust me, this is the voice of experience. Ah, but here's our moment. Come and let me introduce you."

Captain Reynaud pulled Kurt with him and forced himself into the circle surrounding de Gaulle. "Mon General," he said standing at attention, " It is my privilege to introduce Lieutenant Kurt Auster, who has been assigned to us as temporary liaison."

Kurt drew himself up and saluted. "A vos ordres, mon General."

De Gaulle looked at Kurt for a moment. "Do you speak French?"

"Oui, mon General. I lived in Paris up to the arrival of the Germans."

"Ah. Well, I'm glad you managed to escape. We'll all be back in Paris soon."

With that de Gaulle dismissed Kurt with a wave of his hand, and began a conversation with some of the men around him.

"Well, you got past that, " Reynaud smiled. "He's been known to object to people whose French accent is too poor, but you should hear him attempt to speak English. Atrocious. Now, let's enjoy the rest of the evening. You'll forgive me, if I leave you alone, I have some hunting to do. Here is my address and phone number. Please call me if I can be of service, or if you're in the mood for a drink and a chat."

"Thank you, mon Capitaine. I will. And good hunting." Kurt had enjoyed meeting Captain Reynaud and looked forward to seeing him again.

* * *

There was a musty smell in the hallway of the dingy building to which Clemente Theberge had directed him. Kurt walked up two flights of stairs, and pressed the bell under the name "Theberge." Clemente opened the door instantly, as if she had been standing there waiting for him.

She wore an elegant red dress buttoned down the front, displaying snowy white shoulders. Her perfume overpowered the smell of the hallway.

"Come in, " she smiled. "I'm so glad you are on time."

Kurt looked around. He had entered what the British inelegantly called a Bedsitter. The room was fairly large. In the front there was a small table, four chairs, and on the side a couch. In the rear, a double bed, partly concealed by a muslin curtain hung from the ceiling. Along one wall, there was a shelf holding a hot plate and some dishes, and next to it a small refrigerator. A door led off the room, presumably to the bathroom.

"Hardly the quarters of an Admiral in the French Navy, and a long way from what we had in Oran." Clemente sighed, noting Kurt's inspection. "Please sit down. May I offer you a drink, Lieutenant? And forgive me, but I don't even know your name."

"Thank you. I'll have whatever you're having. And my name is Kurt Auster. Now tell me, how I can be of service?"

Kurt was sure that Clemente wanted him to use his influence with Major Thompson , such as it was, to obtain better housing. But he was wrong.

Clemente brought two glasses containing a dark brown liquid. "I have a little Cointreau left. A votre sant," she touched Kurt's glass with her own, and swallowed everything in hers. Kurt took a small taste, and sat down on one of the chairs. Clemente sank down on the couch, close to Kurt. Her dress rode up, revealing her thigh and the top of her stocking. She ignored it, and Kurt made every effort to avert his eyes from the attractive sight.

"I want to know what happened in Oran. You must tell me. "

"What do you mean?" Kurt asked.

"Look," Clemente said earnestly, bending forward and putting her hand on Kurt's arm. "I know that you and Paul's old friend Adam Bede visited him in Oran. I know that you helped Paul dispose of the three Germans who had imprisoned my daughters and me. I saw you on the ship that brought us from Oran to this horrible place. But why does

160

Paul hate you so much? Why has he broken with Adam Bede and refused to meet with him aboard ship or here? And above all, why this sudden decision to abandon his post and flee here? It's against everything he had said before. Please explain this to me."

"I'm afraid, you'll have to ask your husband. I can't help you, I'm sorry. Incidentally, where are your daughters, surely they're not living with you here?"

Clemente crossed her legs and leaned back. Her skirt crept up even higher above her knees, and Kurt had great difficulty avoiding admiring glances at her well formed legs. The top of her stockings was visible, and Kurt caught a glimpse of bare upper thigh. He forced his eyes away from the charming spectacle.

"Solange took a crash course in English and joined the Wrens. She's at a Naval Station, somewhere. She won't tell me where on her rare visits to London, she's so security conscious. But she has indicated that she will switch over to French forces, as soon as we have facilities for her. Berthe was evacuated to a girl's school somewhere up North. She hates it there, but what can I do, I have no place for my own daughter here. But I can't take no for an answer. Look, we lived very well in Oran, and now look at us. My husband always said that his duty is not to pay any attention to politics, but to obey the legitimate government of France, and that is the Petain government. And then, suddenly, without discussing it with me, he pulls us out of bed and brings us to this place, where I have to live like that, where I don't understand the language, and where I spend my nights in the underground listening to German bombs. Why?"

"Is it not likely, Madame Theberge, that the Admiral is a patriot and decided that the interest of France required his participation in the war on the side of de Gaulle's Free French?"

Clemente laughed bitterly. "Paul's patriotism ends with him, not even with his wife and daughters. And de Gaulle and his people don't trust him. They can't understand why he didn't bring his entire squadron over when he defected from the Vichy government. They're using him as a glorified messenger boy. And the worst is....."

"Yes, Madame Theberge?"

"Oh, for heaven's sake, please call me Clemente. I'm not that old, and it's been so long since I could talk in French to a young man who wasn't connected to my husband." Clemente leaned forward again, very close, and her hand was again on Kurt's arm. This time, she began to caress his upper arm.

"Won't you confide in me, " she purred. "Paul is so unhappy, so angry, why he hasn't touched me since we left Oran. I need, I want…help me, won't you?"

She is flirting with me, Captain Reynaud was right. But this is not what I should be doing. Although, as Reynaud said, she's very appetizing.

Kurt stood up. " I'm sorry that I can't be of assistance. I'll speak to the billeting officer, if you like, to see whether better quarters can be found, but I can't hold out much hope."

Clemente stood up too. She moved very close to Kurt, very close. Her fingers were playing with the buttons on Kurt's tunic. "You're such a handsome young man, " and she opened the first button. " I kept looking at you aboard ship, " another button was opened. "And now you're even more appealing in your new uniform," the last button was open. Clemente brought her hands around Kurt, pulled out his shirt and started to caress his naked chest. "Please, please," she whispered. "Don't disappoint me, I need, I need, " and she pulled open his belt, and knelt before him, burying her face in his crotch.

It had been a very long time since Kurt had been with a woman. To refuse Clemente would not only have been churlish, but would have required superhuman strength of character, and Kurt was not superhuman.

"I want to see you again. I hope you feel the same way, I needed this very much." Clemente said, as Kurt exhaustedly began to dress. "Where can I reach you the next time Paul is away? It's got to be somewhere where they'll understand me in French, and it can't be anywhere Paul could find out."

Kurt thought for a minute. "Here's the phone number of a man called Marcel Levesque. I see him quite often, and I'll make sure he's discreet. Why don't you leave another name - say, Odette, and just tell me when you're free again."

162

The ex-actor was by nature a romantic soul. When Kurt explained that he wanted to use him as an intermediary because he was having a secret affair, Marcel Levesque enthusiastically accepted. During the next few weeks, Kurt saw Clemente three more times and found that her passion for him or rather for his body grew. It was only for his body, he realized, because she really had no interest in him as a person. She never asked him anything about his past or his present activities. She was only interested in discussing the one topic about which he would not talk - Oran, and apart from that she wanted sex. And he enjoyed her talents in that regard exceedingly.

He also determined that Clemente hated her husband Admiral Theberge. Apparently it was not only since Oran that Paul Theberge had not touched his wife. The physical side of the marriage had ended many years earlier. Clemente was quite frank. "He lost all interest in sex a long time ago. All he wanted was his career and to talk about his ancient ships. As long as we lived in Paris, and he was away on his duties for months at a time, I did not mind. There was always a young man around - none as good as you, Cheri, - to console me. But he did not like that. He was afraid that I would be found out and that a scandal would injure his precious career. So he moved us to Oran, and there, in the small colonial society I was forced to be discreet. You can see how hungry I was for someone like you, Cheri."

"Why don't you leave him?"

"I should have done it in Paris. Here, I'm stuck. The only money we have is the stipend your government pays us. If I left him, what would I do, where would I live? I'll never learn the atrocious language they speak here, and how would I support myself? No, I'm stuck all right. But Cheri, this is why I hoped you would tell me what happened in Oran." Clemente began to caress Kurt again. "See, if I had some weapon against him, some information he wouldn't want to be made public, he might give me a little more leeway to enjoy myself. And wouldn't you like that too?"

"I'm truly sorry, but there really isn't anything I can tell you. Just accept that the Admiral is a patriot and saw the light."

"Fine, don't tell me. But I know he hates you, and because he hates you, I want you more. Enough talk. Come here and let me...."

* * *

Kurt was having a drink with Captain Louis Reynaud.

"Well, my friend, tell me about the beautiful Clemente Theberge. Did you..."

"Oh no, she wanted me to intercede with Major Thompson to get them better quarters. And I admit, when she showed me where they live, they deserve better. But nothing is available."

"You're very discreet, " the Captain smiled. "I won't press you. Just one question, do you mind if I try my luck?"

"Of course not, but perhaps you should ask the Admiral for his permission." Kurt grinned.

"We're not quite that civilized yet." Reynaud chuckled. "The Admiral has other problems. He has been playing politics against de Gaulle, but he has lost. De Gaulle really is a master. In spite of his low rank, he won't allow any other officer to get close to the limited power he exercises as a ward of His Majesty, so to speak. I think that Admiral Theberge is beginning to regret that he turned coat."

"What about you, mon Capitaine?" Kurt asked. "If I'm not indiscreet, what made you leave North Africa to join the Free French?"

"You ask because you don't find me sufficiently patriotic?" Reynaud grinned.

"I wouldn't impugn your patriotism, " Kurt smiled, " but I don't have any illusions about your realism."

"Quite right, quite right. I'll give you my answer in one word. Arrogance."

"I don't understand."

"I had some dealings with German officers in North Africa. I am a Frenchman, and in spite of what you may think, proud of La belle France, my heritage and the glorious history of my country. And to be treated like a lackey by these Boche, to watch them strut around as if they were really the lords of the earth, the master race, as they call themselves, was more than I could bear."

"This is not what I would have expected from someone who makes such a virtue of cynicism."

"Well, there is a price even I won't pay for a comfortable life."

"That is very interesting. " Kurt mused. " You know, mon Capitaine, that so far there have been no indications of a resistance movement either in occupied or in unoccupied France. De Gaulle's exhortations have fallen on deaf ears. What will change that, do you think?"

"Two things. " Captain Reynaud answered. "First of all, the French must feel that the balance of power is shifting, that Britain and her allies have at least a reasonable chance of beating the Boche."

"Ah, here's your cynicism again," Kurt smiled.

"No, my realism. I know the French. And secondly, as I said before, German arrogance. It is inevitable. The French cannot, simply cannot, do things the German way. The Germans cannot, are absolutely unable to accept that their orders are not obeyed totally and instantly. Their arrogance will force them to demand more and more. There will be clashes and reprisals. And then there will be resistance. In the meantime..."

"Yes?"

"Let us enjoy what is available to us in London, be it Clemente Theberge or any one else you might find to your taste, my friend."

* * *

In spite of his promise not to send American boys to foreign wars, which helped get him elected to his third term as President of the United States, Franklin D. Roosevelt knew that without American help Britain was lost. So he forced the Lend-Lease Act through Congress. It was passed on February 8, 1941. FDR had explained, " If your neighbor's house is on fire, you've got to lend him your water hose to help."

This was the first ray of light for beleaguered Britain. The United States, that "great arsenal of democracy ", as FDR had called it, began to ship supplies, arms and planes to Britain. The first large American bombers, "Flying Fortresses " which exceeded in capacity and range anything the Germans could muster, arrived in the British Isles in April, and from then on the movement of war materiel and food accelerated geometrically. German bombing attacks continued, but there was a feeling in Britain that the tables were turning. The powerful cousin across the water was stirring and if they held out long enough, would join their battle.

Admiral Morse required Kurt's attendance.

"I have read your reports with great interest. Of course they are incomplete."

"Sir?"

"Just make up your mind that I know everything, that's why I'm head of intelligence. Why didn't you report your involvement with Madame Theberge?"

Kurt blushed. "I'm sorry, sir. I thought that was personal."

"Nothing is personal in wartime. I expect you to understand that and act accordingly in the future. Is that clear?"

"Yes, sir."

"Now, I gather that you believe that de Gaulle is firmly entrenched?"

"Yes, at least until a large section of the French colonies defects from Vichy and joins us. Then the officer who maneuvers that could become a threat to de Gaulle. If Admiral Theberge had brought his squadron with him..."

"Yes, I agree. And I also agree that Theberge is not to be trusted. We'll have to keep an eye on him. Now I also believe that Captain Reynaud's assessment of the French character is accurate. I want to verify that situation on the ground. You will go to France..."

"Sir?" Kurt did not conceal his shock.

"What did you think I trained you for? To service Admirals' wives in London? It's time you joined the war, my friend. Now, here's what I want you to do. You will fly to Lisbon. You will be a Swiss citizen, employed by Zurich

Oerlikon, the large armaments manufacturers, who are being courted by Germans so that they will produce for them. And of course, they will. The Swiss are always available for the right price.

You will be a messenger. Because of your youth, you can't act like a senior executive, but that's all right. As a messenger you will be able to travel with impunity. You will be provided with the appropriate documentation and clothing. You'll report to this address on Curzon Street for that. Here.

Now, from Lisbon make your way through Spain to unoccupied France. I want you to contact all the people of Goldoni's network, but just feel them out as to their attitude toward forming resistance cells. Don't reveal yourself.

Then get into occupied France and do the same. I'm particularly interested in Goldoni himself. He could be very useful, if he could be trusted.

I expect you back here in no more than six weeks. Go in, check around, get yourself back into unoccupied France and get back to Lisbon. Marcel Levesque tells me that your French pronunciation has improved drastically, but as a Swiss you'll be forgiven an accent. Now go to Curzon Street. See Commander Riley. He'll brief you further. And good luck."

* * *

CHAPTER VI

The "factory" in Curzon Street had become the home of some of Britain's best forgers. Kurt was equipped with a Swiss Passport including all necessary visas and transit stamps, a French Carte d'Identit d'Etranger, a briefcase containing all kinds of correspondence from Zurich - Oerlikon, some of which was addressed to the most prominent French industrialists, and civilian clothes. He made sure that his clothes showed the marks of Swiss haberdashers and that his shoes too, were demonstrably not English made.

Kurt left instructions with Marcel Levesque to advise "Odette" when she called that he had been sent out of town for a few weeks, said farewell to Adam Bede, and was on his way. He had been on a plane briefly when he took his first - and he fondly hoped - his last parachute jump - he could still feel the jumpmaster's boot on his back, - but now he boarded a civilian plane for the first time.

Even though the plane was operated by British Airways, through a complicated leasing arrangement it was allowed to sport the Portuguese colors. They were displayed prominently in the hope that a passing German warplane would realize that this was a neutral, civilian aircraft.

Kurt loved Lisbon. After the gloom of a British winter aggravated by the blackout and bombings, to find himself in a white city with cafés filled with people, a warm sun blazing from a cloudless sky, seemed unreal. Unfortunately, he had little time to enjoy the atmosphere. The train to Madrid, where he would change to a train for Marseilles, was scheduled to leave shortly. Kurt barely had time to sit at a café in the huge Praca Rossio, sip a fruit drink, and enjoy the passing parade.

At a table near him, he overheard Viennese German. A family of four, father, mother and two teen-age children, were anxiously discussing the problem of getting on a ship to America. Apparently their American visa was due to expire. There was only one ship within their time frame, and no tickets were available. Kurt understood the worry and fear of these people. He heard them express their concern that the

Nazis would enter Spain and Portugal to take Gibraltar and thus cut off Britain from the Suez Canal and her Empire. It seemed a logical fear, and the family, obviously Jewish refugees, were panicked at the thought.

Kurt felt very close to that family. *If I could only help them. They are my people but I can't even speak to them to give them encouragement. It would be too dangerous for the role I am playing. I hope they make it.*

And in his heart of hearts, Kurt felt a twinge of envy at the togetherness of the four people. Seeing them, made him feel even more alone.

The train to Madrid left on time, and eight hours later, early in the morning, Kurt found himself in the Spanish capital. The train to France left from another station, Atocha Station, he was told, and to get there meant crossing Madrid from West to East. Kurt took a taxi, and asked the driver in a combination of French and Latin, with the liberal use of his hands, to drive past the main sights. The taxi drove along a broad boulevard, past what the driver pointed out was the "Palacio Real," another wide street, and through a medieval square which reminded Kurt a little of the Place des Vosges - " Plaza Major" the driver said, again a wide boulevard, squares filled with fountains, and to the Atocha Station.

A beautiful city. I hope one day I can come and look at it. But it is made so ugly by the many swastika flags hanging from flagpoles together with the Spanish flag. It's certainly a reminder that Franco is Hitler's ally.

There had been no problem crossing the border from Portugal into Spain, apparently Kurt's papers were acceptable. There was no problem leaving Spain at the border crossing North of Barcelona. Then the train stopped again. There was a sign "Perpignan," and French customs officials came aboard.

"Vous tes Suisse?" the officer asked. "What is your destination?"

"First Paris, and then home to Zurich."

Kurt's baggage was searched, and his briefcase underwent a cursory inspection. Fortunately, there was only a glance at his papers, and Kurt was in unoccupied France.

I fought so hard to get out of here, and now I'm back.
All I have to protect me are the papers the "factory"
produced. Will I be able to get back to Lisbon and England?
Kurt was very uneasy, and of course quite afraid. But he had
a mission!

The train to Marseilles seemed to take forever. Kurt
asked the French conductor who checked his ticket.

"Aren't there any faster trains? We seem to stop an
awful lot."

"There used to be express trains. But now, we don't
have enough rolling stock, so we must make every stop along
the way."

"What happened to the rolling stock?"

The conductor shrugged his shoulders. "So many
trains have been transferred North to help in the war effort,
we're lucky to be allowed to keep what we have."

Eventually, after a very long and exhausting journey,
Kurt arrived in Marseilles. As he walked through the
cavernous station a man sidled up to him, trying to grab his
suitcase.

"Are you looking for a hotel? I can find you one,
clean and cheap. You know it's hard to get a room. Just
come with me."

"No, thank you." Kurt had to wrestle his suitcase
away from the man. But, as soon as he saw the man
importuning another passenger, he left his suitcase and
briefcase at the luggage checkroom.

Marseilles' main street, the Canebiere, led from the
hill on which the station was built down to the port area a
mile or so away. Kurt remembered Goldoni's instructions,
and walked down the bustling street almost to the port.

He noted that there were very few cars and that they
all were equipped with a contraption burning charcoal.
Obviously there was no gasoline for the civilian population.
He also noted that in addition to the regular police, there
were a number of young men in dark blue uniforms with the
word "Milice" on their shoulder patches.

As he continued to walk downhill on the Canebiere
the port area came into view. Marseilles was France's
principal port on the Mediterranean, and in peace time Kurt
was sure that the port would have been filled with cargo and

passenger vessels, loading and unloading. Now there seemed to be very few ships, and certainly not much activity. In the distance Kurt saw a small island with a large gloomy looking building occupying almost its entire mass.

This must be the infamous "Chateau d'If," where Dumas' Count of Monte Christo was imprisoned. I wonder whether it's still used as a prison. I hope that I'll be able to stay out of it.

Close to the port, in a small side street just off the Canebiere was the "Odeon" bar Kurt had been looking for. He entered a large, dark room, chairs and tables along one wall and the bar, covered with the traditional zinc, along the other. Photographs of sports figures decorated the walls. There were a few people occupying some of the tables, but none stood at the bar.

Kurt sat down on one the few barstools, ordered a beer, and looked around some more.

The man he was looking for occupied a corner booth. He was very fat, bald and wore an open collared red shirt and trousers held up by flower decorated wide suspenders. He fit Goldoni's description exactly.

He was talking to a short, slight man, and from his gestures, Kurt surmised he was issuing instructions. The slight man kept nodding his head and then left with an obsequious bow.

Kurt approached the fat man.

"Monsieur Carnotti? Bon jour. May I speak with you for a moment?"

Carnotti gave Kurt an unblinking hostile stare.

"Who are you?"

Kurt bent down and whispered into the man's ear.

"I am a friend of Silvio Goldoni. May I sit down?"

"Are you really?" The hostility did not abate. "Well, sit down and convince me."

"I worked for Monsieur Goldoni for two years, until the Germans took Paris. He told me to look you up whenever I got to Marseilles."

"Anybody can say that. Do you have any proof? For all I know, you're a police informant. I have nothing to say to you."

Kurt considered. " I have never been in Marseilles before but I made several trips for Monsieur Goldoni to Toulon. Perhaps you know someone there who can verify my identity."

"Hm, what is your name, and who did you know in Toulon?"

"My name is Kurt Auster. I'm not going to tell you the names of the people I saw in Toulon. If you don't know them, we may have nothing more to say to each other."

For the first time Carnotti smiled. It was not an attractive sight. "Go, have another beer. If I decide that I want to talk to you, I'll let you know."

Kurt carried his beer to a booth in the corner of the bar and sat down. Carnotti motioned to one of the men seated at another table to approach and gave him some instructions. The man walked through a door in the rear of the bar.

It's exactly like Goldoni had explained it to me. Carnotti operates from here without ever leaving his booth.

While Kurt sat in his corner, nursing his beer, he observed a number of men come into the bar, wait to be recognized by Carnotti, talk to him briefly, and disappear again. Eventually, the messenger Carnotti had sent out after speaking to Kurt emerged from the rear of the bar and whispered something to his boss. Carnotti motioned to Kurt to join him.

"So," he said, " it's possible that you're the young man who used to work for Silvio. I'm still not sure but I'm willing to listen. What do you want?"

"I need a place to sleep, where I won't be disturbed by the police."

"That's easy enough. What's your story?"

"I've been in hiding in a small village in the mountains since the Armistice. I'm going out of my mind with boredom. I want to get back into action, in fact, I want to get back to Paris and rejoin Monsieur Goldoni. I'd appreciate your advice."

Carnotti smiled again. His smile reminded Kurt of the crocodiles he used to see in the Vienna zoo long ago.

"I can understand that, a young active fellow needs the bright lights and the girls. But there aren't any bright lights in the mess we're in."

"How bad is it? How much influence do the Germans have in unoccupied France? Has the Petain government been cracking down on your business?"

"Well, I'll tell you. The Petain people do exactly what their masters in Berlin tell them to do. But as long as industry delivers to the Boche what they want, they pretty much leave us alone to run our own affairs. Unfortunately, there isn't much activity in the port, and that's where I had a lot of my business. But as long as you're not Jewish, the police is not a problem. They're spending a lot of time and effort rounding up Jews. What a waste of time.

Of course, there's rationing, shortages of food and fuel, but " and here came the crocodile's smile again, " that's an advantage for people like us. Makes up for the business I lost in the port."

"What do you hear from Monsieur Goldoni? I'd really like to get back to Paris and rejoin him."

"There isn't too much communication between the unoccupied and the occupied zone. I haven't heard from Goldoni in a while, but trust him, he's not the kind of man who'd let the Boche interfere with his little activities. It's a lot harder to get around in the occupied zone, though, you've got to have really good papers."

"How would I go about getting there?"

"Well, if you've got the papers, you can just take a train. There aren't too many people going North. Getting out of there is much more of a problem. Now, it's time to eat. Join me, will you."

An enormous platter of spaghetti, meatballs, tomato sauce was delivered to the table. A bottle of red wine was opened.

"Bring an extra plate for my friend here," Carnotti ordered. "Dig in, young fellow." He motioned to one of his hangers on. "When we've finished, take my friend over to Marie-Therese's, tell her to give him a room in the back where he won't be disturbed by the activities, and tell her to let him have one of the girls, with my compliments." He turned to Kurt again. "Tell Silvio Goldoni he can always count on me and that any friend of his is always welcome."

* * *

During the next three days, Kurt wandered the streets of Marseilles, read the newspapers, kept his ears open, and engaged people in conversation whenever it was possible to do so without arousing suspicion. While he found the usual grumbling about conditions, notably food and gasoline rationing and restrictions on travel, he also found no sign that the disaffection was strong enough to rouse people to risk their lives by armed resistance. On the contrary, there was considerable confidence in the old Marshall, the hero of Verdun, who had come out of retirement to save France from the disaster her former leaders had caused.

The Milice appeared to be an organization of volunteers more or less on the line of the SS in Germany which had sworn to defend France against the onslaught of the Jew. Every newspaper, many magazines and posters warned about the Jew. In this respect, unoccupied France had begun to resemble Germany.

Kurt noted with amusement, that while it was impossible to eradicate the national anthem, the Marseillaise, from French consciousness, it was only the third stanza that was sung at official functions. After all, the first and second stanzas were written to arouse the population to fight against ferocious invaders, and to make sure that their blood would fertilize the holy soil of France. This was clearly impolitic under the circumstances. The third stanza was for the young - "We will begin our careers when our elders are no longer with us, and protect France then…"

Kurt boarded a train for Lyon. This major city was very close to the line of demarcation between "free" and occupied France. Here Kurt had been many times on behalf of Monsieur Goldoni. He was recognized and welcomed by Aristide Dupont in the suite of offices he had visited before. Whereas Carnotti looked and acted like the thug he was, Aristide Dupont appeared quite different. He was slender, slightly under average height, which meant, as a Frenchman he was short. Possibly to compensate for that he held himself

174

rigorously straight. He was always dressed at the height of fashion, his hair and small black mustache perfectly in order, and his manners extremely polite. This did not mean that he was any less dangerous than Carnotti when crossed. His offices were furnished in the most modern manner, all blond wood and the most up-to-date communications equipment.

Kurt felt more comfortable in his quest for information about the mood of the population.

"It's not so bad," Aristide Dupont commented. "Of course, if you're Jewish you're in trouble. But I think most people don't mind at all that Jews get out of our hair, they're such tough competitors. As for the rest of us, if you keep your nose clean, you can get along. Of course, the shortages are a problem, but," he winked, " we can always manage, and make some money in the process. And once the war is over, we'll be all right."

"Who do you think will win this war?"

"How can you even ask? It's obvious that Germany will win. Look what they've accomplished. A touch of German discipline would do us a world of good. It's what Marshall Petain keeps talking about. We must have order, we must be more disciplined and work hard. Then we can do just as well as Germany did."

"Even people like us?"

"Even more so. We won't have all these independent operators interfering with our business. Proper territorial allocation, and organization is what we need."

Kurt wandered around Lyon for a couple of days and found that the general attitude was not very different from Aristide Dupont's. It occurred to Kurt that the first sign of resistance would be some posters, some graffiti, perhaps de Gaulle's cross of Lorraine scribbled on a wall. But he saw nothing.

There was no alternative. If Kurt was to fulfill his mission, he had to place his head in the lion's mouth. It was obvious to him that there were small prospects for an effective resistance in unoccupied France. But how did people feel who were directly under the German boot?

The train to Paris was almost empty. Carefully, Kurt placed an enamel pin showing the Swiss colors in his lapel. At the line of demarcation a French Gendarme, accompanied by a German soldier, checked Kurt's papers. The soldier was very friendly. He spoke to Kurt in German, apparently very happy that he could say something instead of just listen to a language he probably didn't know.

"So, why are you going to Paris?"

"I'm visiting some friends, and then I'm going back home to Zurich."

"Ah, you lucky fellow. You'll be back in the land of Swiss chocolate and plenty of food. One of these days, we'll come visit you and help ourselves to all that good chocolate."

* * *

This time, Kurt checked only his suitcase at the railroad station, and kept his briefcase with him. *If the Germans stop me, I'll have something to justify my wandering around.* He remembered the first time he had come to Paris, looking for Herr Langler, without knowing his way around the city. Now, he knew the streets, the buildings, and the language. But how had Paris changed under the occupation?

At the Place de l'Opera, to Kurt the heart of Paris, a huge Swastika flag hung from one of the buildings facing the square. Below it, there was a large sign: "Kommandantur". Two armed German soldiers stood at attention at the entrance. Obviously, this was the headquarters of the German proconsul.

Kurt strolled the boulevards. The first thing he noticed was the absence of people just wandering as he was doing. The famous Parisian flaneur, who enjoyed the sights and sounds of the city, was gone. People walked purposefully, keeping their heads down, without looking left or right. As soon as Kurt became aware of this, he too changed his gait and walked rapidly and purposefully.

There were a lot of German uniforms around. The officers and soldiers wearing them were the ones who had taken over the pleasant task of wandering the streets of the beautiful city. Many behaved like tourists, pointing cameras, admiring buildings, and enjoying the outdoor cafes. Even though it was still cold the cafes were open. Few civilians occupied the chairs, but many Germans did. Here and there,

176

German soldiers were accompanied by young French women. Kurt noted that the passing French civilians averted their eyes when they saw such a group.

Most of the soldiers Kurt saw were Wehrmacht in field gray uniforms, but occasionally a black uniformed member of the SS strolled by, and Kurt felt most uncomfortable and afraid when he saw the eyes of one of them turn toward him. But the man went on without stopping, to Kurt's vast relief.

Kurt noted that the buses passing by were few and far between, and that they all were using charcoal burners for fuel. He entered the Metro and waited a long time for a train that eventually deposited him near the Place des Vosges.

There was a small bar nearby where Monsieur Goldoni usually stopped for an aperitif before going out to dinner. Kurt considered it wiser to wait for Goldoni in a public place from which he could readily escape if necessary. Even though Monsieur Goldoni had considered him a protégé and been kind to him, Kurt did not know how ten months of living under German occupation had affected the man. One thing, Kurt was sure of - whatever Monsieur Goldoni did would be good for Monsieur Goldoni. All else was secondary.

Kurt was very familiar with the bar. He had joined Monsieur Goldoni and others for drinks here many times. The bartender standing behind the zinc bar recognized him, and offered his hand.

"I haven't seen you in a while. Welcome."

They shook hands. Kurt shrugged his shoulders. "You know, the times."

"Ah yes, the times." Those comments, Kurt had learned, excused everything without the need for further elaboration.

"I guess you're waiting for Silvio Goldoni," the bartender said. "He should be in soon. What would you like to drink in the meantime?"

Kurt ordered a beer, and withdrew to a booth at the far end of the bar. He sat with his back against the wall so that he could observe anyone coming into the establishment.

Suddenly, there was a sound of many motors and sirens. Kurt looked at the barkeep questioningly.

"Razzia," the man said composedly. "A raid - the Germans are looking for Jews."

At each end of the street, a German troop transport drove up, accompanied by a car containing French police. The vehicles stopped crosswise and the soldiers jumped out forming a cordon at each end of the street. A French policeman used a bullhorn:

"Everybody out into the street. Bring your identity papers for a check. Anybody found in the buildings will be arrested. Everybody out. Everybody out."

The bartender looked at Kurt. "Do you have a problem? There is a way out through the sewers."

Kurt considered briefly. By saying yes, he would place himself in the power of the barkeep. Whether indeed there was a way out through the sewers was a question. It was equally possible that the barman would call the police the moment Kurt said yes, and thus would receive a reward or at least demonstrate his loyalty.

So far, Kurt's papers had passed scrutiny. He hoped they would again.

"No, thank you." Kurt said to the barman. "I have no difficulty. How often do they do this?"

"Oh, they keep busy." Kurt and the barman followed the other patrons of the bar out into the street. People were pouring out of the houses. The French police made them form into a line. Some German soldiers, rifles in hand, began to enter the houses to make sure that they were empty.

Suddenly, there was a commotion near one of the buildings. Two German soldiers dragged an elderly man out. The other Germans clustered around him.

While this was going on Kurt reached the head of the line, showing his Swiss passport and Carte d'Identit to the French policeman, and was dismissed. He made a concerted effort to keep his face from showing the tremendous relief that he felt.

Out of perhaps one hundred civilians being examined, another three were kept on the side. The rest were allowed to return to their homes. The three unfortunates and the elderly man who had been found upstairs, were loaded into a

German vehicle and within a minute or two the entire force of Germans and French police disappeared.

"Eh bien, another lucky break," the bartender smiled.

"Why lucky? If your papers are in order..." Kurt asked.

"Your papers may be in order, but your face may displease the high and mighty Germans. Or they haven't filled their quota. They take whom they please."

"And what happens to them?"

"Oh, that depends. Forced labor in Germany if you're lucky. Of course, if you're Jewish ...."

"Yes?"

"Better not to ask. Just be glad you're not."

Kurt returned to his table in the rear. It was getting dark, and if Goldoni was going to show up, it should be soon.

So life in the occupied zone was certainly harsher and more dangerous than South of the demarcation line. Kurt kept thinking of Captain Reynaud's comments that it would be German arrogance that would foster a spirit of resistance.

And then, he noted Silvio Goldoni coming in. The bartender handed Goldoni his regular aperitif and nodded toward Kurt. Goldoni looked over at Kurt and then almost ran over to him.

"What are you doing here? I thought you'd be safely away from Europe. You're in great danger."

"I'm so glad to see you, Monsieur Goldoni." Kurt smiled. "Don't worry about me. Tell me how you are."

Goldoni sat down heavily at Kurt's table. "Not so good. Business is terrible. The Boche won't let an honest man make a living. But this is not the place to talk. Come, we'll eat together and you'll tell me where you've been."

The two men walked slowly to the small restaurant where Goldoni was accustomed to dine.

To Kurt's surprise the restaurant was shuttered with a sign on the door saying "Ferm".

Goldoni led Kurt into a courtyard and knocked at the door. An eyehole opened, they were inspected and permitted entrance.

It was the same restaurant, the same waiters, several small tables covered with checkered tablecloths, booths along one wall, candles on the tables, just as Kurt remembered it. He looked at Goldoni questioningly.

"It's the only way to keep the Germans from showing up. I own this place, and I want only French people I know and trust in here. Besides, it's hard to get the kind of food I'm used to. Rationing is getting worse, and I'm not going to allow the Boche to eat good French food."

"And no doubt the Frenchmen you trust and who come here are willing and able to pay the proper prices." Kurt smiled.

Goldoni clapped Kurt on the shoulder. "Ah, I've missed you. You do understand business, don't you. Now let's sit down, have a glass of wine and tell me where you've been."

Kurt obeyed. He had a sip of a very fair Sancerre, looked around at the very few occupied tables and saw some people he had had business dealings with on behalf of Goldoni. Then he launched into his prepared explanation.

"I couldn't get out of France. I tried to get into Spain, but the Germans got to the border too quickly. So I went East and found myself in a small village in Provence, in the unoccupied zone. It was safe and comfortable there. I spent many months just vegetating and waiting to see what would happen. But you know me, Monsieur Goldoni, I like action..."

"And the ladies." Goldoni interrupted.

"That too, " Kurt continued with a grin. "I was going out of my mind with boredom. Then I found out that there was a Swiss consul in Nice. Actually, it was a Swiss businessman who held the position part time. Well, you know the Swiss, always ready to do business. So here I am, a full-fledged Swiss citizen, and as a neutral, I hope, immune from the Germans. In fact, my papers were checked in the raid just before we met, and I passed with flying colors."

"Well, good for you." Goldoni chuckled. "But I wouldn't trust the Germans to be so careful of Swiss neutrality. It wouldn't surprise me if they decided to add Switzerland to their empire one of these days. How are things in the free zone?"

"I stopped to see Carnotti in Marseilles and Aristide Dupont in Lyon. They both send their regards and told me that they are always at your service. They seem to be managing all right. With the shortages and ration cards they are able to do enough business to make up for the loss caused by the lack of international trade. "

"What do they think of the war?"

"They seem convinced that Germany will win and that Petain is really the hero who will save France by putting us on the side of the victor. But you, living here under German occupation, what do you think?"

Goldoni sighed despondently. " I don't know who will win the war. I wouldn't count out the British Empire so quickly but I must admit it doesn't look good. The Germans seem to have the upper hand everywhere they go. Look, by now they've conquered the Balkans. They are even doing well in Libya and are threatening the Suez Canal. If they take that, Britain would have a tough time surviving without its supplies from the East."

"And how is life in Paris?"

"They're not bothering us too much. Of course there are constant checkpoints, and you'd better have your papers in order. It's a blessing that you are Swiss. I hope when you became Swiss you made sure that you're not Jewish?"

"Of course."

"They've been going after all foreign born Jews, but, so far, they haven't gone after French Jews except in special cases."

"What kind of special cases?"

"Oh, if they want something you've got, or if they don't like your face … you know the kind of thing. My problem is that there's been a real crimp on business. My only flourishing enterprises are the nightclubs in Pigalle, and that's because they service German soldiers. No French go in there any more, and of course we've lost the tourist trade completely. And I hate to do business with the Boche. I can't even blame the girls who don't want anything to do with them. And that cuts into income considerably."

"What do you think of de Gaulle? Is there any support for him?"

Goldoni's eyes lit up. "He has maintained our honor, not like those brown noses in Vichy. If France ever regains her soul, it's because of him and his supporters. But I tell you that I'm one of very few people who feel like that."

"Do you think there is any resistance against the Germans?"

"You mean armed resistance? I doubt that you'll find many people willing to risk their lives in a hopeless cause. If the situation changes, if the Germans start to lose, then perhaps..."

"I must say I agree with you. " Kurt shrugged. "I haven't seen any signs of resistance, not even chalk marks on the walls. But I detect something in you. Don't tell me that Silvio Goldoni is a patriot and would fight against the Germans?"

"Don't sell my patriotism short." Goldoni was very firm. "I'm a good Frenchman, and the honor of my country is very important to me. On the other hand," he smiled, "you know me well enough to know that I'm not an idealistic fool. If there were a chance, if I could really believe that it would matter, I would..."

"You would what?"

"Well, we'll have to see when the time comes, if it ever does. For the moment, I think we'll just have to accept the situation as it is. Now, as for you, you'd better move back into one of my houses. I don't think you should go back to your old apartment and suddenly show up as a Swiss."

"You're absolutely right. Thank you very much. And I hope I can be of service to you again."

"Oh, we'll find something, never fear. Now, let's eat."

* * *

Rene Mayer's restaurant was shuttered but the Mayers still lived in the apartment upstairs. They received Kurt with great surprise and pleasure.

"Come in, come in," Rene Mayer took Kurt's hand in both of his. "Come and have a glass tea. But you're in great danger, the Nazis are looking for all foreign Jews, particularly those who fled from them before."

"Have they been bothering you?"

"We're French, we've been French for generations. They wouldn't dare bother us. The French police is bound to protect us. But of course, my business is dead. I had to close the restaurant. There is no way to get kosher food. Besides, it is not wise to have a number of Jews gather in one place."

"Are the synagogues closed?"

"No, the Nazis don't want to look too bad. After all, there are still a lot of foreigners here including Americans, and the Nazis don't want to give America a bad impression. If there's anything, I think, they're afraid of, it would be America's entry into the war against Germany just like in 1917."

"Well, America has begun to help the British with Lend-Lease."

"Oh, if only the Americans would join the war." Rene Mayer clasped his hands and looked up at the ceiling prayerfully.

"Are there still many foreign Jews in Paris, do you think?"

"Unfortunately, fewer every day. Those that can, try to escape to the unoccupied zone, but that's getting more and more difficult. And I don't even know whether they're safe there."

"I don't think they are, but there's a better chance for them to get out from there. Is there any organized attempt to help these people?"

"There are organizations, but they are tolerated by the Nazis and can't get involved in anything illegal. In fact, most of the time, I feel that they are being used by the Nazis to keep track of people who then get arrested. I'm sure that's not what they want to do, but it seems to work out that way."

"Tell me, if we were able to work out a system of getting Jews into the unoccupied zone, would you be able to spread the word discreetly, without having the Germans find out about it?"

Rene Mayer looked at Kurt. "Could you really do this? There are lives to be saved."

"Let me work on it."

* * *

This isn't what I should be doing. I am a British soldier now. They even made me a British subject at my request. I owe my loyalty to the British and to Admiral Morse. He gave me a mission. I have the information he wanted, and I should get back over the demarcation line into unoccupied France, and then back to Lisbon and London. That's what I must do.

But there are Jews here whose lives are at risk. I was lucky to get out of France and to come back here with Swiss papers. If it hadn't been for that, I'd be in the same mess they're in. How can I walk away? Where is my greater loyalty?

And if I don't go back right away, how will it hurt the war effort? What will Admiral Morse do to me?

My report to Admiral Morse will say that there is no resistance movement in France, nor is there likely to be one, at least until there is a sign that the tables are turning. What if he gets that wonderful assessment a few days later, so what. The Talmud says that he who has saved one life is as one who has saved the entire world. I must try.

Silvio Goldoni sat in his accustomed armchair behind his large desk.

"I have a business venture to propose to you." Kurt said.

"I'm glad to hear it. Tell me what you have in mind."

"I would like to organize a way for people who are in jeopardy from the Germans to escape to the unoccupied zone, and perhaps onward to Spain. I'm sure that we could charge a hefty fee for this service."

"And who are these people, Kurt?"

"Right now, most of them would be Jews who had fled their countries of origin, and are presently in France with Cartes d'Identit d'Etranger. They are the ones who are being arrested by the Germans whenever they can be found, and who are being deported. I'm certain that they would pay handsomely if we could get them out."

Goldoni smiled. "And the fact that you are one of them has nothing to do with your proposition? What do you think I am, an altruist? These people have no money. And besides, the risk is great. You'd be acting directly against the Germans."

"I believe the money can be raised, as long as we're not too demanding. And I thought you'd be willing to tweak the Boche's beard a bit."

Goldoni considered. "What you're proposing is a sort of underground railroad…"

"I beg your pardon?"

Monsieur Goldoni chuckled. "You think that I did not have a proper education? Before the American civil war in the middle of the last century, which resulted in the end of slavery over there, escaping slaves were transported North to Canada by a system of secret stations later called the underground railroad. In Canada they would be free. The opponents of slavery who undertook these ventures risked their necks for the principle of freedom for all human beings. And you want me to do the same thing?"

Kurt was impressed. Goldoni had unexpected dimensions.

"There is a considerable difference. I doubt whether the black slaves could pay for their freedom. I think this could be a profitable venture. And besides, you would be saving lives."

"And you think that matters to me?"

"There is another point. You spoke of the honor of France. France has given asylum to these people. Is it not our obligation to protect them?"

Goldoni smiled. "I should watch what I say to you more carefully. Well, let me think about it. Go for a walk. We'll talk more tomorrow."

* * *

Again Kurt walked the streets of the city he loved. Again he observed how its new masters, the Germans, had taken over. There were street signs in French and German at the principal intersections. There were German offices with only German signs on them and all French offices had French and German signs. The French walked past boisterous groups of German soldiers averting their eyes. In the cafes frequented by Germans he overheard waiters attempt to communicate in their language.

Kurt again found himself in the Place de l'Opera. On impulse he walked over to the Palais Garnier, the lovely building which housed the Paris Opera. To his surprise he noted that performances were scheduled. In fact, tonight "Tosca" would be performed, with Esperanza Gonzalez in the title role.

Do I dare? She does not know that I am not Swiss. I could see her and tell her about my few days with Sarah. She deserves that. Poor Sarah. When he thought about the golden girl, he felt a twinge of pain.

Kurt walked over to the box office. There were tickets available, high up in the last balcony. "It's the only place where you won't be bothered by our guests," the ticket vendor shrugged.

Indeed most of the patrons at the Opera were in German uniform. The orchestra seats were filled with officers, many accompanied by lovely young ladies showing white shoulders and lots of jewelry. *There are a lot of French women who do not have any problems entertaining the enemy*, Kurt thought. The lower balcony was the area for lower ranks, and here or there, a civilian. Only up, in the rarefied air of the top floor, there were no Germans, but mostly young opera enthusiasts of both sexes.

The great Gonzalez was as good as ever. In spite of her age and heft, she portrayed the fiery Tosca convincingly because of the miraculousness of her voice.

Kurt left his seat just before the end of the performance and managed to sneak backstage, while everyone observed the many curtain calls Madame Gonzalez and her colleagues received. As Madame Gonzalez walked from the stage surrounded by a host of admirers, many in German uniform, Kurt stepped out. "Madame," he called out.

La Gonzalez looked at him without any sign of recognition and walked on. Suddenly she turned, grabbed his arm, and pulled him into her dressing room. She closed the door firmly in the face of her admirers and looked at Kurt.

"You're the young man who helped my Sarah. What are you doing here?"

"I thought you might want to know what happened."

"I know all about it. Sarah wrote me. She said you saved her and then she had to leave you behind. She's very worried..."

Kurt did not hear another word. *Sarah is alive. She's alive. What a miracle. But how,- who cares, she's alive!*

Madame Gonzalez recognized Kurt's shock. "You didn't know? You didn't know she had reached England safely? Look, just sit down, let me get rid of those vultures out there, and then we'll talk."

Kurt sank into a deep sofa at one end of the spacious dressing room. Madame Gonzalez opened the door, allowed the herd of her admirers to enter, and disappeared behind a screen. Kurt was so absorbed by his thoughts, by the realization that Sarah was indeed alive, that he paid no attention to what was going on around him. Eventually, the dressing room emptied and Madame Gonzalez emerged from behind the screen dressed in street clothes, and sat down beside him.

"I have to go to a reception at the Kommandantur. I have no choice. So let's talk briefly. Sarah wrote to me how wonderful you were. She felt terrible about leaving you behind when she boarded a British ship."

"But how did you get mail from her?"

"Via Spain. I have a home there and it is being forwarded to me. Sarah will be happy to hear you're allright..."

"I was told that the warship she was on was sunk?"

"I don't know anything about that. " Madame Gonzalez said. "Sarah did write to me that she was transferred to another ship because she had some information with her that you had obtained, that had to be brought to London quickly."

"Where is she now?"

"She's somewhere in England, doing her bit, you know. But she didn't tell me what her bit is. I must write to her about you. What are you doing?"

"Please don't write about me. If your letter is intercepted, it could cause me harm."

"But Sarah is worried about you?"

"Still, I must insist. Please promise me, that you won't mention our meeting - to anyone".

"Oh, very well. I guess you have a right to ask that."

"One more thing, Madame Gonzalez. What is Sarah's real name? You may remember you introduced her only as Sarah Brown."

The Diva smiled. "Her father, the bastard, is Lord Harrington. Sarah is the Honorable Harrington-Brown."

"Thank you, and good bye, Madame Gonzalez."

Incredible. She's alive. And she's of the British aristocracy. I suspected something like that. I'm glad she's alive, and I'm glad she thought enough about me to write to her mother. But any connection between us is a fantasy, and I must try to forget about it.

She's a Lady, and I'm a penniless refugee. But at least, she's alive, and I hope, happy.

* * *

Silvio Goldoni had a large and detailed map of France spread out on his desk. He looked up at Kurt with a smile. "Quite a challenge you've posed, haven't you. How are we going to get people across the demarcation line without getting caught? An interesting problem."

"So you've decided?"

"Not so fast, my friend. I want to establish what can be done. Then a lot will depend on how much money we can make. I'm not in this business for my health, you know."

Kurt saw a completely different Monsieur Goldoni from the depressed, unhappy man he had had dinner with just two days ago. Goldoni was alert and eager to act. Very much the same man he had first met years ago.

"Now listen to me, Kurt." Goldoni said. "I want you to go to Tours and see Arsene Martin, you've met him before. Talk to him about the possibilities, and if he doesn't come up with a better idea, mention Chenonceau to him."

"Chenonceau?"

"Just get going. He'll understand."

Kurt was on the next train to Tours and five hours later in the office of Arsene Martin. Martin was a small thin man of about fifty, with tremendous nervous energy. He could never sit still. He fiddled and moved constantly, and that made it a little difficult to conduct a conversation with him. Kurt presented the problem strictly as a business proposition emanating from Monsieur Goldoni.

"Hm," Martin mused, rubbing his chin. "The demarcation line is tightly closed. There are guard posts on all roads South, and the terrain here is too open. It's too easily patrolled. There may be better possibilities in the mountains further East, but that would require only people with the stamina to attempt such a crossing. I fear that it's too difficult around here."

"Monsieur Goldoni said I should mention Chenonceau to you."

Arsene Martin burst out in laughter. "What a man. Silvio is really a genius. Of course. Nothing easier. I can arrange everything. Tell him he has my admiration. No wonder he's the man we all look up to. Still as cunning as ever."

"Would you explain this to me, please? " Kurt asked. "I'm at a loss…"

Martin smiled. "You know that around here we have some of the finest renaissance chateaux in existence. The chateaux of the Loire are a major tourist attraction. This was the favored area for the kings of France and their nobles to build the most elaborate and beautiful residences."

"Yes, I've heard about them, " Kurt said, " but I've never had the chance to visit any of them."

"Now you will, but I don't think you'll be able to do much sight seeing. The Chateau de Chenonceau is one of the jewels of the area, a sixteenth century chateau that housed Marie de Medici. And it has a particular feature. There is a two story gallery that leads over the Cher River. Well, the Cher is the line of demarcation here. On the other side is unoccupied France."

"But wouldn't the chateau be guarded too?"

"There is no tourism a this time, so all the chateaux are kept up by the caretakers who have lived there for a long time. They are not private property. They belong to the

Patrimoine National, in other words to France. I am sure that the road leading to Chenonceau is patrolled. I can easily ascertain when the patrols go past, and when they can be avoided."

"And the caretaker?"

Arsene Martin grinned wolfishly. "Don't worry about him. He'll cooperate. Now, how much do you think we can get per body? You know, there'll be expenses. I have to arrange transport to the chateau, check on the patrols, handle the caretaker, and so forth."

Kurt settled down to a period of hard bargaining. This was something he was good at, but in the past he had bargained about the price of products, now he dealt in lives.

* * *

"Well, it now boils down to price and a trial run." Goldoni said when Kurt had finished his report. "We also have to make arrangements with Aristide Dupont in Lyon to pick up our passengers and to deliver them to the nearest railroad station from which they can continue South. Now, let's talk money. I think you got a good price from Martin for his part of the deal. We'll have to take care of Dupont who may not be so generous, and of course there has to be something for us. I think a fair price would be " and he mentioned a fairly high price.

"Let me talk to the people involved." Kurt said. "I presume you're talking per family and not per person."

Goldoni chuckled. "Your father must have been a capable business man. He taught you well. No, my friend, the price should indeed be per person."

"Hardly the same for children as for adults?"

"Well, find out what they can pay and we'll talk further."

"Fine, I'll get back to you. Incidentally, if we try it, I'll go along on the trial run. I know Dupont and can make further arrangements with him."

* * *

Rene Mayer took Kurt's hands in both of his. "If we can only save some of these people before the Nazis take them back to Germany, it's worth the effort. I'm sure we can raise some money from the Jewish community in Paris, but not very much, and most of the refugees have no funds. Still, let's see what we can do. Give me a day."

"We have to make a trial run. No more than four people for the first trip. And warn them of the risk, please. It may not work, and if we're caught…"

"You, you will go along?"

"I must. I am the one who can make arrangements once we've crossed the border."

Kurt persuaded Monsieur Goldoni to charge a relatively modest fee, and that only per adult, at least for the first run. Goldoni enjoyed the bargaining, but Kurt was perfectly aware that his mentor was not doing this for the money alone in spite of his protestations, but for the challenge and for the pleasure of doing something the Germans would not like. Goldoni was reluctant to be directly involved, he always preferred to deal through intermediaries. However in this case it was better for the smallest number of people to be in the know. So he consented to meet Rene Mayer and to work with him in the future.

When Kurt had taken the train to Tours, he had had to pass through a document check at the Gare d'Austerlitz in Paris, his papers had been checked again on the train, and he had to identify himself once more before being allowed to leave the platform at Tours. His Swiss papers were accepted without question in each case. But obviously, this was not the way he could travel with a family of refugees

"Are you coming back to Paris or will you try to get out of Europe this time?" Goldoni asked Kurt.

"I don't know yet, but I promise you that you'll see me again. And I believe it won't be very long. I'm sure we'll find other ways to tweak the Germans' noses."

Goldoni embraced Kurt. "Good luck, my friend. I hope to see you safe and sound in better days."

Kurt met the Taubs at Rene Mayer's apartment. Herr Taub had been a manufacturer of glassware in Leipzig. When the Nazis took over his business, without compensation of course, he and his family crossed the border into Belgium at night and from there had made their way to Paris. They did not even have French Identity Cards, and so they were at risk every moment of their lives. They had spent most of their time in France in the homes of other Jews, without daring to go out except for a rare and risky breath of air.

Herr Taub was about forty five, of medium height, heavy from his sedentary occupation, balding and exceedingly nervous. His wife was thin, elegantly dressed, and seemed the stronger of the two. There were two daughters, twelve and fourteen, who apparently were cowed by their experiences. They clung to their parents as much as possible.

The timing had to be exact. Kurt did not want to be on the streets with his charges any more than necessary, but he also had to be careful not to violate curfew. So, at the beginning of the evening, he led his group to the nearest Metro, from which they took a train to the Porte de Sevres station.

This was the most dangerous part of their journey. There were frequent raids during which papers were checked carefully, and people like the Taubs whose papers were not in order, were caught. It was dark when they emerged from the Metro at Porte de Sevres. A square spread out before them with several roads going off in different directions. Kurt saw a truck parked across the street.

"Please wait here." he whispered to the Taubs in German, pointing them toward a small alleyway. "I'll be right back."

Kurt crossed the square to the truck. The driver was leaning against the cab, nonchalantly smoking a Gauloise. "Jean-Pierre?" Kurt asked. The driver nodded. Kurt swung up into the passenger seat next to the driver and waited for the man to join him.

"Over there, " Kurt pointed. The driver started the truck and drove around the square, stopping in front of the alleyway. Kurt jumped out of the cab, lifted the tarpaulin covering the back, and motioned to the Taubs. He helped Herr Taub up into the back of the truck, and lifted Frau Taub and the girls until they could be assisted in. "Just make yourselves as comfortable as you can, " Kurt whispered. "We have a five hour drive. And, please, make no noise if we stop."

Kurt returned to the front of the cab and the truck took off. The driver avoided the principal highways whenever possible. They drove on secondary roads through sleepy villages using only parking lights. It was a dark night. Kurt wondered whether the driver really knew his way. He did not have to worry. Nearly five hours later, just as dawn was breaking, the truck arrived on the outskirts of Tours. The taciturn driver, who had avoided all of Kurt's attempts to engage him in conversation, stopped the truck in front of a shuttered garage.

"Upstairs," he said. "You'll be picked up tonight."

Kurt retrieved the Taubs from the back of the truck and the truck disappeared down the road.

Behind the gas pumps there was an open door leading to a staircase. Kurt led his charges upstairs. There was a waiting room, obviously to be used by customers awaiting repairs. A couple of shabby, plastic covered benches, two chairs and a low table completed the furnishings.

"We must wait here until evening." Kurt said. "Please relax. Do not attempt to go downstairs. I have to leave for a little while, but I'll be back with some food."

The older girl whispered to her mother. Frau Taub approached Kurt. "Is there a bathroom around here?"

Kurt smiled. "Let me check. I'll be right back."

A filthy toilet was in the back of the garage. Like so many toilets in the countryside, there was no seat, but only two footrests over a sump hole. With regret, Kurt pointed it out to the Taubs, and left.

* * *

Arsene Martin was accustomed to going to bed very late, and rarely got up before noon. Here it was barely dawn, and there was a loud banging at his door. He jumped out of bed - the Germans, who else could it be? *Where to go, what to do?* His maid appeared, also in her dressing gown, unaccustomed to this early hour.

"It's a young man, he says his name is Kurt Auster."

Thank God, it's not the Germans. But what nerve, he'll hear from me. Who does he think he is?

Martin put on his dressing gown, combed his sparse hair, and with as much dignity as he could muster, walked into the living room. Kurt was pacing up and down.

"It's about time," Kurt said. "I have a bone to pick with you."

"You have a bone to pick with me? " Arsene Martin was so angry, he almost sputtered. "Who gave you permission to come to my home in the middle of the night and to wake me like that?"

"Never mind that," Kurt replied calmly. " I want to know whether you are interested in proceeding with the venture Silvio and I are organizing. If you are not, just say so and I will report this to Silvio and we will find someone else to work with in Tours."

Silvio - he calls him Silvio. No one calls Monsieur Goldoni by his first name. This character must be related to Goldoni. Perhaps his son? Entirely possible. And he threatens to replace me? Does he have that kind of influence? Then it would be better not to antagonize him.

"What is the problem? Everything is organized…"

Kurt sat down, stretched his legs before him, and said. "Why don't we have some coffee to wake up with, and I'll tell you what's wrong."

Martin was overwhelmed by the young man's nerve. He must really be in with Monsieur Goldoni to be able to behave like that.

He ran into the kitchen and ordered his maid to provide coffee and croissants.

"Now, tell me the problem." Martin asked more calmly.

"You are dealing with human beings, not cattle." Kurt said quietly. "The people we will try to get across to the unoccupied zone must be treated with respect. I understand that they have to be sequestered during the day until you can arrange to get them to Chenonceau, but I am sure you can arrange better quarters than the waiting room above the garage to which you had us delivered. Furthermore, you must provide food and drink for the day they have to spend in hiding. If you are unable to do this, I will have to make other arrangements."

Martin said with some embarrassment: "We can't provide the services of a luxury hotel…"

Kurt interrupted. "Please don't tell me that. You know perfectly well what I'm talking about. Someone of your abilities and connections surely can find a more suitable place, and provide food. This time there are only four passengers, but if this trial run works, we expect to send much larger numbers along on subsequent trips, and that will increase the profit. Now, please make the proper arrangements, and I'll let you get back to bed."

* * *

The little cottage in the woods to which Arsene Martin had them transferred was far more comfortable than the waiting room in the defunct garage. To begin with, there was a clean and proper bathroom. It even had a bidet in addition to a functioning tub. There were two bedrooms, and a couch in the living room. There was a kitchen and Martin had supplied bread, cheese and fruit and even a bottle of vin ordinaire. At Kurt's suggestion, after cleaning up and eating, everybody went to sleep. They had had an active night, and the next night promised to be even more active.

Kurt had found out that the Taubs' sole documents were still valid German passports, with the large red letter J printed over the title page to indicate their religion. Herr Taub and his wife hoped to be able to make their way to Marseilles, where they would try to obtain a Spanish visa from the consulate there. If that proved impossible, they would attempt to find passage on a boat to one of France's African possessions, as far away from the German occupation as possible.

Kurt suggested that they might be able to find someone in the Gendarmerie to issue Cartes d'Identite, since without them they would not be able to obtain ration cards, and were subject to arrest by the French police. Perhaps someone in the Jewish community in Marseilles had the proper connections. Kurt did not think that Monsieur Carnotti would be interested in assisting Jewish refugees.

195

Late that night, the same taciturn trucker picked them up, and drove as quickly and as quietly as possible the short distance to the Chateau de Chenonceau. There was no moon, but by the lights of the stars, Kurt noted a magnificent avenue of plane trees on the approach to the chateau. The truck drove through the entrance gate which some kindly soul had opened wide, over a drawbridge above a moat, and then around toward the back of the chateau,.

Kurt barely made out a large rectangular mansion with turrets at the corners. An elderly man wearing a beret helped them out of the truck. "Vite, vite, depechez vous," he urged them on.

Their guide, no doubt the caretaker, led them up a narrow staircase to a long gallery with windows on both sides. The only light came from the stars outside. The caretaker said:

"You will cross the river Cher and as soon as you reach the other side, you are in the unoccupied zone. There is a gate, normally locked, but open now, please close it behind you. I am told that someone will be waiting for you there. Please hurry, and please be very quiet. Good luck."

Kurt and his charges followed the instructions to the letter. There was enough starlight so that they could traverse the gallery without difficulty. On both sides of the gallery, there were heavy pieces of furniture, paintings and wall hangings. Kurt regretted not being able to inspect any of the art along the walls and not being able to appreciate the beauty of the chateau. He promised himself, that one day, after the war had been won and peace reestablished, he would spend time in the valley of the Loire visiting the chateaux. Perhaps with someone he cared for. *Sarah? Forget it. But Admiral Morse must have known she was alive. Why didn't he tell me?*

The Admiral is a ruthless manipulator and may have had his reasons, which he'd better explain to me to my satisfaction.

They had reached the other side of the Cher. Behind them the river flowed silently, its soft waves reflecting the dim light; on the other side the massive bulk of the chateau blotted out the sky.. Indeed, there was a gate, which Kurt closed obediently behind him. A few steps down from the gallery a narrow lane lead away from the river. They followed it in silence. A truck was waiting at the end of the road. Kurt approached the driver who seemed asleep. "Aristide Dupont?" Kurt whispered.

The driver opened his eyes, nodded, and motioned to the travelers to get in. Just before dawn, they arrived at the railroad station in Lyon.

"I must leave you here." Kurt said to the Taubs. "You should be able to get to Marseilles easily. I hope no one stops you to ask for your papers. Good luck."

Herr and Frau Taub embraced Kurt with gratitude, and the two girls shyly shook his hand. *I hope they make it,* Kurt thought. *Now to see Aristide Dupont and make arrangements for a regular pickup from Chenonceau.*

* * *

Kurt spent one more day in Lyon with Dupont. He was able to convince the man to use his connections to obtain a supply of Cartes d'Identite which could be used by future passengers on the "underground railroad." Then it was time to leave France and to return to London. Three days later, after strenuous train travel across the Spanish border to Madrid and another change of station, Kurt got on the train to Lisbon. *What a blessing Swiss citizenship is. Nobody gives me a second look.*

In Lisbon Kurt reported to the address he had been given, and prompt passage by air to London was arranged. While he was on the plane, Kurt began to compose his report to Admiral Morse.

Should I tell him about the arrangements I made with Goldoni to rescue Jews? He may, no, he will disapprove. Who cares? I'll give him the facts, and if he doesn't like it, let him not use me any more. If worst comes to worse, I'm a British lieutenant, and I'll fight in the infantry like so many others. He can't stop me from fighting in this war.

In any case, once I confront him with my questions about Sarah, he won't feel so kindly toward me. I don't feel so kindly toward him.

* * *

CHAPTER VII

Kurt stopped in his rooms to retrieve his uniform, and reported to Admiral Morse's office. He delivered his written report and was told to wait. So he waited. And waited. And waited. He had had enough military experience to know that " Hurry up and wait " is the motto of all armies, and that it was undoubtedly so when Hannibal crossed the Alps and when Alexander the Great cut the Gordian knot.

Men in uniform walked in and out of Admiral Morse's office. Occasionally a well dressed civilian, undoubtedly a high ranking civil servant, was ushered in. Kurt waited.

So you risked your life behind enemy lines. How important are you, and after all, what have you accomplished? All your information is negative, it's not what they wanted to hear.

Late in the afternoon, Admiral Morse's Wren, a lovely young lady who looked extremely sexy in her severe Navy uniform, emerged from the inner sanctum. "Lieutenant Auster, the Admiral suggests that you report to Major Thompson and continue your liaison duties. He will contact you when he needs you. In the meantime, you are not to discuss your recent travels with anyone. Anyone. The Admiral was very emphatic about that."

Kurt left crestfallen. *It isn't that I expected to be greeted like a conquering hero. I haven't conquered anything. But not too many people, I'm sure, got in and out of occupied France. Is this punishment because I exceeded my orders? I'd do the same thing again.*

Major Thompson was exceedingly glad to see Kurt. He did not ask where he had been. Thompson's devotion to the Army was such that he automatically assumed that wherever Kurt had been was in obedience to orders. And if the Army wanted Bill Thompson to know, he would be told.

"I can't stand our French charges any more," he complained to Kurt. "Will you, please, stay here and answer all their calls and complaints. And above all, don't tell me about them. Just say no to whatever it is they want. But be diplomatic, for Heaven's sake."

Adam Bede had not been home when Kurt arrived. But that evening, Bede returned from a short visit to Oxford. " Kurt, I'm glad to see you back. Can you talk about anything, where have you been, what have you been up to?"

"I can't discuss it, sorry, orders, you know. But I have a question for you. I told you about Sarah, and you were there when I found out that the Dauntless had been sunk. Did you know that she had been transferred to another vessel, and is alive and well in England?"

"Is she, by Jove. How wonderful." Adam Bede exclaimed.

"Are you certain that you had no idea?" Kurt asked.

"What are you talking about? If I had known, wouldn't I have told you? I know how upset you were."

"But Admiral Morse knew."

"No one knows what Morse knows or does not know. I think sometimes he keeps secrets just in order to keep secrets, whether there is a point to it or not. He may have his reasons. But as I remember, you didn't know her real last name. Do you know it now?"

Kurt hesitated. *Was Adam Bede telling the truth? Was there anyone he could really trust? Did it matter? Perhaps Adam would be able to help him locate Sarah. And then what would he do?*

"Her name is Sarah Harrington-Brown. Her father is Lord Harrington." Kurt said slowly.

"Aha!" Adam exclaimed. "I'm beginning to understand."

"Come on, Venerable, what do you mean?"

"Lord Harrington was a member of the Chamberlain cabinet. He has been a German sympathizer for a very long time, and is credited - if that is the right word - with having been the most persuasive voice in Chamberlain's circle in favor of the Munich agreement. He has been a quiet supporter of Sir Oswald Moseley's British Nazis, in fact the only reason he was quiet about it, was his involvement with the government. His often expressed view is that Britain and Germany, as the two strongest Nordic nations, should stand shoulder to shoulder against the onslaught of the Communist sub-humans from the East."

"He must have had a shock when Hitler and Stalin became allies."

"Well you can ask him about that if you ever meet him. After Churchill became Prime Minister, he was eased out of his cabinet position, and to the best of my knowledge, has been in retirement on one of his estates. I can't guess why Admiral Morse did not tell you about Sarah but I suppose her father's identity to be the reason."

"But what does her father have to do with her? She knew perfectly well I was Jewish. Her father's anti-Semitism did not seem to affect her."

"Maybe. It could also be said, that she used you and discarded you when you were no longer necessary to her."

"That's not what happened." Kurt remembered how he had urged Sarah to board the Dauntless. "She refused to board the British ship without me, and I had to almost force her to do it."

"Well, you know best. "Adam Bede mused. "It's entirely possible that Admiral Morse has in mind to use your connection to Sarah at some convenient time. You can ask him when you see him next, if you dare."

"If I see him next," Kurt said bitterly." The fact that I just accomplished a somewhat dangerous mission on which he sent me, does not seem to interest him enough to want to debrief me in person."

"He's a busy man, and he has to husband his time. You will see him, when he finds it necessary."

* * *

Marcel Levesque was very glad to see Kurt again. "Have you been doing your exercises? The paper in front of your lips? The R R R R? Let me hear you talk."

"Never mind that. I think I can pass now. Don't you?"

"You're doing much better with your French pronunciation than when I first took you in hand, but since you also speak English a lot, you can backslide very easily. Now try it again - R R R R ."

"Tell me how you and Madame have been?"

"All is well, except for the nightly bombing. We're all getting so tired, so tired, of sleeping in the underground, and never knowing whether our house will still be standing in the morning. How long do you think this will go on?"

"I'm afraid you'll have to ask Hermann Goering. I don't think I'm qualified to answer." Kurt smiled.

"Oh," the old actor bubbled, " I almost forgot. Your lady friend has been calling every couple of days trying to find out whether you're back from your trip. In fact, here's the number of a friend of hers. Just call this number, she said, and leave word that you're back, and she'll arrange for a time and place. I guess her husband doesn't do much for her, does he?"

* * *

Should I start with Clemente again? Now that I know Sarah is alive? It was a lot of fun. What do I mean a lot? It was wonderful fun, but there was no romance like there was with Sarah. Idiot, you never even made love to Sarah, and do you really think Lord Harrington's daughter will commit miscegenation with a Jew? Well, I have to find that out before I condemn Sarah for the sins of her father.

If I decide not to see Clemente again, I have to tell her in person. That's only fair.

Before or after you've had sex with her, you hypocrite?

Well, that depends. I don't even know where Sarah is. Adam Bede promised he would ask around, and he knows the right people, but it's wartime, and secrets are being kept. Anyway, first things first. I'll see Clemente. After all, she'll bring me up to date on the activities of her husband and the Free French.

Sure, that's why you're going to see her. Only for that. Not for sex. Oh, no.

* * *

The address to which Clemente had directed him, with very flattering enthusiasm at his return, was in the fashionable West End. Kurt found himself in front of a small but elegant Victorian mansion. He rang the bell and was admitted by a tall, slender blonde of about forty. She wore no make-up and was dressed in a long white robe. Kurt noted that she was barefoot. *It's early afternoon but she looks as if she had just gotten out of bed*, he thought.

"You're the young man Clemente raves about," the blonde looked him over from head to foot. "Well, we'll see. My name is Carol. Just follow me."

She led him up a winding staircase to a well-furnished living room. A mahogany desk stood on one side of the room, at the other end a couch, several leather armchairs and a small coffee table. Paintings covered the wall, and if Kurt had had any experience in art, he might have admired a Degas, a Delacroix and a Turner among others.

"Clemente is back there. She's eagerly waiting for you." Carol pointed to a door at the other end of the room. Somewhat taken aback at her brusqueness, Kurt followed her directions and opened the door. The first thing he saw was a huge, circular bed, unmade, and on it reclining totally nude, Clemente.

Clemente jumped up with a glad cry. "Oh, good, you're here. Quick, come on" and she threw herself at him and started to open the buttons on his tunic and trousers. Before Kurt had a chance to finish undressing, she took him into her mouth voraciously. After tasting him for a long moment, she emerged to help get the rest of his clothes off.

"Ah, I've missed you," she whispered. "I can't help it, I still prefer a man."

She forced Kurt on his back on the bed - without getting too much resistance from him - and resumed her activities. He looked down at the busy head, and caressed her shoulders.

The door opened and Carol came in.

Kurt tried to jump up, but Clemente would not allow him to move without risking to lose a very precious part of his body. He watched as Carol took off her robe and joined them on the bed. She brought her breasts to Kurt's mouth and ordered: "Show me what you can do."

It was a new experience for Kurt, but he did his best to satisfy both ladies. However, in spite of his best and frequent endeavors, there came a moment when he knew that there were no circumstances in which he could recuperate sufficiently quickly to perform again. At that point, he watched with considerable pleasure the two white bodies of his hostesses intertwined and enjoying themselves without him.

After a while he felt definitely de trop. He dressed quietly, and with an admiring glance at the two busy naked bodies, walked downstairs and let himself out of the house.

* * *

The pipeline of lend lease supplies was now wide open, and planes and ammunition came in considerable quantities to enable the beleaguered Royal Air Force to take the offensive. Some of the American planes, notably the Flying Fortress bombers had ranges that far exceeded the ranges of the German planes. And the British began bombing raids on German targets. In desperation, Hermann Goering's Luftwaffe redoubled its efforts, destroyed Coventry and in April of 1941 executed the most massive raid London had ever suffered. But the cost for the Germans was tremendous, and within weeks of that most destructive raid, the bombing attacks began to diminish drastically.

Winston Churchill declared that the Battle of Britain was won, and made his famous speech in which he praised the Royal Air Force: " Never in the history of mankind have so many owed so much to so few."

"I have a treat for you," Adam Bede said. "There will be a performance of Gilbert and Sullivan's "H.M.S. Pinafore" at the Savoy and I have obtained two seats. This is the first time in a long while that the Savoyards will be back in their old home."

Kurt had never heard a Gilbert and Sullivan operetta and was delighted at the prospect.

In spite of the blackout, this promised to be a gala affair. The Savoy theater was part of the building which housed the elegant Savoy Hotel on the Strand. Not far, there were many bombed areas, but the Savoy had suffered little damage. In spite of the shortage of petrol, many limousines disgorged their elegantly dressed passengers in the driveway which led to the entrance of the hotel and to the front of the theater. Obviously, the aristocracy of Britain, be it by blood, money or military rank, was gathering to enjoy this performance.

"If a bomb hits the theater, Britain will be decapitated." Kurt whispered to Adam Bede, as they entered the vestibule.

In addition to Kurt's devotion to Grand Opera, which his mother had fostered, he had also frequently enjoyed the typical Viennese operettas by Johann Strauss, Franz Lehar, Emmerich Kalman, and others. Gilbert and Sullivan's operetta was different. There was none of the saccharine sweetness he had expected, even though the music was as wonderful as any he had ever heard. But Gilbert's words had a tartness that he found particularly enjoyable.

After the performance, Adam Bede led Kurt to the huge bar of the Savoy Hotel and ordered drinks.

"I can tell you the difference between the British and the German character, which make an alliance between the two nations, as Sarah's father fantasizes, impossible." Kurt said.

Adam sipped his brandy. "I look forward to this tremendous insight, prompted no doubt by the performance we have witnessed."

"Indeed it is. Don't laugh," Kurt smiled. "The British can make fun of their own, they worship their institutions, but accept their faults. No successful German operetta could have a song in it, like the First Lord of the Admiralty's description of his career. The German sense of humor tends toward Schadenfreude."

"I'm not familiar with the term?" Adam asked.

"Precisely. Schadenfreude is the joy you take in someone else's disaster. It's the laughter when someone else slips on a banana peel. I think it's significant that neither French nor English have one word that has the same meaning, in fact I wonder whether any other language does. One day, when I have the time, it might be fun to explore that question. In any case, German humor would never make fun of the establishment that rules Germany in the same manner that Gilbert and Sullivan so successfully did."

"What an insight. And this after seeing only one of their pieces. I can't wait for the way you will solve the problems of the world after you've seen "Mikado" or " The Pirates of Penzance" or "Patience" or some of the others." Adam Bede chuckled.

"You may be right. It's just that I'm so tremendously impressed with the music and with the incredible and very funny logic of the piece. And, incidentally, now I understand why Captain Corcoran of the Dauntless was the subject of so many jokes. Poor man."

Suddenly Adam Bede saw that Kurt had turned pale and almost dropped his glass. Kurt was staring fixedly at the steps leading to the entrance of the bar. Adam followed his gaze.

"What's the matter with you, Kurt? Are you all right?"

Two couples were standing on the steps, waiting for the headwaiter to meet them to escort them to their table. The two men were senior naval officers, one Captain and one Lieutenant Commander. They were accompanied by two women, dressed in evening gowns with bare shoulders, jewelry sparkling from their throats and wrists. Both were blond and slender. The older one, fortyish and heavily made up, hung on the arm of the Captain.

Adam saw that Kurt kept looking at the younger woman, who was at the side of the junior of the two officers. He could understand Kurt's admiration. She was beautiful, vivacious and charming as she glided down the steps, talking to her companion.

"Let's leave." Kurt said brusquely.

"Why, what's the matter?"

"It's Sarah. Can't you see? That's her."

"Well, go on, say hello. She'll be thrilled to see you."

Yes, Kurt thought, *and so will Carol. Will she tell her how we spent the afternoon last week? And then what will Sarah think of me?*

"No, not now, Adam. Please trust me. Let's leave."

Adam called for the check. Kurt watched as the two couples were seated at a table not far from them. He turned away - but too late.

"Kurt" - a voice he thought he'd never hear again called out. "It can't be. It can't be." She ran up to the table. Kurt got up, and Sarah grabbed him by the shoulders. "Is it really you? Are you really here?"

He looked at her. His voice broke. "Yes Sarah. I'm so glad to see you well."

"But I don't understand. I left you in France, and now you're here, and " she looked at his uniform, " a lieutenant in our Army. How did that happen? Unbelievable. Why didn't you contact me? I've been so worried, and I felt so guilty about leaving you."

"It's a long story, and this is not the time or the place, Sarah. Will you be in London long?"

"Worse luck. I'm leaving for Sussex in the morning. My father has a major birthday coming up, and I've got to be there. But you must join us. I can't let you walk away. You must explain how you got here. It's a miracle."

Sarah looked at Adam Bede. "You must join us, please. I must talk to your friend here." She pulled Kurt over to the table where her companions had been seated. Adam followed.

"This is my friend, Lieutenant - " she smiled at him fondly, " Kurt Auster. He saved my life in France and I just met him again. I must find time to talk to him. Will you entertain Kurt's friend."

Kurt hesitated. Adam Bede intervened. " My name is Adam Bede." The Captain spoke up. "Are you the legendary Venerable Bede who can determine the size of an enemy squadron from the color of the cook's handkerchief? I've heard a lot about you."

"That is a small exaggeration," Adam smiled. " But yes, that is what I am attempting to do."

Sarah had not let go of Kurt's hand. "This is my stepmother, Lady Carol Harrington, my uncle, Captain Everett, and my friend -" she blushed a little, " Lieutenant Commander Cyril Blamington. Why don't you all have a drink together, while Kurt and I catch up."

Lady Carol gave Kurt an impenetrable look. Remembering his last view of her, with her blond head buried between the legs of Clemente Theberge, Kurt made sure to greet her as a complete stranger. He also did not fail to notice that Cyril seemed quite unhappy at being excluded from the little reunion Sarah organized.

Sarah led Kurt to another table, waved to a waiter, ordered drinks, and still holding Kurt's hand, bubbled:

"Now talk. I can't believe I'm sitting here with you. You have no idea how much I've worried about you."

Is that really possible? That this golden girl feels about me as I have not dared to feel about her? Or is it just curiosity and her warm heart? This Cyril seems to have a very proprietary interest in her. And of course, he's of her class. And her stepmother? What a coincidence. She certainly won't want me around. I'll have to assure her of my discretion when the opportunity arises.

"I had heard that the Dauntless had been sunk," Kurt said, " and I was certain that you had gone down with her. I found out only a few days ago that you had been transferred to another ship and, thank God, were safe and sound."

"They transferred me because of the dispatches you took from the German soldier you…" she couldn't bring herself to say "killed." "Apparently they were quite interesting, and intelligence wanted me to tell them exactly where you got them. They were quite unhappy that poor Captain Corcoran refused to take you along."

"I was devastated when I heard that the Dauntless had gone down and you with her." Kurt said, tightening his grip on Sarah's hand.

"Oh, yes, poor Captain Corcoran, and poor Pudgie. You remember Pudgie?"

Kurt did remember the officer who had refused to allow him to board. He was not quite as distraught by the loss.

"But you haven't told me how you managed to get here, Kurt." Sarah caught Cyril's angry look, and gently disengaged her hand from Kurt's.

"Tell me first, this Cyril, is he your boyfriend, your fiancé, or what?"

"Oh, the family has been expecting us to marry ever since we were toddlers. But nothing is settled. I'm certainly in no hurry for that." Sarah looked into Kurt's eyes. *What is she telling me? Is there hope for me? Nonsense. But Kurt felt himself suffused with an incredible feeling of joy.*

Sarah continued. " Now, enough about me. Tell me."

"It's a long story, and some of it I'm not allowed to talk about. I was picked up by another British vessel. I was able to perform a slight service for Britain, and thus allowed to come to England and to enlist in the British Army. And here I am, as liaison to the French government in exile, nurse-maiding some of the most arrogant and demanding clients anyone ever had. Now let's get back to you. What are you doing and where do you live?"

"I'm studying nursing, and I'm stationed at the Naval Hospital in Plymouth. After all, we all have to do our bit. I came to London to pick up Carol, and tomorrow we're going down to the farm for father's sixtieth birthday party. Look here, I want you to come."

Kurt smiled at the lovely girl's enthusiasm. "I have duties here, and besides, I hardly think your father will want me."

"Look, I'll get you the weekend off, if I have to. I've still got connections, like my uncle there, in spite of what they think of Daddy today. And my father will be glad to see you. These days he does not get too many visitors. Wait and see. I'll take care of it. I'm not letting you go, now that I've found you."

She forced Kurt to give her his address at Adam Bede's home, and his duty station with Major Thompson. Kurt could not take his eyes off the beautiful young woman. He looked at the white shoulders so close to him, and remembered the moment he had kissed her nipple the night after he had killed the German dispatch rider.

Cyril towered over them. "It's time to leave, Sarah," he said. "You two have an early train to catch tomorrow."

Considering the direction of his thoughts, Kurt was a little nervous about getting up to say goodbye to Sarah. A napkin came in handy to prevent him from making a spectacle of himself. Cyril hardly looked at him, while Sarah hugged him and whispered " Soon." Then they walked back to their table where Sarah's companions were already up and moving out. Kurt bowed in their general direction and gratefully sank down in his seat, where he was joined by Adam Bede.

"Well?" the Venerable Bede questioned.

"Well, what?"

"You know perfectly well what I'm talking about. Everyone at the table saw you looking at Sarah like a starving puppy waiting for a bite. Well, what are your chances of being fed?"

"Who knows? Was I really so obvious?"

"Oh yes, my friend. And don't think Sarah did not know it. I think she enjoyed making Cyril jealous."

"She's not like that." Kurt was offended that anyone would attribute such base motives to his goddess.

"Of course not. How could I have thought that she had human failings?" Adam smirked, as they left the bar.

* * *

The next morning a formal invitation was hand delivered to Kurt's rooms. It desired Lieutenant Kurt Auster's attendance at the estate of Lord Harrington to help celebrate the Lord's sixtieth birthday. A separate insert gave specific instructions on how to reach the estate by rail or road.

Major Thompson easily gave Kurt permission to absent himself for three days. Adam Bede gave Kurt instructions on the behavior expected from him on a weekend in one of the stately homes of England. "It is fortunate that you are in uniform, otherwise you would have to go out and spend a fortune on the different kinds of clothes you would need."

With just a small satchel, Kurt set out to what Sarah had called "the farm." He left London on a train that seemed to make innumerable stops at stations with odd names. By early afternoon, he finally arrived at Slocum Under The Vale, the station he had been told to reach. Slocum Under The Vale was the stop after Slocum Over The Vale, his instructions read, and the stop before Slocum Beyond The Vale. *Not to be confused with Lower Slocum, Upper Slocum, or just plain Slocum,* he thought.

He descended from the train and looked around. Nothing. There was a small station master's house, the platform where he had gotten off the train, and fields of barley and clover as far as the eye could see. No other building. He looked for the station master.

"How do I get to Harrington Hall? " he asked.

The grizzled man before him looked at him suspiciously. "Why would you want to?" He spat and barely missed Kurt's well polished shoe.

"That's hardly the point." Kurt could not afford to offend the man. "I need to get there."

The station master looked at Kurt's uniform. "You're a soldier and you want to get to the hall? Is it official business?"

If that's what will get me the information, that's what it is.

"Yes."

"Well, just walk down the lane here. It's less than three miles. Keep on straight. You can't miss it."

"Is there a telephone here? Can I call the Hall from here?" Kurt asked.

"Not from my phone, you can't." The man spat again. "I'll have nothing to do with that traitor."

"Well, thank you."

Kurt set out on the walk to the Hall. *If that's the attitude around here, no wonder that Sarah could invite me. I suspect that there won't be too many guests celebrating Lord Harrington's birthday.*

An hour later Kurt saw a massive building in the distance. It was certainly not as big as the Imperial Palace in Schoenbrunn or the Royal Palace at Versailles, but if Kurt needed to quarter a regiment of troops, he could do worse than this place.

Kurt entered a gate through a wall which apparently surrounded the entire estate and was somewhat taken aback by the fact that the gate was unattended. He strolled through beautifully kept formal gardens, where lilies, tulips and roses began to bloom in the soft May sunshine. As he approached the building, he saw more clearly that its dimensions indeed were huge. It was rectangular, three stories high, with many chimneys. A number of large French windows fronted the gardens on both sides of the massive entrance door.

On either side of the main house as well as apparently to its rear, there were several smaller buildings, presumably stables or garages, or perhaps housing for some of the help.

It must take an army of servants to keep these buildings in shape.

One member of that army, dressed in a chauffeur's uniform, was polishing a Rolls Royce in the driveway fronting the Hall. He gave Kurt a suspicious look then turned away. Kurt approached the main door, but before he could knock, it was opened. A corpulent man in a black jacket, striped waistcoat and black trousers, looked at him.

"Good afternoon, Lieutenant Auster. I'm sorry you had to walk. Jones here," he indicated the chauffeur, "was ready to pick you up at the station."

He knows who I am. I must be the only low ranking officer to be invited. Won't it be fun to hobnob with the high and mighty. But I'm prepared to suffer for another chance to be with Sarah.

"The station master was reluctant to let me use his phone to call here." Kurt answered.

"Oh yes, I'll have a word with him. My name is Stevens. Please enter, sir." The man took Kurt's grip out of his hand, waved to a maid, and handed it over to her.

Kurt entered a large entrance hall. In the rear, a monumental staircase rose. Oriental carpets covered a stone floor. The walls were decorated with hunting trophies, stags and boars heads, an occasional tiger skin, and other animals Kurt could not immediately identify. Several large double doors led off the entrance hall in various directions.

"Please follow Maisie to your room, sir. She will take care of you. The dinner gong will be struck at 8 p.m. That is," the butler consulted a large watch he drew from a pocket of his waistcoat, " in less than two hours, but it should give you time for your bath."

Kurt did as he was instructed. Maisie seemed to have some difficulty carrying his grip up the stairs and Kurt wanted to take it from her, but then he thought better of that. *Have to behave like a Lord, don't I?*

One flight up there was a wide corridor extending left and right from the landing. Maisie turned left and took Kurt to the third door down the hall. "Your room, sir," she opened the door and allowed Kurt entrance. The room was large, dominated by a four poster bed, at one end a small desk with one chair in front of a stone fireplace, near the wall a dresser.

The furniture was massive and old. Carpeting covered the stone floors and the walls were hung with paintings of hunting scenes. Kurt approached the two windows and looked out at the gardens through which he had walked. When he turned, he saw that Maisie had opened his suitcase and was busily unpacking his things.

"The bathroom is through here, sir. May I draw your bath?"

"Certainly" said Kurt enjoying the experience of being served.

The maid showed Kurt the bathroom, which, while old fashioned, was complete with all necessities, including a brocaded bathrobe. "There are no other shoes in your suitcase, so please hand me yours so that I can polish them while you have your bath, sir."

Kurt obeyed. He luxuriated in the bath for a while, then emerged into his room to see his shoes polished, his uniform, ironed and brushed, laid out on the bed, and the rest of his clothes neatly hung in the closet. He decided to shave once more, got dressed and waited for the famous gong. *One could get used to this treatment.*

While he was waiting, he looked out the window at the beautiful garden scene. *There should be more cars for the big celebration. Interesting.*

The gong was struck Its reverberations could clearly be heard throughout the big mansion. *Should I go down immediately, or wait a polite ten minutes? Adam did not tell me. Hell, I'm a soldier and used to being punctual. Well, off into the fray.*

He left his room, walked down the staircase and was guided through an open double door into a huge room. *They don't have small rooms in this building.* Again, oriental carpets covered the stone floor. One wall to the front, had three French windows separated by bookcases filled with leather covered volumes. In the rear, there was a fireplace with a fire crackling against the chill of the early May evening. The walls were hung with portraits of ladies and gentlemen in various period costumes. *The ancestors, no doubt.*

The room was furnished with several couches, armchairs and massive tables, all of the same antique style

Kurt had observed throughout the mansion. In one corner of the room, there stood a complete suit of armor, probably of the late Middle Ages. In the other corner, Stevens stood ready behind a small bar.

"Good evening, sir." The butler enunciated in his fruity tones. "May I offer you something to drink?"

Kurt accepted a small sherry and looked about. Only one other person was in the room. A tall figure rose out of one of the armchairs and approached him.

"Well," the man said, "you look familiar, Lieutenant. Have we met?"

"Yes, Colonel." Kurt drew himself to almost attention. Not totally, after all this was a social occasion. "My name is Auster. I served under you in the training battalion in Londonderry until a few months ago."

Lieutenant Colonel Wheat looked Kurt up and down disdainfully. "I don't remember a subaltern named Auster?"

"Sir, I was a private being trained." Kurt answered politely.

Wheat looked closer. "I remember you now. You're that insubordinate…." he almost sputtered, " and now you're an officer. Your people always seem to have the right connections, don't they?" Lieutenant Colonel Wheat turned his back to Kurt and resumed his seat.

My people! Well, I don't mind his knowing that I'm Jewish. If he doesn't like it, too bad. First he stopped me from dining again in that nice hotel in Derry, and now this. I must keep in mind that we're on the same side in this war. For the moment, at least.

Kurt took his drink and stationed himself near the windows. For fifteen minutes no one else appeared and there was silence in the room. Stevens stood like a statue at his post. Wheat sat unmoving in his armchair and Kurt sipped pensively at his drink.

Finally, the glacial silence was broken by the sound of laughter and the steps of high-heeled shoes. Carol and Sarah came down the staircase arm in arm. Both were dressed in evening gowns. Carol's blond hair piled high above a gown of blue velvet, which left her shoulders bare, a diamond choker around her throat, and diamond bracelets on both wrists. Sarah, his lovely Sarah, wore her hair long over a white gown which also left her shoulders bare. She wore no jewelry but her sparkling eyes, which found Kurt's immediately.

"Please forgive us, gentlemen," Carol said. "It's the privilege of women to be a little late." She looked around despondently. "No one, no one else has arrived?" She turned to Kurt and Colonel Wheat. "Arthur is in conference with two other guests and will be here shortly. I assume you have met each other?"

Kurt couldn't resist. " Oh, yes. We know each other. We dined together once."

Wheat's face turned red with suppressed anger, but he said nothing.. Sarah moved over to Kurt, linked her arm into his and drew him away. "What a disaster. Poor father. All his old friends are snubbing him because of his political views. What a way to celebrate his sixtieth birthday. He sent out invitations to all his friends and not one seems to have responded."

"Not even Cyril?"

"Are you jealous, my pet?" Sarah smiled. "Poor Cyril. By now he's somewhere on the high seas. I'm sure he would have come, for my sake, if not for father's. But let's not talk about him. Are you quite comfortable in your room? I made sure it's just across the hall from mine."

"Oh yes, I'm very comfortable . Thank you. " *And I'll think about you in bed so close to me.* Kurt blushed at the vision of Sarah in bed.

Sarah continued animatedly. "Tell me more about your adventures. I still don't understand how you got to England and into the Army."

"I'm just so glad to see you, Sarah. I can't tell you how unhappy I was when I thought you were dead." Kurt could not keep his eyes off the girl.

At that point there were voices in the hall, and three men walked in. The tallest, clearly, was Lord Arthur Harrington, Sarah's father.

It wasn't that Kurt saw a resemblance to Sarah, it was that the two men who followed Lord Harrington could not have been relatives of his golden girl. Those two resembled each other in their stocky build, the brutality of their expressions and their military postures. Both were clean shaven and appeared to be in their mid-thirties. Kurt immediately thought of them as Tweedle-Dee and Tweedle-Dum. Lord Harrington was taller, painfully thin, sporting a small gray mustache and with black hair slightly graying at the temples. He walked bent forward, perhaps to compensate for his height. All three men were dressed in dinner jackets, the appropriate British uniform for this gathering.

Lord Harrington's eyes swept the room. "So, no one came," he muttered half to himself. Sarah took Kurt by the hand and led him up to her father.

"Father, this is Lieutenant Kurt Auster, who helped me get out of France last year."

Lord Harrington looked Kurt over from head to foot. "What were you doing in France at that time?" he asked, without acknowledging Sarah's introduction.

"Escaping from the Germans, just like your daughter." Kurt replied.

"You're not British?" Lord Harrington asked.

"No, I was born in Vienna."

"Then why are you not in the German Army?"

"I'm Jewish." *Didn't he know? This is odd.*

"Hm." Lord Harrington turned away and spoke to Carol. "Let's get this charade finished. I have work to do."

"Very well, Arthur." Carol answered stiffly. She nodded to Stevens who went out into the hall and returned quickly with several other servants.

"The staff wishes to congratulate your lordship on your birthday." Stevens intoned. Kurt noted that in addition to Maisie, the maid who had taken care of him, and the chauffeur, there was only one middle aged woman of ample girth, evidently the cook, and a wizened man in rough clothes, clutching a cap to his chest, probably the gardener.

Lord Harrington responded: " Thank you all. I appreciate the extra work you are all doing since so many of your colleagues have left to participate in this war. I hope they will return shortly."

The staff left, and Lord Harrington nodded to his wife. She took the lead: " Shall we go in to dinner?"

She led the small group through another door into the dining room. Again this was a huge room, with a fireplace at one end. The room was dominated by a refectory table covered with a damask tablecloth, set with gleaming crystal and porcelain. The table was set for at least forty guests. High backed chairs stood behind each setting. Ancestral portraits and old battle flags decorated the walls. If Henry the Eighth had appeared in their midst, he would have found nothing strange in the surroundings.

Lord Harrington walked to the head of the table and sat down, Tweedle-Dee and Tweedle- Dum, whom he had not bothered to introduce, to his right and left, and Lieutenant Colonel Wheat, after receiving a nod from his host, next to one of them.

Carol moved to the foot of the table and sat down, with Sarah next to her. She waved to Kurt to sit down at her side, facing Sarah. The distance between the two groups was enormous.

And now began the strangest meal in which Kurt had ever participated. No one spoke one word. Stevens served first Lord Harrington and his group, then made his way to the lower end of the table and served Carol and Sarah and finally Kurt. At one point, Kurt attempted to break the silence, but before he had a chance to utter one word, a warning glance from Sarah shut him up.

The meal was finished in less than half an hour. No wine was offered, the plates were whisked away as soon as they were empty, and when the last trifle had been served, Lord Harrington rose.

"We will dispense with the port and cigars." He left the room with his silent followers and Wheat trailing after him.

As soon as they had gone, Carol rose and with an enigmatic glance at Kurt walked out without a word.

Sarah looked at Kurt.

"I'm very sorry I exposed you to this, Kurt. I had no idea how bad the situation had become. I haven't been home since I got back from France, and I did not realize that father would be completely ostracized by all his old friends, and what this has done to him. In the past, he was always a kind man, and I was sure that he would want to thank you personally for helping me. Carol told me he had become very bitter, but I never thought it would be this bad."

"Don't worry about me," Kurt smiled. "As long as I'm with you, I'm happy."

"Oh, you're sweet." Sarah said. "If only Johnny had been able to come. Father always favored him, and he could always make father laugh. "

"Johnny?"

"My brother. Or half brother, I should say. Carol's son. But he's off on the high seas somewhere. I just hope he's safe. Come, I'll get a wrap and we'll take a walk in the garden."

As they were walking among the fragrant early blooms, Kurt took Sarah's hand. "Just one question," he asked. "Who are Tweedle-Dee and Tweedle-Dum, the two men who sat next to your father?"

"Is that what you call them, how appropriate." Sarah laughed. "You see, he used to be the most courteous of men, and now he doesn't even bother to introduce dinner companions. According to Carol, they are members of a more radical offshoot of Sir Oswald Mosley's Union of British Fascists. They are here, ostensibly , to protect father from attacks by the many people who disagree with his politics, but I can't believe that. Who's going to bother to attack father? He's out of it."

"They must not have been happy to see a Jew at your table." Kurt mused.

"Oh, fiddlesticks. I don't see you as a Jew. I see you as Kurt who saved me." Sarah linked her arm in Kurt's and they strolled on. This seemed to be as good an opportunity as any. Kurt put his arms around Sarah, turned her toward him, and kissed her.

She responded ardently. He pressed her entire body against his, and felt the deliciousness of her breasts against his chest. She opened her mouth and for the first time, he tasted her tongue.

After a few moments she stepped back. They continued their stroll in silence, this time with Kurt's arm around Sarah's waist and her head on his shoulder. As they approached a stone bench along the path, Kurt suggested that they sit down. Again he turned to Sarah, and they began kissing. Her scarf slipped from her shoulders and Kurt's kisses followed the line of Sarah's throat, down to the valley between her breasts. He slipped the side of her gown down, and one breast emerged to be captured instantly by Kurt's hungry mouth. Sarah held his head against her as he tasted her nipple. She pulled his head up, and again they kissed, this time while Kurt's hand eagerly explored the contours of Sarah's firm breast. At that point, she pulled away from him, looked into his eyes, and said:

"You're driving me crazy. We mustn't..."

"I love you Sarah," he whispered and recaptured her mouth, immersing himself deeply in it. Her tongue played with his, then she pushed his head back down to her breast where he could savor the tender nipple again. Kurt moved his hand toward Sarah's knee and allowed it to stroke her thigh under her dress. Almost without volition his hand rose caressing the inside of Sarah's thigh, past the top of her stocking to the soft flesh. For a moment, she opened her legs, and he touched the depth of her.

Sarah jumped up. "No, no, we mustn't. Not here, not now."

He rose and recaptured the girl in his arms. She pressed herself full length against him, kissed him briefly, and said softly: " Soon." Then she pulled herself out of his arms, and ran back to the house.

Kurt stood there filled with conflicting emotions. He had never been so aroused in his life. *She must love me. She wouldn't have allowed me so much. What did she mean by "Soon "? Do I dare go to her room now? I could spoil everything by being too aggressive.*

Kurt was totally confused. He began to explain to himself that a woman like Sarah could not immediately take him to her bed, particularly in the mansion of her father.

But there was certainly hope. He would see her in the morning, and the hospital in Plymouth where she was being trained was not so far from London that visits could not be arranged.

He wandered around the garden filled with longings, rethinking every moment when Sarah had been in his arms, remembering the feel of her skin, her hand on his head pressing him to her breast, the touch of her body against his.

Suddenly he realized that he did not know where he was. It was dark There were clouds and neither the moon nor stars were visible. He walked slowly along the path he found himself on, and eventually came to the wall surrounding the property. Wrong direction He turned to retrace his steps. Eventually he could make out the bulk of the massive building in front of him. He walked along its sides in the hope of finding the French doors through which Sarah and he had emerged a while ago. All was quiet, all the doors were closed.

He turned a corner and saw a light. Finally. He approached along the wall and was just about to call out asking to be let in, when he heard a voice:

"But this is murder."

Murder? What are they talking about?

He crouched underneath the open window and raised his head slightly to get a quick glimpse of the interior of a small room, clearly a study. Lord Harrington was pacing up and down. Tweedle Dee and Tweedle Dum were standing almost at attention near the door, and Lieutenant Colonel Wheat was seated in an armchair.

Harrington had been speaking. He continued: "You really don't see any other way?"

Wheat shook his head. "Look, if he hadn't been captured, we'd be in a different position. We could have brought him to the House and proved their good intentions toward us, and explained their plan to eliminate the Red Menace once and for all. We could have toppled the government and put you in so you could make the peace Britain needs. But now you know very well he'll be kept incommunicado as long as Churchill is in charge. What's worse, I wouldn't be surprised if Churchill warned the Russians."

"And if I kill him?"

"There will be a change of government. Our people will try to liberate Hess and we can proceed with the original plan. You probably will not be Prime Minister, but your act will go down in the annals of our country as a most selfless and heroic deed. And you know very well that Churchill alive is an insurmountable obstacle."

"And it has to be me?"

"Who else has access? Who else can enter 10 Downing Street without being searched? Only a peer of the realm, a former cabinet minister. It is an historic opportunity to change the course of events."

"When do you think…?"

"No later than the day after tomorrow. If there is no word of any changes here, Hitler may call off or postpone Operation Barbarossa."

Kurt was so fascinated by what he heard that he became a little careless. He slipped and broke his fall with a hand which struck a twig. It snapped with a sound that seemed to Kurt louder than a cannon shot. "What's that? " someone in the room called out.

Quickly Kurt crawled backward around the corner, then stopped not daring to breathe. He heard nothing further. He decided that he knew enough. *Now to find another way into the building.*

He walked slowly around the entire circumference. *Ah, an open window.* He climbed in and made his way out the door in the darkness, carefully skirting walls, not knowing where in this huge building he was. Finally, by sheer chance, he found himself in the entrance hall. There's the staircase up to his room. In the bathroom he cleaned himself off as much as he could and packed his grip. *I can't wait until morning. I've got to get back to London and report this.*

The door to his room opened. Carol came in.

"I must talk with you, " she said. She had changed from her evening gown into an elegant long robe, which almost reached the ground.

"If you're worried about my discretion," Kurt said, "please don't be. I promise…"

"Never mind that," Carol interrupted. "You don't understand us. Marriages in our circle are dynastic arrangements. I have done my duty and produced an heir. Arthur does not begrudge me my little pleasures, as I don't begrudge him his. In fact, if you tell him, he'll only regret that he wasn't there to participate."

"Then what is it?"

"I want you to leave Sarah alone. I've seen how you look at her, and what's worse, I've seen how she looks at you. She must become Lady Blamington. Once she has done her duty and had her children, she will be free to enjoy herself any way she wishes. That means you may have to wait a few years, but you don't have to give up hope to have her in your bed."

Kurt was totally shocked. He found he had nothing to say. Carol continued.

"I'm sorry to be so blunt, but I want you to leave right now. You can walk to the station and take the 4 A.M. milk train to London. You walked here. The return walk will not be a problem for a healthy young man like you. You may not to see her again for at least the next few years. If you don't do as I ask, I will tell Sarah about the first time we met."

Kurt looked at the woman. He had never seen such cold determination.

"Don't you care about Sarah's feeling at all? " he asked.

"I love Sarah as if she were my own daughter. That is why I want to make sure that she marries Cyril Blamington and takes her proper place in society. Romantic love has nothing to do with it."

"What will you tell Sarah? She'll expect to see me at breakfast."

"Never mind. It's wartime. I'll tell her you had an emergency call and orders to return immediately. The point is you must agree to leave, and what's more, to leave Sarah alone. Is that clear? "

"Very well." Kurt sighed. *I have to get out of here anyway. But I'll see Sarah again, in Plymouth or London or wherever. There isn't any point in continuing this discussion, but Sarah will have to make her own decision.*

"Good, that's sensible." Carol smiled. She looked at her watch. "You don't have to leave for another hour. Would you care to spend it with me?" She began to open her robe at the neck. It was obvious that she wore nothing else.

"You are the most cold-blooded woman I've ever met." Kurt said. "No, thank you. At least not now and not here."

"Too bad. Well, perhaps we'll meet in London. Clemente knows how to get in touch with me. I enjoyed our last encounter." Lady Harrington swept out the door in the most dignified manner possible.

Kurt finished packing his grip, quietly descended the staircase and went out the front door closing it behind him as silently as possible. As he walked toward the gate, he reviewed the evening he had just spent in the heart of British nobility.

* * *

He left the estate behind him and followed the path. It was quite dark, but the clouds opened up occasionally so that he could see his way by starlight and was able to proceed at a rapid pace. Suddenly he stopped. Tweedle-Dee and Tweedle-Dum stood before him barring his way. They each had cricket bats in one hand, which they swung nonchalantly.

"Where do you think you're going, Jew?" One of them asked as they advanced toward Kurt.

With a brief prayer of thanks to his unarmed combat instructor, Kurt threw his grip with full force at the stomach of Tweedle- Dee. He pivoted and hit Tweedle-Dum in the vulnerable place between his legs with the point of his heavy army shoe. Tweedle-Dum dropped his bat and grabbed his injured testicles, bending forward in agony. Kurt swung his fist straight into the injured man's carotid artery, and he collapsed.

Kurt turned and kicked straight at Tweedle-Dee's knee. Tweedle-Dee fell down. Kurt picked up the bat Tweedle Dum had dropped and with full force hit Tweedle-Dee's kneecap. He felt it shatter. He then turned to Tweedle-Dum and administered the same kind of stroke to that man's knee with the same result. The adrenaline was pumping and for a moment he considered breaking the men's other kneecaps.

No. Let them limp for the rest of their lives. Now they will have a good reason to hate and to remember at least one Jew.

The entire episode had taken just a few seconds, and there had been silence. But now, the moaning of the two injured men became too audible for Kurt's taste. One after the other he pulled them away from the path into the bushes. *Let them stay here. They'll be found in the morning.*

Will this affect Lord Harrington's plans? Should I try to steal the Rolls and drive it to London? I'll never find the way. All the road signs have been removed or altered to make a German invasion more difficult. No, I think these two brutes were sent here by my good friend Carol just to ensure that I obey her wishes. Did they intend to kill me or just injure me? No matter. This was personal. Lord Harrington may not even be aware of it. In any case, I have to get to London as fast as I can.

Kurt walked as quickly as possible toward the railroad station. *I enjoyed this*, he thought, *but how could I have been so brutal? I crippled these men for life. They may have deserved it, but who am I to make that decision? Would my parents have approved? I doubt it. But I feel good about it. Strange.*

It was still dark when he reached the railroad station, but there was a glimmer of light on the horizon. In May, in these latitudes, the days were getting longer, and dawn would break soon. Kurt looked for the station master. No one in sight.

He walked over to the station master's house and banged at the door.

"Just a minute, just a minute, don't break the door down. What is it?" a querulous voice called out. The station master opened the door. His hair was tousled and he wore only a pair of pants, which he must have put on in haste since the buttons on his fly were still open.

"What's the emergency? Why did you wake me in the middle of the night? What's going on?"

"I apologize," Kurt said, " but it's very urgent that I get back to London immediately. Really very urgent. I need your help."

"Ah, it's you, Lieutenant. Back already from that place? Didn't like the   company?"

The man mumbled as he adjusted his trousers. "What can be so urgent that you had to wake me? I'm entitled to my sleep, ain't I?"

"Please forgive me, " Kurt pleaded. "But it's really very important."

"Just wait for the milk train. It'll be here at 4 A.M. It'll get you to London eventually."

"That's not good enough. Look, I know you're a patriot. Please believe me, this is a matter of national importance."

The station master looked at Kurt for a long while. He must have liked what he saw.

"Very well. There's an express freight train passing through here in about half an hour. It makes no stops to London, so you'll be there by eight A.M. But it's not scheduled to stop here either. If I halt the train, I could get into a lot of trouble."

"Look." Kurt said. "You don't know me, but please, please believe me that this is vital. I'll make sure you will not have any problems, in fact you'll get a commendation. Here's my name and address, so that you can contact me. But please, don't tell anyone from Harrington Hall about this."

That last statement was the clincher. "Oh well, I believe you. Come in and have a cup of tea, while we're waiting. " He went out and set the signal which would stop the express freight train.

A cup of tea was just what Kurt could use. Ii wasn't long before he heard the rumble of an approaching train. "Come on," the station master called, and he led Kurt to the front of the platform.

With a screech the train came to a stop. A figure bent down from the locomotive. "What's the matter?"

"Hello, Charlie," the station master called out. "This is an emergency. You've got to get this soldier to London quick as lightning. Trust me on that one."

"If you say so, Joe." The figure reached a hand down to Kurt who swung up into the cab of the locomotive and the train pulled out of the station.

* * *

Kurt was in Admiral Morse's office before that redoubtable figure had arrived, but the pretty Wren who guarded the doors was there already, brewing the Admiral's morning tea.

"Good morning," Kurt said. "I must see the Admiral most urgently. Please get me in to see him."

224

"Not a chance, Lieutenant. He has meetings all day long. I'll tell him you want to see him, and he'll let you know when it's convenient. He's a busy man, you know."

"Yes, I know. Please believe me this is not an idle matter. I have information he must have, and he must have it now. I hate to use a cliché, but it is a matter of life and death."

The Wren smiled. " Whose? Yours? I don't think Admiral Morse would allow even your imminent demise to interrupt his meetings today."

"No, not mine." Kurt said almost in despair. "Please give me a piece of paper and an envelope and at least promise me you'll make him read my note the moment he comes in."

The Wren looked at Kurt speculatively. "You're a persistent young man, Lieutenant. Oh, very well."

Kurt wrote: " I have information about a plot to assassinate the Prime Minister today or tomorrow. Please let me explain." He sealed the note in the envelope provided to him by the Wren, and sat down in the anteroom to await the Admiral's arrival.

In what seemed to Kurt an eternity, but actually was not more than ten minutes later, the Admiral stormed in, with his usual " I have no time " attitude. He glanced briefly at Kurt who had jumped out of his seat, and without a word entered his private office. The pretty Wren followed him.

A few moments later she came out and beckoned to Kurt to go in.

"You've got two minutes, Auster. Explain this absurd statement." Admiral Morse frowned.

Kurt gave as concise a report of the conversation he had overheard as he could. He concluded with a brief mention of his encounter with the two British Fascists, but did not mention anything about Sarah or Carol.

"You are certain they mentioned the name Hess?"

"Absolutely, Admiral."

Admiral Morse picked up the phone and dialed. "Who's this? Ah, Bellows. Morse here. I'm coming over to see the P.M. right now. No, it can't wait. I'll need ten minutes as soon as I get there. Oh, and Bellows, if Lord Harrington arrives to see the P.M., do not allow him access.

Just divert him politely until I show up. Understood? Thank you."

"Auster, you stay here." The Admiral called to his aid. "Cancel my appointments for the morning. Keep Lieutenant Auster here until I come back. He is not to talk to anyone, anyone. Is that clear?" The Admiral stormed out without waiting to hear the Wren's "Aye, aye, sir."

"Well," the pretty Wren looked at Kurt. "You've certainly caused a stir. Now what am I going to do with you?"

Kurt felt as if a burden had been lifted from his shoulders. He had transmitted the information and he knew that it was in good hands. He smiled at the Wren.

"The first thing you could do, is tell me your name. I've been thinking about you all this time as the Admiral's pretty Wren, but since I'm now in your care, I ought to be able to call you something else."

The girl blushed a little. "I'm Ensign Diana Fordyce. Of course I know who you are. The Admiral has few secrets from me."

Kurt doubted that last statement. An experienced spymaster like Admiral Morse probably had secrets from himself. Suddenly Kurt realized how tired he was.

"Thank you, Diana. May I call you Diana or must it be Ensign? I'm Kurt. What I'd really like is a place to lie down and close my eyes. I haven't slept in more than twenty-four hours."

The Wren smiled. "I can fix that, Kurt." She led him to an empty office. "This is Commander Nelson's office. He's away until tomorrow. Just make yourself comfortable."

Gratefully, Kurt took off his jacket and shoes, sank down on Commander Nelson's office couch, and closed his eyes.

* * *

"He mentioned Hess and Operation Barbarossa?"

"Yes, Prime Minister."

"Well, Morse, here's something even you may not know. Rudolf Hess, Adolf Hitler's deputy and second in command, parachuted into Scotland from a Messerschmitt 110 two days ago, on May 10. He broke his ankle and was captured in a field near Glasgow. I have just authorized Duff Cooper as Information Minister to make the matter public."

"But that is incredible. What does he want?"

"I have had him interviewed, of course. He wants us to make peace with Germany and aid the Nazis to defeat the great Red Menace."

"And that would be Operation Barbarossa?"

"Most likely. Now from what you tell me, there is more of a conspiracy involved. Clearly they consider me the principal obstacle to such a devil's deal. I can't imagine that many people in Britain would be willing to go along with it."

"With your permission, Prime Minister, I'll handle the conspiracy."

"Please do so, Morse. But discretion, please. I don't want an announcement that a peer of the realm has been arrested and I don't want a treason trial. It's hard enough to keep up the morale of this beleaguered island. Oh, and the young man who brought you this information. Make absolutely sure that he keeps his mouth shut. Totally shut."

"Rely on me, Prime Minister. One last question. Do you intend to warn the Russians?"

"What, warn them? The best thing, next to America's entry into the war, would be a German attack on the Soviet Union. Think of the pressure it would relieve on us. No, if I warned Stalin and he moved a few divisions to the West, Hitler may have second thoughts. Let him think he'll win quickly against the Russians, I suspect they won't make it that easy for him."

"Yes, Prime Minister."

As Admiral Morse left Winston Churchill, he reflected that it took a hard man to guide Britain through this major crisis in her history, and that the British were to be congratulated on having found such a hard man to be their leader. He wondered briefly whether the Prime Minister had given much thought to the Russian and German lives that a word of warning might have saved.

* * *

Late that same morning, Lord Harrington presented himself at 10 Downing Street. "I need ten minutes with the

Prime Minister, Bellows, " he said to the guardian of the inner sanctum.

"The Prime Minister is very busy, your lordship. And you have no appointment." Bellows dared to say.

"I need no appointment. I am a peer of the realm, and a former cabinet minister. Now announce me immediately, do you hear. I will stand for no insolence." Lord Harrington said arrogantly.

Bellows removed himself from the Lord's presence, returned shortly, and bowed his lordship into a room next to the Prime Minister's office. "Why here?" Harrington asked. "Why not in the PM's office?"

"Because I am here, your lordship." Admiral Morse said politely. "Please forgive me, but there has been a threat on the Prime Minister's life, and we have orders to search everybody who wishes to see him."

Lord Harrington paled. Then he began to bluster. "Search? You must be joking. Do you know who I am? I have been going in and out of this building freely for more years than you know."

"Again, I ask your forgiveness, your lordship. But I must search everyone without exception."

"Well, you're not going to search me." Lord Harrington announced. "I will not be insulted like that. Very well. I'll see the Prime Minister another time." He turned and began to walk out of the room. His path was blocked by one of the policemen assigned to the building.

"Sorry, your lordship." Admiral Morse could not have been more obsequious. "But now that you're here we'll have to search you anyway."

Lord Harrington looked at the Admiral and saw no pity in his glacial eyes. He collapsed into a chair. "This is what you are looking for." He pulled a small revolver out of his breast pocket. "I carry it for protection," he stammered.

"Of course you do, your Lordship. London is so dangerous when you drive through it in your Rolls." Morse permitted himself a small smile. "Enough of this charade. I know why you are here, and you know that I know."

"Are you going to arrest me? " Lord Harrington quavered.

"Perhaps. But there is an alternative."

"What is it?"

"We can have a show trial where you will be charged with conspiracy, attempted assassination of His Majesty's first minister, treason, dealing with the enemy, and anything else we can come up with. Your name will become as well known as Guy Fawkes, and centuries from now, children will play the villainous Lord Harrington. As for you, I doubt that in this day and age Britain will execute a peer of the realm. It's been centuries since that was a regular hazard of the position. More likely you will be sent to prison for life. You might find it interesting to see how His Majesty's prisoners are treated in Dartmoor."

Lord Harrington shuddered. "You mentioned an alternative?"

"You could have a nervous breakdown. I will arrange for you to be kept incommunicado in a sanitarium under my control. When the war is won, you will recover miraculously and will be released with your miserable life and your position intact. But there is a price."

"What is it?"

"A full confession, written out in your own handwriting, giving complete information about the entire conspiracy, names, dates, and all participants. You may wish to consider that your messenger, Lieutenant Colonel Wheat is already in our hands and has begun to talk. Very freely, I might add."

Lord Harrington thought for a moment. He whispered to Morse: "I did not want to say so before, but you must listen to me." He looked around to make sure no one could overhear. "We have support from the highest quarters. The King..."

Morse recoiled. "I will not listen to your talking treason about King George."

"Not him." Harrington continued to whisper. "The real King. Edward VIII, whom those conspirators forced to abdicate five years ago. Look here, when he comes back to the throne, you will be rewarded if you help me now. Why, an earldom is not out of the question."

Morse looked at the quivering man before him without pity. If that is his fantasy, he really is having a breakdown. True, there had been rumors last year that the former King had been approached by German agents in Lisbon, and had been offered the throne of a conquered Britain, but there was never any indication that the now Duke of Windsor had ever seriously considered the matter. Still, the rumors were enough for the British government to appoint him to the nominal governorship of the Bahamas where the Duke and Duchess of Windsor could sit out the war in comfort and safety.

"Do I take it that you refuse my offer, Lord Harrington?" Morse asked coldly.

Harrington collapsed in his chair. Suddenly, he seemed a much smaller man. "No," he sighed, "I will do as you say."

* * *

Two other peers of the realm suffered nervous breakdowns that week, Lieutenant Colonel Wheat was convicted of forging mess checks based on his own confession, was drummed out of the Army and sentenced to five years imprisonment. Two limping British Fascists found themselves transported to India so serve as medical orderlies in a hospital high up in the Himalayas. A small handful of high-ranking officers suddenly were assigned to minor posts in the outer Hebrides or in the Falklands. But all that took some time. After a flurry of activity to set all these matters in motion, Admiral Morse turned his attention to Kurt.

Kurt was dreaming of Sarah in his arms, when he felt a soft hand on his cheek. He opened his eyes and looked at the pretty face of Diana Fordyce.

"Time to wake up. The Admiral wishes to see you now. You may wash up here, " she pointed to another door, " and then I will announce you."

Kurt jumped up. The few hours of sleep had made him feel very much better. A quick few moments in the bathroom, and he reported to the Admiral. This time Morse looked at him in a very friendly fashion.

"Well, my young friend, it appears that you have done Britain another service."

"May I ask what happened, Admiral?"

"No, you may not. The matter has been attended to. That is all you need to know." Admiral Morse was no longer quite as friendly as before.

Now Kurt got angry. "With all due respect, sir, the information I brought you concerned the father of the woman I love. She may never speak to me again. I think I'm entitled to know whether I still have a chance with her."

Admiral Morse leaned back in his chair with a smile. "I hardly think that your love life falls within my purview, but I will tell you this. Lord Harrington has had a nervous breakdown and has been admitted to a private sanitarium for the foreseeable future. A similar fate has befallen some others. Is that good enough for you? I don't think anyone in this matter knows about your involvement, except for the P.M. and me."

"Thank you, Admiral." Kurt sighed with relief. Sarah may not be totally lost to me.

"Now let us talk about you. I don't know what to do with you. You have done good work, but you are insubordinate. You can't run the war to suit yourself."

"So, you read my report on France, sir?" Kurt said with some bitterness.

"Of course I did. Most attentively. And your conclusions are correct. They have been verified from other sources. The French are far from ready to resist the Germans. On the contrary, most middle class and almost all upper class French are enthusiastic collaborators. They are all making money. But what possessed you to organize what you called your underground railroad? That was not part of your brief, and you risked capture and thus failure of your primary mission."

"When my people are at risk, I have to do something." Kurt said. "I can't believe, Admiral, that you wouldn't have done the same thing."

"Hm. It's all academic now, anyway."

"What do you mean, sir?"

"Word has reached us that Field Marshall Hermann Goering issued an order to all governmental authorities in countries under German control, including unoccupied France, that no more exit visas for Jews are to be issued in view of the imminent final solution of the Jewish problem."

Kurt jumped up. "But this is terrible. What does he mean "final solution?" What can we do about this? There are many millions of Jews at risk."

"I don't know what he means, Auster, but the only thing we can do is try to win the war as quickly as possible. And I regret to say, our chances are getting slimmer every day. You saw that even here at home, there is opposition to continuing."

"Why slimmer, sir?" Kurt felt flattered that this exalted personage took the time to discuss strategy with a lowly lieutenant.

"Our only chance, only chance, mind you, is to hold out until the Americans come in. And I'm not sure we can. We are at tremendous risk until then."

"Why now, sir?"

"You know that the Germans control most of the Balkans. If Rommel's Africa Corps takes the Suez Canal - and they're very close to it - we're done for. Without the connection to the East, we cannot survive."

"But what can we do, sir? This is terrible. Here I've been having a good time in London, when all I want to do is fight Germans."

"Hm, you're giving me an idea, Auster. I've always thought of using your talents in France, but that seems pointless for the moment. But you are of course also fluent in German."

"It's my native tongue, sir."

"Let me think about it for a few minutes. Perhaps I'll send you to Egypt. I see the beginning of a plan. I assume you'll go wherever I send you?"

"Of course, Admiral, as long as it helps in the war effort."

"Well, go down to the canteen and have something to eat. By the time you come back, I may have something for you. Diana," the Admiral called out, "take Lieutenant Auster to the canteen. Same instructions as before, understood?"

Diana stuck her head into the Admiral's office, acknowledged his orders, and led Kurt downstairs. Kurt failed to see the trace of a satisfied smile on the face of that master manipulator, Admiral Morse.

An hour later, Kurt appeared again in Morse's office.

"Very well, " the Admiral said briskly. " All is organized. Diana will drive you to the airfield at Tewksbury. A Lancaster bomber is waiting to take you to Alexandria with a refueling stop in Gibraltar. Report to Brigadier Geoffrey Thornton, head of theater intelligence, and give him this envelope. I wish you good luck. " The Admiral shook Kurt's hand and hustled him out of his office.

"But Sarah, and my friend Adam Bede. They won't know what happened to me. " Kurt said to Diana as they rushed to the car park.

"You can write them each a note while we're driving, and I'll see that they get it."

* * *

"Is he off, Diana? " Admiral Morse asked.

"Yes, sir."

"Give me the letters he wrote." The Admiral ordered.

"How did you know, sir? Must I? I'm sure, they're private."

"Make up your mind that I know everything." Admiral Morse smiled. " Now give me the letters, and then get back to work."

Diana obeyed reluctantly, and went out. Morse took the letters and without hesitation opened them. He read the letter to Sarah without smiling at the expressions of love and devotion, then slowly tore it into small bits. He resealed the note to Adam Bede and placed it into his out basket.

For a moment, he sat there quietly. A good man, Kurt Auster, he thought. He could have been useful in France after Operation Barbarossa begins. Well, perhaps he will survive the mission I sent him on, after all. The important thing is to get him out of England and to make sure that he does not talk.

Admiral Morse, too, was a hard man.

* * *

Sarah woke up feeling happy. She stretched and remembered her evening with Kurt. Quickly she jumped out of bed, went to the bathroom and began to draw her bath.

She dropped her nightgown and stood in front of her full length mirror inspecting herself.

She looked at her firm breasts. Maybe they're a little small, she thought. She remembered Kurt's mouth on her nipple, and blushed, warmth suffusing her body. He certainly seemed to like it. She stretched out in the bath and remembered more. Here is where he touched me, her hand slid down between her legs. And I remember the effect I had on him when he held me close. Do I love him? I don't know what that means. He's the most exciting man I've ever met. An adventurer. A foreigner. He saved my life. Cyril - and all the other men I know, they're so boring, so predictable. But Kurt? I wish he had come to my room last night. Perhaps, I wasn't explicit enough. Well, today, certainly.

She climbed out of the bath and as quickly as possible completed her toilet. She dressed in a warm country suit with boots. I'll take him for a walk, that way we'll have privacy. And again, she blushed as she thought of what they might do.

When she came down the stairs to the breakfast room, only Carol was there sipping her tea. "Good morning," Sarah called out cheerfully. "Where's everybody?"

Carol looked up. "Your father had to go into town, and I assume he took his bodyguards, in any case I did not see them. Lieutenant Colonel Wheat left very early this morning."

"And Kurt? " Sarah had a foreboding of something unpleasant.

"He's gone too."

"He can't be. Not without saying good bye to me. What really happened, Carol?"

"I don't want to hurt you, dear, but I think his leaving is a very good thing."

Sarah grabbed Carol by the arms. "Please, Carol, please tell me what happened."

"Well, if you insist. Perhaps it's just as well, it will teach you to stay with your own kind. I don't know what happened between you two in the garden, but when he came back to the house he was crazed. I met him in the corridor and he tried to rape me."

"What? I don't believe it."

"He said that you had aroused him to a painful extent, and if he did not get immediate relief, he'd suffer. He grabbed me, tried to put my hand on his - you know - and promised me an incredible experience if I went to bed with him then and there. I hit him and escaped. By the time I came back with Stevens, he was gone. And good riddance. You just can't trust these foreigners."

Sarah was devastated. Is it my fault? No, how could he, is that what he meant when he said he loved me? Just a body? Any body would do? She burst into tears and ran up to her room.

Carol poured herself another cup of tea and smiled.

CHAPTER VIII

Brigadier Geoffrey Thornton was a small man. This certainly had caused him problems at Sandhurst where he was always the smallest of any group. Perhaps it was that factor that had made him go into intelligence. He was born in India of military parents, spoke fluent Hindi and Urdu, and had learned Arabic as well at subsequent postings. Like so many officers in the British Empire, he had spent only a few years in the country he called home. His real home, where he felt comfortable, was the East. His smallness was a major advantage to him when he went out disguised as a native on his various intelligence missions. He had not done that in some time. With advancing rank he became more of an administrator, but he had a soft spot for the derring-do of all field agents.

His problem as Chief of Intelligence in Egypt was the fact that most Egyptians were strong supporters of Germany, not for any ideological reasons, but merely because they wanted freedom from the British Yoke. The old Middle Eastern saying - "The enemy of my enemy is my friend " - applied very much. And now, with Rommel's Africa Corps approaching the Egyptian border and threatening Suez, Thornton had his hands full trying to ward off Egyptian sabotage and obstruction. He hardly had time to devote to his other passion, Bible Study, with a particular emphasis on Archeology.

Kurt reported to the Brigadier. He saw a small man, impeccably dressed in British tropical uniform, clean shaven, thin and fit looking, with piercing blue eyes which presently were focusing on Admiral Morse's letter.

"Hm, the Admiral thinks highly of you, and he has an idea that might be of help. Let me think about it for a while, and see how it could be implemented. In the meantime, report to Bachelor Officers Quarters and draw some tropical uniforms. You must be dying in these heavy woolens."

"Indeed I am. Thank you, sir."

Thornton looked at the retreating back of the young officer and returned to Morse's letter. He had not failed to grasp the implication when Morse suggested that the mission he had in mind might be called Operation Uriah. Thornton remembered well the appropriate quotation from King David: " Send Uriah into the midst of the battle so that he might be slain." He wondered what Lieutenant Auster had done, but since he trusted Morse totally, set about to organize the mission.

* * *

Feldwebel Horst Behnke was proud to serve in the Africa Corps. His photograph in the special Africa Corps khaki uniform, with the soft forage cap popularized by General Erwin Rommel, was in a place of honor over the mantelpiece in his home in Oldenburg. All his life he had thought of Africa as the most romantic of continents, Arabs in burnooses, mysterious women in veils whose flashing eyes promised paradise, tropical sun and blue seas, camels and stomping race horses.

The reality was of course quite different. Back in Oldenburg, he had never imagined the heat, day after day, turning into freezing cold in the desert night, the sand flies, the dust storms coating everything he touched or ate with gritty motes of sand, the lack of water which meant that a bath or shower were an infrequent and very welcome bonus.

He was used to the many colors of the Oldenburger Moors near his home. Here there seemed to be only one color - yellow, in various shades ranging from brown to red. The desert shimmered in the noon heat. The blue of the ocean was far to the North and invisible from here.

Horst Behnke was in command of a Kuebelwagen, a car armed with a machine gun set on a post in the rear, with two men under his orders. His mission was to look for the British lines, but not to make contact. His commander merely wanted to establish where the British would make what General Rommel hoped would be their last stand, before allowing the Germans to sweep through Egypt to the Suez Canal.

They proceeded Eastward slowly. Other Kuebelwagen to the North and South of them were on similar missions, but at this point, Behnke saw no other German troops. The three men felt totally isolated in the trackless desert. Only Behnke's compass confirmed the exact direction in which they were advancing.

"Stop for a moment, " Behnke ordered his driver. " There is something ahead of us."

He lifted his heavy field glasses. "This is odd. A motorcycle coming toward us - it's weaving back and forth as if the driver were drunk. Let's approach, slowly. And keep your weapons handy."

"Zu Befehl, Herr Feldwebel, " (at your orders, Sergeant,) Henkel, the driver, muttered, while Meinen, the machine gunner took a firmer grip on his weapon.

As they approached, the motorcycle made a stuttering noise and stopped. The driver of the motorcycle descended hesitatingly and allowed his vehicle to fall over on its side. He tottered a few steps forward, sank to his knees, got up with great difficulty, sank down again and appeared finally to have collapsed.

"Slowly forward, " Behnke ordered. " Be careful, this may be a trick. Stop here, and cover me."

He advanced slowly toward the recumbent figure. Odd, it looks like a German uniform. Yes, there's the swastika. That uniform. Almost looks like Navy. What would a German naval officer be doing in the desert?

He pulled out his pistol and carefully bent over the man. "Wasser, " the man croaked out of blistered lips. Behnke ascertained with a quick search of the stranger's body that there were no weapons anywhere around. He then took his field canteen, uncapped it, and gave it to the man. "Slowly, slowly, or you'll get sick," he allowed the stranger to drink his fill.

Behnke helped the man sit up. All that time, he kept his men in the Kuebelwagen on full alert. " Meinen, take the field glasses and sweep the horizon. Let me know if you see anything." He turned to the stranger.

"Who are you and what are you doing here?"

"I'm Oberleutnant zur See Gottfried Hagen, " the man whispered. He took another drink from the canteen Behnke held out. " I was a British prisoner. I stole the motorcycle. Are there any pursuers? We have to get back. Do you have other troops? They'll catch up with us. "

"Peace, peace, " Behnke consoled the man. "Don't worry. We'll get you back safe and sound. You must have eluded them. Good job."

"Meinen, keep looking," the Sergeant ordered. " Henkel, come here and help me load the Lieutenant into the car. " After this was accomplished, Behnke walked over to the motorcycle. There was no way to take it along in the Kuebelwagen, but it should not be left for the British to repair and reuse. Anything the enemy lost was a gain for the Fatherland.

Behnke noted the dispatch case attached behind the driver's seat. He opened it. It was filled with papers. "Hm, this, we must take along. Intelligence could use it. " After taking the dispatch case, Behnke opened the gas tank and threw a lit match into it. There was a small fizzle but nothing more. " You must have been riding on fumes the last few kilometers, " Behnke told the lieutenant, then he threw a hand grenade at the motorcycle.

The explosion destroyed the vehicle.

Behnke took careful note of the mileage on his car to be able to report accurately where he had found the naval officer. "Time to go back", he ordered.

Hauptmann Raederer was one of the intelligence officers on General Rommel's staff. He spoke English fluently, and had taken a quick look at the contents of the dispatch case. " Gold, pure gold," he muttered. " If it's true. Now let's have a look at this naval officer who brought us this treasure."

Oberleutnant zur See Hagen was stretched out on his bed in the field Lazarett - the infirmary. Raederer sat down next to him. "It's all right, nurse," he waved the male nurse away. " I'll take care of him."

"Well, Kamarad, tell me about your adventures. But first, how do you feel?"

Hagen tried to sit up, but collapsed again.

"I'll live," he croaked. " Can you get words to my parents that I'm safe? I'd be so grateful."

"Of course, Kamarad. Give me their address. I'll get a message out immediately."

"Helmut Hagen, 12 Pestalozzigasse, St. Poelten, Ostmark. And thank you very much."

"I thought I detected an Austrian accent. " Hauptmann Raederer smiled. "How did you get into the Navy from landlocked Austria?"

"My father was a naval officer in the old Austro-Hungarian Navy and told me so much about life at sea that I wanted to try it too. When the Fuehrer brought Austria home into the Reich, my chance came. I enlisted immediately. My father still had some connections that got me into officer's candidate school. May I ask where I am? "

"You are in the forward depot of the Africa Corps. We are very close to the Libyan-Egyptian border. With any luck, we'll be at Suez soon. Come, let me help you up."

Hauptmann Raederer assisted the young man up from the cot and led him to the door of the tent. He opened the tent flap. In the brutal desert sunshine, large numbers of gasoline trucks and tank carriers were parked, covered with camouflage netting.

"This enables us to move so swiftly, " Raederer said with pardonable pride. "When the orders come down from the General, you will see how quickly this depot can be moved. But now, to you. How did you get here?"

"I served on the Schnell-Boot Haifisch off Crete. We were sunk by a British destroyer. Only three of us survived, only three of my good comrades."

"Take it slow. I understand your sorrow, " Hauptmann Raederer patted the naval officer on the shoulder.

"We were picked up by the destroyer and taken to a large port. I assume it was Alexandria. As we were marched down the gangplank, I saw a motorcycle with the engine running. The driver was standing next to it talking to someone. I own a motorcycle myself, it's an old hobby of mine. This gave me an idea. I vaulted over the railing into the seat of the motorcycle, kicked the driver who was trying to hold on to it, and took off."

"There must have been pursuit? "

"Of course there was. But the streets are very narrow and winding, and I could get away from foot pursuit easily. Cars had trouble following me in those streets. Fortunately there did not seem to be any other motorcycles around. "

"What an adventure," Hauptmann Raederer looked admiringly at the young officer. "And then?"

"Once I had found that there was little pursuit, I started to head West, figuring that that was my chance to encounter our own troops. I passed a large number of British troops, but no one paid much attention to me. I guess they couldn't imagine that an enemy could be riding in their midst. Eventually, I left all British troops behind, and just kept going West. I just about ran out of fuel, when I met the patrol. And apart from dehydration and too much sun, I feel fine. "

"Just one more question, and then I'll let you rest, Kamarad, while I see about contacting your parents. What about the dispatch case? "

"What dispatch case? " Hagen asked.

"You don't know? On the back of your motorcycle, there was a dispatch case containing enormously valuable information regarding British troop dispositions. I wouldn't want to be in the shoes of the dispatch rider who allowed you to get away with that. Now rest, my friend. I'll be in to see you again."

* * *

General Erwin Rommel had already demonstrated the qualities which had made him the most popular officer in the German Army and eventually brought him a Field Marshall's baton. In the few months since he took command of the Africa Corps, he had reorganized it into a superb fighting force, defeated the British in a major tank battle, and was now threatening Egypt and the Suez Canal. At his staff meeting, in his tent located as far forward as possible, he listened to Hauptmann Raederer's report with his usual courtesy.

"If the dispatches are accurate, " Hauptmann Raederer finished, " we are facing three extra divisions we knew nothing about, two divisions of Gurkhas from India, and one Anzac division. And they have formed a defensive line along the border from the Mediterranean South to Khan Shaar."

Oberst Wedemeyer, Rommel's chief of intelligence, interjected: "Indeed, if the dispatches are accurate. They may be a trick. In 1917, a small British force besieged the

Turks in Beer-Sheba, which, at the time, was considered impregnable. There was a cavalry skirmish near the fortress, and a British dispatch case was found by the Turks after the fight. From its contents the Turks gathered that a major British force was approaching and they abandoned the fortress without a struggle. There was of course no such force. It was all a trick. I know, because I was there as a German liaison officer, and I was unable to dissuade my Turkish counterpart from his cowardly action."

"It all depends on the bona fides of Oberleutnant Hagen, Herr Oberst." Hauptmann Raederer replied. " I am inclined to believe that he is who he says he is, but it will take us at least three days to get confirmation from OKW (Oberkommando der Wehrmacht - Supreme military headquarters)."

"We can't take the time. Waiting may be just what the British want us to do. " Rommel decided. "Let's have another look at the maps.

There is a wadi just South of Khan Shaar. If this is a trick, it would be the logical way for us to approach to avoid the concentration of forces further North, and the British will be waiting for us there. If it is not, this would be an excellent place to cross the border and then roll them up from the South where they do not expect us. This is what we will do. Our main force will proceed with all possible dispatch to here, " the General pointed to a spot on the map. " In the meantime, send out patrols in strength to probe the British positions both North and South of Khan Shaar. Depending on what they find, we will strike where it will do us the most good. Any questions? "

"Only one." Oberst Blach, Chief of Procurement, spoke up. " We are getting very short on gasoline. By moving this far South, we risk running out of supplies."

"We will get more supplies from the enemy." General Rommel decided with his usual boldness. " This is our chance to strike a major blow, and we must take it."

* * *

"Well, how do you feel now, Hagen?" Hauptmann Raederer sat down next to Hagen's cot.

"Almost like a new man." The Naval Officer sat up. " I'm ready for action. What happens to me now? "

"Well, we'll send you back to headquarters with the next transport and then you'll be able to rejoin your branch of the service. In the meantime, I have notified OKW of your unexpected visit to us, and have asked them specifically to contact your parents. You should be leaving in the morning. We're just about ready to attack and non- essential personnel and wounded will be sent back."

"Attack? I wish I could join you. "

"Wrong service for that, my friend. Too bad, serving under General Rommel is a privilege. The man is a military genius and a great officer."

* * *

It is cold in the desert night. The heat of the sun dissipates quickly, the sterile sands do not store it for any length of time. Most of the troops trying to sleep before the action promised for the morning were huddled in their blankets or, if rank permitted, in their tents. Only a solitary sentry or two paced the perimeter of the forward depot.

In the hour after midnight, when the human metabolism is at its lowest ebb, a ghost-like figure emerged silently from the small tent which served as a field hospital. He looked around - the moon was just a sliver in the sky, but multitudes of stars were visible, far more than could be seen from the great cities of the world. They gave off sufficient light, so the man could identify his surroundings.

The field hospital tent was located at the side of what appeared to be a gigantic parking lot: forward several tank trucks, obviously filled with gasoline, and a number of other smaller trucks, filled with cans clearly containing the same product; behind them , a number of battle tanks and tank carriers. In the rear, a number of other trucks. " Normal doctrine." the man known as Hagen muttered, " the gasoline and the ammunition trucks separated as much as possible."

He made his way to the rear of the parking area, keeping in the shadows as much as possible. When a sentry came by, a distance away, he ducked under a truck to keep out of sight. Eventually, he reached the last row of trucks. He vaulted into one of them and began to search its contents. "Food, only rations, " he muttered. Out of that truck and into the next, and then the next again. Finally he found what he had been looking for. A case of hand grenades. He pried open the case, and distributed as many hand grenades as possible around his body. Fortunately, contrary to the British and American models, German grenades all have handles. Easily fifteen or sixteen fit into his belt by the handles, others inside his shirt and jacket pockets.

Carefully, oh very carefully, he eased himself out of his truck.

"I am very disappointed in you, Hagen or whatever your real name is. " a voice addressed him. Hauptmann Raederer stood before him, a Luger pistol pointed directly at his stomach. " I really believed you, but I had to make sure. I would dearly like to kill you now, you traitor, but I think the General would like the answers to some questions first."

"You wouldn't want to shoot me here, and explode all these, " Kurt Auster pointed at the hand grenades surrounding his body. "Remember, there's an ammunition truck behind me."

Raederer hesitated for a moment. Then he lowered his pistol and pointed it a Kurt's knee. "Very well, but I warn you, I'm an excellent shot. I'll shoot you in the legs if you do not obey instructions. Now, move away from the truck."

"No."

"No? You dare? Very well. Sentry, sentry." Raederer called out.

At that point, Kurt jumped. Raederer's gun went off. Kurt felt a white hot flash of pain in his thigh. He ignored it as best he could, pulled one of the hand grenades from his belt, and pummeled the German officer with all his strength in the face and head. At the same time, with his other hand, he grabbed Raederer's gun hand and tried to force it away from him. Raederer fell backward and Kurt straddled him. He grabbed at the Hauptmann's gun hand with both hands and managed to turn the gun toward the German's head. It went off. The body under Kurt relaxed.

Kurt took a deep breath and got up. His thigh was throbbing painfully, but he could put weight on it. Obviously, sentries must have heard the two shots, if not Raederer's cry. Time to move.

Kurt armed the hand grenade with which he had attacked the Captain by pulling its pin, and threw it into the truck. Whoosh - a mighty explosion - shrapnel, flames in all direction. Kurt had taken shelter behind another truck, but even there he was not immune. Some debris hit him. None, fortunately, too damaging. He noted in the glare of the fire, that the ammunition truck he had destroyed had caused two other trucks to explode.

Ignoring the pain in his thigh, he raced forward toward the gasoline carriers, throwing hand grenades into other trucks as he passed them. Behind him, explosion after explosion. In front, finally a sentry. The man looked at him in astonishment.

"Quick man, fire, alert the post." Kurt yelled out to him. The soldier turned and ran off, calling out : " Sergeant of the Guard, fire, fire."

Kurt continued his progress. He stopped throwing hand grenades into the trucks he passed. *They may be ration trucks. No sense wasting grenades.* He reached the line of tanks, and finally the gasoline trucks. Running from one to the other, he lobbed hand grenades into them as quickly as he could move. Whoosh - whoosh - explosion after explosion. Finally, he ran out of grenades. He turned and looked around. In the desert night, dozens of major fires flared, explosions continued here and there, soldiers were shouting. He saw running figures outlined against the flames.

With a grim smile Kurt turned and started to walk East along the dunes, into the desert. His leg throbbed but he could walk. *Time to look at it later*, he thought. *Now to get away and find my support patrol.*

* * *

General Rommel listened calmly.

"Eight casualties, three lightly wounded, four severely wounded from flying shrapnel and debris, one not expected to survive. And Hauptmann Raederer - murdered. Six gasoline tankers totally destroyed, four ammunition trucks destroyed, two others badly damaged, several more in varying states of damage but we expect to be able to repair them."

"Well," the general sighed, " that takes care of our plans."

"With your permission, Herr General, " Oberst Wedemeyer interjected, "may I send patrols in force to capture the British spy?"

Rommel thought for a moment. " No. We do not know how far the nearest British troops are. I can't imagine the spy did all this without knowing that they are close. I do not want to risk any of our men and have them encounter an overwhelming force for the sake of catching one man."

"But he murdered Hauptmann Raederer. We've got to get him." Oberst Wedemeyer protested.

"I share your wish for revenge," the general said, " but it is not a priority. Right now, we have to make other decisions. Obviously, we cannot proceed with our attack, we certainly do not have enough gasoline. How long before we can be resupplied, Oberst Blach?"

"I'm afraid it will be at least a week before we can get more gasoline from Tobruk. We are very short there, and we expected a new shipment by ship only three days from now. " Blach sighed. " I just hope it arrives safely, and that the British Navy hasn't intercepted it."

"Very well, we have no choice." General Rommel decided. "We will retreat toward Tobruk, and try again as soon as we are resupplied. And since the British may be approaching, let's move. Now. Understood?"

The chorus acknowledging General Rommel's order was far less enthusiastic than when he had proposed crossing the Egyptian border the day before.

* * *

Hot, yellow sun. Hot, yellow sand as far as the eye could see. Low dunes, high dunes. Trudging up a dune, trudging down a dune. *Where are they? Did I get lost? They were supposed to be here and to look out for me? Where are they?*

The leg had been bleeding but the blood had coagulated. Still, there was pain. *That's good, if there were no feelings I'd worry. Should have taken a hat. Well, a piece of shirttail will do, and it might protect my eyes a bit. Should have taken a canteen. Should have. My father always complained. Should have bought butter when butter was cheap. Should have sold cheese, when cheese was expensive. Should have stayed home with my parents. There it was nice and cool, and plenty to drink. Don't think of drinking. Keep looking out for our soldiers. Where are they?*

Hard to breathe. The pain in the leg is getting worse. It looks infected. I don't want to touch it. I don't want to look at it. Just keep going. One foot and another foot. Hot, dry, hot, dry.

No pursuit? Why not? They must know I got away. Too much confusion? Or are they afraid to meet my support troops? If they only knew I can't find them myself.

Fell down. Should rest a while. Not in the sun. Up, find shade. No shade anywhere. Romantic African desert. Where are the romantic sheiks? Where are the camels or dromedaries? What's the difference between a camel and a dromedary? Who knows? Do they know? Do they care?

Breathing is hard. Lungs on fire. Must stop. Can't stop breathing, you idiot? Why not? Anyone tried it? One foot and another foot.

Sun is going down behind me. Been doing this all day? Well, sun behind me means I'm going East like I'm supposed to. But where are they?

Shadows getting longer. Good, soon it'll be dark and cooler. Too cold, perhaps. Keep on. Up a dune. Down a dune. Legs are heavy. Dragging injured leg. Won't support me much longer. Never knew legs are so heavy. Up a dune. Down a dune.

Dark now. Why am I not cold? Feverish? Good, that'll keep me warm. No one ever thought fever was good for you. New discovery. Must report it to the world. Fever keeps you warm. Up a dune. Down a dune.

Better lie down for a while. Get lost in the desert without the sun. If I really were a sailor, I could steer by the stars. Starlight, starbright. Up a dune. Down a dune. Just lie down for a while.

Sun is hot again. I must have slept. That's good. Up and at'em. Leg still hurts. Hard to walk on. All blown up. Drag it, come on, drag it. Up a dune, down a dune. Toward the sun. East. East.

Papa and Mama are waiting. I'm late for Shabbat dinner. Go on. Can't make them wait. He's starting the Kiddush prayer. Don't start without me. I'll be there, I'll be there, I'm coming. Up a dune. Down a dune.

Can't. Can't. Leg collapsing. Wait for me, Papa. Please don't start without me. " Wahi erev we wahi boker. And it was evening and it was morning - "See, Papa, I can begin the Kiddush myself. But wait for me, wait for me.

Kurt collapsed. The sun burned, but he could no longer move.

* * *

In 1917, during what was then called the Great War, Britain was in desperate straits. Acetone, which was essential in the production of munitions had always been imported from Germany, and now with Germany the great enemy, if a substitute could not be found, Britain would be unable to continue fighting. Russian born Chaim Weizmann, the great chemist and Zionist leader, was able to develop synthetic cordite and thus solve the problem. As a reward for his efforts, he asked and received, a declaration issued by Lord Balfour, the British Foreign Secretary, which said:" His Majesty's Government view with favor the establishment in Palestine of a national home for the Jewish people."

This declaration was issued on November 2, 1917. Of course, the British were offering to give away something they did not possess. Palestine had been a Turkish province for more than four hundred years, and was governed by the Sultan in Istanbul. On the other hand, the Turks were allies of Germany and Austria-Hungary in the Great War, and the British were fighting them in the Middle East. In fact, on December 4, 1917, British General Allenby dislodged the Turks from Jerusalem, and in the final peace treaties which settled the war, Britain took on Palestine as a League of Nations Mandate.

As Nazi Anti-Semitism began to rage, more and more German Jews attempted to enter Palestine. About sixty thousand succeeded out of a total German population of 600 000.

But the Arabs did not like this. There were major Arab riots in 1936 and subsequently. A British Royal Commission recommended partition of Palestine into Jewish and Arab sections, but the British Government did not agree. So they issued a "White Paper" in 1939 which limited Jewish immigration into Palestine to 15,000 souls per year for five years with a total cut-off after that time. This, at a time, when the survival of European Jews depended on a place to which they could flee.

How the British attitude had changed since the Balfour declaration was issued can best be illustrated by a comment in a private letter written in September 1941 by Anthony Eden, Britain's Foreign Secretary, to his private secretary Oliver Harvey: " If we must have preferences, let me whisper in your ear, that I prefer Arabs to Jews."

The Yishuv, the Jewish settlement in Palestine, consisted of fewer than five hundred thousand people at the beginning of the war. David Ben Gurion, the Head of the Jewish Agency, the quasi government of the Yishuv made a famous statement: " We will fight the war as if there were no White Paper, and we will fight the White Paper as if there were no war."

Vichy France signed a protocol with Germany allowing the Germans access to all naval and air bases in Lebanon and Syria, which had been French protectorates since the end of the first world war. Germany also got access to the West African port of Dakar. Iraq, which had been under British tutelage, revolted and a pro-German government was set up.

Besieged North and South, the British Authorities in Palestine had no choice but to allow members of the Yishuv to participate in the British Africa Corps. 130 000 Jewish settlers volunteered, but the British were reluctant to arm and train Jewish settlers with whom, they knew, they would ultimately find themselves at odds. They finally accepted 30 000 men, who formed Jewish companies in which Hebrew was spoken among the men, but who served under British command.

These Jewish companies participated in the successful invasions of Syria, Lebanon and Iraq, which resulted in British dominance of these countries. 20 000 Vichy French soldiers were permitted to return to France from Syria and Lebanon. The Grand Mufti of Jerusalem, Haj Amin al Hussein, who had been supportive of the pro-German efforts in Iraq, fled to Berlin where he met with Hitler, and where he spent the rest of the war broadcasting propaganda to the Arab world on behalf of Germany.

Other Jewish companies fought on the Southern front against Rommel's famed Africa Corps. One patrol from one of these companies was now probing the Libyan desert to determine the extent of the German advance.

They were driving an American made jeep - one of the first to reach their area, now that the cornucopia of American production was fully functioning on behalf of the British. It was only a two man patrol, but a machine gun mounted on the jeep gave them a considerable amount of firepower.

In front of them - the trackless dunes of the Libyan desert. Behind them, the same. Equipped with a compass and familiar with the desert from their birth, the two soldiers felt completely comfortable in their desolate surroundings. Both of them were sabras - the term used for Jews born in the Holy Land, named after the fruit of the cactus - prickly on the outside, soft on the inside.

"Hold it, Yitzhok," the driver said. "There's something lying at the bottom of the dune there. Let's go closer."

"It looks like a man, Moshe." Yitzhok had taken out his binoculars and was studying the figure lying on the sand.

They approached carefully. Yitzhok descended from the jeep and approached the body, while Moshe stood at readiness behind the machine gun looking all around.

"He seems to be dead." Yitzhok reported. " It's a German, but how odd, he seems to be wearing a naval uniform. What would he be doing here?"

"Careful, the body may be booby-trapped. Check that out first, and then perhaps, we'll find some clues in his pocket."

Yitzhok stood as far away from the body as he could, and pushed it with his rifle so that it would move. In this manner, he hoped, any explosives attached to the body would go off without hurting him. Suddenly, he stopped and approached the body.

"What is it, Yitzhok?" Moshe called out.

"I think I heard a groan. Maybe he's still alive." Yitzhok knelt close to the body and put his ear on the man's chest. "Yes, he's alive. I can hear his heart beating."

He took out his canteen, and tried to give the man some water. Experienced in desert lore, he started out by wetting the German's lips, then slowly allowing some water to trickle into the man's mouth as it opened.

"It looks as if he's been shot. Look at his leg - it's all blown up, must be infected. I think we ought to get him back to base as soon as possible."

"He's a German, Yitzhok." Moshe said. "Why bother saving his life? We have a mission to perform. Let's just leave him. Take what's in his pockets and we'll see whether there's any information there."

"No, Moshe. We can't do that. He's our responsibility now. We must save his life if we can."

"Oh, you're such a Jew." Moshe smiled. "Do you think the Nazis would feel the same way about a Jew they found like that?"

"But that is the difference between us. And don't tell me you are not proud that there is such a difference. Now, come on, help me get him into the jeep. And then let's get back as fast as we can, before he dies on us."

The two men lifted the German and installed him in the back seat of their vehicle. Moshe turned the jeep around and they started to drive back, while Yitzhok continued to administer water to the dried lips of the man. The German began to swallow, first a little, than more, greedily, until Yitzhok withheld the water for fear of causing injury. The German began to babble - incomprehensible croaking sounds. Yitzhok bent over the man and tried to listen.

"I don't believe it. Moshe, do you know what he is saying?"

"He's singing the Nazi anthem. How would I know?" Moshe said irritably.

"No, my friend. He's saying the Friday night Broche. He's davening (praying) in Hebrew."

Moshe was so shocked that he brought the jeep to a screeching halt.

"What? A Jew in a Nazi uniform? And here, in the desert? There must be an explanation." He restarted the jeep and accelerated as much as possible.

* * *

The first time Kurt opened his eyes, he saw a giant fan overhead, circling, circling to move the stale, hot air. A moment of following the fan with his eyes, and he was asleep again. The next time, he looked a little closer. He was in a bed - there were sheets, there was a pillow in a pillowcase. He didn't remember the last time he had slept in a bed. Trying to figure out this important problem, he fell asleep again.

When he woke up he found that he was enormously thirsty. He looked around again. His leg was bandaged up to his groin. There was something connected to his arm, from which some liquid appeared to be dripping into him. He saw that he was in a very large room, with white washed walls, and there were other beds occupied by recumbent figures to his left and to his right.

Bright sunlight came in from several large windows, so bright that he had trouble making out the figure that bent over him.

"Oh, good, you're awake." The figure revealed herself as a nurse in a starched white uniform. She sat down on a chair next to Kurt's bed, helped him lift his head and allowed him to drink from a glass of water. " Not too much all at once," she said, " you've got to take it slow."

Gratefully Kurt laid back on his pillow. "Where am I? " he croaked.

"You're in good hands," the nurse answered. "You're in the military hospital in Alexandria. I'm Sister Roberts, and I've been taking care of you for the last two weeks. Doctor Tanner, who operated on you, will be in to see you shortly. You'll be fine."

"Two weeks!" It was too much for Kurt. He closed his eyes and slept again.

When he woke up again, he felt much more alert.

Sister Roberts helped him sit up and fed him his first meal of porridge and soft vegetables - slowly and carefully. Eventually, Doctor Tanner made his appearance. He examined Kurt from top to bottom.

"You are a very lucky young man," the doctor said. "When we got you, your fever was going through the roof, and the infection from your bullet wound made me fear that you might have to lose your leg. I was also very concerned about the effect of sunstroke on your nervous system, particularly your optical nerves. Fortunately, you have a very strong constitution."

"What about my leg, Doctor?"

"We saved it for you. We had to operate twice, first to get the bullet out and then to ease the infection. But you'll be alright. You'll need some rehabilitative therapy, but I see no reason why you won't regain complete use of the leg eventually. And now you must rest again. I'll see you tomorrow."

The next time Kurt woke up he had another visitor. Brigadier Thornton was seated in the chair next to his bed.

"I'm glad to see you're recovering, Auster."

"Thank you, sir."

"I know the results of your mission, but I want to know the details. Are you strong enough to report?"

"Yes, sir." And Kurt recounted briefly what he had done. He ended with " I can't imagine why I didn't meet my support when I left the German encampment. I thought I was going in the right direction where they were supposed to be."

Thornton did not reply, but a shadow passed over his face.

"Now I understand." the Brigadier said after a moment. "We knew that Rommel withdrew toward Tobruk without attempting to attack. I was hoping that your disinformation package had that effect, but it seemed too good to be true. Frankly, the best that I had expected was that it would give us a few more days to prepare for the assault while Rommel tested the information in the dispatch case with combat patrols and aircraft. You achieved his total withdrawal by destroying his vital fuel supplies. That gave us the time we needed to resupply ourselves. God job, Auster."

"Thank you, sir. May I ask how I got here? "

"You were found by a patrol from the Jewish companies from Palestine attached to us here. Apparently you spoke in those people's language in your delirium, so instead of bringing you to the German prisoner of war camp, they brought you here and insisted on getting you the best medical attention immediately. Eventually, word reached me about the mysterious German naval officer who was a Jew. But you really owe your life to that patrol. I think they're planning to visit you when their duties permit. Now rest some more. We'll talk again."

With a friendly clap on Kurt's shoulder, Brigadier Thornton took his leave.

* * *

"Memo to Admiral Morse.
From Brigadier Thornton.
Top Secret - For your eyes only.
Following your instructions I sent the subject of Operation Uriah " in the forefront of the hottest battle and retreated from him, that he may be struck down and die."

Contrary to expectations, the subject accomplished his mission superbly, and managed to escape with his life, albeit severely injured.

As you will see from the enclosed report, he has rendered a signal service to our country. Personally, I would be honored to have him under my command at any time.

Assuming that the reason for your concern is information the subject has and may disseminate wittingly or unwittingly, I interrogated him several times with great intensity, and was unable to obtain any but the most cursory information about his background.

In view of the subject's evident discretion, and in view of his service to our cause, I urge you to reconsider your plans for him. I will watch his further progress in our ranks with considerable interest.

I am always at your service."

Admiral Morse finished reading the memo and the attached document, and walked over to the window. He stared out at the view of the Park with unseeing eyes. He was a hard man, but not an unjust one.

* * *

Kurt was seated in a wheelchair on the verandah of the hospital. Before him a well kept lawn stretched out to the shores of the Mediterranean, where long, low waves broke on a wide, sandy beach. *Oh, if I could just have a swim, that would be delightful.* But he looked at his bandaged leg, which was a long way from healing, and knew that he had to abandon that idea for a while.

"So, Chaver, you look a lot better today." Kurt looked up at the originator of the statement. He saw a dark-haired, clean-shaven man of his own age, in the uniform of a British soldier. He was of slightly less than average height, but looked very fit. Next to him, another British soldier looking almost like a twin brother to the first, smiled and stretched out his hand.

"I'm Moshe, and this is Yitzhok. We found you in the desert."

Kurt took both men's hands into both of his. "I owe you my life, " he said. " I can never thank you enough."

"Thank your parents for teaching you to pray, Chaver." Moshe said. "We couldn't believe that a Jew was in German uniform, so we brought you here just out of curiosity. So, tell us."

"Don't mind him, Chaver." Yitzhok smiled. "He'd save a kitten, if he could, so it was no big deal. But tell us anyway."

They sat down next to Kurt. He saw the Star of David on their uniforms, heard them call him "Chaver" -

friend in Hebrew - and felt enormously close to these two representatives of the Jewish settlement in Palestine.

"I'm a serving British officer, " Kurt said, " but I was born in Vienna where the Nazis killed my parents. I crossed over to the Africa Corps in the guise of a German naval officer with some disinformation. When I escaped to rejoin my support unit, I must have gotten lost. I never would have made it back, if you hadn't found me. Thank you, again."

Moshe's and Yitzhok's eyes met. "That is why there was no attack. You must have done more than just supply disinformation. We expected to be overrun by the Nazis after our recent defeat. Now, there is time to regroup and to get reinforcements. And you did that? But why as a naval officer?"

"Well," Kurt smiled. " If I had been disguised as an Africa Corps member, they would have found me out right away. My cover story as a naval officer was pretty accurate. I took the identity of a German who, in fact, is a prisoner of war here."

"So, Chaver, when will you join us in Palestine? We need people like you to build our state." Yitzhok said warmly.

Kurt felt very much at home with his two rescuers. " I will come. You can count on me. But first, we have to defeat the Germans. Now tell me about Palestine."

"Well," Moshe said. "It's hot, there are deserts and swamps, the Arabs keep attacking and killing us, the British favor the Arabs and stop us from defending ourselves, we are short of money and weapons and supplies. All in all we are in a mess. But it's ours, and we'll have our state. The first Jewish state in two thousand years. We'll have it."

"And I'll be there with you. " Kurt said enthusiastically. " I promise."

They talked for a long time. Kurt learned much he had not known about the Yishuv, and more about the two men he now considered friends. He was eager to join them. But he looked at his leg, and knew that it would be a long time, before he would be of use to anyone.

* * *

Brigadier Thornton came to visit Kurt again.

"Good morning, Captain Auster," he said jovially, clasping Kurt's hand.

"Sir?"

"You've been promoted. " Brigadier Thornton smiled. "It's the least we can do after your exploit. In fact, I've also proposed you for a decoration, but we British are pretty chary about handing out medals. Promoting you was within my power, and it's done."

"Thank you, sir. Thank you very much."

The Brigadier pulled up a chair. "You have done more than you know when you destroyed Rommel's fuel supplies, Auster. We have ascertained from other sources that Rommel had planned to mount his attack further South, where we had practically no troops. He had to change his plans when you eliminated his gasoline supplies. We would have been in very serious trouble otherwise. Why, there were some Egyptians in Cairo who were already making plans for Rommel's triumphant entry into the capital. But now, let's talk about you, Captain Auster. "

"Yes, sir."

"Your doctors tell me that you need several months of rehabilitation to get your leg functioning again. There are much better facilities back home. A hospital ship is leaving tomorrow and you'll be on it. When you have fully recovered, I would be pleased to have you return here and serve with me. I will advise Admiral Morse accordingly. How do you feel about that?"

"I will gladly serve wherever I can do the most damage to the Nazis."

"Spoken like a true British officer. I'm delighted to hear you say that. Well, good luck, and I hope we'll serve together again." With a warm handshake, Brigadier Thornton left.

* * *

HMS Edith Cavell was named after the heroic British nurse who had ministered to many wounded soldiers in German occupied Belgium during the first World War, and who had been shot by the Germans as a spy toward the end of that conflict. The name was appropriate for a hospital ship.

Newly minted Captain Kurt Auster found himself in officer's country on the ship in a cabin shared by only one other officer. While he had been provided with crutches, he had also been instructed that they were not to be used on shipboard where his footing was not very secure. Remembering the problems Adam Bede encountered on the Drake, he took this advice very much to heart. He spent his nights in the cabin. During the long summer days in the Mediterranean he was carried to a lounge chair on deck. He enjoyed observing the two destroyers moving on station next to the hospital ship, and occasionally circling it like terriers protecting their charges against enemy attack. And he spent a lot of time staring out to sea and thinking.

He had found himself waking frequently with Hauptmann Raederer's face before him. Of the Germans he had killed, this was the first one with whom he had had a personal relationship, whose name he had known, and who had been extremely pleasant to him when he still had been regarded as a German officer. He knew nothing about Raederer's life, whether he had a wife or children, whether, even, he was an anti-Semitic Nazi or merely an obedient citizen of the German state. Kurt was fully aware of every justification he had in killing Raederer, but it still worried him. He knew that he had to come to terms with this problem, if he wanted to be able to continue to function effectively in the war against the people who had murdered his parents. So, he thought about it a lot. For " conscience does make cowards of us all."

He had been carried to his usual lounge chair on the forward deck by two attentive male nurses, and was watching the ship and her escorts approaching the great rock of Gibraltar prior to entering the Atlantic on her voyage North, when there was the sound of a klaxon from the bridge.

"Now hear this, now hear this," a loudspeaker announced. "This is the Captain speaking. We have just received word that Germany has attacked the Soviet Union on a wide front. I will advise the ship's complement when more information becomes available."

It was the 22nd of June 1941. Indeed, three million German soldiers on an eighteen hundred mile long front from the Arctic to the Black Sea, had begun their invasion of the Soviet Union. Operation Barbarossa had begun.

In Moscow, Joseph Stalin, the Soviet dictator who had signed a non-aggression pact with Hitler, was so stunned that he withdrew into an almost catatonic state for three days, until his subordinates pleaded with him to emerge and take command. During that time, and in subsequent weeks, German troops conquered a vast swath of Soviet territory. In short order, they were at the gates of Leningrad, stood before Moscow, had taken the entire Ukraine, and had reached Stalingrad on the Volga in the South.

The front-line troops were followed by Einsatztruppen, specialized SS and Police units, whose sole mission was to kill Jews. They acquitted themselves very well of this task.

After the Captain of HMS Edith Cavell finished speaking, there was an immediate babble of voices discussing this major development in the war. Captain Mollen, Kurt's roommate, who was lying on the lounge next to him, turned his badly scarred face toward Kurt and said : "This is great news. The Germans will come a cropper in Russia just like Napoleon did."

"I hope you're right." Kurt said. He always had difficulty facing Captain Mollen. The poor man had been in command of a tank during the last disastrous battle with the Africa Corps. A well aimed '88 artillery shell had destroyed his tank, and caused Captain Mollen to lose one leg, part of an arm, and an eye. In spite of that, he was a cheerful companion and always had interesting strategic theories on the conduct of the war.

"Of course, I'm right. The Germans will face General Winter, just like Napoleon's Grande Armee. And I wouldn't want to have to fight in a Russian winter," Mollen said, and with admirable self-depreciation added, " that is, if I could still fight anyone."

"I don't want to sound too pessimistic," Kurt responded, " but remember, in 1917 Germany defeated Russia."

"But there was a revolution in Russia, then."

"Yes, and what tells you there won't be one now? What, if some of the colonies of holy Mother Russia, such as the Ukraine take the side of Germany? You saw what happened with the Finns. They are not pro-German, but they fought against the Soviets. And the Baltic states? I fear we can't underestimate Hitler. If he invaded Russia, he must have at least a hope of winning."

"No, No." Mollen insisted. "This is the beginning of the end for the Huns. Mark my words. The only other thing that we need is for the United States to come in, just like in 1917. Then, we'll know we've got it won."

"I hope you're right."

* * *

While the conversations swirling around him continued to cover the topic of Germany's Russian invasion, Kurt had other concerns. With every mile that HMS Edith Cavell advanced toward England's green and pleasant shore, he came closer to Sarah.

I left her without a word after that lovely interlude in the garden. And then, I denounced her father and thwarted his plots. Of course, she does not know about my part in that. Or does she? I had to do it, how could I have remained inactive? One day, I will have to tell her that it is because of me that her father is being held incommunicado in a psychiatric hospital. Of course, I'm committed not to talk about this until well after the war. That's a long time from now. What kind of an honest relationship can there be between us, if I don't tell her? A relationship must be based on trust. Did she get my letter? Did she understand that I had no choice but to leave her? Her brother is a sailor and has to obey orders, she'll understand about orders in wartime.

What nonsense. You really think that there could be a serious relationship between the daughter of Lord Harrington and a penniless foreigner, a Jew? How absurd.

But she kissed me. And she permitted more than that. And she said, soon. That was a promise of sorts, wasn't it?

Well, if it was a promise for a fling, you missed the boat, my boy. And would that golden girl really go in just for a fling? I hardly think so, she's too good for that.

Why too good? What's so wrong with an honest enjoyment of sex? She certainly was passionate enough in the garden.

These thoughts kept Kurt busy. Of course, he came to no conclusion. He decided to contact Sarah as soon as possible after he had arrived at the rehabilitation hospital to which he was being sent, and to confront her immediately with the question that so bothered him. Did she love him at all?

While this strategic question was more in Kurt's mind then the German advances to the East, HMS Edith Clavell completed her voyage without incident. Kurt and a number of other wounded including Captain Mollen, were transferred to a rehabilitation hospital in the West Country, close to the rugged shoreline that had repelled many would-be invaders.

From the verandah of this hospital, Kurt saw a lawn sloping down to sharp and threatening cliffs. Occasional sprays of high waves battering against them sometimes obscured the view of an angry Atlantic when the winds were strong. Kurt considered the difference between this perspective and the similar but so different view from the hospital in Alexandria, and tried to draw a parallel between the stubbornness of the British and the soft submissiveness of the Egyptian Arabs. He was still prone to fast and unwarranted judgments.

The doctors and nurses who manned the rehabilitation hospital were very knowledgeable and experienced in their duties. They were also very stern and demanding taskmasters. Kurt spent a great deal of time exercising his leg, first in a whirlpool, then with various weights. He was able to get around quite comfortably on crutches now, and had been promised that he would be able to walk with the help of a cane fairly soon.

He had been kept so busy that it was several days before he had access to a telephone. His first call was to the Harrington estate.

"I would like to speak to Miss Sarah, please," he said with some trepidation.

"May I ask who is calling, sir?" The unmistakable dulcet tones of Sanders, the butler, came across the wires.

"Kurt Auster."

"I'm sorry, sir, but I have been instructed not to accept any calls from you."

Click. The phone was disconnected.

Hm. He has been instructed. By whom? By Sarah? By Carol? Kurt remembered that Sarah had mentioned working in a military hospital in Plymouth. After some difficulty, he was connected there.

"This is Captain Auster." - *might as well pull rank* - " I'd like to speak to the Matron supervising the nursing staff."

"This is Matron Hoyes. How can I help you?"

"I am looking for Sarah Harrington-Brown. Is she available?"

"Sarah has not been with us for some months."

"Can you tell me where I might find her?"

"No, I'm sorry. We do not give out personal information about our staff or former staff."

Click. Another hang-up.

Well, now it's up to Adam Bede. I wanted to call him anyway, and perhaps he can find Sarah for me.

It took two more days of effort before Kurt reached Adam Bede at home.

"Kurt! How wonderful. I've wondered what had become of you. I asked Admiral Morse, and he wouldn't tell me. You know that closemouthed bastard. All he said was that you were on a mission. Where are you? When will I see you?"

It warmed the cockles of Kurt's heart to receive a response like that.

"I'm somewhat incapacitated right now, Venerable. In fact, I'm in hospital. But, they tell me that I'll be out of here in another six to eight weeks. Perhaps, there's a chance that you might be able to visit me?"

"I'll make the chance. Of course. Where are you?"

Kurt told him. He wondered whether he should raise the question of Sarah on the telephone but decided that it was better to wait until he could see Adam face to face. He was sure that that inveterate gossip monger would have some information for him.

CHAPTER IX

The Queen! The Queen is coming for a visit! The hospital staff buzzed around, cleaning, scrubbing, painting. Uniforms were pressed, decorations were polished, areas that had not been dusted in months were given great attention. Queen Elizabeth was not only the consort of King George, but was revered because she had insisted on staying with her husband and her people in London throughout the worst of the Blitz. Even when bombs damaged part of Buckingham Palace, she had refused to leave.

On the great day, flags were flying, the doctors and nurses were dressed in their best, and even the uncertain weather cooperated. It was a beautiful hot day in late July. At the appointed hour three Rolls Royce limousines drew up at the entrance of the hospital, preceded and followed by a military escort. The Nursing Matron and the Chief of Surgery bowed low, while the youngest and most attractive member of the nursing staff presented the Queen with a bouquet of flowers. The Queen graciously accepted them and handed them to one of the several ladies - in- waiting who followed her.

Then there came a tour of the wards, with the Queen stopping at every bed with a kind word.

Kurt stood on his crutches next to his bed, dressed in his new and almost unused Captain's uniform. The Queen passed by with her entourage.

Then he saw her. It was Sarah. She followed the Queen, dressed in a high fashion summer frock. She looked as adorable as ever. Kurt called out to her: "Sarah, Sarah."

She turned and looked at him. Then she recognized him and hurried to his side, while the Queen and her entourage moved on.

"Kurt! You turn up in the oddest places. Are you all right?"

"I will be. It's so wonderful to see you, Sarah. I've thought about you so much. What are you doing here?"

Sarah looked at Kurt with some embarrassment. "You can see what I'm doing. I'm one of Her Majesty's ladies-in-waiting. It goes with my title."

"Harrington?"

"No, silly. I'm Lady Blamington now. Didn't you know? I married Cyril two months ago. Oh, it was a grand affair. The King and Queen came. It was in all the papers."

Married. She's married. Kurt turned away for a moment. Then he looked at Sarah again. " I can't congratulate you, I'm sorry. I love you and I thought you had some feelings for me."

"You can say that when you almost raped Carol right after being with me?"

"What? Is that what Carol told you? And you believed her? "

Sarah did not answer.

Kurt dropped his crutches and hopped on one foot over to Sarah. He took her by her shoulders. " Look at me, Sarah. Did you believe her?"

She did look at him. And she said. " No, I did not. Not really. But what difference did it make? I couldn't give up my rank." She drew herself up. " My husband is twelfth in line in succession to the throne. I'm Lady-in-waiting to the Queen. And Cyril stood by me when my father…"

Kurt turned away. He almost fell, and had to hold on to the bedpost. " I really thought you cared for me."

"But of course I do, my pet. My being married has nothing to do with that. I'm very fond of you, you know. You must come and see me in London when you're well. Cyril is at sea so much. I'd love to be with you. I remember our last evening together too." Sarah blushed a little as she said that.

"I see." Kurt said slowly. "Will you give a message to Carol for me?"

"To Carol? Of course."

"Just tell her, that she was right. And now, good luck to you."

Kurt turned his back and stared out the window. A little non-plussed, Sarah looked at Kurt's back, and with a small shrug ran out to catch up with the Queen.

Admiral Morse called his aid into his office.

"I want you to telephone Captain Auster in the rehabilitation hospital."

"Captain Auster, sir?"

"Yes, Captain. My old friend, Brigadier Thornton got him promoted. He deserved something, he did a good job in Egypt, but a promotion like that was far too much. I think Thornton did it out of guilt. I thought he was tougher than that. I have to keep that in mind."

"Guilt, sir? Why?"

The Admiral looked at the pretty Wren. "Never mind. You know a lot, but it's better that you don't know everything. Now, here's what I want you to tell Auster, and be sure to talk to him personally by phone, nothing in writing, is that clear?"

"Yes, sir."

"Tell him I'm very pleased with his accomplishments in the desert - use that phrase; that I wish him a speedy recovery and that I want him to report to me as soon as he is released from hospital. And, this is vital, remind him in the strongest terms, that he is not to talk about anything, anything, he has done, whether in Africa, on the continent, or in Britain. He must be silent about everything. Emphasize the part about Britain."

Ensign Diana Fordyce acknowledged her orders.

* * *

"May I talk to you frankly?" Adam Bede had come to visit and had found a very depressed Kurt. Now, they were walking along the paths around the hospital, that is Adam was walking and Kurt was trying to keep up with him on his crutches.

"Of course, you may." Kurt shrugged.

"I think of you as a dear friend," Adam continued. "I admire you greatly. I do not know the details of any of your missions, but it is my understanding that you have acquitted yourself extremely well. I respect the fact that you yourself have told me nothing about them, nor for that matter has

Admiral Morse, but he has indicated that he thinks very highly of you. But, I am more than twice your age, and I will presume on our friendship to tell you to forget it."

"Forget what?"

"Your romantic attachment to someone who never existed."

"Never existed? " Kurt grew angry, but restrained himself. Adam was his friend, and meant well.

"Please answer me " Adam said " How much time altogether did you spend with Sarah?"

Kurt hesitated. "All right, altogether probably seven days. But that doesn't mean anything."

Adam continued. " Tell me her favorite color. Tell me what she likes to eat for breakfast. When is her birthday? Tell me where she went to school. Tell me what kind of books she likes to read - or does she read? Does she prefer ballet or theater? What kind of music does she listen to?"

"I see your point." Kurt said. "It's true we didn't have much time together, but she could have waited to give us a chance."

"Why should she? Look at her position. Her father in disgrace and in a mental hospital, her stepmother urging her into a most favorable marriage with a man of her class whom she knew well and certainly liked if not loved; a marriage that would put her at the top of British society, - and you expect her to give all this up to get to know a penniless foreigner? Please forgive me if I sound harsh, but if you understand Sarah, you may not be so hurt. Tout comprendre est tout pardonner."

"And a week ago, she just about offered to take me into her bed. And she - just married."

"More fool you, if you did not take her up on it. I didn't detect such scruples with your other friends. Oh, I don't know who they were, but I certainly know that you indulged in the joyous sport. And why not? But Sarah, whom you don't know, is supposed to be pure so that she may deserve your love. Well, that's not the way of the world."

"Of course, you're right." Kurt said slowly. "But that does not mean I'm any less disappointed."

"Of course, you are. But I will say only one more thing and then not presume on our friendship any more. You have set yourself the task, as all of us have, of getting rid of Hitler and his war machine. That is our priority. In the meantime, like all warriors of old, take your pleasures wherever and whenever you find them but ignore sentimental attachments until the war is won. That is my heartfelt advice to you. I hope you'll take it. And now, to another subject."

Kurt had listened attentively to the Venerable Bede. But his absolutely unbeatable logic did nothing to subdue the pain of Kurt's broken heart. At least not that day.

* * *

September of 1941 was a beautiful month in Britain. The Autumn rains had not come yet, flowers bloomed everywhere, and London had begun to recover from the Blitz. The bombed areas were neat looking piles of debris, streets had been repaired, and people slept in their own beds - those at least, who had beds to sleep in.

The German Juggernaut had continued its advance into the Soviet Union, and behind the troops came the SS Einsatztruppen and the Police Battalions. In less than three months, over 200,000 Jews had been murdered in the occupied territories. In two September days alone, over 33,000 Jews from Kiev had been shot in a ravine called Babi Yar, near that city. But the world did not yet know the extent of Germany's crimes.

Kurt's leg had not healed quite as fast as he had hoped, and it was late October before he was discharged from the hospital and was able to return to Adam Bede's rooms in London. He still walked with a cane, and had strict instructions to perform a number of leg strengthening exercises daily, but at least he was able to report to Admiral Morse.

Ensign Diana Fordyce welcomed him warmly, and he was admitted very quickly into the inner sanctum.

The Admiral received him in a very friendly manner.

"Brigadier Thornton has reported to me fully about your accomplishment. It was certainly lucky that you were in the right spot at the right time to delay Rommel's invasion plans."

Lucky? Kurt thought, but did not voice a reply.

"How is your leg?" The Admiral continued.

"I'm sure, I'll be able to undertake any mission you choose to send me on in short order, sir. I'm eager to get back into action."

"I see you still need your cane. So, we may have to wait a while before sending you out into the field. In the meantime, resume your duties as liaison to the Free French. Major Thompson will be glad to have your assistance again. The situation has changed very much in the last few months, and it will be interesting to hear what they will tell you unofficially. Report to me if you hear anything of value."

"Yes, sir."

"And, enjoy yourself a little, while you're in London. I'm sure there are a lot of attractive young ladies around, who would be glad of the attentions of a wounded hero," the Admiral said with a grin. Then he turned serious. "One more thing. I cannot emphasize enough the need for total silence on any actions connected with my service." The Admiral leaned forward " Anything, whether it happened here in Britain or abroad. Do you understand me, Captain Auster?"

"Yes, sir. I understand fully."

* * *

"It's good to see you again, mon ami. And promoted to Captain, no less. And wounded. You must tell me all your exploits. Here, amid the fleshpots of London the chances of distinguishing oneself so as to earn promotion are fortunately very slim." Capitaine Louis Reynaud was his cynical self.

"Oh, my cane? I fell down some stairs. Nothing heroic about that. I'm sorry I can't tell you anything more interesting. I think I got promoted just so I can be of the same rank as you, and so le grand Charles doesn't ignore me totally. " Kurt smiled with pleasure at meeting the irrepressible Capitaine Reynaud again. " How has life been treating you here among those famous fleshpots? Tell me all the gossip, mon Capitaine."

"Now that we are the same rank, you must call me Louis, and I will call you Kurt. a va?"

"I'm honored, Louis. So tell me what you have been doing. Any romances?"

"Oh, I have my little pleasures - nothing difficult about that. In fact, you remember that delicious Clemente Theberge? Her husband, the Admiral has gotten himself more and more into disgrace with le grand Charles, but I have been able to console Clemente here and there. Too bad, though."

What a relief. I won't be bothered by her again. Although, I can't say I didn't enjoy her." But why too bad, Louis?"

"Because she's got an even more delicious daughter, Solange, who now works in our headquarters. It just wouldn't do to pay court to mother and daughter at the same time. It might be a little embarrassing if they talked to each other."

"Scruples? From you? I can't believe it." Kurt smiled.

"Not scruples, mon ami. Self-preservation. Although if those two women were truly liberated, enjoying them both at the same time would be a special treat. Have you ever met Solange? If not, I recommend her to you."

Kurt did remember the lovely girl with whom he had spent many hours on the ship that brought them from Oran to England. He had admired her courage in insisting on talking to him in spite of the obvious disapproval of her parents. But even though he had no intention of resuming his liaison with Clemente Theberge, the prohibition expressed by Louis Reynaud about a relationship with both mother and daughter applied to him as well.

"Tell me what's going on in France. I've been somewhat out of touch." Kurt changed the subject to one he considered more important.

"Ah, the German attack on the Soviet Union made quite a difference. The best organized group, who could conduct resistance activities, are the French Communists. After the Hitler-Stalin pact, on orders from Moscow, they cooperated with the Germans, who, after all, were Stalin's allies then. But after the Germans violated the non-aggression pact and invaded the Soviet Union, again on orders from Moscow they began resistance and sabotage. They may call themselves French, but they are totally under the thumb of the Soviets. I believe they will be a great danger to the stability of France, after the war is won. "

"How does General de Gaulle feel about that?"

"He can't stand it. To him the French Communists are traitors and he does not want to have anything to do with them. What is worse, unless organized resistance can be developed from other quarters, they will be the only ones who will get credit for fighting the Germans. The General is farsighted enough to worry about France after liberation, and none of us here want to see a communist France subservient to Moscow."

"But isn't there any other resistance at all?" Kurt wondered.

"From what we hear, none, although, the general feeling is that invading Russia was not to Germany's advantage, and that quite possibly, Germany may lose the war. But that's contradicted by the continuous German victories and advances on all fronts. Nevertheless, I'm convinced that all will change soon."

"What makes you say that, Louis?"

"Because the Germans punish resistance indiscriminately. They will shoot ten or twenty hostages for every act of sabotage or resistance. They do not care who committed these acts. That means that many French who are not Communists and who would not normally have resisted, will now be affected if their loved ones are shot. So, I think, with their usual arrogance, the Germans will help us develop an underground very soon."

"What will you do about that?" Kurt asked.

"Me? I hope nothing. I like it here in London. I'll be glad to send other people out to fight the Boche, but I'm not risking my neck if I can help it. What would all those lovely ladies do without me?"

"You are incorrigible, mon ami." Kurt smiled.

* * *

A few days later, Kurt presented himself at Admiral Morse's office. He noted that the usual quiet decorum in his anteroom was constantly interrupted by telephones ringing off the wall, messengers scurrying frantically about, and a very harassed Diana Fordyce greeting him very absently. "Is it urgent, Kurt? "she barely glanced at him, as sheaves of messages were thrown at her from all sides.

"What's going on?" Kurt asked, taken aback.

"Haven't you heard? The Japanese have attacked the United States. Germany and Italy have declared war. The United States is with us now, thank God."

Kurt sat down, as the import of those words began to sink in. Now, for the first time, he knew, he knew with absolute certainty, that, whatever time it would take, the forces of evil would not triumph. The great Colossus overseas could not be defeated.

"I didn't know, Diana. I'll leave. Just tell the Admiral, I'm at his service for anything at all."

* * *

On December 7, 1941, a "day that shall live in infamy" according to President Franklin D. Roosevelt, Japanese Air and Sea Forces attacked the main United States Naval Base in Pearl Harbor, Hawaii, and destroyed a major portion of the United States Navy. Japan's Axis partners, Germany and Italy declared war on the United States. Now it was truly a world war.

In spite of the somewhat subdued rejoicing in London, 1942 began on a very bad note for the Allied cause. The Japanese sank several British battleships, conquered the Philippines, Singapore and a number of other strategic Pacific islands as well as all of South East Asia. The Germans stood at the gates of Leningrad, Moscow and Stalingrad after conquering the Ukraine and a major portion of the Caucasus. The Balkans including Greece were all in German hands.

In late January of that eventful year, Kurt finally was summoned by Admiral Morse.

"Sit down, sit down, my boy." Since Kurt's return from Africa, he had noticed a much friendlier attitude in Morse.

"Sir, you and I know that it was your intention all along to use me in occupied France. I believe the time has come for me to go there. I believe that a resistance movement is beginning and that we should develop liaison and communications and if possible, supply the resistance with weapons and ammunition."

Admiral Morse smiled. "And what makes you think the time is ripe?"

Kurt recounted the conversation he had had with Capitaine Louis Reynaud and added to those facts others he had gleaned from numerous other meetings with Free French officers. "It is not my business to tell the British government whether it wants to get involved in the disagreement between the French Communists and De Gaulle, but I feel that we should use any and all means to fight the Germans, and if the French Communists are the only ones who want to fight, we must work with them, just as we are supporting the Soviet Union today. Besides, now that the United States is in the war, I would not be surprised if a some of the non communist French finally came to the conclusion that our side is bound to win in the long run."

"I must say, it's very decent of you to allow the Prime Minister to decide policy toward the French Communists," the Admiral said amusedly, " but I am inclined to agree that the time is approaching rapidly when we would want to take a more direct part in any resistance in France. I see you are still limping. How is your   leg?"

"Getting better, thank you sir. I'm sure it won't stop me from doing my duty."

"Well," the Admiral said, " you will hear from me when the time comes. I don't think I'd want to send you on a foray into France until your leg is completely healed. I have another job for you and I don't think your leg would be a handicap there. I have been asked by the Home Office to supply an officer who can pass as a German soldier. There is a problem in a prisoner-of-war camp in Scotland they need help with. I believe you could use your persona as Oberleutnant Gottfried Hagen, and solve the matter in short

273

order. I don't know the details. Report to Mr. Lanyard at the Home Office and he will brief you. Just let me know when they've finished with you, and you're back in London. And good luck."

"Thank you, sir."

* * *

Mr. Lanyard was a gray man. He looked like all the other civil servants who wandered around London in their bowler hats and striped pants, carrying tightly furled umbrellas regardless of the weather. He received Kurt in a small and dingy office in the large building that served as temporary quarters for the Home Office, whose original more luxurious suites had been damaged during the Blitz.

"There is a jurisdictional problem you may be able to help us with, Captain Auster," Mr. Lanyard began. He did not steeple his fingers, but Kurt fully expected him to do so momentarily.

"Yes, sir?" Kurt was very polite.

"Prisoner of War Camps are under the jurisdiction of the Army, of course. However, there have been three suspicious deaths in one camp. If these deaths were caused by disease or accident, we have no difficulty. If, however, there was foul play, the Home Office must investigate. All crimes committed in these British Isles fall under our jurisdiction. It is not at all clear whether these deaths were murders or not. The Army prefers to consider them accidents and to forget about them, rather than to allow us unrestricted access to investigate. We must know the facts. There is another point. If there are murders in the camp and we do not put a stop to them, we are in violation of the Geneva Convention. This could have unfortunate repercussions for our prisoners in German hands."

"What were the circumstances of the three deaths? " Kurt asked.

"Many captured German officers are being kept in an old castle on the estate of the Duke of Waterstoun in Scotland. The other ranks in our hands are in three camps where they live in tents or huts spread out throughout the countryside in Scotland or Wales. We have no trouble in any of those camps. In the officers' prison, however, in the last four weeks three prisoners have fallen to their deaths out of high windows in the castle. Those windows are not barred because they overlook the sheer castle walls over a ravine, which makes escape through them impossible. It seems unlikely that all three falls were accidents or suicides, but we have no indication that they were not. No witnesses have come forward."

"How many officers are kept in the castle?"

"Almost five hundred. The Camp Commandant, Major Brattlewaite, insists that the camp is well run and that the three deaths were not the result of foul play. He suggests that they may have been escape attempts. This seems very unlikely considering the physical situation, but we have absolutely no evidence to the contrary."

"What would you like me to do?"

"I would like you to become one of the prisoners and investigate from the inside, so to speak." Mr. Lanyard finally steepled his hands as he leaned back in his chair. " I particularly do not want Major Brattlewaite or any of his staff to know who you really are."

"Do you have any reason to distrust them?" Kurt asked.

"Just a feeling, just a feeling. If this is going to be done, it must be done right. If there are bad apples among our own people, we must weed them out, weed them out. Root and branch, root and branch. Don't you agree?"

"Of course. Now if I go in as a German prisoner, how do I get out? Is there anyone you trust with whom I can communicate?"

"I will arrange for one of our people from Special Branch to be appointed Chaplain. I have someone in mind who could pass for a man of the cloth. His name is Orne, Walter Orne. Trust him but trust no one else. As Chaplain he will have access at any time. Now I understand that your people on Curzon Street can outfit you as a naval officer and that you have played this role before. Contact me when you are ready. I assume that this will be no later than the day after tomorrow. I will arrange to have military police deliver you to the castle."

"Very well, sir."

This is an interesting little digression. I'm going to be a detective. How does this advance the war effort? Do I care how many Germans die, even if they are already prisoners? This is a turf war between the Army and the Home Office, and I really do not want to get involved in it. In fact, even though the Home Office sends me there, as an officer my loyalties really should be with the Army. In any case, I'll try to find out the facts and get out of there as quickly as possible. Admiral Morse ordered me to do this, and he always has more than one objective. I suppose he wants me to practice being a German officer among Germans, in case I have to do it again. At least, this time, I'll be doing it in perfect safety.

Kurt had no idea how wrong he was with this last assumption.

* * *

Mr. Lanyard arranged for two military policemen to deliver Kurt to the Waterstoun Castle. His cover story was that he had just been released from a British military hospital, where he had been treated after having been captured with a wounded leg. Kurt's limp and need for a cane - which had been issued to him at the hospital of course, verified the tale.

Oberleutnant Hagen and his escorts had taken an overnight train to Edinburgh. Tired from a night on hard wooden benches in the third class compartment, they had reported to the transport office at the station, and after many hours, were assigned a small truck and driver to take them North to Waterstoun.

Kurt had decided to exaggerate his limp - which in fact by now, had almost totally disappeared - and to keep his knowledge of English to himself, at least for the moment. They drove for a long time through a snowy landscape, then along a fairly narrow lake, surrounded by soft hills. Kurt overheard the driver explain to his escort that this was the famous Loch Ness, known because it was supposed to be the home of the even more famous Loch Ness monster, assumed to be a species of aquatic dinosaur which, miraculously, had survived for millions of years. There had been many sightings, but no definite discovery of the truth of this story.

However, in peacetime, the driver reported, there were always tourists whose enjoyment of the beautiful countryside was increased by the possibility of seeing the monster.

Long before the time they reached the promontory on which Waterstoun Castle was built the sinking sun covered the tips of the hills in gold and red and the lake took on a darker and more mysterious hue. Kurt could well believe that people considered it the home of a monster. It was quite late and totally dark by the time they reached their destination.,

Kurt paid very close attention to the approaches to the castle. A private road with a big sign " No Trespassing - Military Reservation " led away from the main road which circled the Loch onto a promontory sticking out into the lake. About a mile into this road, there was a guard post, manned by two armed soldiers. Kurt's escorts identified themselves and Kurt noted that one of the guards dialed a phone, obviously to notify the castle of their imminent arrival.

Another half mile onward the road narrowed into a causeway with the waters of the lake lapping against both its shoulders. In due course they reached their destination. There was another guard post. Kurt noted a machine gun mounted on a swivel that permitted it to be turned 360 degrees. Then they clattered over a drawbridge over a wide moat and between high, forbidding walls, into the castle courtyard.

A sergeant and two soldiers awaited them. Kurt climbed out of the truck with great difficulty, favoring his injured leg, and limped slowly, leaning on his cane, to the entrance of the guardroom the sergeant had indicated. His escort received the appropriate signature on their paperwork and left.

The sergeant allowed Kurt to sit, completed some more paperwork, asked Kurt to verify his name and rank in broken German, and then ordered Kurt to follow him. Kurt was led to a cupboard, handed two blankets, a pillow, a towel, and a small packet of soap. He had trouble carrying all this while leaning heavily on his cane, but the sergeant made no move to help him. Then he was led through a locked door into an inner courtyard. All around the castle walls rose high and there was the sound of the lake waters beating against the crenellated battlements.

"Officer of the Day" the sergeant called out.

A German officer in field gray uniform materialized out of a door in the inner castle.

"New arrival", the sergeant said and turned around, back to his office.

"Willkommen, Kamarad," the German officer smiled at Kurt. " I am Leutnant Werner Moser." He stretched out his hand. Kurt moved his cane into his left hand and shook Leutnant Moser's hand warmly, while trying to hold on to the material he had been issued. "Let me help you," Moser took the blankets from Kurt.

"Am I glad to find someone I can talk to," Kurt said in German. "I'm Oberleutnant zur See Gottfried Hagen. What is this place?"

"A prisoner of war camp for officers." Moser answered. "As prisons go, it isn't too bad. We are pretty much running the place ourselves. The English stay out of our way as much as possible. Come, and I'll find you a bed."

"What are the chances to escape?" Kurt asked.

"What a fire eater." Moser laughed. " I see you're injured, don't you think you'd want to get well first? But, to answer your question, escape is just about impossible. This castle is surrounded on three sides by a lake and heavily guarded on the fourth side. And the lower windows facing the lake are barred. I fear we have to resign ourselves to staying here until the end of the war. Now come along, I'll find you a bed on a low floor, since you have difficulty walking."

They entered the room from which Moser had emerged. It was a small room, with a wooden table and two chairs. "One of us is always required to be here in case the English want us. Come along."

A door opposite the entrance to the small room led into a huge hall. "This is the refectory hall, where we eat, play and socialize."

The hall was high ceilinged, stone walls and stone ceilings with one huge fireplace at one end, and in the distance a winding staircase going up. Very long wooden tables on trestles stood along both walls, and wooden benches completed the furnishings. The walls showed engravings of arms and armor, and high up along the walls there were some old and torn flags hanging. Moser noted Kurt's inspection. "You'd expect Lohengrin to come down these stairs, wouldn't you? We've been told that the castle had not been used since the Middle Ages, but was refurbished just for us. It's damp, cold and drafty, but not too uncomfortable. Normally, the hall is filled - there are almost five hundred of us - but it's past curfew and everybody is in bed by now."

"Is there no place to be outdoors?" Kurt asked.

"We're permitted to use the inner courtyard for exercising and the occasional soccer game, but it's quite small, and so our commandant has set up a rotation system of one third of us for two hours at a time. But the hall is larger than you think, and with this Scottish weather, being indoors is no hardship. Can you make it up the stairs all right?"

"Yes, as long as we go slowly. Thank you for carrying my things. They told me in the hospital that my leg will be better in a few weeks, if I do the exercises they taught me."

"You'll have to tell me how you were wounded, but I fear we'll have lots of time to talk. In any case, a doctor comes once a week, and he can look you over on his next visit. Ah, here we are."

Moser had led Kurt up one flight of stairs. Above him, the staircase ascended into the gloom, and Kurt could not tell how many floors there were. Moser led Kurt down a corridor and opened a door. The room into which Kurt was shown was square and again had stone floors, stone walls and stone ceilings. The wall facing the door was pierced by two very narrow windows, barred, through which a sliver of moonlight entered. On each side of the other walls were two bunk beds, one on top of the other. In the middle of the room a rough wooden table and two chairs, and next to the bunk beds two wooden closets completed the decor.

"Not like at mother's," Moser grinned. "Well, this is your new home."

Three of the bunk beds were occupied. Moser clapped his hands. "Attention, lazybones. I want to introduce your new roommate, Oberleutnant Hagen. He's injured. It would be nice if one of you offered him a lower bunk."

A tousled head appeared on the left. " He can have mine," a voice growled and a figure threw his blankets into the upper bunk, swung himself up and returned to sleep. Kurt's other two roommates paid no attention to him and went back to sleep.

"Well, you'll get acquainted tomorrow." A slightly subdued Leutnant Moser said. " Have a good night's sleep. We'll see each other tomorrow. And tomorrow, and tomorrow."

He left the room. Kurt placed his blankets on his bunk, threw off his clothes, and stretched out on his bed. He tried to review what he had learned about the prison but fell asleep quickly.

* * *

A beautiful girl was bending over him. Odd, her hair was not blond. It wasn't Sarah. He tried to make out the face and just saw dark hair. The girl shook him. He woke up.

"Wake up, wake up." Moser whispered. "The Commandant wants you now. Now. Hurry."

Kurt sat up. " You. I was just dreaming of a beautiful girl and you interrupted me." He yawned. "What time is it? "

"It's 3 A.M. And never mind girls. When the Commandant wants you, you hop. Quickly now."

"All right, all right." Kurt got out of his bunk with difficulty, slipped on his trousers, uniform jacket and shoes, and took his cane. Moser rushed him as fast as he could limp out the door and back down the stairs to the refectory hall. At the end of the hall, next to the tall fireplace - so tall that two men could stand in it without crouching - there was a door. Moser knocked. A muffled "Enter" was heard. Moser opened the door, ushered Kurt inside, and withdrew.

Kurt found himself in a large well-furnished room. The walls and floor were stone, as in all the other rooms of the castle, but here a carpet covered the floor, there were several leather armchairs and small tables, book cases along the walls, and at the far end, a large desk.

The man seated behind the desk got up, extended his right arm in the Hitler salute, and barked: "Heil Hitler."

Kurt stood at attention, transferred his cane from his right into his left hand, and raised his right arm in the same greeting. "Heil Hitler," he responded.

The man behind the desk sat down. "Report," he ordered.

"Oberleutnant zur See Gottfried Hagen reporting to the Commandant." Kurt replied in as military a manner as he could.

"Very well. I see that you are injured. You may sit down."

Gratefully Kurt sank into a chair in front of the desk. He kept his military manner and sat upright. He finally had a chance to take a look at the Commandant. He saw a medium sized slender man, gray haired, clean-shaven, in the uniform of a Lieutenant Colonel of the Wehrmacht. A Ritterkreuz, the highest military medal, on its distinctive band, was hung around his neck.

"My name is Werfel. Now tell me how you got to join us here," the Lieutenant Colonel ordered. His manner of speech was extremely military. No one could confuse it with a conversation between equals. It was very clear who was giving the orders and who had to obey them. His accent was Northern German. Kurt surmised that he was Prussian. His entire bearing spoke of a long military tradition.

As Kurt began to speak, he noted another figure seated in the shadows in a corner behind the Commandant. He could not make out the other man's face or rank.

Zu Befehl, Herr Oberstleutnant." (At your orders, Lieutenant Colonel) Kurt began. "I served on the Schnellboot Haifisch out of Dieppe. We ran into a mine and were blown up. I was the only survivor. After several hours a British frigate picked me up and took me to a British port."

"And this is how you were injured?"

"No, sir. I was actually uninjured in the explosion. When I was taken off the frigate there was an opportunity to escape. I vaulted over the railing and started to run. Unfortunately, one of the guards was more alert than I had hoped, and I got two bullets into my leg."

"Do you think it was wise to try to escape? What would you have done, alone in enemy territory, if you had succeeded?"

"I feel it is my duty to fight on as long as I can, Herr Oberstleutnant." Kurt was as military as the Lieutenant Colonel. "My hope was that I could find a boat and escape from England. If I had not been able to do so, at least I could have done the enemy some harm by acts of sabotage. To my great misfortune I was prevented from doing so. May I ask a question, sir?"

"You may." Did Kurt detect a slight warming in the Commandant's tone?

"Is there an escape committee here? I would like to register so that I may make an attempt to escape at the earliest opportunity."

"You are injured. How long do you think your wounds will incapacitate you?" This time there was definitely a warmer tone.

"The English doctor who operated on me indicated that I should be back to normal in a few weeks, if I do the exercises he prescribed, Herr Oberstleutnant."

"Ah," the Commandant asked. "Do you speak English?"

"No, sir. There was an interpreter at the hospital."

The figure behind the Lieutenant Colonel bent forward and whispered to the Commandant. Werfel nodded and addressed Kurt again.

"Escape from here is almost impossible, but nothing is impossible to loyal soldiers of the Fuehrer. Are you or anyone in your family party members?"

"My father, Herr Oberstleutnant." Kurt made an effort to speak with considerable pride. " He was an illegal party member in St. Poelten while the Austrian regime prohibited membership, and was proud to wear his party emblem from the first day that the Fuehrer brought Austria home into the Reich."

The figure behind the Commandant got up. Kurt recognized the distinctive runes of the SS on his lapel. This was a tall, thin, almost cadaverous man of about thirty-five. His hair was cropped so close as to give the impression of baldness.

"With your permission, Herr Oberstleutnant." The man addressed the Commandant and then turned to Kurt.

"I have the impression that you are a loyal German. Is that correct?"

"Yes, sir." Kurt did not recognize the SS rank and hoped he would not be caught because of this lack of knowledge.

"You took the Fuehrerschwur when you joined the service. Will you repeat it now?"

When Adolf Hitler became chancellor and then dictator of Germany, he changed the usual oath taken by the military swearing loyalty to the country, to an oath swearing personal loyalty to him, Adolf Hitler. The fact that the highest officers of the Wehrmacht agreed to this change indicated their submission to his total power. Ever since then, the Fuehrerschwur - the oath to the Fuehrer - became an integral part of many military ceremonies.

"It will be my honor." Kurt got up with difficulty, moved the cane to his left hand, stood at attention and raised his right hand. The other two officers also stood up, and Kurt repeated after the SS officer.

"I Gottfried Hagen, swear total loyalty and obedience to Adolf Hitler, Fuehrer of the German Nation...."

As he repeated the words, Kurt wondered at the relationship between the two officers facing him. It seemed to him, that the SS officer actually exercised control.

When the oath was completed, Kurt was permitted to sit down again. The SS Officer spoke:

"We are in a difficult position here among our enemies. There are people among us who do not deserve the name of German officer, who are defeatist and have shown disloyalty to the Fuehrer. I must warn you against such people, and ask you to report immediately any defeatist sentiments you hear. Is that understood?"

"Yes, sir."

The SS Officer continued.

"Furthermore, it is also difficult for young men to live without women for such a long period. I remind you that you belong to the German nation, body and soul. Your essential essences are the property of the Nation, and in due course,

will be used to create more pure Germans, when you have
returned home. If you hear of any of our people who indulge
in activities that would waste this property, either by
themselves or even jointly, you must report them
immediately as well. Is that understood?"

*Does he mean masturbation and homosexuality are
forbidden here? In a prisoner of war camp of five hundred
young and vigorous men? And I must be his spy? Of course.*

"Yes, sir. I understand and will obey."

Lieutenant Colonel Werfel spoke up. " Do not give
up hope of escaping from here. I want you to concentrate on
getting well. Trust the Fuehrer. He has not forgotten us even
here among the enemy. We maintain strict military
discipline here and keep ourselves in readiness for anything
the Fuehrer may ask of us even here. You will be assigned
chores like all other officers and you will be expected to
participate in all required exercises and classes."

"Zu Befehl, Herr Oberstleutnant." Kurt snapped in
his military manner.

Oberstleutnant Werfel continued. " Because of your
injury I will exempt you from your chores until you have
been examined by the British doctor and he has reported to
me. Now, we all must learn from each other. As a naval
officer, no doubt you are familiar with celestial navigation. I
will expect you to teach a class in that. If you have any other
knowledge that could be useful, please write up a proposal
for other classes you may teach. I will give you a few days
to get acclimatized to our way of doing things here, and you
will report to me again. And now, dismiss."

Kurt saluted "Heil Hitler" and as smartly as he could,
given his cane and limp, left the room. Moser was waiting
for him.

"Wow, what a session." Kurt sighed. "Who is that SS
Officer?"

"Sturmbannfuehrer (Major) Fratzer. I advise you to
stay on his good side. If you don't, it could be dangerous."
Moser whispered looking around the empty hall, just to make
doubly sure that no one could hear him.

"The brass seems to be doing well for themselves," Kurt wanted to hear as much as possible, if he could get Moser to talk.

"Well, as I told you, we're pretty much running our own show here. The Commandant gave his parole to the British and assured them that there would be no escape attempts. The result is, no British officer ever enters the inner keep, except for Major Brattlewaite, their commanding officer. He and Lieutenant Colonel Werfel get along famously. The British deliver our food and supplies to our door, and we take care of ourselves. Of course this means, that junior officers like you and me have to do K.P. and other chores, but it keeps the British out of our hair. Naturally, the top officers take the best for themselves first."

"So there really is no possibility of escape?"

"I'm afraid not."

By the time Kurt returned to his room, dawn was breaking. He was deeply concerned about the order to teach celestial navigation. *What I know about navigation, I could teach in one minute. I'd better complete my investigation and get out of here before they find out that a naval officer does not know anything about such a basic subject. I wonder when Mr. Lanyard's agent, the Reverend, will show up.* He collapsed on his bed for what seemed just a few minutes, when the hustle and bustle of his roommates getting up awoke him again.

* * *

"Reveille. Time to get up." The man from the bunk above him, who had sacrificed the lower bunk for Kurt, shook Kurt gently.

"Must I? I haven't slept at all." Kurt grumbled.

"Sorry, Kamarad. If your bunk is not made up when the Commandant comes around for inspection the entire room is in serious trouble. We would all be held responsible for your dereliction. Besides, you wouldn't want to miss breakfast."

Kurt got out of his bed with difficulty and started to throw on his clothes. His companion said: " I'll make up your bed for you this time, so you'll know what's required."

He rolled up both blankets, placed one at each end of the bed, with the pillow centered between them.

"Thank you very much, " Kurt said. "My name is Gottfried Hagen."

"Yes, I remember Moser mentioning your name when he woke us. I'm Horst von Greifenklau. And in the real world, I was in the air force."

Kurt looked at his companion more closely. Von Greifenklau was tall, in fact slightly taller than Kurt, and very blond, so blond, in fact, that his very short hair and blond eyebrows made him look almost like an albino. On his clean-shaven face, there was a deep scar going from the left eyebrow across the entire left cheek up to the jaw.

Von Greifenklau noticed Kurt looking at the scar.

"You haven't seen a real Schmiss before, have you, Kamarad?"

A Schmiss was a scar inflicted on the participants in a ritual duel with sabers between members of rival Burschenschaften - fraternities - at some of Germany's most prestigious universities. Only members of the aristocracy and their hangers on still participated in the brutal sport, but among those classes, a Schmiss was considered a badge of honor.

"No, I haven't. In the Ostmark where I come from, we don't practice the sport anymore."

"Well, among us it's still a very important test of courage. Come on now, time for breakfast."

Kurt followed von Greifenklau down the stairs to the main hall. The tables which had been along the walls, had now been moved forward and occupied the center of almost three quarters of the hall. Most seats on the benches fronting the tables were occupied by officers. Kurt expected noise from almost five hundred men, but was astonished to note total silence.

Von Greifenklau motioned Kurt to follow him. Kurt had seen by Von Greifenklau's uniform that he was an Oberleutnant, a first lieutenant, and von Greifenklau led him to a table occupied by officers of the same rank.

Kurt's assumed naval rank, Oberleutnant zur See, was actually the equivalent of Army Captain, but Kurt decided not to make an issue of that fact at this time.

There was a table set at right angles to the long row of tables, at the head, just in front of the huge fireplace. This table held no more than six or eight seats, and it was still empty.

Suddenly there was a word of command. As one the officers rose and stood at attention. Lieutenant Colonel Werfel, followed by Sturmbannfuehrer Fratzer and six other officers entered and stood behind their chairs. Werfel raised his arm in the German salute:

"Heil Hitler."

In one voice, the assembly responded, raising their arms:

"Heil Hitler."

Werfel's sharp glance swept around the enormous room. Then he intoned. "At ease." At that point the assembly sat down, and finally a buzz of voices filled the hall. Plates of food were delivered to the tables by officers assigned to that duty, and the usual bantering comments about the quality of the food and of the service were exchanged.

Von Greifenklau introduced Oberleutnant Hagen to the other men at the table. Kurt noted that the tables were organized by ten, and with little success, tried to remember all the names that were thrown at him. He saw that the officers around him all wore the same light blue air force uniforms that his mentor, Horst von Greifenklau, wore.

"I see I am surrounded by the Luftwaffe," Kurt smiled. "Are there so few naval officers here?"

"Very few, it appears." Von Greifenklau answered. " Most of the officers here were captured in the early days of the war, except for us in the air force. A lot of us are here because we were shot down attacking the British."

"So many?" Kurt said. " We were not told about so many losses."

The officer sitting across from Kurt looked up from his meal. "Aha," he exclaimed. "Haven't I told you that our Minister of Propaganda keeps the truth from the people? You see, they don't get told anything."

"Watch your mouth." Von Greifenklau said sharply. " Please do not criticize our government in my presence."

The officer across from Kurt said nothing and resumed his meal. Another man spoke up.

"Since you are the last arrival, please tell us what's been going on in the war. The British give us no information."

"Well," Kurt began. "The war with Russia is going very well. Our troops have reached the outskirts of Leningrad and Moscow. The entire Ukraine is ours, and we are at the gates of Stalingrad on the Volga. It can't be much longer before the Russians surrender like the French did. And our allies, the Japanese have been winning victory after victory over the British and Americans in the Pacific. Half the British Empire there is now in Japanese hands, and the Americans are impotent after the destruction of their fleet."

"What an optimistic assessment." The officer across from Kurt muttered.

"I apologize," Kurt said to him. "I did not get your name?"

"My name is Hugo Bratter, and I am the pessimist at this table."

"But why? The war is going very well. We are conquering Russia, our Japanese Allies have taken enough of the British Empire, so that the colonies won't be able to help their masters, and the United States has lost its fleet. Once Russia is out of the war, the British will have to sue for peace."

"You have forgotten something, my optimistic friend." Oberleutnant Bratter said.

"What?"

"One, the stubbornness of Winston Churchill and the British people, and two - far more importantly, the power of the United States."

"America will have its hand full, fighting the Japanese Empire."

"Nevertheless, you underestimate the Americans. We here, in the air force, know what they did to us even when they were ostensibly neutral. They have supplied the British with fighters and bombers that far exceed the quality of our own planes. Their incredible productive capacity is far greater than ours."

"That's enough, Bratter." Von Greifenklau interrupted. "There will be no defeatist talk at this table. We must trust the Fuehrer. He has brought us so far, and we must believe that he will bring us all the way to the inevitable victory."

Bratter muttered something unintelligible and withdrew into a heavy silence. For a few moments nothing was heard at the table except for the sounds of forks and knives and the occasional " Pass the salt, please."

As soon as the meal was over, there was another call to attention. The assembly rose. The officers at the high table stretched out their arms: " Heil Hitler." The proper response was given. Kurt found the large group of officers standing at attention shouting in one voice "Heil Hitler " a frightening spectacle, but of course he participated in full voice and with outstretched arm.

The brass left, and the rest of the officers began to mill about. However, Kurt noted that there was a purpose to all the movements. One group moved the tables back against the wall, other groups assembled in various parts of the great hall and began different kinds of drills or calisthenics, and some groups climbed the stairs, probably to find rooms where some of the lectures were being given. The impression Kurt got was not that of a group of prisoners patiently waiting for the end of the war and their release, but a unit of professional, highly disciplined soldiers, preparing for the next time they would be in combat.

Kurt had noted that the two tables of ten on each side of the high table were filled with officers in the distinctive Waffen SS uniform. Now he observed how some of those officers wandered from group to group, occasionally stopping to exhort or criticize a performance.

Since he had been given freedom from assignments for the moment, Kurt limped about observing what he could. Soon, he was spotted by one of the ubiquitous SS officers.

"What is your assignment, Kamarad?" he was asked.

"I have no assignment until my leg is better," Kurt answered. " I am looking for a spot where I can do my exercises so that it will improve."

"Follow me, Kamarad." The officer led Kurt to a door Kurt had not observed earlier. The door led to another hall, much smaller than the main hall, but still sizable. It was filled with groups of men practicing various drills. Kurt was led to a corner and told, " This will be your spot until you can report yourself as fully fit for duty."

Kurt began his stretching exercises, making sure that he demonstrated considerable difficulty in his movements, and occasionally giving forth a groan or two.

Lunch was a repetition of the ceremony of breakfast. After lunch, half of the officers were marched out into the open courtyard. Kurt heard comments about soccer games. In the middle of the afternoon there was a fifteen minute break during which the officers all milled about and conversed.

Dinner followed the same ceremonial routine. However, when it was over, no one left the tables. Songs were sung, some of which were the same songs Kurt had enjoyed as a boy scout in Vienna. Then, at the end, the assembly stood at attention and began the Horst Wessel Song, the official anthem of the Nazi Party, named after its composer, a young National Socialist who had been killed during one of the riots in 1923. Kurt sang along with a growing feeling of fear and discomfort:

"Die Fahne hoch, die Reihen dicht geschlossen,
S.A. marschiert im ruhig festen Schritt.
Kameraden von Rotfront und Reaction erschossen,
marschieren im Geist in unseren Reihen mit."

"High the banner, close the ranks,
S.A. marches in quietly firm steps.
Comrades shot by reds and reactionaries
march in our ranks with their spirit."

If they knew who I am, they would tear me limb from limb. Kurt was very afraid. The song reminded him of groups of young Nazis strutting in the streets of Vienna.His parents had always turned the next corner so as to avoid any confrontation. *I wish there was a corner I could turn now.*

After the Horst Wessel Lied was over, the assembly was dismissed. The tables and benches were pushed back against the wall, and the young men started to wander about

290

in the center. Here and there card games started; in the open space in the middle, there were athletic contests; and some groups formed around one officer who appeared to be haranguing them. Kurt walked about, favoring his cane, and making sure that his limp was very noticeable. He stopped at some of the groups and listened to its leader expounding some point of Nazi doctrine, often very specifically the racial doctrine that established very definitely the Teutonic superiority over the rest of mankind. Kurt noted with some interest that rarely two officers were alone with each other for more than a passing minute.

The free time period after dinner lasted for no more than forty-five minutes, when word spread quickly - five minutes to lights out. The assembly dispersed into their rooms. Climbing the stairs painfully with his pronounced limp, Kurt was one of the last to reach his quarters. He barely had the time to get out of his uniform when the lights went off. There was a small glimmer of starlight through the narrow window. As soon as Kurt's eyes had gotten adjusted to the lack of illumination he was able to complete his toilet and slip into bed. From the bunk above him, von Greifenklau whispered: " Tomorrow you'd better give yourself more time. Good night." Then there was silence.

Kurt could not sleep. *I am surrounded by the murderers of my parents. This is worse than in North Africa. There the German soldiers were busy fighting, and had no time to pay much attention to me. Here, they have nothing else to do, and the SS officers keep indoctrinating them. I have to be very careful, and try to get out of here quickly.*

Then a thought struck him. Ratzersdorfer. Ratzersdorfer, the murderer of my parents. I know nothing about him, but his name and that he is in the SS. It would be too much to hope that he is here, but surely, among the SS officers here there must be someone who knows him. Perhaps, I can find out more about that man. One day, I'll find him, and this may be one way to him.

And with a wolfish smile, Kurt Auster went to sleep.

***

CHAPTER X

He had always known that the accident had changed his life, but for many years Jack Shaughnessy had thought that the change was for the better. And then, slowly at first, and then with accelerating swiftness, he began to realize that the opposite was true. More and more he regretted the way that his life had turned out. As he began to hate, he also longed for the innocent times of his childhood, which he idealized beyond recognition.

Jack was the seventh and last child of Seamus Shaughnessy, a tenant farmer on the estate of the Duke of Chalmerston, which was located near Londonderry in the six "lost" counties of Northern Ireland. As Catholics and staunch supporters of Irish independence his family never accepted the division of the country that had created the Irish Free State in 1921, and left the six counties - Ulster - in the hands of the British. Jack was ten when these momentous events occurred, and remembered well the sense of betrayal and unhappiness in the discussions of his elders.

But what did this have to do with the life of a boy? As far as Jack was concerned, life was good, it was glorious, as long as he had access to the love of his life - the Duke of Chalmerston's stables. The Duke was a renowned breeder of horses, for racing and hunting and for show. When the Duke was in residence at the manor house on the estate - not more than three or four times a year for a few weeks at a time- there was great action in the big house and in the stable yard. During those times, Jack's mother Mary often helped out in the kitchen, and Jack's father Seamus acted as head lad for the trainer.

When the Duke was not in residence, Seamus devoted his time to maintaining his farm. Jack had access to the stables, and when the Duke was not about, had even begun to learn to ride. He loved being around horses. He loved their smell, the glossiness of their coats which he learned to brush, the responsive way in which they would accept a caress, and the nobility of the highly bred racehorses when they were led out for their daily runs.

By the time Jack was twelve, his ambition in life was to become the trainer for the Duke. To be master of the stables and all the horses, to control their destinies - subject, of course, to the will of the Duke, was all he wanted from life. These days, when he remembered those dreams, he resented bitterly the limits of his ambition, and the willingness with which he accepted everybody's subservience to the Duke.

Then came the day. The Duke was in residence. On a cold Fall morning the horses were being readied for the great Hunt. The Great House was filled with guests. Both of Jack's parents and his older siblings were fully occupied in assisting the permanent staff of the House to care for them. From far and wide other neighbors arrived for the Hunt, bringing their favorite horses.

It was cold and a mist rose over the fields. A pale sun began its slow ascent as the members of the Hunt gathered. The men were resplendently dressed in their red hunting jackets, the ladies in a variety of riding costumes. The master of hounds and his assistants were busy keeping the braying and barking dogs in check. Servants moved about the prancing horses carefully, holding trays with stirrup cups for those members of the Hunt who needed something to fortify them against the cold.

Jack was busy helping some of the guests mount by holding their horses. Some of the older members of the Hunt needed more assistance. Stools and strong backs were provided to help them. And here came the Duke, emerging from the great doors of the House, surrounded by friends and family. The Duchess was not going on the Hunt that day, for reasons that had caused some snickering among the staff and some gossip about the possibility of a male heir coming along. The Duke's only child, Lady Maud, stood beside her father, dressed in a forest green riding costume which undoubtedly cost more money than the entire Shaughnessy family would see in a year. Jack had seen Lady Maud often on the family's previous visits to the estate. She was two years younger than he but so far above him in station that he had never exchanged a word with her.

Now he was ordered to lead her horse to her, as she was standing on the steps with her father. Her horse was a black stallion named Gordie, very spirited. The stablemaster had originally thought he would be too much for Lady Maud to handle. It had taken an order from the Duke, after considerable entreaties by his daughter, to allow her to ride Gordie for the Hunt. She had, as the experts said, a good seat and had ridden Gordie before, but never at the Hunt and in the presence of so many other horses and the hounds.

Gordie was somewhat skittish as Jack led him from the stables. The stallion had never seen so many horses and so much commotion before. Jack caressed his neck and whispered soft words into his ear as he brought the horse to the steps where the Duke and Lady Maud were standing.

"Are you sure you can handle him?" the Duke asked. " Of course, I can. Stop treating me like a child." Lady Maud was quite angry. Obviously, this discussion had been going on for some time. Quickly Lady Maud climbed aboard Gordie. "Let go, boy." she ordered. Jack let go of the bridle and Lady Maud took the reins. Gordie danced about a bit.

"He's a little nervous, what with all this crowd." Jack dared to say.

"I'll show him nervous." Lady Maud muttered and raised her riding crop. "Don't!" Jack wanted to yell, but it was too late. The crop fell on the horse's withers, he reared up, Lady Maud lost her seat and slid off the saddle, but her foot was caught in the stirrup.

She was hanging upside down while the horse neighed and stamped. Jack ducked under the hooves trying to grab the reins but Gordie could not be controlled. Jack held the reins as tight as he could and was dragged about by the maddened animal. The other horses in the vicinity started to get upset and their riders had a very hard time trying to control them. Every time Gordie reared and bucked, Lady Maud's head was getting closer to the cobblestones of the yard. Jack threw one arm around Gordie's neck and tried to hold him down. Then he reached for the stirrup and freed Lady Maud's foot. The girl was released - Jack grabbed her before she could hit the ground, eased her down as quickly as possible and covered her with his body to protect her from the flashing hooves of the horse. Dimly he heard shouting -"Get the bridle, hold the horse" but he could not see what was being done. All he worried about were the hooves. He cowered on the ground above Maud, and for a brief, a very brief moment was conscious of the soft, female body under him. Then Gordie's hoof descended and hit Jack's knee with a shattering crack.

***

"Well, what more do you want me to do? After all, he's just the son of a tenant farmer."

The Duke was pacing up and down in his study, occasionally glancing at his cousin, Sir Edward Hughes.

Calmly Sir Edward continued to fill his pipe. "He saved your daughter's life. And, he's permanently injured."

"It was an accident. And after all I provided him with the services of the best surgeon in Harley Street." The Duke smiled.

"I appreciate the compliment. It was fortunate that you invited me to the Hunt and that I was able to operate immediately. Any delay probably would have cost the poor boy his leg. As it is, he'll walk with a limp the rest of his life. But, accident? That's not what Maud thinks. She feels responsible, and I think she's right. And she considers the boy her savior."

"Oh, she's a romantic. Didn't I do enough? He spent the last three months living in my house while he was recuperating from your butchery, Edward. What more do you want from me?"

"Don't act like a saint, my friend. You weren't in the house for most of that time, and the place is so big that you wouldn't notice the presence of a cavalry squadron. It was certainly better for the boy to recuperate here, close to his family, than to send him to a hospital or nursing home, for which, incidentally, you would have had to pay."

"Oh, very well, stop your blathering. What do you want me to do?"

Sir Edward leaned forward. "Look here, the boy cannot go on with his life the way it would have been before the accident. He can't ride. He can't work on a farm. He will drag his leg for the rest of his life. He needs to make his living in some kind of sedentary occupation. I have talked to him a few times. He's smart. I think you should send him to school. Perhaps, he'll grow up to be a bookkeeper, or a teacher, or something like that."

"Is that what you think, Edward? Any special school? Will Eton or Harrow do?"

"Come on now, you're joking about a boy's life. A boy who has deserved well of you."

"Oh, very well," the Duke grumbled. "We'll find him a boarding school around here, and we'll see how far he will go. But if he can't keep up with his studies, he's out on his ear."

Sir Edward smiled. He knew that the Duke's protestations were merely an aspect of the gruff character he liked to project, but that in reality the Duke knew perfectly well what he owed to the boy.

***

And so Jack's new life began. He was sent to Kearnleigh, a private school - called public school in the British Empire - a school he could never have aspired to as the son of a tenant farmer, an Irish Catholic tenant farmer at that. And here he met a new world.

The part of that new world that he liked, and grew to love, was the world of the mind. Indeed, Jack was smart, and he was very happy to discover that in himself. He had hardly had any education before - barely enough to read and write and do simple arithmetic. And now he found himself in a position to learn, and he couldn't get enough. He not only was absorbed in the challenges of the classwork, but in his spare time, he read anything that he could get his hands on, history, philosophy, science, politics and biographies. Those particularly, the biographies of people who had made a difference, appealed to him.

And in spite of the hard and unaccustomed work, Jack found that he had plenty of time for himself. There were two reasons for that. First of all, because of his bad leg, he was excused from participation in all sports. That was unfortunate, because had he been able to excel in at least one sport, that might have helped him overcome the second and much bigger reason.

Until the Industrial Revolution, British public schools had been the exclusive purview of the landed gentry. Land ownership was the measure of wealth which permitted the sons of the nobility access to education. With the rise of the middle class to wealth - the word millionaire came into vogue only at that time- anyone with the necessary funds could aspire to a place in one of the prestigious public schools from which the leaders of the nation would emerge. The sons of those nouveau-riche were inscribed in the register of those schools, which heretofore had catered only to the aristocracy, as "sine nobilitad" abbreviated as "s. nob-"without title", from which, of course , the word snob emerged.

Particularly because Kearnleigh was a school of the second, or more likely third rank, snobbery was paramount. The students were, for the most parts, sons of upper civil servants or of commercial barons who had not yet made it high enough up the ladder of success to get their heirs into better schools. Some were the sons of minor colonial potentates, who, while suffering discrimination because of their color, at least had the aura of their exotic origins to recommend them. And of course they were all fanatic about their sports activities.

How could an Irish Catholic, a member of the underclass in Ireland, the son of a tenant farmer, be accepted in this group? Jack was shunned at best, and made fun of at worst. And some of the "childish" pranks played on him were as truly vicious as teen age boys could devise.

So Jack's refuge was his books. And his dream. He realized that his dream was only that, but it did not leave him. Maud had been very grateful to him, during his convalescence in the Great House. She visited him whenever she was in residence, and Jack thought that she looked at him with admiration for having saved her. A sort of friendship had indeed developed. Jack had visions of growing up, becoming eminently successful in some as yet unspecified field, and being accepted by Maud as an equal and potential suitor. The unlikeliness of this could not prevent the dreams of a teenager from taking shape. So he dreamed, and read, and studied, and suffered the taunts and worse of his classmates.

On school holidays Jack went home. Whenever Lady Maud was in residence he would see her, and if there were no other guests spend time in her company. The Duke was pleased with the reports of Jack's scholastic achievements. In fact, there was a dinner party at the Great House when Jack was home for the Christmas holidays the year he had turned sixteen. The Duke called Jack in and paraded him about the room to demonstrate his generosity.

Jack remembered his embarrassment, dressed as he was in his father's best hand-me down suit. He saw all the gentlemen in uniforms or dinner jackets and the ladies in their finery, white shoulders gleaming and jewels sparkling, look at him as if he were an animal in a zoo, while the Duke demonstrated that his tenant farmer's son had some brains. Jack remembered not only his embarrassment but his fury when he caught Lady Maud's eye. She looked at him with what he was sure, was pity. That was not the emotion he wanted to arouse in her.

As he was parading about the table, feeling like a pet lapdog, the Duke pronounced not only his satisfaction at Jack's success in his studies, but promised that he would assist Jack to go as far as his abilities would take him. Surely he did not anticipate that Jack would take him up on this. But it was something Jack took with him from that terrible evening.

He began to look at himself and to think about his future. How could he make a success of himself? To enter commerce he needed capital, to enter the law he needed connections; his leg prevented him from joining the Army or Navy and becoming the hero Maud might admire. He remembered the kindness of Sir Edward Hughes, and the story of how he had taken charge after the accident, and operated on Jack's knee on the great kitchen table and thus saved Jack's leg. Medicine might be the answer. A career where hard work and talent might enable Jack to make the success of himself he craved.

From then on his dreams about Maud involved his doing some great deed of derring-do, performing an operation that would save Maud's father's life, or discovering the one vaccine that would protect the Empire from the ravages of a dread disease. And Maud would look at him with admiration, not with pity.

Once Jack had made the decision, he applied every effort and all his considerable talent. He concentrated his studies on biology, chemistry and anthropology. When the time came, he used the good offices of Sir Edward to remind the Duke of his promise. Reluctantly the great man agreed and Jack was sent to the University of Edinburgh to study medicine.

The years passed. Jack saw Maud rarely - when his visit home and the ducal family's coincided. He heard rumors about Maud's wild escapades in London's fashionable world, but he refused to listen to them. His dreams continued.

Six months before he was due to take his final exams and acquire the title of Doctor, his dream was destroyed. By that time Jack's mother Mary had become head housekeeper of the great house. She and Seamus had moved into quarters there, leaving their cottage to Jack's eldest brother. Jack was at the kitchen table below stairs in the great house, enjoying his parent's company. They heard a car pull up at the front door, with the horn blaring. Maud had arrived unexpectedly with some of her friends. Mary went to meet her. "We did not expect your ladyship," she curtsied," but we'll try to make you comfortable."

"That's allright, Mary" Maud said. "We were in the area and decided to stop by.. We'll all stay in the green room", she giggled, looking at the two young men and one girl she had brought along. "We just want something to eat and drink and then we'll be on our way. You can fix us up, won't you?"

"Of course, your ladyship."

Jack stayed in the shadows below the stairs. He saw the two couples wander over to the green room bantering and laughing, and felt very out of place. Even though he was almost a doctor, he did not see himself ready to speak out and greet Lady Maud when she was with her friends. He retired to the kitchen and watched his mother prepare plates of sandwiches, and send one of the maids up with a few bottles of wine. "Wild thing she is," his mother muttered. "If his lordship were here, she wouldn't carry on like that. This is not London, after all."

Jack sat in the dark kitchen for a long time. His mother had gone to bed, complaining about the demands of the young people of the day. He sat there, staring at his cold cup of tea, visualizing Maud and her three friends in the green room. The green room was a smaller, secondary dining room, only used when just a few people dined together. It contained a table for no more than six, which was surrounded by comfortable couches along three walls. The fourth wall surrounded the windows, usually covered with heavy drapes. Jack remembered how cozy and warm the room seemed to him on the few occasions that he had been in it. Now he thought of Maud and her friends, joking, drinking and eating and enjoying themselves. And he? Well, once he had achieved his goal, once he was a famous physician, a great surgeon or renowned researcher, Maud would look at him with admiration, and perhaps with more. In the meantime, let her enjoy herself, after all she's still a child. She never had to deal with the seriousness of life as he had. And yet, and yet, he was bitter at being excluded from the warmth and fellowship he imagined going on in the green room.

Then he heard voices: "You can't go out like that Maud ," a male voice remonstrated. "Sure I can, we need more champagne." Maud's voice was slightly slurred. And the door opened to the kitchen. Maud switched on the light. In its blaze, Jack saw her - totally nude, a cigarette dangling from her lips. "Now, where's that champagne?" she began rummaging in the large refrigerator. "Maud!" Jack spoke without thinking. "Oh, hello Jack. Where do you think - Ah, there it is." Totally unselfconsciously, Maud took two bottles from the refrigerator and went out of the kitchen. "Who was that?" the male voice asked. "Oh, it was only Jack." And the door to the green room closed .

Only Jack. Only Jack. The words reverberated in his head. He saw the nude body that the others had been enjoying , but that did not mean as much to him as the words:" Only Jack." As if I were a piece of furniture, of no importance.

For a long time, Jack stood still as if struck by lightning. Only Jack. Slowly he went over to the bathroom adjoining the kitchen and looked at himself in the mirror, for the first time really looked at himself.

He saw a black-haired, slight young man, short - he was only 5 foot 7 inches high, actually somewhat shorter than Maud. Somewhere in his genes there must have been one of the Spanish sailors who were shipwrecked in Ireland when King Philip's Armada failed in its attempt to conquer Queen Elizabeth's England three and a half centuries ago. His constant studies had given him a slight stoop. He wore glasses and of course, something the mirror did not need to show him but of which he was always conscious, he dragged his left leg. And I thought she would look at me? Of course "Only Jack. Only Jack."

The bile rose in his throat. Then he began to hate. I'm not good enough for her, the proud Englishwoman. They treated me like a lapdog, like a pet. One day, one day, I'll show them. I will do such things, I do not know yet what they are, but such things…. He did not know that he was paraphrasing King Lear, but his anger grew and grew. All the slights suffered in school, all the insults swallowed here in the great house, all of them came to him and he sat for hours beginning to hate and to hate.

The next six months passed in a blur. He continued his studies, passed his final exams, but did so mechanically and out of habit. He constantly had before him the vision of Maud's white body, her pink tipped breasts, the golden fleece at the juncture of her legs, and he kept hearing the words "Only Jack." His love - that is what it had been - for the girl had turned to hate, but his desire had remained unabated. On the contrary, his fantasies now included a helpless, naked Maud, with whom he could do as he willed, whom he could punish and whom he could enjoy.

And finally he received his certificate. He was a full-fledged physician. He was duty bound to report to Maud's father, the Duke of Chalmerston, who had paid for his education, but first he needed to know whether his application for a prestigious residency in surgery at the world-famous hospital in Edinburgh or his research grant were accepted. His first choice was surgery, but he would be almost equally happy doing research. In fact, to his solitary and reclusive nature, a career in research seemed ideal. He had graduated at the top of his class, and so was certain that one or the other of his applications would be granted.

The list of residencies was posted and he strolled over leisurely to view it. He did not need to press close to the wall in the shouting throng of students. "Where are you going?" - " Look, what they gave me ."- "Oh, how dreadful, this is not what I want." He knew that at least in his medical studies he had no equal among his peers in the class.

When he read the list, at first he could not find his name. Then he finally saw it - close to the bottom. Residency at the local hospital in Balmoren, Scotland. The two choice spots he had wanted had gone to others. He looked. Of course, never mind the grades, both were sons of English aristocrats. He stormed into the Dean's Office.

"I know why you're here, Shaughnessy," the dean harrumphed." I'm sorry, but you've got to understand the way of the world."

"What do you mean? I'm so much better than those two idiots. My grades …"

"Yes, yes, your grades. But if I need to spell it out for you, I will. Do you think that the two most prestigious residencies would go to an Irishman when Englishmen want them?

Be realistic, man. Accept who you are. Now the hospital you're going to is a nice, small country hospital. It's a bit out of the way, but there won't be that much pressure, and you'll get along fine with the population it serves."

"Sheepherders and farmers in the Scottish highlands . Oh, yes. But I want to study. You know I can do much better than those two."

"Now look here, Shaughnessy," the Dean grew angry. "Do you want the assignment in
Balmoren or not? Just make up your mind. I'm busy."

Another dream shattered. Again the English. They took my country, they took everything from me. If I could destroy their vaunted Empire, their aristocracy, their feeling of superiority, if I could just kill them all.

And so it began. Jack went to his assigned post in the small hospital in the Scottish highlands. He wrote an obsequious letter of thanks to the Duke, hating himself all the time for doing so. And he began to concentrate on his hatred for all things British. His work was easy. Taking care, under the supervision of senior staff, of the ailments and minor accidents of the local population, required no effort. When a serious case appeared, a major accident or a difficult to diagnose disease, his seniors handled it without giving the young doctor much of a chance to learn. He was not popular with the staff. His glum demeanor and solitary manner rebuffed any friendly opening.

Then he was assigned to make a weekly visit to Castle Waterstoun. The castle had become the home of a group of German prisoners of war. Jack was sent there once a week to check on any medical complaints that they may have, and of course, he had to make himself available in case of emergencies.

There he saw almost five hundred German officers, locked up in a castle, but apparently still totally devoted to their cause. Five hundred men, who could be used to damage the British Empire. Slowly, a plan emerged in his brain. Execution depended first of all on his finding a German who spoke English - Jack did not speak German, of course - and whom he could persuade that he could be trusted. Jack began to plan in great detail. He sat over maps at night. He studied the area and the news. Soon, he knew exactly what he wanted to do. He could strike a blow at the Empire, a very damaging blow, and if he timed it right, he could even fulfill his fantasy and have Maud in his power. With the same intensity and dedication that made him, a tenant farmer's son, head of his class in his medical studies, he now proceeded to execute his plan.

***

"Ratzersdorfer, you know my old friend, Franz Ratzersdorfer?" SS Untersturmfuehrer Priebke smiled. "Where do you know him from? When did you see him last?"

"Just after the Fuehrer brought Austria home into the Reich." Kurt tried not to show his nervousness. This could turn out very badly. Perhaps he shouldn't have asked. But now it's done.

"Well, the last time I saw him, he was an instructor at Schloss Kleinfeld. Heydrich himself has taken an interest in Franz, and I wouldn't be surprised to see him in another position by now. That boy will go far." Priebke was very friendly.

"I always thought so. He was very devoted to the cause." Kurt said.

"Oh, yes. If there's any one of us who epitomizes our motto - Our honor is Loyalty - it's Franz."

"Well, one of these days, we'll see each other again." Kurt sighed. "I wonder when."

"I wouldn't give up hope that it'll be soon." Priebke smiled. "Trust the Fuehrer."

"Is anything going on?" Kurt was very eager. "If there is, I want to be part of it."

"Well, keep your mouth shut. But I'll talk to the powers. After all, an old friend of Franz Ratzersdorfer can be trusted."

Kurt wandered away in deep thought. *I've learned quite a bit. Ratzersdorfer's first name is Franz. But what's more important, for my mission here, I've learned that there are indeed escape plans. Where in heaven's name is that Walter Orne, who's supposed to be my outside contact?*

"Oberleutnant Hagen?"

"Yes?"

"The British doctor is ready to see you now. Please follow me."

Kurt followed the young officer to a room not far from the commandant's office. The room was furnished as a medical dispensary. His guide left him. He looked around and saw a young man in civilian clothes, wearing the usual white coat and with a stethoscope around his neck - the standard doctor's uniform. The physician was short and slight, his eyeglasses were dangling from a black ribbon worn around his neck, and Kurt noticed that the doctor dragged his left leg as he moved.

"Come in, come in." The doctor said in English. Kurt obeyed. "Take off your shirt," the doctor continued.

"Ich spreche kein Englisch" (I do not speak English), Kurt replied, shrugging his shoulders.

"Of course". The doctor muttered and motioned to Kurt to take off his shirt. He then examined him carefully, listened to his chest and finally motioned Kurt to remove his trousers and to stretch out on the examination table. He then paid particular attention to Kurt's wound, made him move the leg in various directions - which Kurt did with appropriate exclamations of pain - and when he was done, said." Your leg is healing nicely."

The doctor then brought his face close to Kurt and whispered. "You can trust me, I'm in touch with M.I.6 - do you have anything for me? "

Was this Walter Orne? No. Mr. Lanyard had told him that his contact would pass as a man of the cloth - not as a doctor. And in any case, he had not identified himself by name.

"Ich verstehe nicht." (I do not understand). Kurt answered.

"Come on, Hagen. You know where I'm from. Don't act so surprised. Give me your report so that I can pass it on," the physician insisted.

"Bitte, ich spreche kein English" Kurt was adamant.

"Allright, you can go." The doctor motioned to Kurt to leave, and Kurt obeyed.

This is very odd. A British doctor acting as if he were an intelligence emissary. Of course, it's possible, but why wasn't I warned? If he is real, he should have been able to identify himself better, he should have mentioned some names that I know, like Lanyard, or Admiral Morse. I don't trust him. I wish that Walter Orne would make an appearance.

Kurt limped over to the mess hall to take his accustomed seat at the dinner table. The dinner proceeded as usual. When the men had been dismissed, Kurt was approached by one of the several adjutants the commandant liked to have around him.

"You are wanted in the commandant's office, Hagen".

"On my way." Kurt jumped up and followed with alacrity.

Again he was led into what appeared an even more luxurious room now that he had become accustomed to the bareness of his quarters. "Ah, Hagen," the commandant smiled. "Sit down, I may have some good news for you."

"Not so fast," Sturmbannfuehrer Fratzer stood up from his customary seat slightly to the rear and left of Oberstleutnant Werfel. "First, I have some questions, with your permission," he looked at the commandant.

"Go ahead." The Oberstleutnant nodded.

"Oberleutnant Hagen. You remember your orders as regards reporting any defeatist talk or any unauthorized sexual activity?"

"Yes, sir."

"Well?"

"I have no knowledge of any such unauthorized activity, sir. " Kurt thought quickly.   " However…" he hesitated.

"Well?"

"Sir, dinner table conversation among fellow officers is hardly…."

"I understand your reluctance, and it does you honor. But you are required to answer, and answer fully."

"Yes, sir. Then I must report that Leutnant Hugo Bratter expressed some very defeatist sentiments."

"Ah." Fratzer and Werfel exchanged knowing glances. Fratzer resumed his seat, and the commandant spoke again.

"When you first came here you asked about the possibility of escape. Such a possibility exists now. It requires total dedication and of course great risk, but it also presents us with the chance of doing considerable damage to the enemy. Are you ready for such a task?"

Kurt jumped up, stood at attention and spoke out strongly:

"I have sworn to give my life for my Fuehrer and for the Fatherland, if necessary. Please give me the honor of proving this."

The two officers smiled. "This is nothing less than what I expected to hear." Werfel commented. " Dr. Shaughnessy has reported to me that your leg is almost as good as new, and should not prevent you from proceeding. Now, you are the only naval officer we have here. What do you know about British warships? Specifically, would you know the most vulnerable spot in British ships lying at anchor? The spots where some explosives could do the most damage?"

Kurt had to hide his astonishment that the British doctor, whose name apparently was Shaughnessy, had reported to a German officer, who, after all, was a prisoner of war. *I knew that there was something fishy about this doctor. But now, how do I answer the question? I've got to find out more about the plan.*

"Of course, Herr Oberstleutnant. At the Naval Academy, we studied the Navies of all our enemies. And the best place to damage or destroy a vessel would be an explosive either in the munitions bunker or as close as possible to the engine room."

"And you would know, where these areas are in each ship of the British fleet?"

"Well, sir, it's been a while since I studied the British fleet, but, yes, I believe that I should be able to point them out. Yes, sir."

"You know about the Firth of Forth?"

"The main homeport for the British Navy in the North Sea? Of course, I do."

"If our plan succeeds, you would have a chance to demonstrate what you know about the British Navy. Think what a blow we could strike if we could damage or destroy a substantial portion of the British North Sea fleet. Wouldn't that be worth every risk?" Werfel's eyes gleamed with enthusiasm.

"Indeed, it would, sir, but how would we go about that?"

"You will find out in due course, Hagen. Now your job is to try and recollect every detail you remember from your studies about the British fleet. I want you to draw pictures of every kind of British vessel, and write out detailed instructions as to how a force of four or five men, with a minimal amount of explosives could cause the greatest damage. "

How in heaven's name am I going to do that? I can't tell one ship from another.

"Zu Befehl, Herr Oberstleutnant "

"Priebke" Oberstleutnant Werfel called out. The SS Officer who had known Ratzersdorfer appeared at the door.

"You and Hagen will be a team. Now that Hagen knows something of the plan, there will be no further discussion with anyone about anything. Priebke, you will help move Hagen into your quarters and make sure that he remains undisturbed so that he can do the work that I have assigned to him. You will not leave him alone at any time. Is that clear?"

"Yes, sir." Priebke stood at attention.

"Very well. Hagen, I urge you to get to work immediately. We should be ready to move very shortly. And now, dismiss."

Kurt jumped up, saluted, and left the room, closely followed by Priebke. He took a good look at his new partner, guard or jailer - whatever the case may be.

SS Untersturmfuehrer Priebke was a giant. He was at least half a head taller than Kurt, who was quite tall himself. He had a head that appeared a little too small for his body, resting on a thick neck above massive shoulders. His arms and legs were thick. He seemed to be in superb physical condition. *He is just the kind of man who would have enjoyed tramping through the Jewish section of his hometown, beating Jews and destroying their property, and then relaxing in a beer garden over a dozen steins. My new partner. How am I going to get past him, so that I can get out of here and warn the fleet? But I have no idea how Werfel and Fratzer expect to get us out of here and over to the Firth of Forth, which after, all, is quite a distance, and how they expect to get weapons and explosives. Until I know that I really have nothing to report. I must hang in there and find out more. Where in heaven's name is Walter Orne?*

Priebke led Kurt to his old room and helped him gather up his belongings. To the questions of his former roommates, Kurt merely answered " Orders" and gave an expressive shrug. Priebke then led Kurt up the stairs, up, up more than seven flights up to the top room of the tower. "Must we go so high?" Kurt complained. " My leg …"

"Orders, my friend. But I'll help you." And Kurt allowed Priebke to half carry him up the stairs, while Kurt constantly complained about the pain that this trip caused him. *This should make him a little less watchful,* Kurt hoped.

At the top of the tower, Kurt entered an octagonal room, simply furnished, with two beds, a closet and a wooden table with two chairs. "Here," Priebke said. "You can do your work here, and they'll send up our food so that you won't be distracted. We only have one or two days, before everything starts."

So he knows the plan. Good. Kurt dragged himself to the windows. There were eight windows in the room and the view from all of them was magnificent. Four windows overlooked the Loch. The water seemed very cold and forbidding. The wind, which whistled through the tower room, produced waves . Kurt opened a window and leaned out. The waves just below the tower hit the rocks with considerable force. He looked up. The roof of the tower appeared to extend a bit out over the rocky shore.

The view through the other windows was to the land side of the castle. Just below was the causeway. Here there was a sheer drop down to the ground.

"Well, we should be safe here from any attack by armed knights." Kurt joked. Priebke did not smile.

"I am glad that you had a good look out." The SS man said grimly." This window has served me very well in disposing of traitors to our cause. And do not think for a moment that, friend of Ratzersdorfer or not, I would hesitate to do the same to you, if I am ordered to do so."

He produced paper and pencils and motioned Kurt to the table. "And now, you'd better get started."

"I need a ruler," Kurt muttered. He looked around the room. "Here, try this." Priebke pulled a silver cigarette case from his breast pocket. " I got this from a Jewish banker," he snickered. "A gift, you know." The case was rectangular and large enough so that one side could indeed serve as a ruler. Kurt set to work.

Well, I have the answer to the question Mr. Lanyard asked. The three deaths were indeed murders, and I know the murderer. But the problem here is much greater. The escape attempt could really cause a lot of harm. I must get to this elusive Walter Orne and get out of here so that I can make my report. In the meantime, how do I handle the task they have set me without arousing suspicion? The only British war ship I've ever been on, was the destroyer that took me to Oran and then to London. I have no idea where the munitions bunker or the engine room are on that ship, but I might as well start and make something up.

He started to draw a schematic representation of a ship, named it "destroyer" and began to write detailed instructions about finding the third staircase from the bow and going down to the fourth level, and so forth. Priebke came over, helped himself to a cigarette from the silver case, offered one to Kurt who declined, and sat down on one of the beds smoking quietly. Every time Kurt looked up, he found Priebke's eyes on him. It made Kurt quite uncomfortable.

After a while, Kurt got up and stretched. " Where's the latrine?" he asked. "Down two flights. Is it urgent?" Priebke replied. "I'm afraid so. Would you help me? I don't do so well on the stairs." With a bit of grumbling, Priebke assisted Kurt down and then back up. *Going to the latrine together must be a bonding experience,* Kurt thought. As he leaned heavily on Priebke on the way back up the stairs, he said. " I'm a bit worried. Do you really think we can trust the English doctor? "

He did not anticipate the reaction. With a broad smile, Priebke said: "So, they told you the plan? I'm not surprised. I thought that a friend of Franz Ratzersdorfer was trustworthy."

"Of course, they told me." Kurt sighed. "But I'm worried about the Englishman."

"That's because you don't understand. He's not English. He's Irish . That makes all the difference."

"You're right. I don't understand. English, Irish - they're the same."

"No, they're not. The Irish have been oppressed by the English for centuries, and we're going to liberate them. They're on our side. Don't you worry."

"Well, you reassure me. But I'm still worried. Getting out of the castle isn't a problem, but afterwards.."

"That's where the doctor's plan really makes a difference. It's the Poles. That's the beauty of it."

"I guess you're right. In any case, we must rely on our superiors to know best." Kurt was afraid to ask more . He did not want to arouse Priebke's suspicions, but he hoped the SS man would continue to talk. Unfortunately, by now they had reached the top of the tower and were back in their room. Kurt sat down and continued his work, and Priebke resumed his silence.

The Poles. What could the Poles have to do with an escape from here?

***

"Come in, doctor. What is the news?"

It was fortunate, Jack Shaughnessy thought, that Lieutenant Colonel Werfel had spent considerable time as military attaché with the German Embassy in London. Not only did that mean that his command of English was excellent, but it also meant that he had studied the nuances of British politics, and needed no explanation about the disaffection of an Irishman from the British cause.

"We must move tomorrow night." Shaughnessy said.

Werfel paled.

"What? So soon? I'm not sure we're ready. Why tomorrow?" Lieutenant Colonel Werfel had enjoyed the planning and the conspiracy. But now it was going to be serious. He was very comfortable as the commanding officer of this prisoner of war facility. Did he really want to risk his life on a hopeless, or almost hopeless venture? He really wasn't that fanatic a Nazi. But did he have a choice?

"I'll tell you why. " Dr. Shaughnessy sat down and stretched out his legs - he always felt better when he could take the weight off his damaged knee. "Tomorrow is Saturday. Tomorrow night a dance has been arranged in a village about twenty miles North of the Chalmerston estate. The Polish battalion which is training on the estate has been invited. That means that almost all the men will be absent, and you'll only have to deal with a small cadre. Similarly, Saturday night the guards here are rotated off, and you will have only a handful to worry about. They won't be expecting anything. And here is what I consider most important: The Duke of Chalmerston, his wife and daughter and several guests of similarly exalted standing will be in residence at the Duke's Scottish estate. They would make very useful hostages on our trip to the Firth of Forth. They could insure us against bombing attacks by British planes, once we have captured a ship that could take us to Germany."

With some reluctance Werfel translated Jack's speech for the benefit of Fratzer. That Fratzer should jump up with enthusiasm, grab Shaughnessy's hand, and exclaim "Yes, yes, let's go," did not surprise the more cautious Werfel.

"I suppose you're right." Werfel said, with an inward sigh. " Let's go over the plan once more."

***

Kurt worked along as slowly and carefully as he could, drawing schematics of invented British warships and using his imagination to describe complicated ways of reaching the engine rooms and munitions bunkers of these ships. *If only the Venerable Bede were here, he could certainly add verisimilitude to my efforts. But when and how do they expect to get out of here? I've got to find out more, and then I've got to find a way to pass on a warning.*

Someone banged at the door. Priebke opened, and welcomed Fratzer. " How are you doing?" the SS Officer asked.

Kurt jumped up and stood at attention. "Please , sir, look at my work." He proffered the sheaf of drawings to Fratzer. Fratzer threw a cursory glance at the sheets, folded them and placed them in his pocket. " Fine, I'll study them later. Keep it up," he said to Kurt.

Then with a nod to Priebke, asking him to follow him, he left. As soon as Priebke was out the door, Kurt rushed over to it and opened it slightly. On the next landing Fratzer and Priebke were in intense conversation. Kurt could not make out Fratzer's soft voice, but every once in a while Priebke's booming baritone was audible.

"Tomorrow night? Wonderful."

- - - -

"Oh, I'll make him keep up."

- - - -

"I understand. I hope it won't come to that, but I'll do it."

- - - -

"I can't wait to get started. I just hope that one of the Poles is my size, or I'll have trouble finding a uniform."

- - - -

"Zu Befehl. Heil Hitler."

Kurt rushed back to his table and worked very studiously when Priebke returned to the room. "Well, my friend," Priebke smiled, "get as much done as you can. Then we'll try to get a good night's sleep. You never know what tomorrow may bring."

Kurt started to think. He remembered the summer of 1940, his flight from Paris in the company of Sarah - whom he thought about with a sense of loss, but less bitterness than earlier. *There were Polish troops being embarked on British vessels near St. Jean de Luz. There may be a Polish unit nearby. The doctor would know about that. If he can get almost five hundred German officers out of here, he could lead them to the Polish bivouac. They would not have many arms, just what they could get from the guards here at the castle, but with surprise, they could overwhelm the Poles, take their uniforms and weapons, and march in broad daylight down to the Firth of Forth. Who here in Scotland, would know that these foreign troops are German escapees instead of Poles, particularly if they avoid as much contact as possible?*

How do I get out of here to prevent this?

Priebke was snoring very loudly, when Kurt noted the false dawn - it must be two A.M. He rose from his bunk as quietly as he could and climbed out the window of the turret room onto the slanting roof. Carefully he looked about. It was hard to see much, there was just a sliver of the moon in the sky and it was frequently covered by heavy, dark clouds. *Does this roof get me anywhere?* One side seemed to end in a sheer drop down to the cobblestones of the courtyard. Kurt could not find any way to climb down - there appeared no hand-holds, that he could see. *This might be easier in daylight,* he muttered, *but even then I can't see how I could get down there.* The other side of the roof appeared to stretch a little further. Kurt walked over, very carefully. He noted that the slant ended and a straight, narrow ledge appeared. Following this, he realized that the roof extended over a small pier jutting out into the lake. He stretched out full length and looked over the edge. Below him - water. The roof covered the pier but stretched beyond it, so that any vessel docking there would also be covered. *When their local lordships get out of their boat, they mustn't get wet if it rains. But how do I get down?* There seemed to be no way. Kurt looked at the water below. *It seems calm, but who can tell in the darkness. But it's got to be deep enough for a boat. I wonder how cold it is?* And he jumped.

* * *

Sergeant Bridener was at the guardpost at the end of the causeway having a cuppa, when he saw Dr. Shaughnessy pedaling up on his bicycle. "What are you doing here today, Doc? This isn't your regular day?"

"Absolutely right you are, my boy". Doctor Shaughnessy dismounted, got his medical bag, and entered the guard hut. " Roll up your sleeve, and you too," he said to the two privates who shared the duty with the sergeant. "There's a terrible flu going around, and they sent me a batch of vaccine, with orders to administer it urgently. So, let's go."

Sergeant Bridener obeyed - all soldiers are accustomed to be shot full of strange substances anytime a medical man comes around. " But, if I may ask, why isn't the regimental surgeon here to do this? After all, you're a civilian, doctor?"

"Because this is very urgent, and the regimental surgeon is busy inoculating everyone in sight at headquarters. Your handful of shirkers will just have to do with me. Now sit down. You'll be a little dizzy for a moment after the inoculation, but it will pass. Never mind."

Doctor Shaughnessy administered his injections to the three soldiers. Within seconds all three were sound asleep. He pulled rope from his medical kit, and proceeded to truss them up tightly, placed their own wadded up handkerchiefs in their mouths and taped over them, being careful to allow them room to breathe freely through their noses. He then cut the telephone wire, got on his bicycle, and whistling a merry tune rode on to the main entrance to the castle.

While there were more soldiers to take care of, Jack Shaughnessy had no problems in putting those on guard to sleep in the same manner. This time he did not bother to tie them up. The injection would last long enough for his purpose. He then went into the ready-room, where the off-duty squad was sleeping, and was able to inject six out of the eight soldiers before they woke up. The last two were easily persuaded by his silver tongue to allow him to administer the injection.

With the entire complement of guards asleep, Jack leisurely obtained the keys to the arms room and then opened the main gate to the prisoners compound.

Werfel and Fratzer were waiting for him. " Here," Jack said, "all is going according to plan, get your men and let's go."

Fratzer took two of his men and went into the arms room. Others grabbed the soldiers' weapons and web belts. "And now, before we go -"Fratzer ordered his SS guards-"Kill all the soldiers."

"What? Stop! "Werfel cried out. "You can't do that. They're unarmed prisoners. I forbid this shameful behavior. I give the orders here."

Fratzer grabbed Werfel by the throat. "I've taught higher ranking officers than you who
gives the orders in the cellars in the Prinz Albrechtstrasse. Now you'll keep your mouth shut or you'll stay here with them."

Werfel started to shiver. He had not known. But if Fratzer mentioned the Prinz Abrechtstrasse, he was not an ordinary SS officer, he was a member of the Sicherheitsdienst, the elite SD whose headquarters was in the Prinz Albrechtstrasse in
Berlin. Then, regardless of his official rank, clearly Fratzer was in command. "If we do this and get caught, we are dead men." Werfel tried once more. "And it's dishonorable."

"We are dead men anyway, unless we succeed in our plans. And it is not dishonorable to get rid of any potential enemy of the Reich. Now do your duty." Fratzer ordered his SS men. " Do not waste ammunition, use the bayoncts."

Within minutes all the British soldiers were dead. Fratzer made sure that all available armaments were in the possession of his SS cadre, and then whatever was left over, was distributed to officers whose fanaticism he could trust. Werfel received no weapon.

The men were assembled in the courtyard. Fratzer spoke to them:

"We will strike a blow for the Fatherland that will go down in the history books and may well have a decisive impact on the war. Most of you will die for country and Fuehrer, but those who survive will have glory for ever, and those who die will be remembered in the annals of the Reich during its entire thousand year existence. You will obey all orders without question. There is a complicated plan and it must be followed to the letter. Now we will follow our friend, Doctor Shaughnessy, who will ride his bicycle. WE MUST KEEP UP WITH HIM. We have three hours to cover nine miles. Schnellschritt, forward march."

"I will walk the bike to the end of the causeway. We will start in earnest when we have hit the mainland." Jack muttered to Fratzer. "The causeway is too narrow for such a large body of men to make speed."

"You're right. Let's go."

As they advanced, a machine gun opened up. The first few men fell. Fortunately for them, Fratzer and Shaughnessy had remained with the main body of troops and were not injured.

"What's this? You said they were safely tied up?" Fratzer screamed at Shaughnessy.

"They were, they were. I don't understand. Even the drug could not have dissipated so quickly. What's going on?" The doctor was at a loss.

Werfel pushed himself forward. " Perhaps you need the services of an experienced front-line officer after all." Quickly he gave orders, halting the advance. " Take cover. Armed men to the front. One more attempt. You ten, try to rush the post. You four, give covering fire. Go."

As soon as the ten men Werfel had ordered forward approached the guard post, the machine gun opened up again. Several were hit, two or three remained motionless where they had fallen, the others crawled back.

"Well, we have a problem before we even begin this venture." Werfel almost smiled.

"We are on a very tight schedule. Any delay would get us to Castle Chalmerston too late. The Polish troops would be back from their outing. We must get through. We have to order another frontal assault." Fratzer said.

"And lose more men uselessly? No. There must be another way. Let us look around first." Werfel was in his element. This is something he could handle.

* * *

Kurt had hit the water so hard that he was momentarily stunned. He went in deep, pulled down by his clothes. Frantically, he pushed himself up, and finally emerged into the air. After taking in some great gulps of lifesaving oxygen, he took inventory. *Possibly some bruises, but I'm allright.* Then the cold hit him. *I've got to get out of here.* He began to swim to the causeway and staying close to it, made his way to the shore. Gratefully, he felt rocks and sand underfoot, and with some difficulty pulled himself up and out onto the roadway. The wind whistled through his wet clothes, and he was chilled to the bone. *I've got to find shelter and dry clothes before hypothermia sets in. And I've got to get help. Where's the guard shack?* A cloud passed and by the sliver of the moon, Kurt was able to orient himself. He ran as fast as he could in his waterlogged clothes to the guard hut and knocked at the door. " Help, help. Quick."

Odd, there is no answer. Where are the guards. He opened the door and entered. *All three trussed up and unconscious. So it has begun.*

Doctor Shaughnessy, not a military man, had neglected to remove the soldiers' weapons. After all, there was plenty of time to pick them up when he returned with his army of ex-prisoners of war. Kurt found a bayonet, and quickly cut the ropes and then tried to revive the soldiers. *No good, they're out for good.* Kurt began to shiver uncontrollably.

I've got to get out of these wet clothes. He threw off his clothes, undressed the tallest of the soldiers, and put on the man's uniform. *I'm sorry, I need it more than you do right now.* There was a small stove on which a pan of water for tea was heating. The stove was still warm. Kurt put some additional coal into the belly of the stove, and took a sip of hot tea. It revived him, and there was a noticeable increase of warmth in the small hut.

He had noted on entering that the phone wires were cut. *What should I do? They will be coming soon. But they have to cross the causeway. Where can I go for help? I have no transport and I have no idea where the nearest village is. If I leave, five hundred fanatical*

Germans will roam the countryside, and perhaps be able to accomplish their purpose. The Irish doctor will lead them to the Polish bivouac.

If I stay, and use the machine gun, perhaps, a passing motorist will hear the shooting and sound the alarm. At the worst, I will delay them, and in this, time is crucial.

Kurt swiveled the machine gun so that it bore directly on the causeway. He looked for ammunition. One belt only - they did not expect a siege. I have to be very sparing when I shoot. He took the three rifles the soldiers had carried, loaded them from the guard's pouches, and placed them next to the machine gun. Not much ammunition there either. I have to hope that someone hears me.

He looked toward the castle. Here they come. He remembered his gunnery instructor: "Wait for it - Wait - wait." Then he could wait no longer. He began firing.

* * *

Werfel assembled his army in the courtyard again. "I need a few volunteers who are good swimmers." he announced. Several men raised their hands. "Good, come with me. Take off your clothes and give them to a comrade to carry. You four take bayonets only. You two swim on this side of the causeway, you two on the other side. We will give you enough time to get close to the guard-hut, and then we will begin another frontal assault. There can be no more than three soldiers in the shack, if we can believe the doctor. You should be able to get in unobserved, while they are busy shooting at us. Understood? Go."

Kurt watched the causeway intently. Here they come again. He traversed the machine gun, firing carefully, trying not to waste his few precious bullets. Then he heard a noise behind him. Fortunately he had bolted the door. Someone was trying to open it. Kurt reached for one of the rifles. Perhaps it's help? He called out, in English: "Who is it?" There was no answer. The tip of a bayonet appeared at the bolt, and the flimsy lock was broken. Kurt fired at the German. Another German soldier followed and Kurt shot him as well. Kurt swerved. Two more men had climbed over the window while he was occupied. Kurt grabbed the pan from the stove and flung the hot water at one of the men. Time to go. He took one of the other rifles and rushed out the door, across the road and into the safety of the dark woods. *I did not delay them for very long. Isn't anyone awake in this god-forsaken country?*

Kurt hid in the woods. He watched the Germans, led by Doctor Shaughnessy on his bicycle, in quick march coming over the causeway and disappearing down the road. He noted that no wounded were carried along, but that two SS men stayed to the rear and dispatched their own helpless wounded with bayonets. *I expected nothing else.*

* * *

When Priebke had woken up and not seen Oberleutnant Hagen, he was not too concerned at first. *Probably in the latrine*, he thought, *and did not want to wake me, although he should have.* Then he began to worry. He rushed down the two stairs to the latrine. *No Hagen.* He rushed around up and down stairs. *Nowhere to be found. Fratzer will kill me. Where could he have gone?*
Perhaps he overheard Fratzer instructing me to kill him if he can't keep up, and went into hiding. Well, we're ready to go anyway. Let him stay behind. If Fratzer asks, I'll tell him I did what he ordered. Priebke went down to the courtyard where all the other soldiers were milling about. He kept wandering around, keeping a look out for Hagen, but did not see him. Eventually, after the fight at the guardhouse, he followed the troops, staying at the rear, as per his instructions.

* * *

Walter Orne was middle-aged, middle sized and totally undistinguished looking. His was a face people would forget the moment they had stopped looking at it. He liked it that way, it enabled him to be a good operative. Normally, his clothing would be equally undistinguished, but this time, he was dressed in the black suit and dog collar of a cleric. He had presented himself at the door of Major Brattlewaite , the commanding officer of Waterstoun Castle three days ago,
The major had been very hospitable, offered him tea and only glanced at his papers after an exchange of chat about the weather and the latest cricket scores. "So good to have a new face around here," Major Brattlewaite said, "we're really in the provinces. So, you've

been appointed chaplain to the prisoners? Didn't know they were entitled to such services. Speak their language, do you?"

"I do, Major. I spent some years studying in Germany as a young man. "

"Well, whatever. Fine, we'll ask the Colonel whether he'll accept you."

"I beg your pardon?" Walter Orne was non-plussed.

"That's the deal, and it works very well. We guard the outside of the castle, make sure there's no escape, you know, but they run their own show inside. Their commandant, Lieutenant Colonel Werfel, good chap for a Jerry, speaks proper English. He's the one you've got to convince, not me. I'll send him a note."

And a note came back, thanking the British for their offer of a spiritual guide, but declining it. "We can handle our own spiritual requirements, and do not accept interference in our consciences from other sources."

"Well, that's that." Major Brattlewaite harrumphed. "Sorry, old chap. Would have enjoyed your company."

"You can't tell me that you accept this? Can't we at least make a public announcement and see whether any of the prisoners would like to avail themselves of my services?"

"Sorry. Can't do it. They have their own discipline, and it works well for them and for us. Without this arrangement I'd need a lot more troops to guard them, and you know we can't spare them. "

With his tail between his legs, Walter Orne got back into his car and left. At the next village he tried to telephone Mr. Lanyard for new instructions. Mr. Lanyard was out. Orne found a room in the village pub, and kept telephoning, and leaving his number. Mr. Lanyard was out. Mr. Lanyard was in conference. Mr. Lanyard could not be disturbed.

Three days later, Mr. Lanyard finally deigned to come to the phone. To Orne's remonstrances, he answered "What's the problem? What could have happened to our man? He's surrounded by British soldiers. Just as well to give him time to find out what we wanted to know. Routine investigation, anyway, just for show, you know. Anyway, it's time to get him out of there. I'll arrange to send orders to Major Brattlewaite to have him released to your custody, and you go and get him."

So, finally, Orne was able to drive back to Waterstoun with instructions to get Kurt out of there. He was still dressed in his clerical clothes. He had learned a long time ago the importance of staying in character at all times.

As Orne approached the castle, a rather wild looking figure jumped out of the bushes, brandishing a rifle. "Stop, stop."

The man wore British uniform, although it certainly looked as if the supply sergeant who had issued it had not been a friend of the soldier.

Orne stopped the car. "What is it?"

"There's an emergency. You must take me to the nearest British troop depot. Do you know where it is?"

"Why, here, at the castle? What's wrong?"

The man looked at Orne's clothing. "What's your name?" he demanded.

"Walter Orne. But I don't understand .."

"I'm Kurt Auster. It took you long enough to get here. Now we've got a major problem on our hands."

* * *

After the Fall of France, in 1940, Britain prepared for a German invasion. As part of these preparations, all road signs were removed. This was intended to confuse an enemy, and any one who has ever driven through the lanes of the British country-side, would know how damaging such confusion could be. Jack Shaughnessy had anticipated the problem, and had made many trips from Castle Waterstoun to the Chalmerston estate, so that he could lead his army without hesitating at each crossroad. Lieutenant Colonel Werfel's prestige had soared by his handling of the fight at the guard house, and Fratzer allowed him to utilize his military skills. Werfel had organized his men into squads and companies, given each squad and company names and numbers, and placed experienced field officers at their head. Aware that they had limited time to reach their destination, he forced a quick march on his men, but equally aware of the limits of human endurance, he allowed for a ten minute rest stop every hour. During the last of these stops, Werfel asked Fratzer to join him to review the next step of the plan with Doctor Shaughnessy.

"You are sure that the Polish guards are unarmed?" Werfel asked.

"Absolutely. The British don't want armed foreigners running about on the loose," Shaughnessy smiled. " The Polish MP's and their guards carry batons. Good enough to control an obstreperous soldier, but no match for our men."

"Particularly now that we are armed." Fratzer interjected.

"It would be wiser not to use our weapons yet. Every time shots are heard, there is a risk that the alarm is given, even in this rural area."

"Now, Doctor, you know where the arms are being kept?" Werfel continued.

"Indeed, I do. I will lead you to the building. They are under lock and key, but that should present no problem. First we have to cope with the handful of soldiers who had to stay behind and were not allowed to go to the dance."

"And transport to take us to the Firth of Forth? "

"That will be the same trucks that bring the troops back from the dance. We must have everything under control, so that we can arrest and imprison those troops and then as quickly as possible leave for the harbor. However we have to get to the mansion to take the hostages. If you will give me some men, I'll take care of that." Jack Shaughnessy's primary purpose for this venture had been revenge on Lady Maud. He had fantasized for many months having her in his power. The moment was approaching. But he could not reveal to his allies that that was more important to him than who won the war.

"And the Polish uniforms?"

"There should be enough in storage. Otherwise we will take what we need from the troops we capture."

"There is the question again. " Fratzer said. "Can we leave the Polish troops behind to fight against us another day? I say, we can't. We must kill them as we did the troops at Waterstoun."

"You are talking about several hundred men! I will not allow this. You will have to kill me first." Lieutenant Colonel Werfel was a soldier not a murdering thug, and he meant what he said.

Fratzer did not answer, but gave Werfel a speculative look.

The Duke of Chalmerston's Irish estate, on which Jack Shaughnessy was born, was immense in Jack's eyes, and the manorhouse had been the largest and most luxurious building Jack had ever seen. That is, until he came to Chalmerston Palace, the Duke's ancestral Scottish home. The grounds were so large, that the Polish bivouac together with the substantial areas required for training were totally out of sight and hearing of the main complex. The entire estate was fenced in. There was an open gate through which the soldiers marched. Several miles further on, another fence and another gate enclosed the main part of the estate. The Polish bivouac was within those two fences, but a considerable distance to the West of the main entrance driveway. *We would not want His Grace to be bothered by the sight of soldiers training,* Jack mumbled. *Bad enough that he had to give them space We all have to make sacrifices in war time.*

Jack led his troops through the gate, turned left and they were on the sleepy guards like wolves. In short order, the Germans were in control of the camp. The munitions depot and the supply depot were broken into. Very quickly there seemed to be a heavily armed Polish unit, where German prisoners of war had been.

"Now to set up an ambush for the returning troops." Werfel said. He ordered his men into appropriate positions. "We must take them without firing a shot if possible. We can lock them into the supply depot after the door has been repaired. They will be half drunk and will expect nothing "

Fratzer called his cadre of SS men to the side and gave them whispered instructions. At that point Priebke made himself known. "You took care of Hagen? I do not see him with us." Fratzer asked.

"I obeyed your orders, sir." Priebke replied.

"Good man. Now I have another task for you. You must understand that what I order you to do is necessary for the success of our mission." Fratzer drew Priebke to the side and began to whisper instructions to him.

* * *

Chalmerston Palace was perhaps not quite as large as Buckingham Palace, but it lacked very little to equal it. Another mile or more from the second gate, the visitor first reached a lake. The road curved around one side and up a hill to the main building. A number of marble steps lead up to the front door. The family quarters and main entertainment sections occupied the principal part of the building, large wings stretched left and right which were used by staff . The building had originally been designed by Sir Christopher Wren in the seventeenth century, and its harmonious proportions still showed the traces of the master's hand, but additions and modernizations over the centuries had obscured the original design. The formal gardens in the back, designed by Inigo

Jones, had been maintained for three hundred years and were one of the glories of Scotland.

Lieutenant Colonel Werfel had found a number of officers with a working knowledge of English among his troops. He assigned one of them, Leutnant Moser, to the squad with which Jack Shaughnessy now approached the palace. The hour of Jack's revenge was at hand. He could hardly wait.

The troops banged at the front door, which was opened by a sleepy maid-servant. " Yes sir? What is it? "

"Get the senior staff. Quick." Jack ordered.

A portly personage appeared, hastily buttoning his jacket. " Yes, sir. I'm Groton, the butler. How may I help you?"

"There is an emergency. Please assemble all residents of the palace here immediately. How many would that be? "

"Sir, we only have a skeleton staff now. The war, you know. There are eighteen of us below the stairs…"

"And the family and guests?"

"His Grace, her Ladyship and Lady Maud are in residence, sir. And Lady Maud's friend, Lady Sarah Blamington. That's all. This is not the time to entertain much."

"Yes, yes, I know. The war. Well, get them all dressed and get them down here." Jack ordered.

"Sir, they're asleep - I cannot …."

"You can and you will. I told you this is an emergency. You have ten minutes to assemble every one here."

While Jack was enjoying giving orders to the Duke's butler, Werfel started to worry.

"All has gone well so far," he said to Fratzer. "But don't you think the trucks should be here? How long do these dances go on? "

"Oh, I wouldn't be concerned. They'll be here and we're ready for them."

* * *

First they had to get to a telephone, which in rural Scotland was not easy. Orne turned the car around and as fast as the narrow lanes allowed, drove back to the village where he had slept the last few nights. "There is no point trying to reach Mr. Lanyard," he said to Kurt after having told him about his previous difficulties in reaching that estimable gentleman. "We have to call Army headquarters directly, but will they listen to us?"

"I have an emergency number for the chief of my service. This is not his department, I've been lent to Mr. Lanyard for this job, but he'll get the ball rolling, don't worry."

Kurt called Admiral Morse. The number he had would reach the Admiral wherever he was at all times. Of course, Kurt woke his superior out of the soundest of sleeps.

"Auster? You had better have a good reason for this call or you'll find yourself in Greenland counting penguins." Admiral Morse was not in a good mood.

"Yes sir, please listen."

Morse could be most attentive when necessary and did not have to have things spelled out for him.

"Good job, Auster. I'll get on the horn and alert the military. We'll see what troops can be rounded up. You might get yourself to the Chalmerston estate and see if you can warn them. And try to find out where the Polish troops are. It's Saturday night, and there must be a reason why the break-out occurred now. My guess is that most of the troops are at some festivity laid on for them away from their camp."

Frantic attempts to reach the Chalmerston estate by phone were fruitless. Whether the connection was broken deliberately, or whether the inefficiency of the rural network was to blame, Kurt could only guess, but it was an ominous sign. Now to find out whether a dance or some other festivity was in progress for the Polish soldiers. Kurt had a brilliant idea.

"Let's ask the landlord."

And of course, that worthy knew everything. Many of the young ladies of the area, including his own daughter, had been invited to the village of Ballymantrae, about twenty miles away, where a dance was being held in the church hall, the only one large enough in the area to accommodate such multitudes. The landlord even knew the phone number of the rectory to which the hall was attached. Another frantic phonecall and after a long time, a female voice answered querulously. "It's very late, and it's bad enough there's so much noise from the hall. Now what? Can't you let anybody sleep?"

"This is a matter of life and death. I apologize for waking you, but I must speak to the officer commanding the Polish troops at the dance. Please, please, get him." Kurt pleaded.

"You must be joking? Get me out of bed at this hour? No way."

"Let me handle it." Walter Orne took the phone out of Kurt's hand. "Now, I assume you're the rector's housekeeper, and I'm sorry to disturb your well deserved rest." Orne spoke in the soft, but resonant tones of the cleric. "This is Bishop Orne. It is essential that I speak to the rector urgently. Please ask him to bring the Polish officer to the phone as well. Now I must ask you to do this most urgently, please."

"Yes, your reverence, I'll hurry." The voice quavered.

"So, you're a bishop now. " Kurt smiled.

"I'll promote myself to pope if it'll help get us out of this mess. Can you imagine the damage a band of well-armed Germans roaming around Scotland can do?"

"Particularly if they reach the Firth of Forth." Kurt nodded.

They waited with unrestrained impatience until a male voice sounded on the phone. "This is the Reverend Droughton. Bishop Orne? I do not think I've had the pleasure…"

Orne interrupted. "Is the officer commanding the Polish troops with you? Does he speak English?"

"He is here, but I don't know about his English. What is this all about?"

"Please get him on the phone."

"Commandant Warzuleski "

Kurt took the receiver. "Do you speak English? Parlez vous Francais? Sprechen Sie Deutsch?"

"My best language would be German, I regret to say." The Polish officer answered.

Kurt explained the situation in German as briefly as he could.

"What do you think I should do?" The officer asked. "We have no weapons with us."

"The most important thing, in my opinion," Kurt answered, "is to do nothing until British troops arrive. Particularly, do not return to your encampment at the Chalmerston estate. I am sure the Germans are waiting for you, heavily armed with your weapons, and had intended to take you prisoners and to take your transport. As long as they have no access to your trucks they cannot go far. We are in touch with the Military Authorities. Please stay by this phone until you receive further instructions."

"Very well."

"And now," Kurt said, " what do you say if we go to Chalmerston Estate to reconnoiter?"

"First, advise your chief of what we have done and tell him where we're going."

"Good idea."

* * *

"These are all the weapons you could find?" Werfel was noticeably upset. "That's not enough to equip half our number. What about ammunition?"

The three young men to whom he had assigned the task of checking the ammunitions depot stood before him in a somewhat hangdog fashion. Their leader said quietly: "Just ten rounds for each rifle."

"What about handgrenades? What about machine guns? What about heavy equipment?"

"Nothing, sir."

"And uniforms for only half our people as well?"

"Yes, sir. Obviously this was just a battalion of infantry troops being trained. Not more than 200/250 soldiers, I would judge, to go by the sleeping accommodations."

"What about transport?"

"We found one jeep, but there was little gasoline in it, and we found four cans of gasoline. That's all."

"Shaughnessy betrayed us." Fratzer fumed. " Wait until I get my hands on him. He must be an agent provocateur working for the British."

"Not so fast." Werfel said bitterly. " He's a civilian. What does he know about weapons, about ammunition, even about numbers of soldiers. He said there were a lot of soldiers here. To him 250 or 500 is the same thing. He's not trained to evaluate military matters properly. The fault is ours. We were so intent on escaping gloriously that we accepted everything he said without asking searching questions. The problem is, what do we do now?"

"We can still proceed as planned, once the Poles return from their dance. We'll use their trucks. We'll just be more crowded, and when we get to the Firth of Forth, we'll find more weapons." Fratzer wouldn't give up hope.

Werfel looked at him wonderingly. "You must believe in fairy tales. Look at the time. If the Poles were coming back, they'd have been here. It's almost dawn. What commander would allow his troops to remain at a dance so long? No, they've been warned, and

I'm sure that British troops, heavily armed British troops, are approaching."

"Well, what do you suggest? You seem to know everything? "Fratzer could not hide his disappointment, and something like fear began to appear in his expression.

"Do you see what you have done by murdering the British soldiers at Waterstoun? Any prisoner of war is entitled to make an escape attempt, and if he is recaptured, none the worse for him under the Geneva convention. But you have committed many murders and that puts all of us in jeopardy. What would you do if the situation were reversed?"

Fratzer paled. " We cannot surrender, that's for certain. We still have one chance - the hostages. If Shaughnessy captured the Duke and his family and perhaps some other important personages, we could trade them to the British for a chance to escape."

"I doubt it very much," Werfel sighed. "But we have no alternative. In that case, we must take over the palace. It is certainly more defensible than this camp. And then, when the British arrive, we must try to negotiate." He turned to his captains. "Get the men together, get all the weapons. Forget about the Polish uniforms. Quick march to the palace."

* * *

Groton, the butler, had woken the Duke and Duchess, Lady Maud and Lady Sarah, and they had hastily thrown on some clothes and assembled in the library. All the members of the household staff, from her eminence, the chief cook, down to the lowest upstairs maid, were crowded to one side of the large room.

"Now, what is this all about, Jack? You must have a very good reason for this." The Duke was as imperial as ever. He was in his home and had been interrupted in his soundest sleep by a former protégé and a bunch of Polish soldiers.

"It was necessary, your Grace, and I will explain." Jack preferred to keep the Duke in ignorance of the true situation as long as possible. "But first, would you, please, arrange to have all the guns and all the ammunition in the palace brought here. I assure you, that's essential."

"All we have here are a number of hunting rifles, shot guns, and of course, some historic dueling pistols. Do you mean these as well? You're not planning on a duel here?" The Duke added with a smile. He was somewhat mollified by Jack's earnestness, and of course had no reason to mistrust him

"Everything, please, your Grace. " Jack motioned to two of the "Polish " soldiers. "These men will help you, Groton."

After Groton and the two soldiers had left, Jack turned back to the Duke:

"The German prisoners of war at Waterstoun Castle have escaped and are roaming the countryside. It is entirely possible that they may show up here. We will have to defend the Palace. The Polish troops are establishing picket lines forward, but they are lightly armed. Until British troops arrive, we may be on our own."

"Ah," the Duke's warrior blood fired up. " We'll give them what for if they show up here."

In the meantime, Groton returned with the two soldiers; the three men's arms heavily laden with rifles and shotguns, and even a brace of the famous dueling pistols. As they placed the weapons on the table next to the door, one of the guns escaped the grip of one of the soldiers, and fell heavily on his foot.

"Scheisse!" the man exclaimed.

One of the maid's jumped up. She whispered to Groton, who approached the Duke and spoke to him quietly. The Duke turned to Jack.

"Jack, Esther here is a refugee from Germany. She has advised me that your soldier friend used a very inelegant word just now, but a word in German not in Polish. Could you explain that?"

"Oh well," Jack said. " I wanted to spare you for a while longer." He drew a pistol from his pocket and motioned to his troops to remove the captured guns . "You are our prisoners. I suggest that you do as you're told and perhaps no harm will come to you."

The Duke remained silent. But his look of contempt was something Jack would remember. Maud called out: "But Jack, you're British? How can you betray us?"

"British, am I? You have not shown me that I am. And now, Maud, please follow me."

"Where are you taking her? " Lady Chalmerston held on to her daughter. "Let her stay with us."

Jack motioned to one of his soldiers who brutally forced Lady Chalmerston away from Maud. "You will all have to learn who gives the orders now," Jack said grimly. " I told you to come with me, Maud." He walked out of the library. With a despairing glance at her parents, Maud followed.

This was the moment he had been waiting for. Now, he could make real the fantasies which had tormented his sleepless nights for so long. Jack calculated that it would be at least an hour, perhaps longer, before the Polish troops had arrived and been captured and the Germans using the Polish trucks would arrive at the front door of Chalmerston Palace to pick him up with his soldiers and above all with the hostages. Whether Maud would be among them, alive, he had not yet decided.

He grabbed the young woman by the arm and forced her up the grand staircase. "Which is your room?" Shocked at the attitude of the young man she had known most of her life, Maud obediently led him to her large bedroom. Jack pushed her in, and locked the door.

The room was dominated by a four-poster bed, the covers open and the pillow still bearing the imprint of Maud's head. Along one wall was a dressing table with a large mirror, in front of which there was a stool. A couple of chairs stood about, and two, large open closets covered the other wall.

Jack pushed the girl toward the bed and walked over to the closet. More clothes than he had ever seen in his life. Certainly his sisters would not accumulate so much finery in all their lives. His anger increased. Carefully, he selected a thin alligator belt, hanging from a hook among many others. He then picked out two scarves.

"What are you going to do?" Maud whispered fearfully.

"What should have been done to you a long time ago." Jack pushed Maud against the posts of the four-poster and tied her wrists to each of the two posts at the foot of the bed. He tied them as high as he could, forcing the girl to stretch her arms and to stand on tip toe. Maud had not bothered dressing when she had been called to come downstairs so unexpectedly. All she wore was a thin silk dressing gown over a negligee. With both hands, without regard for any pain this inflicted on his victim, Jack tore the gown and the night dress off the girl's body. Maud yelped and attempted to hide, but her hands were tied.

Finally. This is what he had dreamed about. The nude body of the girl he had loved and then had hated was before him, in his power.

"Don't act as if no one has seen you before. Multitudes have possessed you, haven't they? Haven't they? " Jack pushed his face close to Maud's. " How many men have you slept with? And how many women?"

Maud did not answer. She tried to turn her head away. "Even I saw you naked before." That statement made Maud look up. "You don't remember, it wasn't important to you, bitch. Six months ago, you and your friends had yourselves a time in the Green room at the Manor house in Ireland. And you needed more champagne and came into the kitchen, dressed just as you are now. And who looked at you? Only Jack. Only Jack."

With that, Jack pulled the belt back as far as it could go, and struck the unprotected bottom of the girl with all his might. "Only Jack", he repeated and continued to whip her.
" Only Jack," and another and another stroke hit the white , unresisting body. Jack was in a frenzy.

"Why don't you cry, bitch, why don't you whimper? " An icy shock stopped Jack's arm in mid swing. "You like it, you like being beaten?" He noted that instead of crying out, Maud had a small, voluptuous smile on her face and that her body, instead of trying to avoid the blows, actually seemed to search them out.

Jack dropped the belt and tried to collect himself. Even in this she was victorious. He undid the scarves with which he had attached the girl to the posts. "Yes, Jack, yes,"
Maud cried, " beat me, hurt me. I'm yours. " She dropped to her knees in front of her capture, fumbled with his trousers, and took him into her mouth.

Jack jumped back, totally distraught. " You are evil incarnate. You are the whore of Babylon . You destroy everything." Without another glance at the girl, he opened the door and rushed away, back down the stairs. He walked out the front door and tried to collect himself.

In spite of his medical training, Jack Shaughnessy was an innocent in matters sexual. He had learned the mechanics in school, of course, but his strict Catholic upbringing and his personal unattractiveness had prevented him from experimenting with willing girls of his class. A few times his hormones had driven him to the stews of Belfast , where his relief had been procured for a few shillings in the most unappealing manner. This left him always with so much guilt that it could not even be cleared up by confession and absolution in one of the out of the way churches he would frequent for that purpose. As a result he had just about forsworn sex, and concentrated his young man's imagination all on Maud, first with love and admiration, and then, after the incident in the Green room, with hatred. After all, she had betrayed him. She was evil. He needed to punish her. And now, instead of punishing her, he had given her pleasure, and she, in fact, had punished him.

And for this he had destroyed himself. No, he reminded himself. He was striking a blow against the British Empire, the Empire that had oppressed his people for centuries. That, after all, was the purpose of this venture.

He stood in front of the door of Chalmerston Palace, taking in the cold night air in great gulps. Slowly, he calmed down. Where are the troops? They should be here by now.

Then he saw them. No trucks, but his German Army - as he had started to think about them - coming up the drive in quick march. Why, what has happened? He would soon find out. When Fratzer saw him, he let out a yell and jumped forward, hitting Jack in the face with a balled fist.

* * *

With a small, inscrutable smile Maud rose from the floor, quickly threw on some serviceable, dark clothes and her most comfortable boots, opened the window and swung down from the balcony to the ground, using the same trellis that she had used for the purpose when her parents attempted to confine her to her room. *They have certainly cut the phones in the main house*, she thought, *but they may not know about the extra line in the garage office.* She made her way to the rear of the building, taking as much cover as possible and went toward the outbuildings. *Who should I call for help first*, she wondered.

* * *

Priebke did not like what was going on. While he had not been made privy to the entire plan, he had added two and two well enough to know that their escape depended on trucks obtained from the Polish troops. Now those troops were not arriving and the Germans were ordered to hurry to the main palace, carrying the weapons they had found. Priebke also saw that, contrary to his leaders' hopes, the number of guns and the amount of ammunition were pitifully small. The palace can be defended, perhaps, but it looks to me like this is one of those heroic last stands you read about

330

in the history books. *Not for my mother's son,* Priebke thought. *I'm better off making myself scarce.* He hid in the shadows of one of the tents, and allowed his comrades to rush up to the palace. As soon as they were a distance away, he ran in the other direction, through the main gate, and straight into the arms of his old roommate.

"Hagen, you are here after all?" Priebke said with astonishment.

Then he noted, that Hagen was in British uniform, and that there was a rotund civilian next to him, pointing a pistol. Priebke raised his hands, and started to babble: " I surrender, in fact I left those murderers, because I wanted to surrender. I had nothing to do with the killings at Waterstoun. I just went along; after all, I had to obey orders."

"Where are the others?" Kurt snapped.

"They gave up on getting the Polish trucks. They went up to the palace to take defensive positions; I suppose, that's where they have hostages. But you see, I want nothing to do with them, I just want to go back to a nice, safe, prisoner of war camp. I won't cause any trouble."

Kurt turned to Orne. " It seems that they must have killed some of the soldiers at Waterstoun."

"If they did, they're nothing but criminals. " Orne was furious. "They will have to be tried for murder."

"Of course," Kurt said, "but don't you think first, we should recapture them? And if, indeed, they have committed murder, they will not want to surrender as easily as this example of the Nazi superman." he looked at Priebke with contempt. "And don't forget, they probably have the residents of Chalmerston Palace as hostages."

Orne calmed down. " Well, let's secure this hero. I suggest you tie his hands with his belt, and tie his shoelaces together. That should keep him under control, while you take a rest."

"What, a rest?" Kurt said, shocked, while following Orne's suggestion and binding Priebke.

"You have had a busy time, haven't you, from what you have told me." Orne smiled. "You aren't a superman, either. If you trust your chief, you must know that help is on its way. You can't take on five hundred Germans. Look, dawn is breaking. Try to take a nap. I'll keep an eye on our guest. I'll wake you when our troops arrive."

"Very well, I'll follow your advice. But first,"Kurt turned to Priebke, " a little conversation. I want you to tell me all you know about Franz Ratzersdorfer."

Eager to curry favor, Priebke talked. After a while he began to repeat himself, and Kurt felt that he had no more to say.

Kurt had not realized how tired he was. He had been awake for twenty four hours, had jumped into the coldest water he had ever experienced, had been in a fire fight, and probably killed some people, and had been going on pure adrenaline for a long time. He obeyed Orne's advice, curled up as best he could in the back of Orne's car, cursed its small size, and closed his eyes.

* * *

Major Eustis was in command of the first Battalion of the Royal Scots Regiment, one of the oldest regiments of the line. The regiment had originally been a pure infantry unit with a glorious history of battles fought from Waterloo to Verdun, and throughout the British Empire. But this was a different war, and the regiment was training to be transformed into a motorized unit, to be part of a brigade equipped to transport troops quickly from one location to another. He had been working his troops hard, and had barely slept one or two hours after a comfortable dinner at the Regimental Mess, when his batman woke him.

And now he found himself at the head of his troops, driving toward what could be the first engagement of armed soldiers fought in Scotland since 1745, when the Army of the Hanoverian King George defeated the final attempt by the Stuarts to regain the throne.

Major Eustis had been instructed to get his battalion, as fully armed as possible, to the Chalmerston Estate, and to round up a large number of German prisoners of war who had broken out of Waterstoun Castle. He had been informed that the Germans had a modest number of light arms. He had also been advised to cooperate with Kurt Auster, and to try and protect the lives of all civilians, particularly the Duke and his family of course.

The sun had risen, and the morning dew had burned off by the time Eustis' battalion reached the outer gate of the estate. Orne had woken Kurt out of a very sound sleep when he heard he rumbling of military vehicles approaching. Kurt felt a little less tired, but his eyes were gritty, his face unshaven, and he thought he had not been this grimy in a long time. Walter Orne and Kurt waved to Major Eustis' command car and identified themselves. As soon as they clarified the situation, Major Eustis took his dispositions:

"Company A East, Company B West - set up machine gun positions to enfilade the estate walls. Company C , move around to the rear of the estate and do the same. Headquarters company, remain here." The major turned to Kurt. "I really don't have enough men to cover this large area. We don't want them to get out in small groups and then have to beat the bushes for them."

"May I suggest...." Kurt said, quietly.

"Yes?"

"The Polish troops are still awaiting instructions at Ballantrae. They are not armed, but they are manpower. We need to contact them by telephone."

"Good idea," the Major acknowledged. His communication officer materialized by his side, and a field telephone appeared. After some difficulty, contact was established with the officer commanding the Polish troops. Kurt explained the situation in German, and the Poles were on their way.

At that point, the solitary figure of a police constable ambled along on an antiquated bicycle.

"What is going on here?" The official dismounted and asked the assembly. " We have not been informed of any maneuvers in the area."

The major explained briefly.

"That explains the mysterious telephone call we got a few hours ago. A woman who identified herself as Lady Maud called and said there were German prisoners of war on the estate and that she had escaped and was hiding in one of the outbuildings."

"And what did you do about that?" Major Eustis was quite incensed.

"Well, I'm here, ain't I? To investigate." The constable was quite calm. "Lady Maud has played all kinds of pranks on us in the past, so we don't take her calls too seriously."

"Well," the Major smiled. "This time it's quite serious. Do you know the layout of the estate? The buildings and so forth?"

"Indeed, I do. I've been there many times. Mrs. Bradley, the cook..."

"Never mind your reasons for having been there. Sit down, and draw me a sketch of the estate. Show me where the buildings are, and particularly where Lady Maud said she was hiding."

While the Major busied himself with the constable, Kurt approached Priebke, who had been turned over to a guard of burly soldiers.

"Did you tell Werfel or Fratzer that I was missing?"

"No, I did not."

"Are you sure?"

"On my honor, I didn't."

Kurt did not believe him. On the other hand, in the confusion of all that had been going on, it was certainly possible. Kurt went over to Major Eustis.

"I'd like to make another suggestion."

"Please do."

"I could go in and try and contact Lady Maud. She might know where all the civilians are, and we could try to rescue them or at least know their whereabouts before you begin an assault."

"That seems to me a very dangerous task." Major Eustis said with some respect for Kurt's offer.

"Not if I could go in as Oberleutnant Hagen." Kurt explained how he had spent the last few days. "The problem is, my German naval uniform is back at Waterstoun, in the guard shack, and I'd have to get it. Can you lend me a jeep and I'll see if I can find it? I couldn't make the attempt until after dark in any case. In the meantime, what will you do, if I might ask?"

"Of course, you'll have a jeep." The Major acquiesced. "As soon as the Polish troops are here, and we have drawn a cordon sanitaire around the estate to prevent any of the Germans from escaping into the countryside, I'll approach the palace under a flag of truce. Perhaps, I can persuade them to surrender without bloodshed."

"That would of course be the best solution." Kurt nodded.

"Just one minute." Walter Orne was quite agitated." These Huns have murdered a number of British soldiers at Waterstoun. They must be punished for that."

"Of course you're right, " Kurt agreed. " But what if they turn over those who did it? I suspect the murderers were the SS troops."

"That is not my decision." Major Eustis ended the conversation." My orders are to recapture the prisoners one way or another, and I will do so."

* * *

Kurt reached Waterstoun quite quickly. *It's remarkable how short the distance was in daylight when you know the way.* He found his uniform still wet, crumpled up in a ball where he had left it. He also found several dead bodies of British soldiers, whose throats had been cut. He could not resist a quick run up to the main castle, and retched as soon as he reached it. It was a charnel house. British soldiers, all evidently murdered in a similar fashion, lay about in various stages. On the causeway, there were the bodies of three Germans. *Those are the ones I killed. But that was war.*

He straightened out the German naval uniform as best he could, and stretched it on the jeep's rear seat. *Perhaps, it'll be a bit drier by the time I've got to put it on.* When he returned to Major Eustis' command post, he was just in time to see that officer return with his flag of truce.

"They are holding the Duke and his family, a guest, and a number of servants. They demand safe conduct and transport to the nearest British port, and a ship to take them to Germany. They insist that they will take all civilians with them but that in Germany they will be treated fairly for the duration. If we refuse, they will begin executing them one per hour. They feel they have nothing to lose."

"Did you gain any time?"

"I told them that I would have to consult my superiors and they gave me until noon tomorrow. Then the executions begin."

"Who was their spokesman? "

"A Lieutenant Colonel Werfel, who speaks excellent English. But he kept consulting with another officer."

"Fratzer, no doubt. The SS man who probably ordered the murders. I suspect he calls the shots. What are you going to do?"

Eustis sighed. " I will do what I told them. I will consult my superiors. I cannot take it upon myself to condemn the civilians to death. They have also warned me that they will execute all of them the moment an assault begins."

"In the meantime," Kurt said, " I'd better go in and see what can be done."

Major Eustis looked at Kurt. "Very well, but you will not go in alone. I'll send a dozen of my best men with you as back-up. " He called out: "Jerome."

A battle hardened sergeant appeared. "Take your squad, draw full ammo and weapons, and follow Mr. Auster here. He'll be in command. Don't worry about his wearing German uniform, he's a British officer. I suggest you blacken your faces and wait for dark before you start." He turned to Kurt. "You will have communications with me through one of Jerome's men. I will have a full company follow close behind, in the event that you find a way in, where we can surprise the enemy. I am sure that, ultimately, we will have to fight. We will not submit to blackmail. If you can do something about the hostages, that should be your first priority. Now let us study the map the constable drew, and determine the best place for you to make the attempt."

* * *

It had started to rain heavily, as it does so often in Scotland. Leutnant Bratter was cold and miserable, and had no problem expressing those sentiments frequently and loudly to his assigned partner, Leutnant Schuler. "What a foul-up." he grumbled. "Our leaders really have no idea what they're doing. Where were the trucks they promised us? Now we're stuck here, the British will come and get us, and because of the SS we'll all be executed. And you and I out here, alone, with one rifle between us, are supposed to watch out for the British. In this rain? When I can't see five meters? What nonsense."

"What do you think we ought to be doing?" Schuler asked.

"If we're going to fight, we ought to just take defensive positions inside the house, where at least it's nice and warm and dry. But I think fighting is nonsense. We'll all be killed, and for what? We're not even going to be able to inflict any damage on the British."

"So, do you want to surrender? You'd better not let Fratzer hear you."

"Fratzer and his SS. They're the cause of all our troubles. "

"I agree with you," another voice could be heard.

"Who's there? Identify yourself or I'll shoot." In the dark and the rain, Schuler who had been holding the rifle, had not seen or heard anyone approaching, particularly because of Bratter's incessant complaints.

"Don't you recognize me, Kamarad? It's Hagen, Oberleutnant Hagen."

"Where do you come from?"

"The colonel assigned me to make a tour of the outer guardposts. Lucky for you, I'm not the enemy. Now, have you been in visual touch with the others?"

"You must be joking. Who can see anything? " Bratter continued his grumbling.

"Listen, I overheard you. Do you think a lot of our comrades feel like you do?"

Bratter grew suspicious. "What? Do you want to denounce me to Fratzer as a defeatist?

I will do my duty."

"And die?"

"That's what soldiers do."

"But so pointlessly?"

"So, Hagen, do you agree with me on that?"

"Yes, I do. My feeling is that the British will treat us well if we surrender without causing them any more trouble. But the SS who killed all those soldiers, they'll get theirs. But why should the rest of us, regular soldiers, have to pay for Fratzer's brutality.?"

"So, what do you propose?"

"Let's go back in and talk to the regular officers. Maybe we can get out of this alive. We'd have to overpower Fratzer and the SS and turn them over to the British."

"That's high treason." Schuler interjected.

"No, that's survival. We have a duty to the Fatherland to survive when the situation is hopeless. You don't really think, we can get out of this alive."

"We have the hostages." Schuler said hesitatingly.

"Do you really think the British will care about a handful of civilians, even a Duke? That's fantasy."

"What should we do? " Bratter asked.

"I see no point in being out here, several hundred yards from the palace, in the rain. Let's go back and quietly sound out the others. Only regular officers of course. Perhaps we can get enough support to talk to Werfel about surrendering. After all, there are so many more of us than the SS. Werfel is a good officer. Without Fratzer, he would make the right decision."

"But if we leave our post, the British could…"

"What can you do in this rain and in the darkness? You couldn't even see me approaching."

Bratter and Schuler looked at each other. "Let's go," Bratter said. "What's the difference whether we get killed by Fratzer's SS or by the British? At least we'll be dry."

"Let's split up," Hagen suggested, " so we can talk to as many comrades as possible."

Kurt and his squad had chosen to approach the palace from the outer wall as close as possible to the outbuildings where Lady Maud must be hiding. The guardpost he had just disabled by his silver tongue, was within the two concentric circles of walls. Kurt was sure that Jerome and his men would follow him, and that Major Eustis would be made aware of the break in the links of German guards. He climbed over the inner wall and began to look for the outbuildings. The rain came down even more heavily. His Naval Uniform which had been soaked by his dive into the Loch, was now just as wet as when he had emerged from the lake. He could see nothing. He did not dare to use the flashlight with which he had equipped himself among other useful devices that he now carried.

He banged into a wall. Suppressing an ouch, he moved along the wall to the left, away from the main section of the palace. A door. Quietly, he opened it and slipped in. The absence of the steady rain was very welcome, but the drumming of the rain on the roof was quite loud in the confined space. He moved around the wall, sliding his hand along it so he could orient himself. *What is this smell?* To the city bred Kurt it was not familiar. Than he realized. Manure. *This is not the garage.*

He moved back outside into the rain and continued slowly in the same direction, to the left, away from the main house. The building ended. *Is there another?* He felt like a blind man. Carefully, counting his steps, so that he could return, he moved forward. He banged his head again.

At this rate, I don't need Germans to kill me, I'll do it myself. This building was not made of wood like the others, but of some kind of metal, aluminum siding, perhaps. That encouraged him. *It's newer, perhaps that is the garage.* He moved around, and found a small door. Feeling around it, he noted a large double door, big enough to allow two cars to pass through. Quietly, he opened the small door and went in. Instantly he hit something again, this time not his head only his shin. The bumper of a car. *Here I am. But where is Lady Maud?*

"Lady Maud?" he whispered. "I am a British officer. I've come because of your phone call." He kept whispering the same thing as he circled, keeping one hand against the wall. He reached what seemed to be the rear of the building. Again he hit something. *I'll be in wonderful shape, when this is over.* A staircase going up. Quietly, he moved upstairs, continuing to whisper his litany. Another door. This may be the office. He opened it gently and stood back. He continued his whispering.

"I heard you, I heard you." A young woman's voice answered. "Where are the troops?"

"Is it safe to turn on my flashlight? " Kurt asked.

"I suppose so, in this weather no one will see us."

Kurt pointed the flashlight at the floor to reduce its field, and turned it on. A fury of hands and feet jumped him, something hit his head. "Stop, stop." Kurt whispered and tried to control the angry young woman. "I'm really British, the uniform is a sham to help me get in here .How would I have known about your phone call?"

As quickly as she had started, the young woman subsided. " True. First, have you got something to eat? I'm starving. It's been almost two days."

"We had anticipated something like that. All I have for you is a couple of chocolate bars. I hope that'll help."

Lady Maud grabbed the bars and hungrily started to devour them. Kurt gave her a moment. In fact, he needed a little time to recover from her attack. *I haven't been this banged up since my first attempt at the obstacle course in training.*

"Now, Lady Maud, please tell me what happened."

Maud told him, deleting the specific details of the incident in her bedroom with Doctor Shaughnessy. "But how did you escape?"
"Well, the doctor turned his back, and I slipped out."

"Do you have any idea what they did with your family and the staff?"

"When I escaped they had all been herded into the library, but I don't know whether they're still there."

"All right," Kurt said. A plan was forming in his mind. "Please wait here. I've got to go and get our people."

Kurt went downstairs and left the garage. It was still raining as hard as ever. This time he found it a little easier to orient himself. Counting his steps, he walked in as straight a line as possible until he reached the wall. Then he turned back in the direction from which he had come, again counting his steps. When he reached the area where he thought he might have climbed the wall, he began to whistle softly. After a while, a soft whistle replied.

"Jerome? " Kurt whispered.

"Yes sir. We are here, and A Company is following not far behind."

Kurt explained the situation. " I've got to go in and find out where the hostages are being kept. It would be nice if they were still in the library, but I doubt it. As soon as I know, I'll try to signal you. Once we have them safe, Major Eustis will have to come and get us quickly. There are far too many Germans for us."

"Trust the Major. We're in touch. "

"Very well. Follow me."

Blessing the steady rain obliterating their presence, Kurt led his squad to the garage building.

"I'll go in through the front. After all, I'm one of them. Do not move until you have heard from me."

"Very well, sir."

* * *

I must be used to this Stygian blackness by now, and I can't get any wetter, but where is the main building? Kurt, followed by the squad, moved along the out buildings, keeping his left hand along the walls. There was a space, they crossed it, and Kurt got the impression of massiveness towering above him. "This must be the main palace," he whispered to Sergeant Jerome. " Here's where we separate. I'll look for a door at the front. Good luck."

Moving along, Kurt detected an entrance. Calling out loudly in German, " Friend, - Oberleutnant Hagen here," he opened the door. Two nervous German officers confronted him, only one of them armed. Cursing the rain, and wiping his face, he gave them the same story about having been sent to check on the outposts, and was allowed free passage. He walked along a long hallway, sparsely lit by occasional lamps, noting the paintings of figures in a variety of ancient costumes frowning at him from the walls. *These must be the forebears of the Duke, I'm sure they're not happy to see their ancestral home desecrated by the Huns.*

Kurt emerged in the main hall at the center of the palace. It was huge. The ceiling extended to a cupola which seemed at least four stories high. The room was almost circular. It was so large that in spite of the hundreds of German officers milling about, it did not give the appearance of being crowded. A number of doors went off to both sides of the hall and an ornamental staircase of majestic proportions rose to the upper floors. In the rear, Kurt noted a door likely to lead to the gardens, and a series of tapestries hanging from the wall adjoining it.

There was considerable hubbub, unusual among normally disciplined men. Officers stood about in small groups, discussing their situation animatedly. Kurt noted Werfel and Fratzer standing against the far wall, attended by a number of Fratzer's SS cadre. He made every effort to stay away from them as much as possible. He wandered from group to group; the discussion was indeed about the

340

prospects for the coming battle, or the chances that the British would give in to their demands. Here and there he overheard someone suggest surrender, which, in this assembly was quite unusual. Putting in a judicious word when indicated, Kurt made his way to the door, which Maud had described to him as the entrance to the library where the hostages had been kept. No guard at the door, a bad sign. *They must have been moved.* He wandered into the library. Here, too, a number of officers had settled down. Kurt noted that there were no weapons in evidence, except for the guns in the hands of the SS troops at the side of Fratzer. *The rest of the guns must be with the outposts. There really could not have been many. That is fortunate for us. But where are the hostages?*

Kurt moved to the rear of the staircase. Aha. A narrow green baize door, and in front of it two armed SS officers. He walked over to them, acting very officiously. They barred his way.

"I've been ordered to interrogate the butler. We need more food, and he'll have to provide it. There isn't enough up here, and Colonel Werfel is sure that there is more squirreled away."

"That makes sense," one of the SS men said. "Go ahead, Kamarad, and don't be too easy on him."

"Never fear, he'll tell me what we need to know."

Kurt opened the green baize door and descended into the bowels of the palace. Two floors down he confronted a locked grate. A pale light illuminated an extensive wine cellar. In it, huddled on the floor, he could make out a number of civilians. The key to the cellar was missing. *Fratzer probably kept it. But this is good, they seem to be safe down here. We just have to prevent him from sending his SS down here when the attack starts.*

Kurt moved back upstairs, and told the guards: "No problem, there is plenty of food in another pantry we had not found. The entrance appears to be around by the garden. I'll go and see."

He made his way to the garden door and stepped outside. A few paces away from the building and he was again engulfed in darkness. Sergeant Jerome appeared next to him. "I didn't even see you come," Kurt muttered. "Now listen. The hostages are being kept in the winecellar below. There are two guards at the door. We must prevent these guards or anyone else from reaching the hostages when the attack takes place. Now what about Major Eustis? Have you been in touch?"

"Indeed we have," Jerome pointed at his communications specialist carrying a field telephone. "The Major is taking advantage of the rain and darkness. After you opened the way, we eliminated many of the outer guard posts, and the main body of troops should be here soon to surround the palace."

"Will the Major wait for our signal that we have the hostages safe?"

Sergeant Jerome did not answer. A burst of rifle fire sounded from almost directly to their front. It subsided immediately, but there was an immediate reaction from inside the palace. Kurt hurried inside. Werfel called out. "Attack. Take your defensive positions."

In a disciplined manner the officers dispersed. He saw Fratzer whisper to one of his SS men who hurried to the green baize door. Kurt tried to follow but was prevented by the mass of milling men.

From the outside a series of searchlights suddenly illumined the palace. A voice came over a loudspeaker. " This is Major Eustis. The palace is surrounded. There is no escape. If you surrender immediately, you will be returned to the castle at Waterstoun and treated in accordance with the requirements of the Geneva convention. You have ten minutes. Then we will begin firing."

Even though Major Eustis had spoken in English, the general tenor of what he had said was understood by the former prisoners of war. There were enough among them with some knowledge of English to be able to translate. Those who did not understand immediately certainly grasped the situation. There was consternation and discussion among the men.

Kurt saw Fratzer's messenger emerge from the green baize door, pulling a resisting young, blond woman behind him. Fratzer jumped up on a table.

"Achtung!" He repeated the command several times until there was silence. "We are not going to surrender. I have promised the British that we will execute the hostages if they attack. We will begin with this one, one of their aristocrats. Then we'll see whether they are bluffing or not. Do they want to lose all their people?"

"No." Werfel cried out. " We do not make war on women. Enough. We must surrender."

Fratzer pulled out a pistol taken from one of the murdered British officers and shot Werfel in the chest. The Lieutenant Colonel collapsed. Fratzer brandished his pistol: "SS to me." All the SS men formed up behind him. "The next traitor will be shot also . Now for the hostage." He pulled the girl in front of him and raised his gun.

Kurt shot Fratzer in the head and emptied his pistol at the other SS men standing behind him. A massive blow from a rifle butt wielded by one of the German officers hit his head and he blacked out.

* * *

CHAPTER XI

God, I hurt. But it's light. I can barely see. Then he blacked out again.

This time, when he opened his eyes, he felt a little better. He took inventory. He was in a soft bed, there was a large bandage around his head, and he hurt. He hurt so much that he closed his eyes again.

When he woke up again, he saw a white clad form sitting next to his bed. He had trouble focusing his eyes. "What happened? Where am I?" Was this his voice? He croaked like a frog.

A soft hand touched his forehead. "Everything is fine. Just rest. I'll get the doctor."

Somehow, he fell asleep again. The next time he woke up, he could see more clearly. The nurse sitting next to him smiled and said. " I think you'll live, don't you?"

Kurt considered. This was not an easy question to answer. After long thought, he croaked: "Not if you don't feed me soon."

"Oh, that's wonderful," the nurse enthused. "I'll get you something to drink and to eat and I'll get the doctor. " She raised Kurt up a little. Nothing tasted more delicious than the cold glass of apple juice she held out to him. An elderly man carrying a stethoscope hurried in. "How's our young hero?" he asked going through the usual routine of tapping, listening and examining Kurt. He particularly looked at Kurt's eyes, shining a small flashlight into his pupils.

"Another few days of rest, and you'll be fine. But then for a while, no strenuous exercises. You had a very severe concussion and you must take it seriously. I will look in on you later."

The nurse appeared with a steaming bowl of soup and began to spoon it into Kurt's mouth, preventing him from asking any more questions. Finally, she allowed him to lie back again. The act of sitting up and eating had exhausted him, but after a while he finally could ask: "Where am I? What happened?"

"You are in Chalmerston Palace. The doctor did not think it wise to move you to a hospital over our country roads, and the Duke is only too happy to offer you his hospitality. "

"But what happened? The Germans?"

"The Germans are back in Waterstoun where they belong. I'll let your associates tell you.
They're eager to see you. But first, I think another nap is in order."

When Kurt awake again, Major Eustis and Sergeant Jerome were at his bedside.

"What happened? " Kurt could not wait.

"We were successful in rolling up the German guard posts, and so we were able to surround the palace easily, all thanks to the heavy rain. But we missed one post, and he fired."

"Yes, this alerted the Germans inside. And then?"

Sergeant Jerome took up the tale. " We were just ready to enter, when the shooting began in the main hall. I saw the SS officer shoot the other German and saw you kill him and attack the other SS men near him. So we went in and finished the job."

"What do you mean?"

"We killed and wounded the entire group of SS men standing against the wall there. At that point, one of the German officers jumped up and called out : "Surrender, we surrender. " The Germans raised their hands, Major Eustis' troops came in and it was over."

"And the girl? The hostage?"

"Lady Blamington had the good sense to duck under one of the tables. She's fine. She'll want to thank you. If it hadn't been for you, she's sure she would have been shot."

Lady Blamington? It couldn't be. Sarah? That would be an unbelievable coincidence. I don't want to see her. What difference does it make, anyway. If she wants to come and see me, let her. No, what's the point?

"Well, thank you. What about the Nazis who murdered the soldiers at Waterstoun? "

"A Royal Commission of Inquiry will be set up, and it will investigate. Most of the SS men are dead, but those who are not, and any other Germans who will have shown to be responsible will be punished in accordance with the Geneva convention."

"And the Irish doctor? Doctor Shaughnessy?"

"Ah, there's a mystery. He's disappeared. He must be many miles from here by now. Of course there's a mighty hue and cry out after him, and the ports and borders have been alerted. Sooner or later they'll catch him."

But Jack Shaughnessy was not very far away, not far away at all.

After Nurse Bradley gave him a sponge bath, dressed him in a pair of clean pajamas obtained from who knows which kind soul, and above all shaved him, Kurt felt like a human being for the first time in a long while. The bandage on his head had been changed, and it was a little smaller now than the turban of the Great Turk he had seen in history books, but not much smaller.

"You should be ready for visitors now. His Grace has expressed a desire to meet you."

Interesting, how stilted the language becomes, when even a plain, straightforward person like the good nurse deals with the aristocracy. "I 'll be honored." Kurt nodded. He regretted having done so immediately. His head was not yet ready to be moved.

His Grace the Duke of Chalmerston, her Grace the Duchess and their daughter Lady Maud, promptly made an appearance. Behind them, Kurt saw a familiar face he had not expected ever to see again. Appropriate compliments were exchanged, Kurt's heroism was praised, and Kurt, in turn, having been properly brought up, modestly refuted all praise, and thanked his hosts profusely for their hospitality. Eventually the moment had passed, and the lordly personages withdrew. Maud stayed behind, touched his hand and whispered: " I'll thank you privately, but someone else has priority."

Then he was alone with Sarah.

"You have saved me again. You're making a habit of it." She looked at him with a mixture of embarrassment, and gratitude. *No doubt she remembers our last meeting.*

"I'm glad you're all right, but don't give me too much credit. I didn't know it was you.."

"Would knowing it have stopped you?" Sarah was quite in earnest.

"No, of course not." And, before the matter could go any further. " How is your husband?"

"Who? Oh. He's at sea. He's been at sea for a very long time. Who knows whether he'll ever come back" *Was there a degree of bitterness?*

"Well, wartime, of course." *Couldn't you have found anything more inane to say?*

Sarah sat down on the bed next to him. " Look, Kurt, I never had a chance to thank you properly for the last time." She leaned over, and kissed him full on the mouth. The tip of her tongue snaked between his lips. Sarah got up and closed the door. "How do you feel?" she smiled.

"Fine, as long as I don't move my head. The rest of me is fine," Kurt stammered, totally taken aback.

"Well, let me thank you now and you don't have to move your head. In fact, don't move at all. Let me do everything." Sarah's hand reached down under the sheet and liberated him, then she bent down, and took him into her mouth with a practiced motion.

Kurt looked at the blond head bobbing up and down. *Two years ago I put her on a pedestal. The golden girl, my angel, my virgin.*

But two years ago, when I met her, I was a romantic fool. I had other thoughts.

Two years ago.

When I was young.

* * *

After Jack Shaughnessy had been knocked down by Sturmbannfuehrer Fratzer, he got up and unsteadily made his way into the back garden. Away from the Germans, away from the British. Everything had gone wrong. His revenge was a failure. He could not hurt Maud and he certainly failed in his attempt to hurt the British Empire. His wonderful plan had resulted in the deaths of a number of British soldiers and would undoubtedly result in the deaths of a number of Germans as well. But what did he care about that? His own fate was sealed. He was known as a traitor. In fact, both sides considered him such.

In his musings, Jack wandered far into the gardens. It began to rain heavily. Without thinking about it much, he took shelter in a gazebo, where he sat down on a bench and continued to contemplate his fate.

Suddenly, shadowy figures raced past him in the rain. There was the sound of gunfire, the shouting of orders, the rumbling of carriages. Powerful searchlights illuminated the palace. Jack looked around him. The heavy wrought iron bench on which he sat was so constructed that one would have to crouch down and look directly under it, to see someone hiding there. The space was small but for he first time in his life, Jack felt grateful for his short stature. With considerable difficulty he slid under the bench.

And there he remained. He heard, more than he saw, trucks loading the German prisoners and moving them out, presumably back to Waterstoun, ambulances picking up dead and wounded bodies, and eventually, the British troops marching off to wherever victorious troops may wish to march.

Of course he knew they would be looking for him. Hopelessly, he contemplated giving up. He would be tried as a traitor, and hanged. He had no great desire to live, but he did not wish to give the British the satisfaction of executing him.

But every time he tried to climb out of his hiding place, there were people, soldiers, gardeners, staff. At one point, he even saw the Duke and her Ladyship taking a stroll not far from him. They almost entered the gazebo, but in the last minute decided to return to the palace. He held his gun in his hand. If they had come closer, he was prepared to shoot them both. What after all did it cost him? His life was forfeit in any case.

Then he began to realize that he had to take the risk and move out of his hiding place. If he did not get some food, and above all some liquid into his poor, abused body soon, he would no longer have the strength to crawl out from under the bench. With a grim, amused chuckle he visualized the Duke and the Duchess sitting above his long dead body. He realized, he was becoming light headed, and that he had to move.

After dark, he emerged with great difficulty from beneath the bench. He had trouble standing up straight. Every movement was painful. First food. He moved toward the palace. Voices. Two men emerged from French doors directly in front of him. They stopped to light cigarettes, then they walked, deep in conversation, directly toward him.

Jack moved as quietly as he could toward the wall of the palace. Ah, an espalier to train ivy. Is it strong enough? In despair, he pulled himself upwards with all his remaining strength. There was a balustrade. He climbed over it, and heavily fell to the floor. An open window. Gathering his last ounces of strength, he crawled over to it and peered inside.

A bedroom - a man, his head heavily bandaged lying in his bed. And Maud, her blond head bobbing up and down above the man's groin, servicing him greedily.

Red rage overcame Jack Shaughnessy. The whore. The whore of Babylon. She does not deserve to live. He pulled out his pistol and fired at the blond head. It exploded.

The man on the bed jumped up. At the same time, the door opened and Maud - Maud! stood in the doorway. *Who did I kill? Again, I failed.*

In total despair, Jack Shaughnessy put the barrel of his pistol into his mouth and fired.

* * *

"Guilty? You're guilty? " Adam Bede almost bellowed." How can you say it's your fault? What more could you have done?" He calmed down a little. " My dear fellow, you did everything in your power and more. No one could anticipate the acts of a madman."

They were seated in front of a crackling fire in the Venerable Bede's comfortable quarters in London. In spite of any danger to his injured head, Kurt could not stand remaining on the Chalmerston estate for a minute longer than necessary. He was welcomed by his good friend with open arms, put to bed and allowed to sleep almost around the clock. Adam Bede would not let him tell his tale until he had put a good meal into him, and now Kurt had just completed the story. He reflected that this was one incident about which he could talk, since no intelligence work was involved.

"I should have done something sooner about the Doctor. I had my suspicions about him from the start. If I had only gone to poor Major Brattlewaite earlier.."

"Nonsense, my boy. You had no proof. What do you think would have happened? Nothing. And the Germans would have done something similar a few months later. You saved the day by warning the Poles not to return to their camp. That stopped the Germans dead in their tracks. You should be proud of what you have done."

"But Sarah.."

"Must I repeat a cliché? It's wartime. People die. Civilians die. Did you feel guilty when you thought she had drowned in the warship you had allowed her to board? How much control do any of us have over anything? I know you had feelings for the poor girl, but you must put them aside. You can't allow yourself to brood any more."

"I suppose you're right," Kurt sighed.

"What is more," Adam Bede continued, "You must thank all the gods that you were not injured when the bullet hit Sarah. There are many ways," he said with a small smile," that you could have been hurt, considering the position."

Kurt shuddered when he remembered the moment when the shot was fired.

"Now," Adam said," If you will forgive me another intrusion into your privacy, I think that it is essential that you find yourself a charming and willing companion. Must get back on the horse, immediately, so to speak. Otherwise, you'll just keep remembering."

Kurt did not answer. The last thing he was interested in at this time was a sexual encounter.

* * *

When Kurt reported to Admiral Morse, he was introduced into that great man's office without delay and allowed to sit down . Admiral Morse even offered him a glass of sherry. Kurt had never been treated so pleasantly by that gruff old man.

"I want the complete story from you, even though I have heard the outlines from others."

When Kurt had finished, the Admiral leaned back.

"You did well. It was fortunate that you were there. If the Germans had succeeded in reaching the Firth of Forth, they could have caused incalculable damage. Now the fur will fly. The Prime Minister has taken a personal interest in the arrangements we have for prisoners of war. I suspect the Home Office will lose jurisdiction. But more importantly,

I know that efforts will be made to send as many prisoners of war as possible over to the United States for the duration. There is plenty of room in the ships that arrive here with men and materiel and return to America almost empty. It will relieve us of the burden of guarding and above all feeding them with our limited resources."

"I have a request. " Kurt spoke up.

"Yes?"

"I would like permission to question any surviving SS men in Waterstoun, or in fact any SS men in any other prisoner of war camps regarding a certain Ratzersdorfer. He is the man who killed my parents."

"No, absolutely not." Admiral Morse was very stern and abrupt. " This is a war for survival. We have no time for private vengeance. I will not allow you to be distracted from any duties I assign because of your own agenda. Is that understood?"

"Sir. I repeat my request. I will do so on my own time. I promise not to have it interfere with anything you require of me."

Admiral Morse almost bellowed. "Are you bargaining with me, young man? Are you willing to disobey a direct order? I'll have you court-martialed. "

Kurt smiled. " You won't do that, Admiral. And I repeat, I am always at your disposition."

Morse got up. He paced back and forth without speaking. Then he resumed his seat.

"Well," he said with a small, a very small smile. " If you were not so independent, you wouldn't be much good. Very well. On your own time, only. And of course, you will bring me any useful information you develop. But I want your promise that you will take no action against this Ratzersdorfer without consulting me. If you can find him."

"Yes, sir."

"Now," the Admiral grew friendly again. "You must make every effort to recover your strength. How is your leg?"

"Well, the actions of the last few days did not help, but I'm sure I will be fine."

"And your head?"

"Throbbing and painful, thank you. But the doctors say that's normal."

"Well, you are relieved of all duty until you have recovered completely. Relax, and take good care of yourself. As soon as you feel up to it, report to me. I believe the time is rapidly approaching when you will have to return to France. "

"Very well, sir."

As Kurt left the Admiral's office, he reflected that of all his deeds of daring the bravest had been confronting his chief.

* * *

He woke up with a barely stifled scream. That dream again. Slowly, he came to complete consciousness. His face was bathed in cold sweat, his head throbbed. He got out of bed, and without turning on the light, walked over to the chair by the window. He took in deep gulps of the cold night air. The city was silent, the black-out still on, even though it was very rare these days that a German bomber attempted an attack.

He remembered the dream. Sarah's blond head exploding - her brains and blood covering him and the bed. Exactly what had happened. But then the agony of feeling her teeth clamp down on him, and severing him. He touched himself. Just to make sure. No, he was intact. It could have happened, but it didn't. *So why am I constantly dreaming about it? Probably because it represents one of man's deepest fears. Of course, Professor Freud, what an easy answer.*

Again, as he had done before, he attempted to arouse himself. Nothing. In the past, he would be ready at an instant, all he had to do was visualize a willing and attractive companion. Now, Sarah's mangled head intervened. *Will this be my fate? Impotence, from now on?*

Eventually, he returned to bed, and fell into a fitful, interrupted sleep.

* * *

The doctor finished his examination and, shining his light into Kurt's eyes, peered once more into his pupils. "You don't look well. Your wound is healing nicely, your leg is just about as good as new, but I am concerned about the effects of the concussion. Do you still have headaches?"

Kurt shook his head, proud that he could do so without pain. " Some times, but not very severe, they seem to be getting better."

"How is your appetite?"

"I am not very hungry. After all, just sitting around without exercise …"

"And you don't sleep well?" The doctor asked.

"That is true. I'm still dreaming about those last minutes."

"Understandably." the doctor nodded. "You had quite a shock. Look here, I could give you something that would make you sleep, but I would rather not create a dependency in a soldier who will soon be ready to resume his martial duties. I could send you to one of my colleagues who dabbles in psychiatry, and perhaps he could help. "

"I would prefer to wait before going to a head doctor " Kurt did not want to be labeled as unreliable because of his dreams. If Admiral Morse heard about it, that tough old buzzard would never allow him to go on any other missions.

"Well, here's what I suggest. You're not well enough to resume your duties, but I see no reason why you should sit around and be inactive. I suggest that you walk. Walk as much as you can. London is an exciting city to view right now, with the influx of all these Americans. Tire yourself out walking as much as possible. It will help your appetite and I hope, will enable you to sleep better. And it will begin to get you back into shape. When you come to see me next, we'll see whether that has helped. If not, there's still time to see my colleague."

So Kurt walked from early morning to just before curfew, when the blackout made finding your way around London's narrow streets difficult. He found that he enjoyed his walks and his observations of the city. His appetite improved, and he began to feel stronger, but the dreams continued.

He did not yet feel strong enough to visit the remaining prisoner of war camps in his quest for information about Ratzersdorfer, but the desire to do so was strong, and gave him an additional incentive to get better.

One day he was wandering around the bombed area, which extended from near St. Paul's Cathedral East through Whitechapel to the docks. It was the area that had suffered most during the Blitz. Most buildings were gone, but by now, more than two years after the Battle of Britain, the rubble had been removed from the streets and neatly piled up on the empty lots. The streets and roadways were clear, and the occasional undamaged building stood out like a single tooth in an otherwise toothless mouth.

As he walked toward one such building, he noted a number of well-dressed people hurrying toward it, from all sides. When he came closer, he saw the sign on the front - Congregation Ohab Zedek. Ah, a synagogue. He realized that it was Friday afternoon. He had not attended services in a very long time. He entered.

The atmosphere in the sanctuary enveloped him with its familiar setting. The wooden benches, the pulpit and the Ark of the Covenant, the congregants in their good clothes greeting each other, all reminded him of more peaceful times. He sat through the service, responding appropriately with the familiar Hebrew words, chanting the Sh'ma - the central tenet of faith - Hear, Oh Israel, the Lord our God is One. When toward the end of the service, he stood with all the mourners and recited the Kaddish, the prayer for the dead, he not only thought of his martyred parents, but also thought of Sarah, and tears came to his eyes.

As he walked out after the service was over, a voice called out to him. "Captain, just a moment, please."

The rabbi had been standing at the door, greeting his flock, but held out a hand to Kurt. "Forgive me for asking, but do you have family in London?"

"No," Kurt answered.

"Then, may I have the privilege of inviting you to share Sabbath dinner with my family and me? I'm sure you haven't had a good home cooked meal in a long time, particularly one like my wife serves."

Kurt hesitated, but the rabbi, a small man with merry eyes and a wisp of a graying beard, looked at him with such friendliness that he could not refuse.

So Kurt found himself at the rabbi's table, sharing it with several children, a graybeard, obviously the rabbi's father-in-law, and a few other guests. He had not realized how much he would enjoy the kind of food that was so similar to what his mother would serve on a Friday night. The candles on the table, blessed by the Rebbetzin, the Rabbi's wife, the twisted white bread, the Challah, the chicken soup, the brisket, the stewed prunes, and all the other goodies that make up such a festive affair.

"We are not black marketeers," the Rabbi smiled at him. "We save our coupons and eat very little during the week, but we want to be able to celebrate the Sabbath as much as possible even with the wartime shortages."

"And then you invite guests? Won't you be short of food for the next week as well?"

"We'll manage. It's more important to perform the commandment of feeding the stranger. And no Jew is a stranger here."

After dinner, the familiar Sabbath songs, the Zmirot, resounded and Kurt found himself participating in full voice. The evening ended quite late. Kurt rose to take his leave, but the Rabbi held him back. "I'm sure, your quarters are quite far from here. You cannot walk such a distance in the dark. Please spend the night in our spare room."

Kurt demurred, but finally gave in to his host's insistence. He undressed in the dark - after all it was the Sabbath - and slipped between clean sheets into a bed much too short for him. He curled up, the Sabbath songs still going through his mind. He thought about his parents. "Mama, I miss you so. If you could take care of me like you always did when I was sick...." And Kurt, the warrior, the spy, the killer of men, started to weep uncontrollably.

* * *

It wasn't that the episode at the Rabbi's house was a catharsis, but Kurt began to feel better about himself. The dream still appeared, but with less and less frequency. And as far as his fear of impotence was concerned, he tried to put it out of his mind. He told himself that he was not in the mood, just not interested, and that when the right woman and the right moment arrived, the problem would not exist.

But in his heart of hearts, he did not believe it.

"There was a call for you, "Adam Bede told him. " Lady Maud would like to see you. She's in London at the ducal residence."

"Why? What could she possibly want with me?"

"Thank you, perhaps? " Adam answered.

"She's done that, as have her parents. Besides, I really don't deserve any thanks."

"Be that as it may, I don't think it would be wise to ignore a summons from the daughter of a Duke."

"Oh, you class conscious English. Very well, I will report as ordered."

The residence in Mayfair was only a small mansion compared to the estate Kurt had seen in Scotland, but he was received by a grave butler with as much formality as if he had been of the nobility himself. He was led into a small drawing room, furnished with antiques and ancestral paintings, and Lady Maud appeared. She was dressed very simply in an afternoon frock, which however made her appear far more elegant than when he had last seen her in Scotland. She offered him a drink, which was instantly provided, and then sat down next to him on a damask covered couch.

"I appreciate your coming to see me. I wanted to talk to you about Sarah."

Kurt could not conceal a pang of pain.

"Yes, I know. Yonu cared for her. Sarah was my best friend, my sister, my first lover. Oh, don't be so shocked. I know she thought the world of you, and I wanted to tell you about her. Don't misjudge her - or me, for that matter."

"I don't understand, what do you mean?"

"Sarah told me all about your Odyssey through France. And she told me specifically about the night you spent together in - where was it?"

"St. Jean de Luz."

"Yes, yes. She had expected that you would be making love that night, and she was very taken by your restraint. She knew perfectly well what an effect she had had on you, and she liked you very much."

"So she laughed at me for being too callow or too romantic to take advantage of the situation?"

"Oh no, you don't understand. She respected you for it, and she told me, it made her look forward to the opportunity of your enjoying each other. Unfortunately, that opportunity never came."

"But you said she was your lover?"

Maud sighed. "I suppose I'll have to explain our attitude about sex. In our crowd, we have been fortunate enough to have every whim indulged. Now, marriage is a dynastic matter, we are required to marry and procreate to maintain our estates and alliances, and we can count ourselves fortunate if our marriage partner happens to become a friend. Sex, on the other hand, is entertainment, and we do not see why we should not enjoy all of it. Most of our men enjoy the sexual favors of other men as well as of women, and the same freedom applies to us. Sarah and I experimented when we were young. I believe that we started at fourteen when we were at school, and we have enjoyed each other and participated in sexual pleasures with others, men and women, ever since. What harm is there in that? We do our duty when the time comes. I cannot tell you how much I miss Sarah. We have shared so much together."

"Evidently." Kurt said with some bitterness.

"Don't be naïve. Victorianism went out with the old queen, and even when she reigned, it was a position taken only by the middle classes."

"Why did you want to tell me about this?"

"Sarah had hoped that you would follow her to her room when you visited her on her father's estate. You did not, and then you suddenly disappeared. And the next time you met, she was married, and you did not understand. She really liked you , you know."

"She liked me - but she did not love me."

"Love? I don't know what that means. In other circumstances, in another world, who knows? All I can tell you is that she kept talking about you. You were totally different from the men she knew, and you had made a deep impression on her."

"Well, Lady Maud, thank you for telling me all this, although I do not understand its purpose."

"Don't you? Sarah was my dearest friend. She felt she owed you - and herself - a passionate encounter, and now she's gone, and it won't ever happen. But I can do it for her " - with a small smile, Maud added, - " and for me, as well. Will you let me make love to you, please, for Sarah's sake, and for mine?"

* * *

"Well, how was your visit with Lady Maud, Kurt?" Adam asked.

"She wanted to tell me about Sarah."

"And did that help?"

"I have to think about it. I understand her better now, and I'll always be sorry that she died.".

"And did Lady Maud thank you again?"

"Repeatedly," said Kurt.

* * *

The Spring of 1942 represented the nadir of the Allied forces. In the Pacific, Japan had conquered enough territory to be at the gates of British India. Rommel's Africa Corps threatened the Suez canal, and if the Germans succeeded in taking it, they could link up with the Japanese in a truly global strategy. German troops had conquered the Ukraine and the Caucasus. But the sleeping giant in America was stirring, and the tide began to turn. By the middle of 1942 the United States demonstrated to the Japanese Empire that the losses at Pearl Harbor were far from fatal, and in two naval and air battles, Coral Sea and Midway, halted and reversed the advances of the Japanese; Field Marshall Montgomery defeated Rommel's troops at the battle of El Alamein, and the Suez Canal was never in danger again; and the Russians rallied at Stalingrad and stopped the German advance in a five months long battle that ultimately destroyed a whole German Army. The high water mark of the Axis had been reached and reversed.

It was summer before Kurt got a clean bill of health from his doctors. His leg was fully functional a long time before the effects of his concussion were totally dissipated. He had been bored to tears performing the duties of liaison officer to the French contingent in London.

His search for Ratzersdorfer had been fruitless. There were very few SS officers among the captured Germans, and those he encountered were unwilling or unable to give him any information. Kurt was not in a position to take drastic measures to force their cooperation. He knew no more than what he had learned at Waterstoun from the cooperative Priebke: He knew Ratzersdorfer's origin, his age, his physical description and that he was on a very successful career path within the SS. That was a lot, but the Germans had several million men under arms. Ratzersdorfer could be in any one of the many theaters of war.

Finally Kurt presented himself in the Admiral's ante-chamber in order to report himself fully fit for duty.

Admiral Morse was friendly but quite short.

"I'm glad to see that you're ready for some meaningful work. You will report to the farm for a refresher course, and when you have completed that training, come back to me. It's time to use your talents properly."

The next day, Kurt reported to the "farm" - a training facility run by his service on a small estate in the North. He was taken in hand by a taciturn master sergeant, and spent the next three months doing some of the hardest physical work he had ever done. In addition to the usual routine of obstacle courses, unarmed combat and calisthenics, he was taught very specifically how to kill silently, how to approach potential victims from the rear, where it would do the most good to insert a knife so as to hit the heart instantly, how to use a piano wire and two wooden dowels to make a serviceable garrote, how to avoid being splattered by blood when engaged in such activities, and similar pleasant subjects. Kurt also spent a great deal of time learning the use of explosives and the manner in which ordinary agricultural chemicals can be transformed into lethal weapons. He learned the best way to derail trains, destroy motor vehicles' engines, and how to turn artillery pieces of different kinds into functional scrapmetal by the judicious insertion of small metal pieces where they would do the most harm.

He practiced making Molotov cocktails and fake documentation and fake uniforms of all German and French military and police services. And he worked on his weakest subject, communication by Morse code.

* * *

CHAPTER XII

It was late Fall by the time he reported again to Admiral Morse.

"Well, you are ready. It's time for you to go back to Paris. You will take along a substantial amount of currency, both in French Francs and German Marks, that we have produced here. They cannot be distinguished from the real thing. You will organize resistance and sabotage and you will act as paymaster to the various French groups engaged in this pursuit - except for the Communists, with whom you will coordinate only when absolutely necessary. I will send a radio operator along with you. Your ability to communicate with us by Morse code is not your greatest talent.

You will be taken to Portugal by submarine, and landed near Oporto. Since you will have two large suitcases, you must get to Paris by train. There is a sealed train leaving Lisbon for Switzerland every week. It is the only land communication between Switzerland and the neutral world, and therefore allowed through Vichy France without interference. No customs inspector in Portugal will bother you, knowing that you will go through Swiss customs. You must leave the train in France. You will receive full details at your final briefing. You will again use Swiss papers.

Report to Curzon Street for your detailed briefing and for all the paperwork you need.

Return to see me" - the Admiral consulted his desk calendar, " next Monday at 11 A.M. You will meet your partner, and I will wish you luck. After this, I probably won't see you until we all meet in Paris after the Jerries have been thrown out."

"Sir, I would much prefer to travel on my own. Can I not meet the communication specialist in Paris?"

"I'm afraid not. I depend on you to get both of you and the equipment into France. You have the experience to cope with unforeseen circumstances, as you have demonstrated."

"As you wish, sir."

* * *

"The sealed train is a rather unique phenomenon," the briefing officer sounded very professorial. "You remember that in 1917 the Germans allowed Lenin to cross Germany to Finland in a sealed train, from where he could get to St. Petersburg to foment the October Revolution?"

"Indeed, I do. I remember it well."

The briefing officer was not deterred by Kurt's attempt at levity. "Since Switzerland's neutrality is important to both sides in this war, and Switzerland's geographical location has her surrounded by the Axis, the sealed train is the only solution that would allow Switzerland access to the sea. In effect, the train is considered Swiss territory, although juridically this is not the fact. The train crew is composed of nationals of the countries the train passes through."

Kurt was tempted to make some comments about the niceties of diplomatic fictions in the midst of a war, but thought better of it.

"You will board the train in Lisbon. It makes no stops, except for refueling and taking on water, until after it crosses the Swiss border. It circles around Madrid so as to obviate the need of changing from one station to another. The duration of the voyage is somewhat extended thereby, but the few passengers are not in a position to object. The train is first class throughout with sleeping compartments for all passengers. The trip generally takes about four days." The briefing officer permitted himself a small smile. "You will be in the lap of luxury."

"Now, your luggage will not be checked until you cross into Switzerland, and of course you must not do that. Look at the map with me, please." The briefing officer produced a pointer. "Here, about sixty miles South of the Swiss border the train crosses a ravine and stops to take on water. Most of the cars remain on the bridge over the ravine. You will attempt to get seats as far to the rear of the train as possible. When the train stops for water, you and your companion will simply exit with your luggage, and climb down into the ravine. Wait until the train departs, climb back up, and walk in the direction you have come from for half a mile, where the tracks cross a highway. You will be met there. Piece of cake."

"I'm sure it is, sir." Kurt was not so sure.

* * *

"Now when you reach Paris, you know what is expected of you, " the Admiral said. "Will your gangster friend be of help, do you think?"

"Monsieur Goldoni is no gangster, Admiral, but he is a patriot. The question is what shape he is in at this time. Have the Germans left him alone?"

"To the best of my knowledge, he is still operating in the entertainment field. He could be quite useful to you, if he can be trusted. But that is a decision you must make. It's your neck that's at risk, after all. Now, I want you to meet your partner." The Admiral picked up the phone and said " Send her in, please."

Her? He wants me to travel with a woman. What nonsense.

Solange Theberge entered the Admiral's office.

The last time Kurt had seen Solange was on the ship from Oran more than three years earlier. He remembered her nervousness about her inability to speak English, and her courage in spending time with him in spite of her father's disapproval. He also remembered how attractive she was.

In the intervening years, Solange had matured from an attractive teenager into a beautiful young woman. "Hello, Kurt, it's good to see you again," she said in perfect English with a charming French accent.

Kurt acknowledged Solange's greeting with a smile, but turned to Admiral Morse:

"Sir, I object. This is a dangerous mission, and not suited for a lady."

"I am a French patriot." Solange interrupted. "It is not your decision how I want to serve my country."

"Quiet, both of you." Admiral Morse was quite stern. "I remind you Captain Auster, that you are a serving officer and will obey my orders. And, Miss Theberge, once we have explained the circumstances to Captain Auster, I'm sure he will withdraw his objection. Now, both of you, sit down."

"Now," Admiral Morse continued. " Your cover is that you were married in Switzerland. You are both Swiss of course, went on your honeymoon to Portugal - even in wartime, some wealthy Swiss have been known to do that - and are returning home. Your train tickets are the return portion of that trip. You will remain together until you reach Paris. After that, it is your decision, Captain Auster, what living arrangements are to be made for Miss Theberge, as long as she is able to fulfill her primary function of communicating officer. Miss Theberge has become very adept at transmitting and receiving Morse code, a skill, I must point out, Captain Auster, in which you are sadly deficient. You have been thoroughly briefed. It

362

now remains for me to wish both of you Godspeed, and to express the hope that we will all meet in Paris in the not too distant future."

Admiral Morse had given Kurt permission to say good bye to Adam Bede and to tell him where he was going.

"I wish you safety and good fortune," Adam said emotionally. " I will keep all your possessions and uniforms here until you come back. I'm sure there will be an invasion of the continent in the next year or so, as soon as the Americans have sent enough troops and equipment over here, and then you'll be able to return. This is your home, remember that."

"I can't tell you how much your friendship has meant to me," Kurt, too, felt tears welling up. " I certainly hope to see you again soon."

When Kurt left, Adam stood on the landing and waved. Kurt hoped that this was not his last glimpse of his good friend.

Kurt made sure that none of his clothes, shoes and toiletries were made in Britain. Curzon Street had adequate supplies of such things made in Switzerland or France, so that he was properly equipped. He hoped that Solange had been equally careful and promised himself to check this out with her as soon as they met.

* * *

Compared to a submarine a destroyer was like a cruise ship. After banging his head several times, Kurt had learned to walk in a crouched position. He had become aware of the wisdom of requiring submariners to be on the short side. He had been assigned quarters in the tiny cubby that served as sickbay, where he stayed in a bunk designed, he believed, for the smallest of Snow White's dwarfs. A submarine is not equipped to carry passengers, notably female passengers. The Captain had graciously turned over his quarters to Solange and doubled up with his first officer. This was not particularly onerous since one of them was always on duty.

Kurt had no time to have a word in private with Solange. He ascertained that her clothing could not be identified as British, but beyond that, there simply was no opportunity for private conversation. The submarine traveled on the surface where much greater speed could be achieved, but the passengers were not permitted on the sloping narrow deck. "We may have to dive fast, and you're not trained to hop as fast as you may have to hop, and we wouldn't want to lose you, would we? " the Captain told Kurt genially. As it turned out, traveling through the Channel and into the Atlantic was no pleasure. The waves were quite high and the ship moved constantly in totally unexpected directions. Kurt, who had not experienced any seasickness on the destroyer, felt queasy throughout the voyage. Perhaps, the stiflingly hot air below, redolent of motor oil and other unpleasant fragrances, perhaps the constant very loud thrum of the engines, contributed to his ill feeling. "Wait until we've been under for a while," he was told, "it's much quieter there."

As they traveled further South, there were, indeed, several dives. Whenever the lookout or the radar operator detected even the slightest sign of life on the horizon, the klaxon sounded its harsh alarm and the sub dove. The first time it happened, Kurt looked into himself for signs of claustrophobia - and found them. Oh, how he found them. He was extremely conscious of the tons and tons of water pressing in on them, and the tiny space in which a few dozens humans were forced into a very tight companionship. He could not wait for the voyage to end, and found that he spent most of his time on his bunk, bent almost in half, trying to nap and hoping that the time would pass quickly.

Finally, they arrived. They surfaced in early evening just off Oporto in the North of Portugal. Their luggage was thrown into a rubber dinghy, as were Solange and Kurt, and with a smile and a cheery wave they were off. Two sailors rowed them ashore to a sandy beach, helped them with their bags, and left them standing on terra firma. The two travelers looked at each other with a sigh of relief.

"Welcome to Portugal," a voice intoned in perfect upper class English. Kurt turned and saw a short, swarthy man of indeterminate age, dressed in working man's clothes and wearing a chauffeur's cap. "Your taxi is waiting," he said.

"Who are you?" Kurt asked, even though he suspected that this reception had been organized by Admiral Morse.

"My name is Whitney. I'm deputy security officer at the Embassy here, and I double as a taxi driver and sometimes in other functions when necessary." The man smiled. "Come on, let's get going." He took hold of two of the bags, allowing Kurt and Solange to carry the rest. Just above the beach a highway stretched North and South, and indeed, a Lisbon taxi of the type Kurt had seen on his previous trip to Portugal, was waiting.

As they were driving South toward Lisbon, Whitney continued. "We've got you booked into the honeymoon suite at the Ritz - nothing too good for Admiral Morse's people, and it goes with your cover. Get a good night's sleep, and tomorrow you'll walk over to the railroad station and book your "return" passage to Zurich on the sealed train. The train leaves in two days, so you'll have a little time to relax in beautiful Lisbon. After I've dropped you at the Ritz, you're on your own, but here's a number where you can reach me in case of emergency."

The Ritz was one of the newest and most luxurious hotels in Lisbon. They registered, showing their Swiss passports which identified them as man and wife, and were shown to a large suite, living room, bedroom and bath.

"I'm totally exhausted. I never want to see a submarine again." Solange collapsed on the couch in the living room. " I need a bath desperately, but I don't know if I have the energy."

"I feel the same way," Kurt smiled. " I respect those sailors immensely for what they're going through just being on that boat. I never want to be in one again either. Before you take your bath, there's something I need to say to you, now that we're alone."

"Oh, that sounds ominous."

"No, not at all. Just that when I objected to working with a woman in Admiral Morse's office, this was not directed at you personally. It's just - how can I put it - that I prefer working alone, and that having to be responsible for someone else creates more difficulty. You understand? If I have to work with a woman, of course, you'd be the one I 'd pick, I remember well our conversations aboard the Drake."

"Now, you're getting me angry. You're treating me like a child." Solange jumped up, her eyes flashing. " You're not responsible for me. You're an agent, and I'm an agent. We've each got our jobs to do, and in a pinch, I'd have no hesitation abandoning you to the wolves, as you must never hesitate to do the same. Beating the Germans - that's our job, not taking care of each other. Do I make myself clear? And now, for my bath."

Before Kurt had a chance to respond, Solange stalked off.

Exhausted as he was, Kurt felt the need of a bath himself - the toilet facilities aboard a submarine are notoriously inadequate. He took off his shoes, and stretched out on the couch in the living room. *I'll close my eyes for a minute and as soon as Solange is out of the bathroom...* The last thing he remembered was a vision of

365

Solange soaping her lovely body in the tub, then steam obscured his dream and he fell sound asleep.

* * *

The smell of freshly brewed coffee wafted across his nostrils. He opened his eyes to a vision of loveliness - Solange, wrapped in a white bathrobe, her hair covered by a towel, looking clean and fresh, stood over him holding a cup of coffee in her hand.

"Time to get up, sleepyhead," she smiled. "I've ordered breakfast from room service, and you didn't even hear the waiter come in. Remind me never again to go on a honeymoon cruise with you on a submarine. You may drink this coffee, but then," she wrinkled her adorable nose, " you'd better get cleaned up before you join me for breakfast. Hurry up, now."

Kurt jumped up, swallowed the coffee quickly and hurried to the bathroom. Twenty minutes later, showered and shaved and dressed in the bathrobe generously provided by the hotel, he joined Solange at a table set near the front window of the suite. Below them stretched the main park of Lisbon and in the distance on both sides, the hills covered with white houses.

"I want to apologize again," Kurt said. " I seem to keep saying the wrong thing."

Solange interrupted. "We'll attribute it to your extreme tiredness. Now, enough of that. We're partners, and we'll do our job. All right?"

This girl has a way of disconcerting me, Kurt thought. *She makes me feel - and act - like the schoolboy I was when I left Vienna. But she is adorable. I can't get involved - not so soon after Sarah's death.*

After breakfast they got dressed and sauntered out of the hotel down toward the railroad station. London had been dark and gloomy in the early November days when they had left. Here in Lisbon the sun shone and it was warm and pleasant. "A lovely city and much nicer weather," Solange commented.

As they walked down, they passed a newspaper kiosk. Big, black headlines screamed from the papers. "Just a moment," Kurt said. He did not speak Portuguese, but with his background of Latin and knowledge of French, he could make out the headlines.

"Allied forces have invaded North Africa." He told Solange. " Now it begins. We're on the way finally."

Indeed, an invasion force composed primarily of American elements with some British and Free French forces had landed in the French territories of North Africa.

"Surely, Admiral Morse must have known this was about to happen?"

"Admiral Morse tells you what he wants you to know. But now that it has begun, our efforts in occupied France are going to be more important than ever. We'd better get there as quickly as possible."

But that was not to be so easy. The official behind the guichet at the railroad station communicated to them in sign language and loudly pronounced Portuguese that the sealed train to Switzerland had been canceled. "He must think that talking louder will make me understand him better, " Kurt muttered. He was unable to get any information out of the man as to when the next train would depart. All he got was an expressive shrug, and arms and eyes raised to the heavens.

"Well, we'll have to call the number Whitney gave us and see whether there are any instructions for us." Kurt said.

"The Germans occupied the rest of France as soon as they found out about the landings in North Africa. I guess they expect us to land in the South of France - not an unreasonable expectation. They're going to fortify it as they have fortified the Atlantic." Whitney was very calm and informative. " I don't think that's in the cards so soon. There's a lot of consolidation to be done, and the landings in North Africa were virtually unopposed. We think that the sealed train will be permitted soon. The Jerries have just as much interest as we have in maintaining land communications between Portugal and Switzerland. So, why don't you enjoy yourself in this pretty city for a few days, keep checking with the railroad station - the concierge in your hotel will gladly do it - and let's see what happens by next week."

Kurt came back from the telephone. "You always wanted to enjoy a honeymoon in Lisbon, didn't you, Solange? " he smiled. "Well, we have instructions to do just that, until the train resumes. Whitney thinks that will happen soon."

During the next few days, the two young people acted as if indeed they were on a honeymoon. They wandered the streets of the white city, climbed to the ruins of St. George's castle and lunched there in the small restaurant overlooking the city. They strolled around the waterfront, in peacetime much busier than now, and Kurt wondered about the mass of refugees from central Europe he had seen on his last trip. How many of them had made it to America or another safe destination, and how many were interned by the Portuguese, or perhaps had been sent back?

As they spent time together, Solange talked about her family. She had lost all respect for her father. She had become aware of the fact that his departure from Oran had not been motivated by patriotism, although she had no inkling of Kurt's specific part in the matter.

"No one in the Free French community in London believes in him any more. It is up to me to rescue the honor of the family." She did not mention her mother, but it was clear that she had essentially broken with her family. "Only my sister. We're still very close and she's so sorry that she's too young to do more for the war effort. She's in school outside of London. The atmosphere at home with my parents is too poisonous, and I'm glad she's away."

Remembering his involvement with Clemente Theberge, Kurt kept as silent as possible. He also thought of Capitaine Louis Reynaud's injunction about mothers and daughters, but found it difficult to consider obeying it, when he looked at Solange's gamin face.

One evening they went up the narrow cobbled streets of the Alfama, the oldest district of Lisbon, dating from the eighth to the twelfth century and the Moorish occupation. The tiny little houses in the winding streets and alleys were filled with small restaurants and clubs in which the main attraction was not the food or wine, but the Fado singers. The melancholy, sad songs of lost loves touched their hearts, even though they did not have an understanding of the Portuguese words.

When they returned to their suite, Kurt got ready to sleep in his accustomed place on the couch in the living room. Then the door to the bedroom opened. Solange stood there, in the white bathrobe in which she had woken him their first morning in Lisbon. It was clear that she wore nothing else. Without a word, she approached the couch, took Kurt's hand and led him to her bed.

* * *

A few days later, the departure of the next sealed train to Zurich was announced. In accordance with their cover as a wealthy Swiss couple returning from their honeymoon, Kurt and Solange took a first class compartment. Under their new and most satisfying status as lovers, sharing the bunk bed would be a most enjoyable chore. The trip through Spain to the French border took four days, a good portion of which were spent while the train was being shunted around Madrid. After all, the passengers of the sealed train were not permitted to leave the train at any time, even to transfer from one Madrid railroad station to the other.

Kurt and Solange kept to themselves as much as possible. Breakfast and lunch were served in their compartment, but dinner had to be taken in the dining car. There they observed the other passengers - mostly Swiss businessmen - very few women, but also a sprinkling of what appeared to be German officers in civilian clothes. The military posture of some of them made this kind of identification unmistakable. "I wonder why they are going to Switzerland?" Solange asked. "Perhaps that is not their final destination as it isn't ours, but they'll have an easier time getting off the train in German occupied France." Kurt replied.

Once they crossed the Spanish/French border the train came to a stop. German troops boarded the train, and an armed soldier began to patrol the corridors of each wagon. As provided in the regulations, no one approached the passengers to ask for documentation. The train was theoretically Swiss territory, but the patrolling soldiers were an ominous sign.

"How will we get off the train with those soldiers about? " Solange asked nervously.

"We will have to see. We still have about twenty hours until we reach the bridge.
Fortunately, we'll get there in the middle of the night." Kurt said.

The train moved much slower than the schedule provided. It was often stopped on a siding to allow troop trains to go past. It was almost dawn the next night when the bridge was reached where they had to descend from the train with all their precious luggage.

"Call the soldier into our compartment. Act helpless," Kurt told Solange.

He flattened himself behind the entrance door, and prepared his handmade garrote, consisting of a narrow wire, looped at both ends. Solange went out to the guard. "Monsieur, Monsieur, venez vite, vite, mon mari est malade. Aidez moi."

The German looked at the lovely girl uncomprehendingly, but her pulling at his arm and her gestures made it clear to him that he was needed. Carrying his rifle in one hand, he followed the pretty girl. As he entered the compartment, Kurt threw his garrote over the man's head and pulled with all his might when it reached the neck. The wire bit into the throat. There was a gush of blood, which Kurt avoided carefully, and the man collapsed.

"Is he dead?" Solange asked. "Never mind, let's go." Kurt replied.

They carried their suitcases to the door of the wagon, opened it and threw them out. As they clambered down the steps, Solange stopped. "I've never seen a man die before." "Don't think about it now, let's go, let's go." Kurt whispered.

Quickly, they grabbed the valises and ducked under the railing of the bridge, climbing down and sliding and slipping into the ravine.

"We can't stay here until the train leaves, as we had hoped. If they find the body, there'll be pursuit immediately. Let's get as far away as we can." Kurt suggested.

Carrying their suitcases with difficulty they slid further down into the ravine. At the bottom there was a small stream, fortunately quite narrow and with little water in it , now in late Fall. "That's lucky," Kurt said, "it must have been a very dry Summer."

He heaved the suitcases across the stream and they followed. Then they began to drag them up the opposite slope. "Stop," Solange said. "The train is moving."

With a great clatter, the train began to move and soon accelerated out of sight. "They didn't find the soldier," Kurt sighed with relief. "Let's find a place to hide, and then I'll go and look for the Maquisards who're supposed to meet us."

They pulled their suitcases into a clump of bushes halfway up the slope. "Don't go yet, " Solange pleaded. " I've never seen a man die, and you killed him. You've done this before, haven't you?"

"I have." Kurt said somberly. "You've been sleeping with a murderer."

Solange looked at him, took Kurt's hands into her own, and kissed them. "I've been sleeping with a hero who fights evil. It was a shock to see it happen. I promise I won't be as weak the next time. But, please, don't leave me alone. Can we just stow the luggage here, and look for our people together?"

By this time, there were some groups of French resisters, who had hidden in the swamps and forests of France. They had taken the name Maquis from the word for swampland, and such a group was supposed to meet Kurt and Solange and help them on their way.

With a small smile, Kurt acknowledged Solange's request. They hid their luggage as well as they could, and struggled up the stony slope. On the top they looked around. "They expect us on the other side," Kurt whispered.

"No, we don't. We figured you'd make your way over here, where it's safer," a familiar voice intoned. Kurt looked around. Three men, dressed in work clothes, wearing berets and carrying rifles, stood there. Unshaven, threatening, they looked most unprepossessing. The most disreputable among them, with a four day old beard, torn, filthy clothes and an unlit Gauloise between his lips, stretched out his hand. "Welcome to France, my friend Kurt," he said.

"Thank you, my patriotic friend," Kurt replied.

Capitaine Louis Reynaud chuckled.

* * *

Silvio Goldoni was not a happy man. Business was not bad - the night clubs in Pigalle brought in as much as during peacetime, even more sometimes, and the fact that most of the money spent there came from German soldiers did not bother him at all; the flourishing fake documents division was much in demand; and the black market supply of food and drink was going well. But several things annoyed him. In peacetime, he had always had his little arrangements with the authorities - he was well protected, and he did certain favors for some of the more important members of the government, particularly the police. But the Germans could not be trusted. He had managed to corrupt a few mid-level officers in the Kommandantur, but he knew perfectly well that there were limits on what they would be able to do for him. And there was no protection against the frequent raids that swooped up anyone who happened to be in the street at a given moment, and sent those unfortunates either to slave labor camps in Germany, or, even worse, to be used as hostages against some of the depredations of the Resistance. Several members of Monsieur Goldoni's organization had been caught in such nets and there was nothing he could do to save them.

And now the so-called Free Zone was no more. All of France was occupied territory. This meant not only that lucrative interzonal smuggling had come to an end, but that the escape route he had always kept in mind for himself in case of need no longer existed.

Silvio Goldoni was sick and tired of the occupation, of watching strutting Germans in his establishments, of the dark and gloomy city that his beloved Paris had become.

There was a commotion in the entrance hall. Marthe, his long time housekeeper, opened the door to his office.

"Look who's come back," she gushed. "It's Monsieur Kurt. I thought you were dead, " she addressed Kurt. "It's good you've survived these terrible times."

Goldoni rose and with a few long steps reached Kurt and embraced him. "So did I, my boy. Welcome, welcome. Marthe, bring some food and drink. Are you well? Are you safe or do you need help? Where have you been all this time? "

"I'm very glad to see you, Monsieur Goldoni, and you too, Marthe, " Kurt said. " I'm well, and I think we have a lot to talk about. How have you been?"

"Not so well. The occupation is wearing me down. We've lost some very good people, and things are very depressing. But enough about that. First tell me where you've been?"

"No, Monsieur Goldoni." Kurt said. "First one question. Do you want to do something about the Germans, even at the risk of your life and all you own?"

Goldoni paused and looked at Kurt for a long moment. "That is quite a question."

"I know you're a patriot, and I'm not asking just to make conversation. If you say no, we'll have a drink together and I'll disappear again. I know I can count on your discretion. But if you say yes, we have a lot of work to do."

Goldoni paced up and down his spacious office. He knew perfectly well what Kurt was talking about. Up to now he had stayed clear of the Resistance, preferring to cultivate his own garden as Voltaire's Candide would have said. Now he was asked to make a decision that could cost him his life.

"Kurt, my friend, I have been so bored without you. So you're going to bring some excitement into my life? Well, it's time we did something to those strutting Boche. I'm with you."

* * *

Madame Esperanza Gonzalez was totally worn out. She had just completed a very strenuous performance of Turandot, and then, as so often, had been required to attend a party thrown by the commanding General, von Weitzensberg. Every time some visiting dignitaries from Berlin appeared in Paris - and this was very often, Paris was certainly a destination much favored for inspection tours, much more so than visits to the Eastern front - she had to be trotted out as principal diva of the Paris Opera. That way those dignitaries could tell their wives about the cultural event they had witnessed and about the great Opera Star they had met. This would presumably keep the wives from asking about any of the less cultural activities the visitors may have indulged in. Activities for which Paris was at least as famous as for the glories of its Opera.

Madame Esperanza had just collapsed in her best armchair, taken off her shoes, and with great satisfaction begun to massage her toes, when her maid came in.

"There's a young man at the door. He insists on seeing you."

"At this hour of the night? Tell him, I don't receive visitors here. Tell him to apply to the office at the Opera."

"He said to remind you of a train ride in the Summer of 1940."

"What! " Madame Gonzalez exclaimed. "Could it be? Well, send him in, send him in."

Kurt entered carrying a bouquet of roses, which had been particularly hard to find in Paris in November.

"It is you." La Gonzalez exclaimed. "Still among us, are you? " She received the roses gratefully and handed them to the maid. " Put them in water and bring us some champagne and then you can go. I'll take care of myself tonight."

After they had clinked glasses, Madame Gonzalez turned to Kurt and said, "All your efforts to save poor Sarah turned out in vain. Did you know?"

"Yes, I know. Do you know the details of how she was killed?"

"I was told that she was killed by German prisoners of war during an escape attempt from a camp in Scotland. Do you know any more than that?"

"No." Kurt said, "That is all my sources reported to me. I am here to ask you just one questions. Do you want to take revenge on the Germans? "

Madame Gonzalez looked at Kurt. " I thought so. You're involved in the Resistance. Do you know I've just come from a dinner party with General von Weitzensberg? And you know I'm Spanish, and Spain is an ally of Germany."

"I know all that. And I repeat my question. Do you want to take revenge on the Germans for murdering your daughter?"

"And if I say no? By rights I should call the police right now and report you."

"You won't do that. But if you say no, that's the end of it. I'll disappear and you won't hear from me again. And before you answer, think of the risks to which you would expose yourself if you say yes. Think hard."

* * *

In 1943 the tide of war turned and anyone less fanatical than the leadership of Germany and Japan would have sued for peace on the best possible terms. A complete German army was destroyed at Stalingrad. The Germans withdrew from the Caucasus and from then on fought a series of delaying battles against the Russians as they gradually were forced back toward the German heartland. Rommel's Africa Corps was destroyed and all of North Africa was in Allied hands. The Allies invaded and conquered Sicily, invaded Italy and Mussolini's regime fell. Germany occupied the Northern half of Italy and the Allies were forced into a series of battles inching their way up the Peninsula. In the Pacific, the Americans implemented their island hopping strategy, defeated the Japanese in a series of air and sea battles and with considerable difficulty and many casualties took several strategic islands. The outcome of the war was no longer in doubt, but the Allies had demanded unconditional surrender, and certainly neither the Nazi thugs of Hitler nor the militarist leaders of Japan were ready to give up.

Everyone awaited the Allied invasion of France. The Soviets demanded this " second front" but the Allies waited until they were ready. Yet it was certain, that sometime in 1944 the invasion would take place.

And in the extermination camps of Poland and the Ukraine, the crematoria were working full blast, and the ashes of one third of European Jewry darkened the landscape.

* * *

Kurt remembered the winter of 1943/1944 as among the happiest of his life. This was odd, because he was in constant danger and there was never a moment when he could feel safe. Monsieur Goldoni had arranged for Solange and Kurt to take over a small apartment in a lovely eighteenth century building on the Ile St. Louis. This was a very quiet section, an island in the Seine just east of the Ile de la Cite where Notre Dame attracted a lot of German tourists. There were no nightclubs or restaurants on the Ile St. Louis. It was essentially an upper class enclave, so that there were no special attractions that drew German soldiers to wander about it. Because it was upper class, and so many of the upper classes were fervent collaborators, there were also far fewer raids there than in the rest of Paris. When Solange and Kurt went out on their errands, they always carried their Swiss documents and wore Swiss flags in their lapels. Thus they escaped the special attentions of both the French and German authorities.

Through Monsieur Goldoni's connections in the black market there was always a good supply of food and drink available to them. Neither Solange nor Kurt were experienced cooks, but they began to collaborate on learning the culinary arts and had wonderful, giggling times when they concocted a totally inedible dish by incorrectly following some recipe they had found in one of the cook books they had acquired.

Kurt had never lived with a woman before. In the past, when he shared a bed, it was for the purpose of a joyous sexual encounter. Not that there were not many of those with Solange, but Kurt found that the bed was made not only for that, but that sharing the bed meant sleeping in each others arms, talking, sharing their dreams and emotions, cuddling and comforting, and taking care of each other. It was a new experience for Kurt who had been alone so long. So new that in spite of their precarious situation and the dangerous work they were engaged in, the phrase " after the war" began to creep into their vocabulary.

As paymaster, Kurt was involved in all resistance efforts. He even managed to come to an agreement with the highly disciplined communist resistance, whereby they coordinated their efforts. There was no obvious cooperation, but a sort of clearing house was established where plans of attacks were discussed. It would hardly have been productive, if both groups, for instance, made efforts to destroy the same train tracks and to derail the same trains.

Louis Reynaud's Maquis group was only one of several whose activities Kurt coordinated, and sometimes shared. The formerly dapper Capitaine Reynaud whose cynicism clearly had been the veneer to cover a deep patriotism, was tireless and fearless in leading and organizing attacks on the German occupiers. And Kurt used his ability to impersonate a German soldier on numerous occasion. He obtained a number of German uniforms and found a tailoring establishment that could reproduce not only any uniform that he might need but also the insignia of rank and unit that were required. Another well-hidden facility sheltered some of the best forgers Monsieur Goldoni could find, so that not only documentation could be obtained, but on several occasions, German orders could be changed, to the confusion and detriment of the enemy.

And all was coordinated with London. Frequently Solange would take her voluminous handbag with the false bottom, and go for a bicycle ride, a walk in the Bois de Boulogne, or a boat ride on the Seine. Always from a different location, and just for a few minutes, she would communicate with London, her expertise in sending Morse code extremely rapidly standing her in good stead. The replies frequently came in code phrases over the BBC. Of course it was forbidden to listen to the British broadcasts on the radio, but the Germans found it impossible to enforce that prohibition. Every broadcast began and ended with a number of coded phrases intelligible only to the recipient to whom they were addressed. How many of these phrases were meaningless and only designed to drive the German listeners to distraction, only their originators knew.

Every once in a while, more materiel and equipment were dropped by parachute and picked up at specific points by Louis Reynaud's group. There were times when Kurt was present at these drops.

In spite of the number of dangerous missions he undertook, the riskiest of which would find him in German uniform delivering forged dispatches to various headquarters on German motorcycles whose original occupant would later be found dead in a ditch, he was as happy as he had ever been. Returning home to Solange and spending days and nights with her made up for all the efforts and fear and strain of his work. And of course, the fact that he finally felt that he was doing damage to the German war machine gave Kurt a good deal of satisfaction. He was not callous about the Germans who died because of his efforts, nor was he insensitive to the suffering and deaths the Germans inflicted on French hostages which increased every time one of his missions was successful, but he had determined that he had to fight regardless of cost, and that only the end of the war could bring such suffering to a halt.

Occasionally - but only when it was required by the overall plan of a particular mission, he found that he had a member of the SS in his hands. He never failed to interrogate such a man about Ratzersdorfer, before sending him on his way to hell. However, he did not obtain any new information about his enemy.

* * *

General von Weitzensberg's office was the largest and most comfortable room in the Kommandantur, as was only proper for the commanding general. When he sat at his large desk, he could easily swivel around and look out the window across the Place de l'Opera at the Palais Garnier, where he spent some of his most enjoyable evenings attending his passion, classical opera. In addition to his desk, his office was furnished with a large conference section, several leather armchairs, a couch and a coffee table, as well as a wet bar, stocked with all the good drinks a country like France could produce. And what he enjoyed most was his fireplace. April 1944 was very cold in Paris. Most Parisians suffered from the cold much more than in peacetime because the shortages of coal and other fuels made it impossible to heat their homes. The shortages of food did not provide enough caloric intake to keep them comfortable. But the commanding general of the occupation forces did not feel any deprivations.

General von Weitzensberg was standing in front of the blazing fire, warming his ample backside. He was a tall man, who once had been athletic, but had allowed years of sloth and culinary indulgence to give him a body that almost competed in girth with that of Field Marshall Goering. Von Weitzensberg was a very competent administrator. He had never commanded troops in the field, but had been able to control his fief, occupied France, sufficiently so as to provide Germany with the materiel and slave labor that was required. . But in the last year there had been increasing problems with the French Resistance, enough so as to cause him to disappoint his superiors in Berlin on several noteworthy occasions.

"Tell me, " he addressed his aid, Oberst (Colonel) Scharfer. "What do you know about this SS Wunderkind that's supposed to solve all our security problems?"

Oberst Scharfer had been a combat officer until he lost an arm on the Eastern front, and had been seconded to Paris as a reward for his faithful service. The job was supposed to be a sinecure, enabling him to indulge in the pleasures of the French capital. But it hadn't turned out to be that way. General von Weitzensberg had assigned him the task of dealing with the depredations of the French Underground, and he had failed completely. As he frequently said to anyone willing to listen, he had not been trained as a policeman but as a combat soldier.

"As I understand it, our new head of security was an illegal adherent of the SS in Austria before the Anschluss, caught Heydrich's eye right afterwards and under his protection advanced extremely rapidly in rank and duties. After Heydrich's assassination two years ago, he is supposed to have been instrumental in the retaliatory destruction of the Czech village of Lidice and the execution of all its male inhabitants. When the Abwehr (the military intelligence organization) was absorbed into the SD (Sicherheitsdienst - the security branch of the SS), he rose even more rapidly in its ranks. As you know, he is now a full Standartenfuehrer, the equivalent of my own rank."

"So he became a colonel in what - six years? And you - how many years did it take you?"

Oberst Scharfer smiled. "Well, that is one of the differences between us in the Wehrmacht and the gentlemen of the SS. I wish it were the only one."

General von Weitzensberg nodded. "Yes, they are hardly the kind of people one would normally associate with. Not much culture there, eh? But useful,very useful. Perhaps we need their special talents now. Well, he's been cooling his heels long enough in the anteroom. Show him in."

A tall man in his mid thirties, impeccably dressed in the black SS uniform, with the silver insignia of a full Standartenfuehrer, entered. He stood at attention, raised his right arm in the Hitler salute and bellowed:

"Heil Hitler. Standartenfuehrer Ratzersdorfer reporting as ordered."

"Heil Hitler." General von Weitzensberg replied. "This is Oberst Scharfer. Please sit down. Drink?"

"No, thank you." Ratzersdorfer replied stiffly. "I do not indulge."

"Ah. Well. Sit down. You are aware of the problems we have had with the Resistance?"

"Just the general outline."

"Of course, of course. Oberst Scharfer, perhaps you would give us an overview."

"In the last year, " Oberst Scharfer began, " there have been eighteen train derailments, most of them troop trains, three particularly damaging. One carried slave laborers going to factories in the Reich, and many of them escaped in the confusion after the wreck and joined the Maquis; one carried ammunitions toward the Eastern front, most of which were lost in the ensuing explosions and the third..."

"Yes?"

"Possibly the most annoying to our masters in Berlin. It carried a collection of art works taken from some of the greatest collections in France and destined to the private collection of Field Marshall Goering. After the trainwreck the crates containing the art disappeared and we haven't been able to locate them. But that's not the worst of it."

"There is more?" Ratzersdorfer asked.

"Unfortunately yes. On several occasions, motorcycle riders carrying dispatches have been intercepted and murdered. Then forged dispatches were delivered by a man dressed in the messenger's uniform, speaking proper German. These forged dispatches caused untold confusion. However, we have resolved this problem."

"How?"

"We are sending duplicate orders, and require that all orders are confirmed by field telephone to headquarters."

General von Weitzensberg interjected. " This is a temporary solution. If the enemy invades France, as we anticipate will happen this year, we cannot go on like this. In battle conditions, speed and accuracy of communications are essential."

"Of course, Herr General. I understand." Ratzersdorfer rose. "I have brought a number of experienced men with me. I see two interesting avenues of approach. I would like all relevant files, and of course, Herr General, I require an absolute free hand."

"You will have both." General von Weitzensberg said. "But tell me, what are the approaches you see?"

"First of all, the German speaking man who could pass for one of our soldiers. Is he one of ours? A deserter? A traitor still serving with us? How many German speakers can we find in the files among the civilian population? And secondly, the leak."

"What do you mean, leak?" General von Weitzensberg was annoyed. " No one among my officers speaks out of turn."

"Then how were the bandits able to find out the train schedules and routes, particularly the art train? And how would they be able to know what false orders could do the most damage? No, Herr General, there is a leak, and I will find it. And now, with your permission, I will go to work. Heil Hitler."

* * *

On the Avenue Foch, not far from the Champs Elysees, a beautiful old building used to be known as the Palais Rothschild. It had been the residence for many years of some prominent members of the French branch of the old Jewish banking family. Immediately after the German occupation it was taken over by the SS. The organization of the raids against Jews emanated from here, and many prisoners were interrogated and tortured in the luxurious rooms of the mansion. Now, Standartenfuehrer Ratzersdorfer established himself and his senior staff here. His battalion of Waffen SS were billeted nearby.

As soon as he and his officers were properly installed, he convened a staff meeting. He made his assignments, somewhat in line with what he had told General von Weitzensberg, and then dismissed his men, except for one. "Just one moment, Karl-Heinz," he said. "Please stay."

Sturmbannfuehrer (Major) Karl-Heinz Most acknowledged the order. Most was a heavy set, thicknecked man, sporting a very short brush haircut. He looked exactly the image of the SS bully, but that image was misleading. He had come up from the ranks because he had realized that he could do so only by offering special services to his superiors. After the Fall of France in 1940, he had still been in the lower ranks of the SS, but when he was assigned to a unit serving in France, he had made a special effort to learn the language. Thus he not only assured himself of the comfortable occupation duties but also improved his chances for advancement.

"You are fluent in French, are you not?"

"Yes, sir."

"I believe there is something else we should look into," Ratzersdorfer said. " I am certain that the Milieu - the criminal element - is involved or at least aware of the underground activities. I want you to find out who runs the girls, the night clubs and the black market. Don't bother looking for the big boss in Paris, he'll be too well protected. Find me the underbosses in other cities - Marseilles, Lyon, Tours, Bordeaux and so on. All I need is one name. When you have it, I'm sure you'll be able to persuade him to help us catch our quarry."

"I understand, Herr Standartenfuehrer. I will get on it right away."

"Very well, then. Heil Hitler."

* * *

"I believe I will invite Standartenfuehrer Ratzersdorfer to join us at the Opera and then at our soiree here." General von Weitzensberg told Oberst Scharfer. " Will you, please see to it."

"With all due respect, Herr General, do you think the Standartenfuehrer will appreciate opera?" Oberst Scharfer dared the question.

"I see your point, Scharfer, but opera could be a civilizing influence. After all, we have to live with these gentlemen. It won't hurt to show them the finer things in life. Tell Ratzersdorfer he may bring along his two most senior officers, if he likes."

"Zu Befehl, Herr General."

* * *

The officers on General von Weitzensberg's staff had long ago made peace with the fact that the General's obsession with opera did not accept the possibility that anyone associated with him could be less enthusiastic. And of course, Scharfer mused, his obsession extended to the Prima Donna, the principal singer, Madame Esperanza Gonzalez. Scharfer shuddered when he visualized the two behemoths in bed together. Like two elephants making love. He preferred a succession of slim, obedient and above all silent bed companions, who would service him according to his moods and then disappear discreetly. The General often asked Madame Gonzalez to remain in costume after one of her bravura performances and, Scharfer reflected, in this manner he could be in bed with Tosca, Carmen or Turandot, and not the middle aged Madame Esperanza Gonzalez. Well, tastes differ, the colonel thought. As long as it makes him happy. She's Spanish, after all, an ally and friend of Germany.

Standartenfuehrer Ratzersdorfer was very gracious in accepting the invitation. He attended the performance of Turandot without complaint. Perhaps, I've done him an injustice, Scharfer thought. He might be more cultivated than most of the gentlemen of the SS. And he was courtesy itself at the soiree in the Kommandantur after the performance. Madame Gonzalez had remained in the costume of the heartless Chinese Princess, and was absolutely stunning, and Ratzersdorfer knew enough to kiss her hand and compliment her on her performance. It was very clear that Madame Gonzalez was more to General von Weitzensberg than merely an admired opera star, and Standartenfuehrer Ratzersdorfer was sufficiently polished to be knowledgeable and discreet at the same time.

* * *

Arsene Martin enjoyed his evening aperitif at the Café Charlemagne. It was his invariable habit to stop there for half an hour before returning to the bosom of his family. His two bodyguards knew enough to sit at a different table, their boss treasured the moments of silence and quiet in his active day. Even the German occupation had not stopped him from indulging himself in his accustomed manner, although he resented the sight of German soldiers in the Café that he favored.

He looked up with astonishment at the figure of a man, dressed in an excellently cut civilian suit, standing over him. Before he had a chance to signal his bodyguards, the man dropped a packet of Francs on the table.

"These are fifty thousand Francs. A moment of your time, Monsieur Martin?"

Even during the occupation, when German presses churned out Francs at the pleasure of the occupiers, fifty thousand Francs was money. Martin waved his bodyguards down, and nodded at the man.

The stranger sat down, expansively ordered a cognac, then began in German accented French.

"I am Sturmbannfuehrer Most. I am dressed in civilian clothes to preserve your privacy. I hope that we can do business together."

Oh, a corrupt Nazi. Well, there were many. Martin smelled a business opportunity and was all ears.

"You, Monsieur Martin, are the man in charge of all criminal activities here in Tours. No, please don't bother to deny anything, let's not waste any time. I'm not here to interfere with your black market activities, with your nightclubs or the girls you are running. I am not that kind of policeman. I need your help in another matter. But before I continue, let me tell you what I know about you. Your wife's name is Marie-Anne. She was born September 13, 1911 in Vienne. You have two daughters, Therese, aged 12 and Vivienne, aged 9. They both attend school at the Sisters of Mercy in the Avenue Montaigne. You live in the same street, at number 14. You also own a building at 7 Rue des Ecuriers, where your mistress, Armande Lepin, aged 22, lives with her sister Henriette, who frequently joins you in bed. There is more, but I believe that is enough for now. Oh, and one more thing. The four German soldiers you see " he nodded at two tables of two men each," are my men, and if you or your bodyguards make a false move, all three of you will be cut down immediately. Now smile at me and say something pleasant."

Martin was speechless. That he was in the most serious trouble he had ever been in his life, he did not doubt. But how to get out of it? He obeyed with alacrity, and stammered something about the weather.

"Fine," the German continued. "If you continue to cooperate we'll get along famously, and you may even survive. Now return my money to me under the table. You will work for me out of patriotism and loyalty to Marshall Petain, and not for financial gain, isn't that right?" Most's smile was hardly reassuring.

"What is it you want of me?" Martin stammered.

"We have had some trouble with the Resistance, and you of course know all about it. Don't deny anything, please, you don't want to make me angry, do you? I want to know the name of the organizers. In particular, there is a man who speaks perfect German and has frequently impersonated a German soldier successfully. I want him."

"But," Martin objected, " I know nothing about that. I won't deny that I'm involved a little bit in the black market. I'm a businessman and you know the conditions under which we live, but I have nothing to do with the Resistance. Nothing. Nothing."

"That may be so. Then your task is to find out what I want to know. You may have to go to Paris and see your boss. I don't care. I'll be in touch with you again, and the next time I see you, I hope that you have something for me. I wouldn't want to be in your shoes if you don't. And, please, don't think of running away and joining the Maquis. I won't have you followed, I don't want to make it difficult for you to find out what I want to know. But your wife, daughters and mistress will be kept in sight, and the day you disappear will be their last day on this earth."

"My children, you wouldn't hurt my children…"

"I'll show you how serious I am," the German smiled again. Martin did not like to see that smile. "You are right handed, are you not? I'll be generous. Give me your left hand under the table. Now, hold still. I'm going to break two of your fingers. Don't cry out, we don't want to cause a disturbance and get your bodyguards killed, do we? Your doctor, Dr. Malgraux, is waiting for you, the appointment has been made. All you have to do is keep smiling and walk over to his office, and he'll fix you up. I'm doing this for your sake, just so you know that I mean everything I have said."

"Please don't, don't. I'll try to find out, please don't hurt me." Arsene Martin was frightened to the core of his being.

The SS Officer reached under the table, took Martin's hand gently in his own - Martin was unable to resist, almost hypnotized by the German's unblinking stare, and while continuing to look into Martin's eyes, broke his first and second fingers with a swift and brutal movement of his own hand. He then rose, waved a smiling good bye to the stunned Frenchman, and sauntered off.

* * *

"There is a message from Madame Gonzalez." Solange kissed Kurt when he came in and then told him. " She needs to see you urgently. At the Opera, in the usual manner."

"Very well," Kurt looked at his watch. " I can get there easily tonight."

At the end of another glorious performance, a messenger carrying a basket of flowers presented himself at the stage door. He was admitted to the dressing room of Madame Gonzalez without question - no one else wanted to take the large and unwieldy basket from him.

"I have to talk quickly. " Madame Gonzalez whispered to Kurt. " There is a new man in charge of combating the resistance, an SS colonel who brought an entire battalion with him. The general has given him a totally free hand. I've met him. He's very frightening. Apparently he has a reputation for efficiency and ruthlessness. He has taken over a building on the Avenue Foch. It may be wise to keep out of sight for a while."

"Do you know his name?"

"Ratzersdorfer."

Esperanza Gonzalez saw a remarkable transformation in the young man before her. It was a combination of exultation and savagery She was glad that she was not the object of Kurt's attention.

"There is something else. " the diva continued. "There will be a meeting of all the top officers, Navy, Army and Air Force, sometime in the next few weeks to coordinate the defense of the Atlantic Wall against the invasion that everybody is sure will come this summer. Top members of the General Staff from Berlin will attend, and it is even possible that the Fuehrer may come."

"Do you know when and where? This could be most important."

"I don't know any more than that - yet."

"Good work. Thank you."

* * *

385

When Solange was in amorous mood, which fortunately for Kurt was most of the time, she liked to receive him totally nude except for a skimpy apron, when she was occupied in the kitchen. As a result, both of them had learned to eat overcooked or burned foods, and it was miraculous that the apartment had not been set on fire, while they were engaged in the activities Solange's outfit inspired. This time, however, Kurt had to refuse her blandishments.

"We have to contact London immediately. I think there's a chance to strike a substantial blow." He gave Solange the news about the scheduled meeting. "Of course, we must find out where and when this conference will take place, but can you imagine what would happen if we could get rid of every one attending it? What if Hitler himself is there?"

He did not mention Ratzersdorfer. But his hands were clenched. He could almost feel the murderer's neck between them.

* * *

Arsene Martin was in total despair. His bandaged hand throbbed, but more than his broken fingers, his head hurt. What was he going to do? The brutal German would not accept any excuses. Ignorance - and Martin was honestly ignorant about any underground activities - would not be an acceptable answer. Over and over he rehashed the horrible conversation with the SS officer. How would he get out of that? He had no idea.

He had become aware of the fact that German soldiers loitered in the neighborhood of his home, his daughter's school, and his mistress' apartment. In fact they acted as if they deliberately wanted him to see them. He knew that the Sturmbannfuehrer's threats were real.

He was a businessman, that's all he was. He supplied people with what they needed. If some of these needs were illegal, that wasn't his fault. That was the fault of unjust and oppressive laws. But he never did anything deliberately to hurt the government in power, whoever that was. And now this.

He remembered that the Nazi had told him that he might go to Paris to talk to his boss. Perhaps that was what he should do. Silvio Goldoni was a very smart man. Maybe he could come up with a solution.

Of course he would make sure that he wasn't followed. He wasn't the one who would betray Monsieur Goldoni in any way. Not him, he was totally loyal.

So he set out for Paris. And when he reached the neighborhood of the Place des Vosges, he used every trick he knew to throw a potential pursuer off the scent. And then he did not go to Goldoni's office, but went to the bistro where Goldoni frequently stopped for an aperitif. He sat down near the window, ordered a drink, and kept his eyes on Goldoni's building.

Who was that? Someone he knew walked by. He racked his brain. The man could have come out of Goldoni's building, or he could have been just a passerby. But he knew him. He was sure of that.

Oh yes, the insolent young man - for a while he even had thought he was Goldoni's son - who had organized the "underground railroad," the transfer of Jews into the "Free Zone" through the Chateau Chenonceau. That was a brilliant idea by Goldoni.

He hit his forehead with his open hand. I, too, can have a brilliant idea. I remember that the young man speaks German. He spoke to some of our "Guests" in that cursed language. The SS officer wants someone who speaks German well enough to impersonate a German soldier. I'll give him someone. Let him prove that he's innocent. Not my business, as long as it gets me off the hook.

While these thoughts raced through his brain, he threw some money at the bartender, and began to follow Kurt.

* * *

CHAPTER XIII

Between Amiens and Abbeville the river Eure approaches from the North trying to join with the Somme on its inexorable march to the sea. Just as it was ready to enter the Somme, it hit the barrier of a granite outcropping unusual in that region. Following the line of least resistance, the water then turned back in a Northerly direction, formed essentially a large circle and then finally flowed into the Somme. It thus formed almost an island, actually a peninsula of substantial size, several hundred acres, with only one land entrance just a few hundred feet wide at its Southern end. This peninsula was easily defensible, the river forming an unbroken moat around most of its area. In the twelfth century this became the domain of the family of nobles who eventually acquired the title of Euremont. The ancestral seat of this family developed from a twelfth century Norman castle into a large and charming eighteenth century chateau.

In 1769 a miracle happened in this chateau. The Marquise d'Euremont gave birth to triplets and they all survived. Unfortunately, the mother, exhausted by the ordeal, passed away in the process, and in the confusion of the births and her death, no note was made of the sequence by which the three boys entered this world. This presented the Marquis d'Euremont with the problem of inheritance. Which of the three boys would become the next Marquis and what would happen to the other two?

The Marquis decided to postpone that decision. Perhaps one of the boys would enter the church, where his connections would ensure him a cardinal's hat in short order, perhaps another would prefer the military life. In order to separate them and yet to bring them up with all the privileges a putative heir to the estates and titles would be entitled to, the Marquis came up with an ingenious idea. He ordered two exact duplicates of his chateau built on his peninsula, all equidistant from each other. Each of the boys would be brought up separately in each of them.

What the Marquis ordered was done. Soon there were three chateaux which were exact copies of each other. The Marquis' worries about his estates and the fate of the triplets were unfounded. All three and their father perished in the Revolution.

The state took over the peninsula, but because of its location and the confusion of Revolution, Empire and Restoration, the chateaux remained unoccupied They were quietly maintained by the staff of servants living in them, who were happy not to be disturbed by officious owners.

In the late nineteenth century a banker with a reputation for speculative success found out about the area. He formed a public corporation, sold a large number of shares and acquired title to the entire peninsula and the three chateaux. He began restoration work with the intention of creating three luxury hotels with wonderful facilities for sport and entertainment on the property, where privacy was assured because of its easily defensible entrance. Unfortunately, in one of the many stock market crashes of the period, his dream disappeared. Eventually the property again reverted to the state after a series of long and protracted law suits in bankruptcy court.

Thus the chateaux were being maintained at the expense of the state. The order had been given and never rescinded. They were thus in acceptable condition when they were discovered by Oberst Scharfer. The colonel enjoyed going off the beaten track on his regular inspection visits to the Atlantic Wall fortifications in the Pas de Calais.

* * *

Extract of minutes of staff meeting called by General von Weitzensberg:

General von Weitzensberg: "We have been ordered to provide a secure location for a conference lasting between two and three days in which the commanding officers of all Army, Navy and Air Force units guarding the Atlantic Wall and their staffs will coordinate their actions when the expected enemy invasion takes place. Field Marshall Rommel, in command of the Atlantic Wall, will preside. There is even a possibility that the Fuehrer may attend."

Oberst Scharfer: "I believe that I have found the best location for the conference. Please note on the map these three chateaux." (Here Oberst Scharfer digressed somewhat on the history of the three buildings until interrupted by the General)." For purposes of identification, we will call them Chateau A, Chateau B and Chateau C. They can easily be guarded. We are concerned that with such a large group of officers security may be compromised. We can supply all three chateaux with everything that is necessary for the conference and decide only in the last minute which one we will use."

Standartenfuehrer Ratzersdorfer: "Is there a possibility of an armed attack by the Resistance?"

Oberst Scharfer: " It cannot be excluded in view of the importance of this gathering. It is also possible that there will be sabotage. The buildings could be mined and blown up. I believe our best protection will be the fact that no one will know until just before the conference begins, which of the three buildings will house it."

Standartenfuehrer Ratzersdorfer : " I suggest that we take a large number of hostages and place one or two hundred into each of the two chateaux that we will not use. This might give the Resistance something to think about before they attempt to blow up all three chateaux. I would propose that these hostages be among the most prominent and important French literary and artistic figures, well known movie actors, and so forth. People whose loss would be felt by everyone."

General von Weitzensberg: " An excellent idea. We will implement it. Now for the details of this operation. Please continue, Oberst Scharfer."

* * *

General von Weitzensberg was extremely pleased at the outcome of his meeting, and very proud of the solution to a knotty problem that his staff had found. So proud, that he had to boast about it that night after the Opera to Madame Esperanza Gonzalez.

* * *

At the last staff meeting before the battle of El Alamein when General (later Field Marshall) Montgomery took his final dispositions, he relied on Brigadier Geoffrey Thornton's assurances that Rommel's Southern flank had to be anchored at the Oasis of Sidi-Reumah, because the terrain South of that oasis simply was not suitable even for Rommel's tanks. Since Thornton was his chief of intelligence, the General had no choice but to rely on his reports.

But Thornton was a worrier and a perfectionist. In spite of all his previous efforts to be sure of his facts, he had had to rely on reports from others. He had never seen the terrain himself. So, after that crucial staff meeting, he commandeered a half-track and set out to the Southern front.

Just as he reached the oasis, the advance elements of Rommel's Africa Corps reached there as well. British artillery began its work on schedule. A defective shell fell short, hit the half-track, killing the driver and wounding Brigadier Thornton very badly.

When he woke up, weeks later, in the hospital in Alexandria, he learned that his report to General Montgomery had been absolutely accurate and that the battle of El Alamein had been a great victory for the British forces.

He also learned that he had lost his left eye and the use of his left arm, and would be limping badly for the rest of his life. He was duly evacuated to England, and after months of rehabilitation, given an honorable discharge from the Army he had served his entire life.

This would not do. It absolutely would not do. The war was still going on and he was out of it. So, he called on Admiral Morse and offered his services to him in any capacity that wily spy-master could use.

And the Admiral certainly could use an experienced intelligence officer. Slowly, Thornton became indispensable to the Admiral. He was the only one, Thornton thought, to whom the Admiral revealed his worries and plans. Of course Thornton also was aware of the fact that even at best he was not in the Admiral's fullest confidence. Morse would never reveal everything even to his most trusted subordinate.

When word of the impending German staff meeting reached Morse, he showed a flicker of interest. Thornton knew that in other men this would represent an enthusiastic appreciation of the possibilities. He had learned to understand the Admiral quite well.

"You know, Thornton," the Admiral mused," Operation Overlord - the invasion - is bound to be launched in the next four or five weeks. That is not a secret even to our German friends. Of course the exact location of the landings is the major question. Now, once the landings have begun, they will have to be very quick in coordinating their response. If we can get rid of the officers gathered at that meeting...."

"There are lots of other highly trained officers in the German forces." Thornton interjected, playing his assigned role as devil's advocate.

"True, true," Admiral Morse said thoughtfully, " but they will be unfamiliar with their units and will have missed the coordinating meeting. No, all things considered, I believe that it would be worth while to pay close attention to this meeting."

Brigadier Thornton devoutly hoped that the Admiral would never want to pay close attention to him in the same manner.

"The location presents a problem. Let's have the RAF get us some photographs and we'll look at it. Will you, please handle that?" The Admiral was unfailingly polite when he gave an order.

* * *

"I'm sorry, Admiral," Adam Bede said. " I have studied the aerial photographs of the three chateaux for hours. As you know, they are at the three apexes of a triangular area. The Germans have a camp in the center of the triangle with substantial supplies as well as personnel, and probably some tents for hostages as well. There have been heavy tracks to all three chateaux, but it is clear that the distribution of the hostages to two of the chateaux and the arrival of the German officers and their reception at the third one will only take place when the conference begins. I'm afraid if you want to know which one of the chateaux will be the seat of the conference, you'd have to have someone right there to signal to you."

"Well," said Admiral Morse, "Then that's what we'll have to arrange. Thank you for your efforts in any case."

"What is your plan? " Thornton asked.

"That seems fairly obvious." Admiral Morse said. "Bomber command will have to take out the castle in which the conference takes place, the night that it begins."

"But how will we know which of the chateaux..."

"We must have someone there to give the signal. That's what Bede suggested, isn't it?" Morse said calmly.

"But who? How? He'll be killed, too, when the bombs begin to fall."

"Well, you'll have to go to France and convince your old friend Auster that it's his job to get into the proper chateau. You'll bring him a brace of Very pistols, so that he can signal the bombers when they're overhead."

"How can I convince him to sacrifice his life ...?"

"Well, " Admiral Morse smiled, "just tell him it's his duty. And if that won't do, tell him that the bombers have been instructed to make an extra pass before beginning their attack. That should give him time to get away. You could also tell him that if we don't know which of the chateaux the conference is held in, we'll have to bomb all three of them."

"And kill the hostages?"

"And kill the hostages."

"But we wouldn't, we couldn't do that. Could we?"

Morse did not reply.

* * *

The pilots of the Royal Air Force who had fought in the battle of Britain and later on had carried the fight to the enemy now controlled the skies over Europe. They were justly reputed to be among the bravest of the brave. But among them, the most foolhardy was a small group flying out of a secret airfield in Southeastern England, who flew a lumbering, slow, one engine plane - the Lysander. This plane had only one advantage - it could land and take off in a relatively small space. A cow pasture, a farmer's field, any relatively flat area that no one could consider an airfield, would do. And so these planes and their incredibly brave pilots had developed a - could one call it - "underground airline "?

In the darkest night, without lights and using old road maps, straining to see rivers and church steeples in blacked out towns, these planes delivered arms, instructions, and agents to the French Resistance. Minutes before a plane was scheduled to land at one of the designated "airfields", the Resistance operatives would light three torches at three corners of the pasture. The plane would land, shadowy figures would descend and sometimes board, materiel would be dropped, and minutes later the plane would take off and be on its way back to England. And this went on under the noses of the Wehrmacht.

Brigadier Thornton duly scrounged about for two Very pistols together with the proper ammunition, placed them in a briefcase manufactured in Germany for use by Wehrmacht officers, which his procurement section had obtained he knew not how, and proceeded to a secret airfield in South Eastern Britain. This was not the usual large installation for bomber and fighter squadrons surrounded by anti-aircraft installations. This was a small field with one or two dilapidated Nissen huts and a barnlike hangar. He was directed to one of the huts. Inside there were a few armchairs and tables that looked as if they had come from a Salvation Army sale, and at one end a bar.

"Hello, Brigadier. You're expected. I'm your pilot, Flight Lieutenant Michael Thomas - call me Mike." A blackhaired shortish officer stretched out his hand. He looks barely out of Kindergarten, Thornton thought. Thomas must have seen the misgivings on the Brigadier's face. " Not to worry," he smiled. " I've done the run dozens of times, ditched only once, and was rescued right away. Lost the plane, though, got a bad mark for that.
Come, have a drink, it'll keep you warm until we get the word. Just hope that the weather holds. Looks a bit iffy."

Thornton accepted a small whiskey gratefully and sank down in one of the armchairs. There was a companionable silence for a moment, then suddenly there was a drumbeat of rain on the tin roof of the hut, a drumbeat so loud that it was difficult to communicate. Thomas looked up, shrugged his shoulders and said , "I was afraid of that. If it doesn't improve soon, we'll have to postpone until tomorrow. It's hard enough to find your way when it's clear. Even though the Lysander can land and take off almost anywhere, it can't do it in mud. We may have to find you a bunk for the night."

Thornton relaxed. He had learned long ago that there are circumstances beyond one's control.

* * *

Kurt could never sleep properly the night before a mission. He and Solange had made love. Much as he had enjoyed it, it did not help him get to sleep. In any case he had to be up in two hours, well before dawn, to make his rendezvous.

He looked at the sleeping young woman next to him. The blanket had slipped from her shoulders and he admired the clean line of her back. In all their time together, by unspoken agreement, they had avoided, whenever possible, speaking of their future together after the war. Yet they were young, and the young are immortal. There were times when they spoke of places to visit, things to do "after the war". But they, very consciously, did not speak of the possibility of doing these things together. They were both in constant danger and were aware that it was very likely that neither of them would escape unharmed. But now, in the wakes of the night,

Kurt thought about it. How do I really feel about her? And in a moment of clarity, he realized that he loved his brave partner. There was a twinge of disloyalty to the memory of Sarah - one never forgets one's first love - but then looking at Solange he put the past behind him, and felt a sudden gush of warmth. With some sardonic amusement, he pictured the scene of announcing to Admiral Theberge and to Clemente Theberge that he and Solange were planning to remain together. He almost laughed out loud at the reaction this would provoke. Then he looked at his lover again. The blanket had slipped down even more, and with great tenderness, he pulled it up over her shoulders. He thought of waking Solange and telling her of his great discovery - that he loved her. Never, even in the throes of passion, had he said that. And then he reconsidered - why wake her, I'll tell her when I get back from my mission.

For the rest of his life, he would regret that decision.

It was time. He dressed in dark clothes, placed a nondescript cap on his head, and left the apartment. Quietly he descended the stairs. Before leaving the building he scanned the street to make sure that there was no German patrol, although patrols were infrequent on the Ile St. Louis. Kurt was in possession of an excellently forged pass that enabled him to travel around during curfew, but it was always better to avoid attention.

With similar precautions he walked over to the bridge connecting the Ile St. Louis to the Left Bank. He waited in the shadows until a truck passed him and slowed down so he could swing up into the cab. "How are you, my friend?" a familiar voice spoke. "Well enough, Louis. Which one of your elegant airfields are we going to this time?"

Capitaine Louis Renault grinned. "The one in the Barbizon forest near Fontainebleau . If all goes well you'll be back in bed with the delicious Solange before you know it."

* * *

Arsene Martin had returned to Tours and had waited. And he did not have to wait long. He had not varied his usual routine. He was seated at his regular table in his favorite café when Sturmbannfuehrer Most, dressed as before in civilian clothes, sat down next to him.

"What have you got for me, Martin?" he said without preamble.

"I found a man in Paris who fits your description. He speaks German as well as French, and has been involved in activities against the orders of the occupying power."

"What kind of activities?"

Martin hesitated. If he told the truth, he would incriminate himself.

"Speak up, man. Of course you were involved in them or you wouldn't know about them. I'm not interested in minor matters. I want to put a stop to the Resistance. We don't want to have to have to watch our backs when the invasion comes. That'll be enough of a problem for us."

I certainly hope it will, Martin thought. *I hope that these arrogant swine get theirs. And getting rid of one man isn't going to stop the others who'll fight against the Germans when the invasion comes.* Aloud he said. "Well, before, when the demarcation line still existed, this fellow organized a route to get Jews out of this part of France into the free Zone."

"And you made a pretty penny out of it, no doubt. " Most grinned. "Never mind. How do we get our hands on this man?"

"I can give you his address in Paris. I don't know the apartment and I don't know the name he goes under, but I know the building."

"You'll do more than that. You'll come with me and you'll point him out."

"But, but, if I do that, everyone will know…they'll kill me."

"And if you don't, I'll kill you. Now, come along."

* * *

"Hauptsturmfuehrer Winter reporting as ordered".

"Come in, come in, Egon." Sturmbannfuehrer Most was very cordial to his immediate subordinate. "I think we may be getting somewhere. Sit down. This Frenchman, Arsene Martin, sitting so disconsolately in the reception area, may be able to help us find our target. Take one of the panel trucks, and two - no, make it four men, go to the area Martin will point out to you and let him find the man we're looking for."

"Are we sure that's the man? "

Most smiled. "We're sure that finding a man who fulfills our requirements will keep Standartenfuehrer Ratzersdorfer off our necks. Isn't that enough?"

"I understand, Herr Sturmbannfuehrer. Your orders will be carried out."

I'm sure they will, Egon. Heil Hitler."

* * *

Egon Winter had been a successful police detective and had reached the rank of Kommissaer. When the time came to serve his country in uniform, he had been transferred into the SS with the rank equivalent to his police rank, and thus became a Hauptsturmfuehrer without ever having had to go through the usual rise through the ranks. As a result he was often looked at with some disdain by some of the men who served under him or alongside of him. Winter was somewhat older than the average SS man. He was in his early forties, of medium size and a little overweight, and his balding head and the pipe he affected gave him the appearance of a benevolent uncle, an appearance he cultivated. In interrogations in his civilian life, when good cop - bad cop was the game, he always played the good cop and often obtained the confidence of a suspect and thus solved the case. His appearance belied the sharpness of his mind and his powers of observation, but he lacked the political acumen that was required in the situation in which he found himself now.

In accordance with his orders, Hauptsturmfuehrer Egon Winter took his detachment of four SS men and a very unhappy Arsene Martin into one of the panel trucks available to him. He sat next to the driver. His men and Martin were in the back hidden from the sight of passersby. Martin directed them to the proper street and they parked a few meters away from the entrance of the building Martin had pointed out. Dawn was breaking. As soon as curfew was over people would leave their homes to go to their jobs or on their other errands. Winter hoped that this would be true for the suspect, so that they could arrest him quickly and quietly.

The same rain that had prevented Brigadier Thornton's departure, had come to Paris. It was a very hard, driving rain, and it was difficult to make out the figures huddled in their raingear holding on to their umbrellas, as they scurried past.

* * *

"I am very unhappy, querida." General von Weitzensberg liked to show off his somewhat limited knowledge of Spanish. " I won't be able to attend your performance as Turandot next week. And it's my favorite Opera, and you always are so superb in that role."

"But why not?" Madame Esperanza Gonzalez was angry. "I've been counting on you, and there's the party after the performance. I can't go alone."

"Duty, Liebling, duty." Under pressure, the general reverted to his more familiar German.

"Don't tell me duty." The diva stormed. "Aren't you the commanding general? Just send someone else to do whatever it is you have to do. I need you."

"I'm really very sorry, mein Schatz. " General von Weitzensberg was unruffled. He had been through scenes like this before. " Remember the conference I told you about? Well, it's scheduled to start just then. Think of me with that insufferable parvenu Rommel when I could be watching you, and have some compassion and understanding. You know, I'd much rather be with you."

Esperanza Gonzalez permitted her lover to calm her down and finally forgave him.

* * *

"You have to do something about the flowers you deliver." Madame Gonzalez was quite angry on the telephone. " This is not a funeral, it's an opera. Next week for Turandot, I don't want to see lilies. I want chrysanthemums, masses of chrysanthemums. All white. Is that clear?"

"Absolutely, Madame Gonzalez. I understand perfectly. I will do my best."

With a small smile Solange hung up the telephone.

"I have to go out for a little while," she then said to the owner of the florist's shop near the opera. She took her raincoat and umbrella, ran through the rain to the Metro stop at the Place de l'Opera, and took the train to Neuilly. She crossed the street to the entrance to the Bois de Boulogne. It was raining very hard, and hardly anyone was in sight. Quickly she ducked into the entrance to that great public park. Carefully, making sure that no one was following her and by a somewhat circuitous route, she came to a thicket . With another sharp glance around her, she stepped behind a tree. For long minutes she stood there watching to see whether she was really alone. She then continued deep into the thicket, down a slope to a fallen tree. Hidden in the stump was her radio.

* * *

"The rain is a blessing because it delayed you. " Admiral Morse was on the phone with Thornton. " We have word of the date the conference begins. I have instructed bomber command. Now just make sure that Auster does his job."

" I will certainly try." The brigadier said grimly.

* * *

"The sun is shining in Montevideo."
"Aunt Martha has bronchitis."
"Under the apple trees there are snakes."
"The cottage roof must be repaired."
Every hour on the hour for five minutes the British Broadcasting Corporation broadcast a string of nonsense sentences. Some of these sentences had meaning only to the resistance group for which it was intended, others were broadcast just to ensure that the German listening posts were driven crazy by the assumption that there were far more resistance groups than existed in reality.

Kurt had been waiting in the safe house near Fontainebleau for the signal that the Lysander had left England. But as the rainstorm increased in force it became more and more evident that the flight would have to be postponed. Finally the confirmation came on the BBC broadcast: "Alfred has lost his muffler."

"Well, my friend," Louis Reynaud was quite philosophical. " It seems we'll have to wait till tomorrow. I think it's safer that you stay here out of sight. There's always a risk in any trip. Of course, if you think that the delicious Solange can't get along without you..."

"You only think of one thing," Kurt smiled. "Do I detect a tone of jealousy? But you're right. It's better that I stay here. She'll understand when she sees the weather." Of course Kurt was anxious to return to the arms of his lover, and to tell her about his great discovery - that he really was in love with her. But the mission comes first, he sternly reminded himself. There's always tomorrow.

But that isn't always true.

                            * * *

In the afternoon the rain stopped. Eventually a glimmer of
sun shone through the clouds. Hauptsturmfuehrer Winter and his
men remained at their post until dark when curfew began. Then they
returned to headquarters in the Avenue Foch and reported.

Sturmbannfuehrer Most was very incensed. "Are you
playing games with me? If you are, you'll regret it and so will your
family!" he yelled at the hapless Arsene Martin.

"No, no. I can't understand why he wasn't there. I know he
lives there. And you can't sleep elsewhere without police
permission..."

Most paused, a smile came to his face. " Of course you're
right, Martin. Unless, you are prepared to do something illegal.
That means that you may perhaps really have the right man. He must
be out doing some mischief. You'll have to resume your watch
tomorrow, Egon," he addressed Winter, "but, in addition, let's get
some information about the people who live in that building. Get
one of our tame Miliciens to inquire from the concierge. Have him
tell the concierge that it's a routine inquiry and have him bring us a
detailed list of all the occupants."

"Zu Befehl, Herr Sturmbannfuehrer."

                            * * *

Alsace-Lorraine was one of the many territories that had
been shifted from country to country in the European wars over the
centuries. There were times when the area was French; after
France's defeat by Prussia in 1870 it had become part of the newly
re-established German Empire, and after Germany's defeat in World
War I in 1918 it had reverted to France. As a result, many
inhabitants of the area were fluent in French and in their own version
of German.

Jean-Paul Bertholder had been born in a small village near
Strasbourg into a large family, barely supported by his father, a day
laborer of limited accomplishments. Early in his youth, he had been
shipped off to Paris where his mother's brother, who was childless,
operated a small grocery in one of the blue-collar districts far away
from the elegant center. His uncle had promised Jean-Paul's mother
that he would bring up the boy as his own. Having one less mouth to
feed was very important to Jean-Paul's family. If indeed that was the

uncle's intention, his own would have found himself as an unpaid and frequently abused jack of all trades in the grocery, loading and unloading barrels and baskets of food, making deliveries, cleaning and sweeping, and sleeping in a corner of the store. But he did get enough to eat, there was that.

When Jean-Paul was sixteen, he ran away from home and tried to join the Army. But by that time, France had been defeated, and there was no Army to join. Jean-Paul whose formal education had ended when he was fourteen and who had not attended classes even then with any regularity, found another organization which received him with open arms - the Milice. This was a paramilitary organization set up as a mirror image of the German SS, designed to assist Germany in their subjugation of France, and to supply cannon fodder for the war in the East. He was trained as an infantry soldier, indoctrinated in German racial theories, and asked to volunteer to fight the Asian hordes of Communists threatening Europe. Of course he volunteered for the Russian front. In the last minute it was discovered that he spoke German and he was assigned to work for the SS in the Avenue Foch. There he made himself useful as interpreter and messenger and served his masters with the utmost devotion. He admired the victorious Germans and tried to ape them in his behavior toward the French. He wished that he would be allowed to wear the black SS uniform, but the midnight blue Milice uniform he wore gave him the authority to intimidate any civilian he chose.

Jean-Paul was such a devoted servant that there were times when he was given an extra-curricular reward. It was standard practice for any woman below the age of grandmotherhood to be raped by the entire unit prior to and as part of hard interrogation, and occasionally, Jean-Paul was given that privilege as well. Of course he was always the last man to do so. Sturmbannfuehrer Most, who always directed these events, made it a point to be there during the rapes. Clearly, he enjoyed watching as much as participating. He would cheer Jean-Paul on. Jean-Paul worshipped him.

When Jean-Paul was given the task of getting the concierge to obtain information about the inhabitants of the building in which Kurt and Solange had made their home, he enjoyed enormously the power his uniform gave him. He loved acting in the brutal and demanding manner he had learned from his German superiors. That this was unnecessary, that the concierge would have answered all

401

questions unhesitatingly anyway, Jean Paul did not realize. He was, after all, only twenty years old.

Winter listened to the report with satisfaction.

"There are six apartments in the building. Apartment 1A is occupied by a retired army colonel in a wheelchair. A visiting nurse comes in daily to take care of him. Apartment 1 B belongs to the concierge, a widow with two small children, whose husband was killed in the early days of the war. In 2 A there is a family of four - the husband is a banker with Credit Lyonnais, the children are eleven and eight and their mother seems to have her hands full caring for them. 2 B belongs to a young couple. Apparently they both work in a flower shop in the center. 3-A is empty - the occupants were Jewish who disappeared. 3-B belongs to a couple in their mid fifties, the husband has a fairly high position with the post office and the wife is a buyer for Galeries Lafayette. They have a married son living in Toulouse."

"Interesting," Winter thought for a moment. "The young couple - I think we'll go and have a look at them."

Solange was ready to go out when a peremptory knock sounded at her door. She opened and several black uniformed men pushed her way in. *SS - oh my God, I'm lost. How could they* - she stood her ground and demanded:

"What is the meaning of this? What do you want?"

"I'll ask the questions and you'll answer. Identity documents, please." The leader of the men stood before her.

"Here they are." She searched in her handbag and pulled out her papers. "As you can see, I'm a Swiss citizen."

"Are you indeed? And you are registered with the Swiss consulate? "

"Of course I am."

Hauptsturmfuehrer Egon Winter noted that there was a slight hesitation in the young woman's response to his question. The documents seemed in order, but he was fully aware of the fact that competent forgers could produce any kind of fake documentation.

He looked around the apartment. Pleasantly furnished living room, large kitchen, bedroom and bathroom - nothing struck him as suspicious. And then it came to him. Something was missing.

"You'll come along to headquarters with us for further interrogation. Fruechtenicht, Gruber, you two stay here. Begin to search the apartment. Take it completely apart and bring me anything you think worth while. I particularly want to see all reading materials, books, notebooks, letters, anything at all, even if you don't think them important. And be quiet about it. When the young lady's husband arrives, arrest him and bring him to headquarters. Understood.?"

"Zu Befehl, Herr Hauptsturmfuehrer."

Brutally Solange was hustled out of the building into the panel truck. She tried to control her panic. *I must be calm*, she told herself, *they can't prove anything unless I give in. I'm afraid they'll catch Kurt when he returns. But first, he'll have to do something about the meeting at Euremont. That's in forty-eight hours. Forty-eight hours. I have to hold out that long, I can't tell them anything until then. God give me strength.*

* * *

In the former Palais Rothschild on the Avenue Foch, which had become Gestapo headquarters, the cells which so often served not only to detain prisoners but also to torture them unspeakably were not in the basement but on the second floor. The rooms which served as cells had been enclosed with supposedly sound proof materials, but too often passersby heard inhuman sounding noises. Because of the SS guards in front of the building, anyone having to pass it crossed to the other side of the wide avenue. Some of the sounds carried even that far. Pedestrians hurried past as fast as they could with their eyes averted.

"Well, Winter? What made you suspicious? " Sturmbannfuehrer Most asked.

"Two things, Herr Sturmbannfuehrer. First, she hesitated when I asked her whether she was registered with the Swiss consulate. Of course we can check on that."

"And second?"

"This is an apartment occupied by a young married couple. Where are the photographs? Pictures of the couple, of the husband, of the honeymoon, of the parents, or of other family members. Think about your own apartment back at home, Herr Sturmbannfuehrer. Don't you have family pictures displayed? I have never been in an apartment without some photos. This place looked sterile - as if the two residents could walk out immediately and leave no traces."

"That is very interesting, Egon, and very persuasive. I agree with you. I believe you've got a point. Good work, my friend. Let's have a look at this young woman."

Solange was brought in and made to stand before Most's desk. Most looked at the beautiful young woman. Involuntarily, his tongue flicked in and out of his mouth.

"Strip." He ordered.

"I am a Swiss citizen. You can't treat me like that." Solange tried to conceal the tremor in her voice.

Slowly, Most got up, walked around his desk, stood in front of Solange, and with full force slapped her left and right. The young woman fell backwards but Most grabbed her throat, stopped her from falling and squeezed. When he let go she had to fight for breath. Most had returned to his armchair.

"I hope that now you understand, that when I give an order it must be obeyed instantly. Now, strip."

Her head ringing from the blows, her throat on fire, Solange began to undress. First her jacket and skirt, her blouse....

"Everything - quickly." Winter took her garments and searched them, with particular attention to the seams. "So far nothing." He reported.

Most just looked at Solange. She continued. Her shoes. Her garter belt and stockings. Her bra and panties.

Totally nude, she stood before the two men. She crossed her arms in front of her breasts to obtain some concealment, but of course that was hopeless.

"Now, talk. Where is your husband? Why wasn't he home during curfew?"

"He went to visit a friend - and he must have been caught in the rainstorm. I'm sure he'll be home soon."

"Name and address of the friend?"

"I don't know."

"Look here, young lady." Winter interjected. "I'm an old time police officer. The sooner you understand that you've been caught, the sooner you tell us everything, the better it will be for you. Believe me, you don't want to have to undergo hard questioning, you wouldn't like it. You're a beautiful young woman. By the time we're through with you, there won't be much left of your beauty. Now we know, you're in the resistance, we know that your husband is very prominent in it, that he speaks German and has committed a number of crimes against the Reich. Tell us about them, tell us where to find him, and I promise you, that we'll go easy on you."

Forty-eight hours, Solange thought. *Forty eight hours.*

"None of that is true. I know nothing of resistance, nor does my husband."

Sturmbannfuehrer Most got impatient. He had been eyeing the lovely nude body in front of him. "Enough talk. We'll begin. How many men are in the building? "

"Probably twenty or twenty five." Winter answered.

"Well, we'll see how she feels after everyone's had her. Perhaps she'll be more talkative then. I'll begin, and you may be next, Winter, since you brought her in. Let's go."

It was routine for any half way attractive woman caught by the Gestapo to be raped before, during, or even after questioning. In fact one of the rooms on the second floor was equipped for that. Solange was pushed and pulled into that room. There was a bed in the center. She was stretched out, her hand and legs were attached to bedposts so that she lay there spread-eagle.

Winter looked down at her. "I'm giving you one more chance, " he said, not unkindly. "Talk and you'll save yourself a lot of pain and suffering. You'll talk in the end anyway. Everybody does."

Forty-eight hours. Solange closed her eyes. *I must hold out.* She heard the sound of belt buckles and then felt the weight of an unfamiliar body crushing her - the first of many.

* * *

"Come on, let's go." Brigadier Thornton had been dozing in his armchair. Lieutenant Thomas shook him by the shoulder. "Take off time."

A bit groggily, Thornton took his cane and followed Thomas out the door and to a small, one engine plane. Because of his injuries, Thornton had a great deal of trouble climbing into the cockpit. Finally he was bodily hoisted into it by Thomas and the sole mechanic standing by to assist in the departure. Thornton found himself seated directly behind Thomas. The engine came to life, the mechanic removed the chocks and gave the thumbs up sign, and almost instantly the plane was airborne.

Thomas turned and said something that Thornton could not understand because of the engine noise. He saw that they were flying very low. After the rainstorm, the sky had cleared. A sliver of moon and bright stars illuminated the sky. Thomas turned and pointed down. Thornton saw the white cliffs of Dover and white caps on the channel. The plane swooped lower and seemed to be skimming the top of the waves. Minutes later they were over the coast of occupied France. To Thornton, the land below seemed dark and foreboding. There was a river, and Thomas followed its course. Forty minutes later in the darkness below, Thornton saw three flickering lights forming a triangle. The plane went lower. Thornton could not believe that it could land in the tiny area delineated by the lights. But it was down, right in the center of the triangle. The moment the plane touched ground, the lights went out. In the complete darkness, Thornton saw two shadowy figures run up to the plane. With great difficulty he extricated himself from his seat, took his briefcase and was helped down.

"Welcome to France, Brigadier. I haven't seen you since Alexandria." A familiar voice greeted him.

"Thank you, Captain Auster. It's good to see you. You look a lot better than you did the last time I saw you."

"I wish I could say the same for you, Brigadier. You look as if you've been through the wringer."

"My own fault, Auster. We have only a few minutes I'm told, before the plane has to go back, so let's skip the chitchat - hope we'll meet after the war to resume it. Here's the story. You know about the meeting at Euremont. We now know that it will begin in forty eight hours. The Prime Minister and Admiral Morse consider it vital that we take out the high ranking group of officers who will meet there. Everybody knows that the invasion will take place in the next few weeks. The great secret of course is where it will happen. Now what everybody doesn't know, Auster, is that we have barely half the divisional strength that the Germans have."

"But then how do we dare..."

"Hear me out. We will land, they cannot prevent that. The two or three days after the landing are crucial. We must have the time to establish the bridgehead and to consolidate it. If the Germans pull all the forces they have in Western France together and attack during that time, we will be driven back into the sea, the invasion will fail, and a German victory in the war becomes possible. They could transfer their divisions to the East and really give the

Russians a beating. Now, our only chance is that they do not concentrate all their forces on the invasion beaches in the first few days. Partly, that may happen because they cannot be sure that there will not be more than one landing and that the first landings are only a feint. Partly, you could delay them. If you succeed in taking out their principal command structure, the new replacement officers will not be familiar with their units or with the coordinating plan. Whatever extra time that gives us, is crucial."

"I understand, Brigadier. But how can I…?"

"Let me continue. As you know there are three chateaux in the area, which look alike. One of them will be the location of the conference, the other two will be filled with hostages. We cannot know until the meeting begins which of the chateaux to bomb. Unless, we can determine which chateau holds the conference, bomber command has instructions to take out all three."

"But the hostages?"

"Yes indeed, the hostages. They are among the most prominent of French artists, intellectuals, performers, household names the world over. And their families. Women and children."

"But you can't bomb them."

"That is exactly what the Germans think. But we must. It is that important to the war effort. Unless you succeed."

"What can I do?"

"You must get into the conference area. Use your old persona as a naval officer, but you must be much higher in rank. I have brought you a uniform and documents making you a Kapitaenleutnant - a commander. And because you're too young for that rank, your name is Raeder and you are the nephew of Gross Admiral (Grand Admiral) Raeder. Even in the Kriegsmarine, a bit of nepotism is not surprising. You must get into the enclave. I have also brought you two Very pistols. The bombers will be overhead - the Germans are accustomed to that, it's the route to the Ruhr which they take every night. They will watch for your signal. If there is no signal from you on the second night, they will bomb all three chateaux. This gives you two chances - the first and the second night of the conference -to save the hostages. Yes, I know that the conference is supposed to last three days, but what if it breaks earlier?"

"I see."

"Admiral Morse told me to tell you that they will make a pass after seeing your signal to allow you to escape before they drop their bombs."

"Admiral Morse told you to tell me that? But you know, that that isn't true. They will begin bombing the moment they see the flares. They must. If I can get away, so can the Germans."

Thornton looked at the young man whom he was sending to an all but certain death.

"Admiral Morse will say anything and do anything to ensure and preserve the safety of the Empire. He will sacrifice you or me or himself. Or for that matter, if necessary, our good name, if he has to order the bombing of the hostages. He will do anything for a few hours extra security on the landing beaches. It is that important, Auster, it is that important." He handed Kurt his case.

Lieutenant Thomas had been hopping from one foot to another in his eagerness to end this conversation and to take off again. "We must go, we must go." He approached the two men who were in such earnest conversation. "We really must go."

"What will I tell the Admiral, Auster?"

Well, there it is. This is my chance to have a decisive impact on the war. At the cost of my life? Yes. But do I have a choice? No, I must do this. And then I'll join my parents. But it will have been worth it. Too bad. Just when I had found Solange. She'll mourn me and then she'll find another. Let her be happy in a peaceful world.

And Ratzersdorfer? Just when I found him. But I promised the Admiral the mission comes first. Someone else will have to punish him.

"Tell the Admiral that I will do my best."

Quickly, Brigadier Thornton shook Kurt's hand. With great difficulty he was again helped into the cockpit and minutes later the Lysander was gone - back to England. Kurt stood there for a moment, holding the case, then made his way back to the edge of the field where Louis Reynaud was waiting.

* * *

"What was all that about? " Louis Reynaud asked.

"Let's get back to the safe house, and I'll tell you. We have a lot of planning to do." Kurt tried to maintain his equanimity, but the commitment he had made began to loom more and more ominously.

"I can't believe that you agreed to do this, my friend. You know what your chances are? "

They were seated in the kitchen of the safe house, and Kurt had just explained his task. Louis Reynaud was appalled.

"You understand that if I don't do it, all three chateaux will be bombed and all the hostages will be killed as well."

"That's blackmail. You're going to allow yourself to be blackmailed by the British? "

Reynaud was furious.

"Think, my friend." Kurt said quietly. " Do you believe that the British will hesitate for a moment, or will they bomb? You are French, it is your people, and some of the best of them, the ones who represent the best of France, who are at risk. What would you do? Besides, there is justification. We will strike a major blow against the enemy and help materially in Germany's defeat and the liberation of France. Isn't that worth while?"

"Are you convincing yourself or are you trying to convince me? " Louis sighed. " I suppose there is really no choice."

"Now, let's see what we can come up with. First of all, I've got to get in there. But that's not all. I think you've got to collect your entire group and you've got to get the hostages out. If not, I fear the Germans will shoot them all in retaliation for the bombing."

"But even if we get them out, where will they go?"

"Let's get them back to their homes. I am afraid of an instant reaction out of rage. Later on, the Germans may hesitate to rearrest such prominent people. Besides, I have an ulterior motive. If you can get into the area with your men, and I can escape the bombing somehow, I can join you."

"I promise, I will look for you. Even if you are wounded, I'll find you." Reynaud gripped Kurt's hand with emotion.

"Not at the risk of your primary mission - that is to save the hostages. But there is one thing you can do for me."

"I know - tell Solange."

"Not until it's all over. And, take care of her. She… she means a lot to me. Now, let's make plans."

* * *

Oberleutnant Horst Feldheimer took full advantage of his position in charge of the motor pool for the German high command in Paris. Whenever he could free himself from his far from onerous duties, he would borrow a Mercedes usually reserved for much higher ranking officers, and take his mistress, the charming Violette, dining and dancing before spending a passionate night with her in her apartment. He had never been so content. He hoped that he could spend the rest of his life in Paris in that manner. How dangerous it is to wish for something. His wish became true, but not in the manner he had contemplated.

His last evening on this earth went according to plan. He had driven Violette in the Mercedes to a restaurant in the Bois de Boulogne which, these days, catered exclusively to the occupation forces and a handful of their most favored French collaborators. Then they returned to her apartment in Montparnasse. Violette was most affectionate, and he regretted having to leave her before dawn, but it was essential to return the car to the motor pool before the daily inventory check. As he walked out of the building into the fresh early morning air, he was stopped by a man asking a polite question. While he tried to comprehend the man's French, he felt the garrote tighten around his throat and knew nothing further.

The man who had used the garrote and his partner pushed the Oberleutnant's lifeless body into the trunk of the car, after removing the keys from his hand where he had held them in readiness, got into the Mercedes and drove off. The entire incident had taken just a moment, and in the early dawn was completely unobserved.

* * *

"What is your real name?"
Crack, the whip bit into Solange's shoulders.
"What is your mission?"
Crack - this time the whip hit her lower back.
Solange had spent hours being raped by innumerable strangers - no one had questioned her. That was, after all, only the standard routine to prepare a victim. Now the questioning had begun in earnest. Her lips were bloody - she had bitten down on them too often, not to avoid her cries of pain but to prevent herself from speaking out. The questioning and the torture continued until, mercifully, she lost consciousness.

* * *

Ernst Zwingli had been councilor at the Swiss Embassy in Paris since before the war. He had fond memories of the happy and carefree Paris in the last Summer of peace, even though he, more than his French friends, saw the clouds of war approaching to blot out the sun. He was aware of the fact that desperate Jews knocked at the doors of Swiss consulates throughout Germany only to be refused entrance into that haven of neutrality.

Switzerland was not generous in its welcome to the poor and unwanted of other lands. After the German occupation, one of Zwingli's duties was to protect the Swiss citizens living in France from the attentions of the Gestapo, but he was fully aware of that organization's depredations against the unprotected of other nationalities.

When he received a call from Hauptsturmfuehrer Winter inquiring whether a certain name could be found on his list of Swiss citizens he thought for a moment.

Obviously someone who is trying to save her life with false papers. Zwingli was tired of closing the door in the face of desperate searchers for asylum, as was the policy of his government.

"Yes, she is listed with us." He felt that he had finally redeemed himself and saved a life.

Unfortunately, the reverse was true. He had condemned Solange to death.

* * *

Standartenfuehrer Ratzersdorfer was so furious that he could not sit still. He paced up and down in front of his desk and glared at Sturmbannfuehrer Most and Hauptsturmfuehrer Winter.

"Explain to me again, Winter, why the lack of personal photographs means that this young woman is a spy? Tell me where you learned that in your previous profession as a police detective."

Winter stammered," It aroused my suspicions, Herr Standartenfuehrer. Everybody has personal photographs..."

"Except people who have no families, or perhaps have broken with their families. Did you ever wonder why a Swiss couple would live in Paris at this time, when life here is difficult, instead of in comfortable Switzerland? Perhaps their families objected to their being together. Did you investigate that? Did you check out anything before you subjected the young woman to harsh interrogation? Or, Most, were you so taken by this attractive young woman that you could not wait to rape her and watch her being raped? I know your peculiarities and I don't care about them, if they don't cause me trouble."

Most and Winter stood at attention, without reply, with completely hangdog expressions.

Ratzersdorfer continued.

"She's Swiss, you idiot, she's Swiss. Do you realize what you've done? This could cause a diplomatic incident. This could go to Berlin. I've just taken over this post, and now they're going to come down on me - because I've got idiots like you working for me." Ratzersdorfer yelled so loud that the spittle was flying out of his mouth. "She didn't tell you anything, did she?" he tried to speak more calmly.

"No, Herr Standartenfuehrer." Most stammered.

"No," Ratzersdorfer repeated." Because she had nothing to tell you, you idiot." He began to yell again, and then with a visible effort, controlled himself. "Very well, you can't let her go, of course. Not after harsh interrogation. Get rid of her, get rid of her immediately."

"Sir?" Most quavered.

"You have no choice, Most. When does the next N & N transport leave Drancy?"

"Probably tonight, Herr Standartenfuehrer." Most replied.

"Get her on it marked for special treatment. And do the same with your French informer. What is his name?"

"Arsene Martin, Herr Standartenfuehrer."

"Get rid of both of them. And when anyone asks about the two people, deny, deny, deny, that you know anything."

"And if the husband shows up?"

"Well, if he's involved with the resistance, he won't. He'll have found out about your elephantine behavior. You never heard the words discretion and caution, did you? And if he was away just to do some black market trading or to spend the night with some other girl, and comes back to look for his wife, deny, deny. You know nothing. And if the Swiss ask, you know nothing. Understood?"

"Zu Befehl, Herr Standartenfuehrer."

"Now let's talk about the security measures for the conference. We'll have to leave just a skeleton staff here, most of the personnel we have available will have to go to Euremont. Use one of our men and one of the Milice to escort your two prisoners to Drancy."

"Zu Befehl, Herr Standartenfuehrer."

* * *

The railroad station at Drancy, a suburb to the North of Paris, had become the staging area for the trains which carried their unfortunate passengers to the concentration and extermination camps in the East. Some of the trains were filled with slave laborers who had a chance to survive in the armament factories of the Reich, but others, the ones known as Nacht und Nebel - night and fog - went directly to the extermination camps, the most notorious of which was Auschwitz-Buchenwald. There the passengers would undergo a selection process: the strong and healthy among them still had a chance to be assigned as slave laborers; the weak, old, and infirm, the children and most of the women, would immediately be given special treatment - the gas chambers and the crematoria.

Following orders, Milicien Jean-Paul Bertholder brought Solange's clothes into the interrogation room where she had undergone her ordeal. He was shocked at the sight before him. The young woman was crouched in a corner, her back bloody, her legs and hands scratched and her face and lips totally swollen and almost unrecognizable.

"Put your clothes on." Jean-Paul ordered. His voice was a little softer than it normally was when he attempted to imitate the brusque voice of command he was accustomed to hear from the SS men. Solange obeyed with great difficulty. Instead of showing impatience, the young Milicien helped her. She could hardly walk, and he assisted her out the door.

Arsene Martin had no idea what had been happening. He had spent many hours seated in a small anteroom. Every time he saw an SS man passing through, he jumped up in the hope that he would be summoned and be permitted to go home. After all, hadn't he done what was asked of him? But every time he asked for the SS officer who had brought him to this dreadful place, he was simply told in broken French: "Attendez, attendez."

He was hungry and thirsty, and no one seemed to care about him at all. When he could not hold out any longer, he asked for permission to follow a call of nature, and noted that when he was brought to the facilities, an SS man remained outside to make sure that he was properly returned to what, by now, he considered his cell. He was a prisoner. But why? What have I done?

Finally, he was summoned and led to a Kuebelwagen. To his shock, he saw the young woman he had denounced. And what she looked like! He gazed at her broken body with horror and tried to sit as far away from her as the narrow confines of the Kuebelwagen permitted.

The driver was an SS man and next to him sat a young French Milicien, both carrying Schmeisser machine guns. Martin leaned forward and whispered to the Milicien : "Where are we going? What's happening?" The Frenchman turned his head away from Martin and stared fixedly out the windshield without uttering a word.

Fifty minutes later they reached the railroad station at Drancy. There was only one track occupied by a relatively small train - an engine and eight freight cars., The Kuebelwagen drove into the station yard between two SS guard posts. A Scharfuehrer (SS Sergeant) stuck his head into the car on the driver's side.

"Brought us two more passengers, did you? We're just ready to roll. Where's the paperwork?"

Even murder in the well-organized and efficient German manner requires documentation.

"Special treatment, eh? " The Scharfuehrer muttered. "I don't know why they couldn't take care of them here. Waste of time to ship them East." He turned to Jean-Paul.   "Well, bring them along. We'll find room for them - the train's been here for a few days, some of the passengers may be ready to get off." He chuckled.

"What are you doing - where are you taking me? " Arsene Martin began to resist and to complain in full voice. The Scharfuehrer turned toward him and without blinking an eye, hit the Frenchman in his stomach with the full force of his Schmeisser. Martin collapsed. He could not breathe. " Come along if you don't want another. " The Scharfuehrer said in a friendly voice. Martin forced himself up on his knees and then stood up with great difficulty. He stumbled after the SS man.

Solange also had great difficulty just getting out of the car. Jean Paul helped her move along the tracks next to the freight cars.

There was a strange sound coming from the cars - a permanent moaning and groaning - but very quietly, very quietly, as if the people in the cars had no more strength to complain.

The Scharfuehrer opened the door of the first car. " Any dead in here? Bring them out."

There was no reaction. Jean-Paul saw a mass of ragged people lying one on top of the other. With some difficulty, the Scharfuehrer closed the sliding doors again, and locked them.

At the third car, a wailing arose when he opened the door. "Water, please water." Ignoring the outcry, the Scharfuehrer called out again. " Any dead here?" "Yes, yes," a weak voice sounded. A small child's body was handed on over the heads of the people who were crushed inside the wagon. The Scharfuehrer took it and dumped it unceremoniously into the ditch next to the tracks. "Well, get in here," he ordered. Martin was forced into the freight car and after him Solange. There was no room for them, but the Scharfuehrer forced the doors closed and locked them.

"Who are these people?" Jean-Paul Bertholder asked.

"Jews, of course. On the way to resettlement East - those that survive. Except for those like your buddies who are going to get special treatment. They'll be up in the air soon." The Scharfuehrer made a gesture indicating smoke.

Jean-Paul looked at the body of the child the Scharfuehrer had dropped into the ditch. He had never seen a dead body before. Yes of course, Jews were vermin that had to be eliminated from the face of the earth, he knew that. But the child did not look like vermin at all.

"Well, I think we've got a full complement now," the Scharfuehrer waved to the engineer. Slowly the train began to move East.

"You, Frenchie." The Scharfuehrer pointed at Jean-Paul. "Pick up that body and take it over to the pile at the end of the pier over there. I think the disposal unit will be getting around to cleaning it up one of these days."

Reluctantly Jean-Paul obeyed. The little girl's body was almost weightless. Without looking at it, and holding it as far from his body as he could, he carried it in the direction the Scharfuehrer had indicated. There was a pile of bodies, men, women, children, old and young. He could not count how many, nor did he want to linger. Quickly he dropped the small body onto the pile and rushed away - to a corner, where he became violently sick And as he heaved, and heaved, he tried to keep telling himself - Jews are not human. But he didn't believe it.

As befitted General von Weitzensberg's rank, his Daimler was escorted by two armed motorcycle riders in front and two in back. His aid Oberst Scharfer was seated next to him. The General enjoyed the lovely French countryside, the warm May sun sinking low on fields of sunflowers, the trees along the highway in serried and well-disciplined ranks.

They had been on the road for quite some time. "We must be getting close." General von Weitzensberg said. "Probably another half hour. " Oberst Scharfer agreed. Suddenly, in the distance in front of them, they saw the figure of a man standing in the middle of the road, waving frantically. Per standard operating procedure, the car stopped, the motorcycle riders dismounted and took up defensive positions surrounding the car with their Schmeissers pointed in all directions.

The man approached at a stumbling run. As he came closer, they saw a German naval officer, hatless and somewhat disheveled

"I need help. There's been an accident." The man called out.

One of the soldiers from the escort walked up to the man, carefully keeping his gun pointed at him. After a moment of conversation, he brought the naval officer to the Daimler. The man saluted as soon as he saw General von Weitzensberg.

"I am Kapitaenleutnant Raeder. My car ran into a ditch, and I fear my driver is dead."

General von Weitzensberg got out of the limousine, returned the salute, and inquired, "Are you hurt? Do you need medical assistance?"

"No, Herr General. I'm just a bit shook up. And forgive me, I'm somewhat out of uniform." Raeder tried to straighten his jacket and comb his hair with his fingers, to improve his appearance in front of a general officer. "I was on my way to a conference in Euremont, when my driver swerved, I suppose to avoid some animal on the road, and drove straight into the ditch. I fear he had the misfortune of breaking his neck. I could detect no sign of life but I'm no doctor. I hope I'm wrong."

"Well, come on, get into the car with us, and we'll take a look." General von Weitzensberg was very friendly. ""I am General von Weitzensberg and this is Oberst Scharfer. We're on our way to the same conference."

The convoy continued half a mile on and stopped. Indeed, a Mercedes was in the ditch next to the highway. The Wehrmacht lieutenant seated behind the driver's seat held his head in a very unnatural position. Scharfer climbed down to inspect the body. "I'm afraid, you're right, Raeder, " he said grimly. "The poor man is dead."

The General took command. "You'll come with us, Raeder, get your bags. " He turned to one of the motorcycle riders. "Go on ahead and tell them to send an ambulance and a repair crew to clean up this mess. And now let's go."

Raeder climbed down to the car, emerged with his cap, a briefcase and a handgrip. His bags were placed into the luggage compartment, and he was seated in the limousine on one of the fold out seats facing the two higher ranking passengers The convoy started off again.

"So, you are Kapitaenleutnant Raeder," The general inquired. "What is your present assignment? "

"I am on the staff of my uncle, Gross Admiral Raeder. While he, personally, is not involved in the planning for the defense of the West Wall, he has ordered me to attend the conference and report to him." The young naval officer began to relax in the luxurious automobile.

The two Army officers exchanged a telling glance. At von Weitzensberg's level of command, he could understand that the Navy wanted to be in on major decisions the Army would take. And now, he could also understand why such a young man held the rank of Kapitaenleutnant. Raeder's nephew, no less. Well, that was the way it was.

"Well, my friend," the General was very charming. "You've had an ordeal but now you can relax. We'll have you at the conference in no time."

"Thank you for your help, Herr General." Raeder smiled. "What I need, as soon as we arrive, is a hot bath, and to have my uniform cleaned. I would not want to represent the Navy looking like this."

"That shouldn't be a problem." Oberst Scharfer interjected. " Provided Ratzersdorfer's security measures don't delay us too much. Are you all right, Raeder? Is anything the matter? "

The young man had paled. His hands had begun to clench and unclench, and a strange expression had come over his face. After a moment, he seemed to collect himself, and said:

"Please forgive me, the accident must have taken more out of me than I had thought."

"I know what you need." Von Weitzensberg chuckled. He pulled a flask of brandy out of the side pocket, together with a small glass, poured a drink and offered it to the naval officer. "Here's something to calm you down. I can understand how you feel. You're just realizing that you could have been killed just as easily as your driver."

"You are very understanding, Herr General, and very kind." Raeder took the brandy and swallowed it gratefully.

"I apologize, Herr Oberst. You were talking about security measures?" He then asked,

"Indeed." Scharfer continued. He had a proprietary interest in the chateaux he had discovered, and loved to show off their special situation. " Do you know why the conference is being held in that particular spot?"

"I had heard something about there being three chateaux? " Raeder said questioningly.

"Yes." The General looked at Scharfer benevolently. "Oberst Scharfer found the location. There are three chateaux all exactly alike, within a relatively secure area. One of the chateaux will house the conference, the other two will hold hostages. That should ensure our security, don't you think?"

"Of course, Herr General." A Kapitaenleutnant does not disagree with a general officer, even one from another service.

"In addition, my chief of security, Standartenfuehrer Ratzersdorfer has been on the spot   and I'm sure will have taken any measures necessary to protect us. Well, we seem to be getting there."

As they approached a guardpost flanked by two armored cars, an ambulance and a light truck sped by them in the direction they had just come from.

"Ah, here they go to your car," the general said.

The Daimler stopped at the guardpost. An SS officer saluted. " Standartenfuehrer Ratzersdorfer's compliments, Herr General. All arriving officers are supposed to go to the center encampment for identification and check-in, and will be taken to Chateau A by truck immediately after nightfall. However in your case, Herr General, my orders are to allow you to proceed to the chateau directly, but without your motorcycle escort. That would be too risky in case of aerial surveillance. At the chateau your quarters and the quarters of Oberst Scharfer are ready."

"Very well." General von Weitzensberg said. "You might as well go with me, too, Raeder, and get your hot bath. And be sure to tell your uncle that we in the Army are always happy to extend all courtesies to the Navy."

"Thank you very much, Herr General." Raeder said with a smile.

* * *

The ambulance reached the abandoned Mercedes quickly and two medics jumped out, opened the back door and removed a stretcher. The light truck pulled out behind them, and the driver and his helper got off. "Let's just look at the situation first, perhaps we can pull the car out of the ditch with a towrope." The driver said.

"You won't have to bother." A French accented voice said in poor German. " Just raise your hands high. All of you."

Six men pointed an assortment of weapons at the four German soldiers. A few minutes later, they had been stripped and tied and moved out into the fields. Their uniforms were being worn by those of their captors they fit best.

"So far so good." Louis Reynaud smiled at his second in command. "And now we must await darkness and the bombers."

* * *

When the Daimler arrived near Chateau A - the chateau designated for the conference - a soldier immediately guided it into a building that no doubt once had been a stable. There the car was safe from aerial surveillance. Two other soldiers emptied the trunk, while a Feldwebel with all the aplomb of a butler in a stately palace, led General von Weitzensberg and Oberst Scharfer to the great hall. Kurt trailed along.

This was Kurt's first view of the chateau. It was much smaller than the chateaux he had seen in the Loire Valley. Euremont was a large square building, with a number of French doors along all the lower floors. A double entrance door above a series of five or six steps led into the Hall. Kurt had noted turrets along each corner and a large balcony, apparently the only one in the building, directly above the front entrance. Once the officers had entered the Hall, Kurt noted that it encompassed almost the entire length and half the width of the building. It was clearly designed for entertaining large crowds. A formal, winding staircase in the back led to the upper floors.

"Your rooms are ready, Herr General, and Herr Oberst. But I had no instructions regarding another officer." The Feldwebel looked at the General questioningly.

"That's all right. Find a room - and bath for Kapitaenleutnant Raeder." General von Weitzensberg ordered. And with a friendly glance at Raeder he said. "Get your rest, get yourself cleaned up, and I'll see you later."

Both the Feldwebel and Kapitaenleutnant Raeder responded with a smart: " Zu Befehl, Herr General."

Kurt was shown to a small room. His luggage was brought up. He had been extremely nervous about his briefcase which contained the two Very pistols, but he had decided that it would arouse suspicions if he had insisted on keeping it with him. Now, he checked the weapons, made sure that the phosphorous cartridges were properly inserted and that the pistols were ready. Then he took his bath - long and hot - grimly thinking that this may be the last time in his life that he would indulge himself in such a sybaritic pleasure.

He cleaned his uniform as best he could, took his cap and his briefcase and descended the staircase.

The chateau was small. It may have been exquisitely furnished when it was the property of a marquis of the ancien regime, but its vicissitudes since then had left it looking like a second class hotel. The worn leather couches and armchairs standing around the great entrance hall did not disguise the exquisite proportions of the grand staircase. As Kurt descended that staircase, he looked around.

Many other officers had arrived by now. Kurt found himself in a sea of field gray, the light blue of the Luftwaffe, and here and there, the dark blue of the Navy. He made sure to stay as far away from any naval officer as he could. *They must all be assigned to the surveillance of the Channel, but I don't want to have to answer questions.*

The large hall had a festive appearance. Soldiers circulated with trays bringing drinks to parched throats and canapés for hungry stomachs. The only thing missing, that would have made it look like a fancy dress ball, was the presence of ladies in evening gowns and an orchestra playing dance music

"Meine Herren, meine Herren . (Gentlemen, gentlemen)." A voice spoke from the staircase.

A few steps up so as to be visible to every one in the hall, General von Weitzensberg stood, drink in hand, flanked by Oberst Scharfer and a tall SS officer.

That must be Ratzersdorfer. Kurt pressed into a corner and stared fixedly at the murderer of his parents. The bile rose in his throat. He had to restrain himself from jumping at the man and tearing him apart.

General von Weitzensberg finished a brief welcome speech and introduced Oberst Scharfer not only as the locator of the chateau, but also as the administrative overseer of the conference. Scharfer spoke briefly, discussing the modalities - a general conference in the morning, then in the afternoon there would be a break into appropriate groupings of officers who had to coordinate specific activities. Von Weitzensberg spoke again:

"We had hoped that Field Marshall Rommel would attend, but I have been informed that he has been ordered to attend the Fuehrer at the Wolfschanze (the Fuehrer's Eastern headquarters). It is possible that the Field Marshall will come here to talk to us before we are done, but even if he is not, I know all of you will act to make him proud of being our commander. Now, I must introduce Standartenfuehrer Ratzersdorfer in charge of security arrangements - some of you may have met him already - and I ask that you pay close attention to what he has to say. The arrangements he has made must be obeyed."

"Welcome, meine Herren." Ratzersdorfer's voice had the Austrian softness, but he did not look soft. " I apologize for the necessity of bringing you here in trucks from the central encampment. We have gone to great lengths to ensure your safety. We cannot afford to have enemy planes see which of the three chateaux so fortuitously found by Oberst Scharfer is the seat of this conference. Of course you understand that an assembly of your vehicles around this chateau would be a dead give away. For the same reason, I must inform you that no one is allowed outside the chateau during daylight hours. Aerial photography is so advanced that a number of high ranking officers taking the air around this chateau would bring a rain of bombs immediately. You will be allowed to take your walks, if you choose, as soon as it gets dark, but I must insist that you do not smoke when you take your constitutional. Smoke all you wish indoors, unless of course, the Fuehrer honors us with his presence."

This last brought forth a chuckle from the large number of officers who were aware of the Fuehrer's view on smoking.

"Gentlemen," Ratzersdorfer continued. "I implore you to obey these instructions. My men will be on watch inside and outside the chateau and have strict orders to enforce them regardless of the rank of a violator. They are among my most loyal SS and will do whatever is necessary to protect the security of the conference."

There was a moment of silence at these words. Even the highest ranking officers did not feel immune to the SS.

Von Weitzensberg broke the silence. "That is all, gentlemen. Enjoy the evening, take your walks if you choose. Breakfast will be served at 7 A.M. and the conference begins at 8 A.M. Until then, good night."

Von Weitzensberg began to climb the stairs, followed by Oberst Scharfer. Ratzersdorfer remained where he was, surveying the assembly. Slowly, more and more of the officers wandered off to their rooms. Kurt remained in his corner, nursing a drink.

***

CHAPTER XIV

In May daylight in Northern France lasts until well past 10 P.M. The bombers would not pass overhead until after midnight. Kurt needed to find Ratzersdorfer's room if he wanted to have a word with him. As regards the bombers, it would be sufficient to find a window and fire a Very pistol straight up. The bombs would follow.

The Hall had emptied. It was not possible to remain there. Ratzersdorfer had disappeared. Only a few soldiers remained, cleaning up, picking up empty glasses. At the entrance door, an SS Officer sat reading a magazine. *I imagine he does not expect any more guests tonight, but he is on guard. I could go out for a walk, and fire the Very pistol from the outside, close by. This would give me a chance to escape. But Ratzersdorfer? I'm so close. He could be killed by the bombs, but I've got to make sure. And I want him to know who I am.*

Kurt walked over to the SS Officer at the door. "Raeder" he said, stretching out his hand. The officer got up, took the proffered hand and said :" Most."

"I can't sleep." Kurt continued. " I had a bad automobile accident on the way here, and it's shaken me up. No one else seems to be awake. Could we have a beer and talk a little? If you're not too busy, Kamarad."

"Sure. I'm not allowed to go to sleep anyway. My chief insists that I stay here all night in case one of those high muckamucks wants to do something he disapproves of. What a job for a Sturmbannfuehrer. An ordinary Sturmmann would do just as well." Most signaled to one of the soldiers and ordered him to bring two beers.

"You sound Austrian, just like my glorious leader. Are you? "Most asked.

"Yes, " Kurt said. " I was born in the Ostmark, although most of my family is Prussian. My father married into an old Austrian family and we lived on their estates."

"Estates, is it? No wonder you're Navy. We in the SS come from sterner stuff. My father was a bricklayer." Most took a long swallow out of the bottle of beer the soldier had brought him.

"And Standartenfuehrer Ratzersdorfer? He's from the Ostmark too? I thought I detected a familiar accent."

"He's very proud of himself, that one. Another self-made man. But he doesn't deserve it. He brownnosed Heydrich and that's what got him his start. And now he lords it over the rest of us."

"You don't seem to like him very much, Kamarad." Kurt smiled.

"Like him? He never appreciates anything I do. I can work my fingers to the bone, try everything I know to get rid of the blasted French resistance, and he's never satisfied. Why just yesterday… Oh, never mind. Some matters shouldn't be discussed outside the black Corps."

"How about another beer? " Kurt asked.

"Absolutely. There's nothing else to do now anyway. Where's someone to bring one? "

The hall was empty - the cleaning crew had finished their task and had disappeared. All the guests had retreated upstairs to their rooms. Only Kurt and Sturmbannfuehrer Most remained downstairs.

"Come on, we'll find the kitchen. There's bound to be something to drink there. The door's locked, and it's nonsense for me to have to hang out here. He ordered me to do that just to punish me."

Most led the way to a door at the end of the hall. A few steps down there was a large kitchen. A big wooden table in the center. Gleaming equipment and two large refrigerators, cases of food and drink, obviously brought in by the Germans.

"Come on, Raeder. Have something a little stronger." Most found a bottle of Cointreau and two glasses. "The damned French are good for two things only - producing good drink and easy girls, right Raeder? Come, sit."

Kurt obeyed and they drank, clinking glasses. "But why would Standartenfuehrer Ratzersdorfer want to punish you? " Kurt asked. He was happy to let the SS officer talk as much as possible. " Seems to me, you're doing your job."

"You don't know the half of it. Do you think I enjoy hard interrogation? He thinks I do. Well, some of it. When the suspect is a nice attractive girl like the last one, all right, I enjoy it. But I do it because it's my duty. And I was right. She was a spy. But he wouldn't believe me. I would have made her talk - just a little more time for persuasion. Just a little more time. But he had to rush us here so he could preempt the best room in the place. He likes his comfort, our Franz. Don't know where he got used to it, he didn't get brought up on an estate like you Navy gentlemen."

All this time, Most kept refilling his glass. Kurt followed but drank as little as possible.

"What do you mean the best room? Surely that's reserved for the commanding general?"

"Ho Ho, you don't know our Franz. He reserved it for Field Marshall Rommel. And I tell you, he knew all along that Rommel wouldn't come. So now it's his. Only room with a balcony, so he can sit outside and take the air like a lord."

"That must be the room right at the top of the stairs." Kurt sighed. "Me, they got me two flights higher, in the attic, just under the roof."

"Well, you're not any more important than I am," Most complained. "But it's you and me who do the work, and he who gets the glory." He drank again.

* * *

In a Nissen hut in Southern England the aircrews of bomber group 14 and their fighter escorts sat on folding chairs in front of a blackboard for their final briefing for tonight's mission. A large map of Northern France was pinned to the board. The briefing officer explained:

"Today's mission is somewhat out of the ordinary, but probably more vital than most. You will follow the course of the Somme here - " his pointer moved along the map - "to where the Eure joins it. At this point, there are three chateaux on a type of peninsula. One of them is your target for tonight.

You may expect a flare shot out of a Very pistol to illuminate the chateau you are to destroy. If you see the flare, let go of all your bombs and return home. The fighter escort will descend and strafe the area. We do not want a single survivor. But be very careful. Do not, repeat, do not attack the other two chateaux or anyone close to them. Is that understood?"

A hand was raised. "What kind of an idiot will send up a flare knowing what will happen next?"

The briefing officer smiled. "The same kind of idiot that would fly into a mess of Ack Ack to deliver a load of bombs. Next question."

Another hand: "What if there is no flare?"

"You will continue on to the secondary target." The briefing officer removed the map of Northern France and replaced it with a map of the Ruhr. "You will attack the steel works near Essen - here." The pointer moved. "You have been there before. There is, as you well know, a great deal of anti-aircraft protection there. By going there, you will demonstrate the same degree of idiocy than the man whose job it is to set off the flare. You'd better hope he does it, because that would make tonight's mission a milk run for you. Now there are a few more words of explanation. Brigadier Thornton?"

With considerable difficulty Thornton climbed up to the podium next to the briefing officer.

"Let me explain the urgency of this mission, and the particular importance to make sure that all, repeat all, German personnel are killed. There is a conference of almost all the highest ranking German officers of all three services who will oppose our landings, which as you know, as everyone knows, will take place soon. If we can destroy these officers and their plans for coordination when our troops arrive on the beaches, we will certainly have put a crimp in the German plans to counterattack

Now, the other two chateaux in the area are filled with French hostages, men, women and children. It is therefore crucial to avoid hitting them at all costs. The conference is scheduled to last three days. If our man is unable to send the flare up today, we will give him another chance tomorrow."

A hand was raised: "And if there is no flare tomorrow, do we take out all three chateaux or do we forget the mission?"

Thornton did not answer. The briefing officer interjected. " You have your orders for tonight. What happens tomorrow is not your problem." And with a glance at Thornton, he muttered " and thank God, it's not my decision."

* * *

Louis Reynaud and his men, four of them dressed in German uniforms, the others hidden in the ambulance and in the light truck, had driven as close as they dared to the German checkpoint at the entrance to the Euremont estates. There they awaited the sound of the planes.

* * *

"You look like an intelligent man, " Sturmbannfuehrer Most's voice began to slur a little, even as he took another drink. " Let me ask you something. If you live in a nice apartment, in a nice building, with your wife, wouldn't you have family photographs around? Wouldn't you? "

"Probably." Kurt had no idea where this was leading, but there was still time before the planes would arrive. He did have the information he wanted. He was sure now of where he could find Ratzersdorfer.

"That's what I thought, that's what I thought. But he didn't think that was suspicious. What does he know?"

"You mean the Standartenfuehrer?"

"Sure, that's who I mean. Our Franz who knows everything better than anyone else. And let me ask you something else. Wouldn't you be suspicious of a young couple in a fancy apartment who claim they work in a flowershop? Where's their money coming from? I ask you that, I ask you?"

Kurt paled. *He's talking about Solange and me. Did they arrest Solange? What happened to her?* He tried to control himself.

"So what happened? Did you arrest the two people? " Kurt was praying that the answer was yes.

"Not the man. He'd flown the coop. But the girl - oh she was really delicious. But he didn't think they were important. What does he know of police work after all?"

"So you had to release her?" Kurt was praying again.

"Oh no, too late for that. At least not that, let her run around and complain. No, she's gone, she's up there by now -" he twirled his fingers in the air indicating smoke -
"Nacht und Nebel, you know, Nacht und Nebel"

A red mist seemed to form in front of Kurt's eyes. He grabbed a copper frying pan which was hanging from a wall sconce nearby, and hit Most. Hit him and hit him. After the first blow, Most's eyes opened in total wonder at this unexpected betrayal by a comrade in arms. The second and third blow destroyed the face and opened the skull. Kurt did not stop until Most's head was an unrecognizable mass of blood, bone and brain matter.

Kurt dropped the frying pan. His hands were bloody, but he burrowed his face into them *Solange - they've murdered her. And just when I realized I loved her. First Sarah, then Solange. I can only bring misfortune to any women I love. Solange. How could I have exposed her to this danger? It's my fault, again.*

An icy determination overcame him. *What a blessing that I am on a mission that will finally bring me rest. I'll go home to my parents - but first, I can avenge them and avenge Solange.*

He looked about him. There was no one around. Obviously no one had overheard his attack on Most. There was a door at the end of the kitchen. He opened it. Stairs down - probably a wine cellar or something like that. He pulled Most's body by the legs toward the door, and pushed it down the stairs. It rolled down a number of steps - enough to be out of sight to anyone just giving a quick look. *That should do. I don't need much more time.*

He became an automaton. First, he washed the blood off his hands and face at the kitchen sink. Then he opened his briefcase, took out the two Very pistols, checked that the cartridges were properly loaded and put the spare cartridges into his pockets. He inserted the Very pistols into his belt so that his hands would be free for climbing. He turned off the lights. There was a window on the side. He opened it and easily climbed out. No one was outside. He walked to the front of the building. The balcony was just overhead. It was easy to climb up to it by holding on to some of the decorative stone-work along the main door.

As quietly as he could, he swung over the railing. The French doors to the bedroom were open. He looked at his watch. The planes should be coming soon. He walked into the bedroom, well-furnished - dressing table, closets, huge bed. The heavy drapes were not drawn. He looked at the door. There was a key in it. He locked the door, pulled a chair from in front of the dressing table and wedged it into the door. *That will keep them for a few minutes, if necessary.*

Franz Ratzersdorfer was asleep. For a moment Kurt looked at the man who had murdered his parents. He began to shake with anger and hatred. Then he forced himself into some measure of composure. On the night table, next to the bed, Ratzersdorfer had left his wallet, his watch, and his heavy SS dagger. Kurt picked up the dagger. Briefly he considered plunging it into the Nazi's chest. He took a deep breath and changed his mind.

Bending over the sleeping SS officer, Kurt took the hilt of the dagger and hit Ratzersdorfer on the one spot on the side of the forehead that, according to his unarmed combat instructor so long ago, would ensure that his victim would remain unconscious for only a few minutes.

Ratzersdorfer woke up. He was shivering. Apparently someone had doused him with the carafe of water he liked to keep near his bed. His head was throbbing with pain. He attempted to touch it, but realized that his hands and feet were bound to a chair. He felt a tassel. He was tied with the drapery cord. But he was not in his room. He looked about and saw that he was on the balcony outside. He attempted to cry out, but there was a gag in his mouth.

A man was seated on another chair facing him. A German officer? A naval officer; he identified the uniform.

"So, you're awake," the man whispered. He was playing with Ratzersdorfer's SS dagger.

"I have some questions for you. You will answer them in a whisper. If you attempt to make a sound that can carry beyond this balcony, this is what will happen."

With the dagger, the man cut the drawstring of Ratzersdorfer' pajamas and pulled them down. Then he placed the tip of the dagger against the SS man's testicles. Ratzersdorfer felt the tip cut into him.

"Do you understand me? " There was a grim smile on the naval officer's face.

Ratzersdorfer nodded. The gag was removed from his mouth, but the dagger continued to press against his testicles.

"But you are a German officer? Why are you doing this? " Ratzersdorfer stammered.

"I want to ask you a question. Do you remember Vienna, six years ago, shortly after the Anschluss? You killed a Jewish couple, do you remember?"

"I've killed a lot of Jews."

"Please try to remember that particular incident. Would you tell me about it?"

"It was a simple matter." Ratzersdorfer recalled. " I was ordered to take over a Jewish business. I went there with the Aryan foreman and gave the couple the usual fifteen minutes to vacate their apartment. Then I noticed a Jewish religious object, a Torah. Do you know what a Torah is?"

"Yes, yes. Continue." The Naval Officer said in a strangled voice.

"There was a crown and other decorations on it, all made of heavy silver. Obviously, this would be the property of the state. I removed the silver objects and dropped the Torah into the fireplace. The Jew went berserk. He attacked me and I had no choice but to shoot him. Then his wife jumped at me and I had to shoot her as well. As you can see, in this case, my killing these two Jews was actually a matter of self defense."

The Naval Officer took a deep breath. The dagger at Ratzersdorfer's groin did not move. Then he asked in a very quiet voice:

"Do you have any regrets about these killings?"

Ratzersdorfer's face showed total astonishment. "Regrets? They were Jews and we are sworn to eliminate the Jewish plague from the face of the Earth. No, no, they would have been killed anyway, sooner or later, but in a more orderly fashion. This was --- messy."

"Messy." Kurt repeated. He marveled at the fact that he could continue this conversation said :

"Do you remember that there was a son?"

"Oh, yes, I do remember. I believe he escaped. I don't know whether we ever caught him. I was transferred after that. But what is this all about?" Ratzersdorfer still could not believe that this unimportant incident would matter.

The Naval Officer replaced the gag in Ratzersdorfer's mouth. Then he whispered grimly.

"You did not catch him. I am that son. I am an agent of British Intelligence. This chateau and all the personnel it contains will be destroyed soon by British bombers. When they approach, I will signal them with these Very pistols. I will fire the first shot at you.

The phosphorus will cover you and you will be burned to death. While we are waiting, you can think about how messy your death will be."

Ratzersdorfer's face fell. He appeared stunned.

Kurt Auster leaned back in his chair. He held the two flare guns loosely in his hands. *So this is what happened,* he thought.

Papa couldn't stand to see the Torah desecrated. And Mama fought for him as she always fought for me.

There was a brum-brum-brum in the sky. *The bombers are approaching. How appropriate that this is the end for him and for me.* Kurt almost smiled. *Solange, Papa, Mama - I'm coming.*

Kurt looked at his parents' murderer. Ratzersdorfer was struggling against the ropes with a panicked look in his eyes.

With a pitiless glance at the doomed man, Kurt Auster fired the flare gun at the SS man. For a moment, he watched the burning phosphorous engulf the body, he watched the agony twist Ratzersdorfer's face into a grinning mask as the flames licked at his eyes. Then Kurt turned, and fired the second Very pistol straight into the air, reloaded both pistols and fired both of them straight up again.

The lead bombardier had been looking for this. " Here they are, and God help the man who gave the signal," he muttered. The flight of bombers turned toward the target, illuminated as if it had been broad daylight. And the bombs began to fall.

* * *

When Louis Reynaud saw the flares go up, he gave the order to advance as quickly as possible. The ambulance and the light truck drove straight through the German checkpoint. The soldiers guarding it were watching the flares a few miles away, and did not think of stopping what appeared to be German vehicles. In accordance with previous arrangements, the two groups separated, one driving to each of the two chateaux filled with hostages.

Reynaud was driving the ambulance. When they reached their destination, they saw a handful of German soldiers milling about, watching the spectacle of bombers attacking Chateau A, bombs exploding, and fighter planes flying low strafing anything they could see. An Oberleutnant tried to rally the soldiers, but did not appear sure about the action he should take.

Reynaud's ambulance drove up, turned around and, as the rear doors were flung open, the French Resistance fighters opened up on the demoralized German troops with the Schmeisser submachine guns they had liberated. In a few moments all the Germans were dead or wounded. As Kurt and Louis Reynaud had anticipated, only a squad had been assigned to guard the hostages.

Why would more men be required to guard unarmed civilians, many of whom were women and children?

Reynaud opened the door to the chateau. The people inside, awakened from an uneasy sleep by the sound of the bombs and of the battle, were rushing about in panic, looking for shelter. "Vite, sortez, sortez." Reynaud called out to them. "We are French, here to rescue you. Quick, everybody follow me."

With the help of his comrades, Reynaud led, prodded and rushed his group of hostages down the path to the river. Now, if only the boats are here, he prayed.

When the bombers approached, four fishing boats which had been anchored upstream and had appeared to be empty, suddenly began to move. The partisans who had been lying down in the boats under canvas sheets to avoid detection, threw off the sheets and began to row vigorously to the shores near the chateaux. Two boats reached the landing to which Reynaud had led his flock. Quickly he helped as many embark in the first boat as it would hold and they were taken across the river. By the time the first boat was back ready for another load, the second was discharging its passengers on the other side. It took only four more crossings to complete the transfer.

"Are the trucks there? And the other hostages?" Reynaud demanded of the last boatman.

"They are. All is going well. Everything seems to have gone according to plan at the other chateau. Now, it's your turn."

"I'm staying here. I've got to find out if my friend Kurt is alive. I owe him no less."

"That's crazy," the boatman objected. "You'll be killed. You can't pass for a German in spite of your uniform."

"Nevertheless, I must try. I can count on you to take care of our people as planned?"

"Of course. But please, think it over once more. We need you. France needs you."

Louis Reynaud smiled. "There was a time when I would have avoided risking my neck at all costs. But I've been fortunate. I met some people who taught me that life is not worth living if you don't like yourself, and I like myself a lot better now. I must stay. Good luck to all of you. I hope to see you soon."

A handshake and the boat left. Louis Reynaud followed it with his eyes until he saw it land on the other side, be pulled up and hidden on the banks, and his men disappear. Then he turned, straightened his German uniform, and walked quickly toward the sound and sight of the bombs.

* * *

For a moment Kurt stood still. He felt a strange sense of disappointment. For six years he had remembered the name Ratzersdorfer, and now the man who had killed his parents was dead. But so was Solange. The pain cut through him like a knife.

He looked at the shriveled body of the man he had pursued so long. Whiffs of smoke, an acrid odor of burning flesh and chemicals made him gag. He stepped back and looked up into the sky at the approaching planes. He raised both arms to the heavens in a welcoming gesture.

The sounds of explosions, the crashing of masonry, the brrrm brrrm of the planes' engines, and the screaming of victims of the bombs brought him back to full alertness. A sense of self-preservation took over. He clambered over the railing and went down hand over hand along the wall just as he had come up. Around the corner and back inside through the kitchen window. The door to the basement. Perhaps safety there. He rushed down the steps, stumbled over the body of Sturmbannfuehrer Most, fell heavily and tumbled down, down into blackness. His head hit a brick protrusion and he knew nothing more.

* * *

The entire attack took only ten minutes. Anyone left alive would then have seen the planes reform - the bombers in the center, the fighters surrounding them and, gracefully, they swung back toward the West, toward England.

No one around the ruins of what had been designated Chateau A was alive to watch the sky. Here and there, bodies of men who had tried to escape the hell that the chateau had become, lay dead where they had been machine gunned by strafing fighters, but most of the victims were buried in the rubble.

The troops who had remained in the central encampment, and who had not been touched by the attack, were the first to arrive on the scene. Their highest ranking officer, a Major, quickly took command. Messengers were sent to various units in the vicinity to ask for help and equipment, and to notify headquarters of the disaster.

Digging parties were organized, and the slow process of removing debris began. Perhaps, somewhere under the rubble someone was still alive.

In the forest near the disaster scene a Frenchman in German uniform hid behind trees and bushes but watched very attentively. As bodies were brought out, they were lined up along the side of the road. The observer stayed as close to that section as he dared, and in the few instances that he could recognize the dark blue of a naval uniform, he walked over unhesitatingly to inspect the face - if it was recognizable - or at least the rank. Then he disappeared again behind the trees. In the confusion and concentration on the wreckage no one paid any attention to just another German soldier.

* * *

Twenty-four hours had passed. The scene around the rubble of what had once been called chateau A resembled a construction zone. A portable crane had been obtained somewhere. It had been working for several hours lifting and moving some of the largest pieces of masonry. A field kitchen had been set up, and in one corner of the area there was a makeshift morgue and a tent serving as field hospital. Two German Army doctors were waiting for the occasional survivor. There were not many. Those that were brought to them were very seriously injured.

The row of bodies stretched out along the road had become much longer. One of the problems for the rescuers was the difficulty of identifying many of them. The officers had been in bed, most of them wearing all kinds of sleep wear, from pajamas to underwear, and in some cases nothing. Many were so battered by the collapsing building that it was hard to make out any facial features and there were no identifications on most of them. A list of invitees had been obtained in Paris, but the list of those among them who had actually checked in was in Standartenfuehrer Ratzersdorfer's briefcase somewhere in the debris.

Louis Reynaud had sneaked over to the field kitchen whenever he saw a crowd of soldiers around it, and had helped himself to some food with which he disappeared back into the forest. No one paid any attention to him. There were too many soldiers from different outfits working to clear the rubble in the desperate hope of finding some survivors. Reynaud had not slept for thirty six hours. He had taken an occasional catnap, but was afraid that by falling asleep, he would miss finding Kurt Auster. He hoped against hope that Kurt was alive somewhere, and he knew that he would have to remove him from the Germans before they could find out that he was not a real Kapitaenleutnant. And if he was dead, as he almost certainly was, Reynaud wanted to be able to tell Solange that he had seen the body with his own eyes. He did not know, of course, that no one on this earth would ever be able to tell Solange anything.

* **

In Berlin at the OKW - Oberkommando der Wehrmacht - Supreme military headquarters, a stunned staff looked at the list of dead and wounded:
Seven general officers, including four general staff officers and the commandant of the Northern Sector of France, General von Weitzensberg.
One Brigadefuehrer Waffen SS.
Twenty-one officers with the rank of colonel or its equivalent in the other services.
Thirty-four other field grade officers.
Several dozen support personnel of other ranks.
Then they began to comb their files looking for replacements for an Army that would have to face an attack from across the sea in the very near future and that for the moment was leaderless.

* * *

At the Wolfsschanze Adolf Hitler went into one of his famous rages. "Who ordered this meeting? " he screamed, tearing up the report. "What traitor put all my best officers into one building?"
Field Marshall Kluge, who had the misfortune to be in attendance, did not dare tell the Fuehrer that the order for a coordinating meeting had come from him. Nor did he remind him, that there had been gentle objections from the Fuehrer's staff pointing out that precisely the disaster could happen that had occurred.

* * *

Feldwebel Schlosser was in charge of the detail which had been sent to the other two chateaux to collect the bodies of the

German squads which had been guarding the hostages. At the first chateau, after he had supervised the loading of the bodies into the two trucks he had brought along, Schlosser entered the building. Perhaps someone had survived and was in hiding, or was so badly wounded that he could not call out. The hall was littered with the belongings of the hostages who had been kept there, bedding, suitcases, here and there toys and dolls. Schlosser went upstairs to check all the rooms. They were empty, and by their musty odor had not been occupied for a long time. He wandered downstairs, looked around the kitchen and detected a door. It led to a wine cellar, also unoccupied.

Before going on to the second chateau, Schlosser decided to get to the scene of the disastrous bombing raid. There he reported to the Major in charge of the rescue operation.

"Sir, with the Major's permission, I have made a discovery."

"Yes?"

"There is a wine cellar directly under the kitchen area. There are stairs leading down from the kitchen. I believe we should pay particular attention to that section of the building. Perhaps some survivors had time to take shelter in the cellar."

"An excellent thought, Feldwebel. I commend you. Show me exactly where you believe this cellar to be."

The portable crane and the digging equipment were moved to the section Schlosser pointed out. With great care and a lot of hard labor, pieces of masonry were moved, and indeed a staircase was uncovered. One of the soldiers stepped down carrying a flashlight. More debris had to be removed. Finally a call came from below: "There is a body here, unfortunately a dead one."

An SS officer's body was carried up into the light. The diggers continued. More debris, more masonry. "One more, here - he may be alive, I think he's breathing."

One of the doctors ran over and clambered down into the hole. He emerged, shaking his head. " He's breathing, but he seems to be very badly injured. We'll have to lift him out very carefully. I fear that too much movement may cause more hemorrhaging."

With great care, the body of a naval officer was brought up and gently carried to the field hospital. " It is miraculous that he survived so long. There must have been a source of oxygen in spite of the collapse of the walls," one of the doctors muttered, as he worked on the wounded man. " He is totally dehydrated - there are several compound fractures of both legs and one arm, and damage to the head - at least a concussion, probably a subdural hematoma. Is there internal bleeding? We can't find out what damage there is to his internal organs until we have him in a hospital."

One of the medics, recognizable as such by the wide armband with the red cross that was part of his uniform, a tall, blond young man, had wandered off into the forest, presumably for a call of nature. When the man returned, he had miraculously become somewhat shorter and his hair had turned black. His face was covered with grime and dust from the excavation. The soldier appeared intensely interested in the proceedings around the wounded naval officer.

The doctors did their best to stabilize the victim's condition. Temporary splints were applied to his legs and one arm, a glucose drip was attached and his stretcher was hoisted into an ambulance. The blackhaired medic jumped into the ambulance with the stretcher, and the ambulance took off.

A few miles away from the compound, the ambulance driver heard a knocking at the window behind him. The medic who had accompanied the wounded officer made urgent signs to him to stop. The driver pulled off to one the side of the road, opened the rear doors and was just about to ask the reason for the stop when a thin knife entered his stomach with a sharp upward thrust and reached his heart. He was dead instantly.

Louis Reynaud eased the driver's body away from the ambulance and pushed it into the ditch alongside the road. He was totally exhausted from lack of sleep, but the adrenaline of the action and the small possibility that Kurt was alive kept him going. He got into the driver's seat and started the motor. It was getting on to dawn, and he knew that there was no way he could pass any German checkpoints successfully even in the uniform of a German soldier, driving a German ambulance. It was clear to him, that there would be redoubled efforts to find the hostages and their rescuers, and that German troops would be swarming about the area. Furthermore, he was very much aware that he was at the end of his strength.

But if he did not continue and did not find medical help quickly, would Kurt survive?

While he was considering his options, he passed a narrow road, turned into it on an impulse and came to what appeared to be an abandoned farm. There were no animals, no sounds of dogs barking, cows mooing or roosters crowing, to greet the awakening of dawn. But there was a barn. He drove up to it, opened the wide doors, drove in, closed the doors, and collapsed on a heap of straw next to the ambulance.

* * *

He woke up feeling logy and unrefreshed. Only a few hours had passed and it was early afternoon. He looked at Kurt lying on the stretcher in the ambulance. There was very shallow breathing, but at least, he was still alive. He tried talking to Kurt, but there was no reaction - his friend was unconscious. The glucose bag was empty. He searched the ambulance and found another bag in a supply locker. Clumsily, he replaced the empty bag. He opened the barn doors a crack and looked around. No sign of life anywhere. There was a well in the courtyard of the farm house. He went over and pumped some water, all the time looking around very carefully, ready to run to the ambulance and drive off. He drank some of the water greedily, and brought a little to the ambulance. He tried to wet Kurt's lips and to make him swallow some. He had no idea whether this was the right thing to do for the patient, but he was unsuccessful. The body felt hot to his touch. A fever? He hoped not, but was getting more and more concerned. He had too little medical knowledge to be able to help his charge.

He took stock of his situation. Now that he had had a few hours of sleep, he felt he could go on, and his primary concern was Kurt. He needed help, and he needed it soon. He checked the gas gauge in the ambulance - less than a quarter of a tank. Not very much.

It was certainly much riskier to go on in daylight, but did he have a choice? In May, the days were very long and if he waited another five or six hours before leaving his hiding place, what would that do to the wounded man? He was convinced that Kurt's only chance for survival depended on his getting medical help quickly, and he knew of only one way to obtain that. And if they got caught by a German patrol or a German checkpoint, so be it. Abandoning Kurt was unthinkable.

He drove the ambulance out of the barn and tried to stay on the smallest side roads, far from the main road. He drove South and then East so he would circle the approaches to Paris. The gas gauge kept sinking lower and lower. He passed farmers working the fields but did not dare stop. To them, he reminded himself, I am a Boche in a German vehicle.

It was getting toward dusk when he had no choice but to rejoin the main road in the Barbizon forest. In the last hours just before curfew, there was more traffic - the occasional truck. Once a German patrol drove past him. He waved to the soldiers cheerily, and they returned his wave.

The safe house was in the forest, away from the main road. He did not dare drive up in a German ambulance wearing a German uniform. They might shoot first before knowing who he was. He pulled the ambulance into the woods out of sight from the road, left his uniform jacket on the seat, and walked rapidly up to the house, holding both arms away from his sides. He knew he was being watched. The door opened, and a familiar voice said: "High time you got here, Louis, we've been holding dinner."

* * *

At seventy-five Doctor Bernard Charpentier should have retired long ago. But he felt a strong responsibility to his patients, some of whose grandparents he had brought into the world. He was the only physician in the rural area which adjoined the Barbizon Forest. The younger men had been taken into the Army when the war began, or had moved to bigger cities where life was far more pleasant and profitable. Doctor Charpentier promised himself that he would retire as soon as the Germans left - he was certain that the occupation could not last much longer. In the meantime he could not abandon his post. So he made do with the shortage of everything a self respecting physician needed, medicines, bandages, syringes, and all equipment. He used the accumulated wisdom of nearly fifty years, and whatever came to hand, including folk medicines that would have more of a psychological than a medical benefit.

He was seated in the living room of his cottage which served as his home and office, exhausted from a day of making his rounds, when the bell rang. " Oh, no," he muttered as he painfully made his way to the door.

He opened it to see a figure wearing a hood, push past him into the living room. "Doctor, please do not worry," the voice of the hooded man sounded familiar. " We need your help, but we cannot reveal our identities."

"Come on, Franois, " Doctor Charpentier smiled. "Do you think I don't recognize you? I have known you from the moment I helped your mother deliver you. I took care of your chickenpox and your whooping cough, and I've wiped your nose often enough, and your bottom too, when you were a little smaller."

A bit shamefacedly the man removed his hood. "The thing is, Doctor, I'm in the resistance and one of my comrades is very badly hurt and needs help."

"And you think I'll run out and tell the Boche on you? Now I'm really insulted. Let's go."

Doctor Charpentier grabbed his medical bag. "You might want to put on shoes," Franois suggested with a relieved smile. "Oh yes, of course." It was the Doctor's turn to be a little embarrassed as he exchanged his slippers for his well worn boots.

A panel truck was waiting outside. Franois helped the doctor into the back and soon they reached their destination - a small house deep in the woods. .

On the bed a man in a German naval uniform was stretched out. He appeared unconscious. His legs and one arm were strapped in the method used by German medical personnel for emergencies. Charpentier looked at the men crowding around him.

"I'm not going to ask why your comrade is in German uniform. Now give me room and let me examine him. Out, out all of you."

Twenty minutes later, Doctor Charpentier entered the living room. One of the men, who clearly appeared the leader of the group and whom the doctor had never seen before, gave Charpentier a questioning look.

The doctor shook his head sadly. "I cannot give you good news, I'm very sorry," he said.

"There are multiple fractures of both legs and one arm, but they are not life threatening if they are taken care of promptly before gangrene sets in. However, what is most worrisome is internal bleeding. Without X-ray equipment I cannot tell much, but there is major damage to some of your friend's organs. It is vital that his abdomen be opened up and the bleeding stopped - and then one could see what has caused it. He appears to have lost a good deal of blood already, and needs a transfusion above all. Furthermore, there are signs of a concussion, and there may be more damage in the cerebrum. I am sorry to tell you that the prognosis is extremely bad."

"What can you do for him?" The leader of the group asked.

"Not much. He needs a hospital and the services of a fully equipped surgical unit - with some highly skilled surgeons. Even if we brought him to one of the nearby hospitals, the shortage of medications would make it impossible to help him much. If we only had some of the new antibiotic drugs, but none exist in France."

The men looked at each other dejectedly. "One more question, Doctor," their leader asked. "Could he withstand a plane ride? A short, less than two hour plane ride? In a small plane, where he would be crunched up - not stretched out as on this bed?"

"My dear young friend," Charpentier said gently. "You are talking about a dead man. If there is a hospital at the other end of the plane trip, and if he survives the ride, there may be a chance for him. But whether he dies on this bed or in a cockpit - what does it matter? If you have a plane, I will help you make him as comfortable as I can - and then we can only pray."

* * *

Brigadier Thornton burst into Admiral Morse's office. "Auster is alive. He's being flown in on a Lysander. He's badly wounded. I've arranged for an ambulance to meet the plane. We'll take him to St. Mary's - it's not far from the airfield and they have excellent surgical facilities. If you don't mind, I'll go there right now so I can see him and make sure he gets the best care. "

Morse did not seem to share Thornton's enthusiasm. "Well, all right, if you must." He thought for a moment. "You might as well stay there until you can talk to Auster. Please impress on him the need for secrecy. We don't want the French to know that we even considered killing their people in order to get the Germans. We certainly wouldn't have gone so far as to actually do it, would we?"

Thornton was not so sure. "You would have been just as glad if he had been killed, wouldn't you?" He said slowly looking at his chief.

"Oh, of course not." Morse denied. "Just make sure he keeps his mouth shut. And then debrief him. Let me know his condition, will you."

"Of course, Admiral."

* * *

St. Mary's Hospital was in the South of England and far removed from the medical wizards of Harley Street, but in the war years it had become one of the major receiving hospitals for wounded personnel. As a result, its expertise had grown and its surgeons and support staff were the equal of the best in Britain.

Brigadier Thornton arrived a scant half hour after the ambulance carrying Kurt had reached the hospital. The sister receiving him advised: "He's in the operating room. It will be quite a while before the surgeons will have finished with him. You've got a very sick man there. You might as well go down to the cafeteria and relax."

Try as he might, Thornton was not permitted to see the patient or even to confer with the doctors who had treated him. Finally, bowing to the inevitable, he retreated to the cafeteria and drank innumerable cups of weak tea. Eventually, a nurse's assistant came down to call him. " The doctors will see you now."

When he reached the operating floor, two surgeons were just stripping off their gloves.

Thornton disliked looking at their bloodstained gowns, too many memories of his own surgeries and hospitalizations came to the fore.

The more senior of the doctors looked at him with a shake of his head.

"We've worked very hard on your man. All I can tell you is, he's still alive. But how long he will live is very much in question."

"What is the problem?" Thornton asked.

"The problem? The problem is that human bodies were not designed for the kind of abuse this body has undergone."

The younger doctor spoke up. "He's got compound fractures on both legs and one arm. We did what we could, but we couldn't keep him under long enough to do a proper job. We'll have to try again when - if - he's stronger. There was internal bleeding as well, but we were able to stop that."

Now it was the older man's turn: " Bad as this sounds, it's not the worst of it. There was a subdural hematoma pressing on his brain. We had to do a trepanning operation, but I cannot tell whether he will survive the trauma. He has not yet shown any sign of consciousness. Even if he survives all the physiological problems, I have no idea what his mental condition will be. "

Thornton sat down heavily. He had not expected such bad news. He had been overjoyed that the man he had sent to his death had survived. Now it seemed not only that his survival was very uncertain, but that it was possible that he could survive in a complete vegetative state - his mind and personality gone.

The brigadier roused himself. " I know you will do your best for your patient, " he said to the doctors. "This man has served our country and our cause."

"So have all the others whose broken bodies you send us," the younger of the doctors said bitterly.

* * *

On June 6th, 1944 an Armada of 700 ships and 4000 landing craft invaded four beaches on the coast of Normandy. A few days later the Germans responded by launching the first rocket weapons on London, the V-1 (Vergeltungswaffe 1 - revenge weapon 1) from Peenemuende in Northern Germany.

At his headquarters in France, seventy year old Field Marshall von Rundstedt decided that the Normandy invasion was a feint, and that the real blow would be struck at the Pas de Calais. It was a position he had maintained for a very long time, and even the entreaties of his subordinate, Field Marshall Rommel, whom he considered a parvenu and disliked intensely, could not make him change his mind. So he kept the bulk of his forces in reserve.

A week later, he gave in to Rommel's entreaties and allowed him to move half his forces against the bridgehead. He still maintained that the main invasion would land in the Pas de Calais, a belief he held for several more weeks.

In spite of the fact that many of Rommel's officers were recent replacements, the Wehrmacht's iron discipline and training ensured that there were no unnecessary delays and that the Field Marshall's orders were executed efficiently and promptly.

But it was too late for the Germans. By then the invasion forces had consolidated their bridgehead and were able to repulse the German attacks. And more men and more supplies arrived, and soon there would be an attempt to break out.

Kurt Auster did not know that the invasion had taken place. He had been through four operations, the fractures had been brought under control, even though further operations would be required .

* * *

Brigadier Thornton was astonished to find his chief, with his back toward him, staring out the window. Usually, when he entered the Admiral's office, he found him busy at his desk, ready to snap out orders.

"Is there anything the matter, Admiral? " Thornton asked.

"The matter? You know that I was ready to give the order to kill all those French hostages, men, women, children. Prominent intellectuals and artists, and ordinary people. And I was ready to murder them. You know that, don't you?"

"Yes, Admiral. I know that you would have done that if Auster had not made it unnecessary."

"And it would have been for naught. Killing all those German officers made no difference at all. At least, they were the enemy, and deserved to be killed. But if I had given that order, it would have been for nothing."

"Admiral, you could not know. The idea that the absence of so many high ranking officers would make a difference, was right..."

"Yes, Thornton. But is there a price one should refuse to pay? I never considered that. Come back in a little while, Thornton, and we'll talk about today's problems. Come back in a little while."

Gently, Thornton closed the door behind him.

* * *

When the V-1 rockets began to fall on London, it became pointless to sound the air raid sirens. The speed of the rockets was such that they were over London by the time they were detected. So the population of London, inured to horror after five years of war, went about its business. When a V-1, in common parlance a doodlebug - was overhead, there was a moment of stillness below. Only the distinctive sound of the rocket engines could be heard. And then they stopped.

Sometimes the rocket would drop straight down, and sometimes it would choose a parabolic glide path. The people below held their breaths. And then came the explosion, and those unaffected breathed again and continued on their way.

Brigadier Thornton was just coming out of a tobacconers, the thin edition of the Times in his hand (newsprint was in very short supply) when he heard a rocket, and the ominous silence when the motor stopped. He looked about him almost with amusement. He was surrounded by glass - the windows and doors of the shop. The rocket did not have to explode too close to take care of him. But this time, again, he survived. The explosion was a number of blocks away.

With a sigh of relief, he continued on his way to Whitehall. When he reported to his chief - however early he arrived, he found Morse there before him - the Admiral smiled:

"Your friend Auster seems to have made it. Why don't you run down there and give me a personal report on his condition?"

* * *

The senior surgeon whom Thornton had met once before, seemed in a much better mood. "I am happy to be able to tell you that your friend appears to be out of danger. I don't know whether it was the massive use of the new antibiotics, or just the natural powers of recuperation of a young and strong man . In any case, our patient is alert, and able to communicate, although he is very weak. As regards his abdominal problems, they seem to be healing nicely. We may have to repair some of the fractures in one leg, but the other leg and the arm are coming along well."

"Can I see him and talk to him?"

"Just for a little while - he's very weak. But he wants to see you. He wants to know about the war. Of course, we've told him about the invasion and its success so far. It is successful, isn't it? I'm asking because our troops don't seem to have made much progress."

"Oh, yes, doctor. So far, so good. But it will take some time before all the supplies and reinforcement will have been landed before we can attack."

Even though Thornton had prepared himself to find a very sick man, he was shocked at Kurt's appearance. Of course the head and the rest of his body were swathed in bandages, but the face - as much as he could see of it, was incredibly haggard.

Thornton sat down on a chair next to the bed. Kurt's good hand reached out to him and gripped his wrist with more force than he thought the sick man could muster.

"Was it worth it, Brigadier, was it worth it?" The voice was barely a croak.

Thornton hesitated for a moment. Then he looked at the burning eyes in the pale face. "Yes, Auster. It was worth it. Your achievement delayed the counterattack long enough so that we could defeat it. It was worth it," he lied.

The grip on his wrist loosened, and with a sigh, the broken man on the bed closed his eyes. Thornton looked down at him for a moment, then he tiptoed out.

* * *

ABOUT THE AUTHOR

This is a work of fiction.
However, Maximilian Lerner's service as an American agent
during World War II insures the authenticity of its
background.

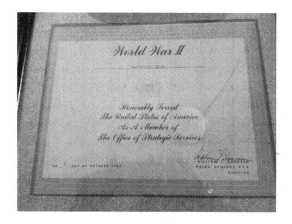

Made in the USA
Middletown, DE
24 May 2017